LANA KORTCHIK grew up in two opposite corners of the former Soviet Union – a snow-white Siberian town and the golden-domed capital of Ukraine. At the age of sixteen, she moved to Australia with her mother. Lana and her family live on the Central Coast of New South Wales, where it never snows and is always summer-warm. She loves books, martial arts, the ocean and Napoleonic history. Her short stories have appeared in many magazines and anthologies. She is the author of the USA Today bestselling *Sisters of War* and *Daughters of the Resistance*.

Also by Lana Kortchik

Sisters of War
Daughters of the Resistance
The Countess of the Revolution
Sisters of the Sky
Angels of War

Sisters of the Storm

LANA KORTCHIK

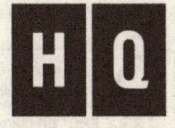

ONE PLACE. MANY STORIES

HQ
An imprint of HarperCollins*Publishers* Ltd
1 London Bridge Street
London SE1 9GF

www.harpercollins.co.uk

HarperCollins*Publishers*
Macken House, 39/40 Mayor Street Upper,
Dublin 1 D01 C9W8
This edition 2026

1

First published in Great Britain by HQ,
an imprint of HarperCollins*Publishers* Ltd 2026

Copyright © Lana Kortchik 2026

Lana Kortchik asserts the moral right to be identified as the author of this work.
A catalogue record for this book is available from the British Library.

ISBN: 9780008656812

This novel is entirely a work of fiction. The names, characters and incidents portrayed in it are the work of the author's imagination. Any resemblance to actual persons, living or dead, events or localities is entirely coincidental.

All rights reserved. No part of this publication may be reproduced, stored in a retrieval system, or transmitted, in any form or by any means, electronic, mechanical, photocopying, recording or otherwise, without the prior written permission of the publishers.

Without limiting the exclusive rights of any author, contributor or the publisher of this publication, any unauthorized use of this publication to train generative artificial intelligence (AI) technologies is expressly prohibited. HarperCollins also exercise their rights under Article 4(3) of the Digital Single Market Directive 2019/790 and expressly reserve this publication from the text and data mining exception.

Printed and bound in the UK using 100% Renewable
Electricity by CPI Group (UK) Ltd

*For Christopher, my football-obsessed karate kid.
And for Sophie, my ballerina princess.*

There's a path that leads to nowhere
In a meadow that I know,
Where an inland island rises
And the stream is still and slow;
There it wanders under willows
And beneath the silver green
Of the birches' silent shadows
Where the early violets lean.

                    Corinne Roosevelt Robinson

Chapter 1

Through Thunder and Steel

8 November 1943

High above the war-torn coast of Catania, inside a screeching C-53D Skytrooper, Andrea Lewis was fearing for her life but trying hard not to show it. She sat still like a mouse, nails digging into the armrest, face pale, nose to the window. Under the wings of the plane, the blue of the Adriatic contrasted sharply with the green of the rolling hills. If only she wasn't so nervous, Andrea would have appreciated the stunning scenery that looked like it belonged on canvas. She would have taken it all in, committed every detail to memory. After all, it had been her childhood dream to visit Italy one day, to see in all its glory the birthplace of da Vinci and Raphael. But, as the plane shook and groaned, she didn't pay any attention to what lay below. She could barely breathe from fear.

The aircraft started to gain altitude and she could no longer see the blue and the green of the Italian coast. 'Look how high we are,' she said to her twin sister Nicole. 'Above the clouds.'

Nicole nodded, her eyes gleaming with excitement. 'Isn't it fantastic? It's like we're moving through cotton wool.'

'They say plane engines are prone to overheating at high

altitudes. Which can lead to mechanical failure. Which can in turn lead to—'

Nicole didn't let her finish. 'That's why we have two engines, silly. Both of them can't fail at the same time. It's impossible. Don't be afraid.'

But Andrea knew anything was possible.

There were thirty of them on this flight, thirteen female nurses, thirteen male medics and a four-man flight crew. Their job was to transport the wounded from hospitals near the frontlines to better-equipped medical facilities elsewhere. Andrea looked at the faces around her, wondering if the others were as scared as she was. Renee was reading a book. Ronnie was knitting. Carrie and Tory were playing cards. Frankie was snoring. No one else seemed worried. In two hours, they would be in Bari, where the wounded and the sick would require all their attention. Andrea knew she wouldn't get a moment of peace once they landed. She should be trying to get some last-minute rest, just like the others were doing. She closed her eyes, took a deep breath and tried to imagine calm waves touching her bare feet. But then the aircraft hit a sudden pocket of turbulence and she jolted upwards, her eyes wide open.

On Andrea's left was her sister, twirling her blonde hair excitedly, turning this way and that, trying to get the best view. It was their first time on the plane and it showed, albeit in different ways. Although Andrea and Nicole were mirror images of each other on the outside, on the inside they were nothing alike. Where Andrea was timid, Nicole was brave. Where Andrea was shy, Nicole was outspoken and argumentative. Nicole was afraid of nothing, not even moving through the air at neck-breaking speed onboard a troop carrier.

On Andrea's right was her husband Brian, who was reading through some notes seemingly without a care in the world. It helped that it was his third evacuation flight. He was practically a veteran. He had been away in Texas for a few months, training as a flight surgeon at the School of Aviation Medicine at Randolph Field and Andrea had missed him terribly. She watched his face for a minute, his eyes moving as he scanned the paper. She reached out and took his hand, squeezing his fingers. He looked up and smiled at her, reassuringly, she thought, even though his attention was clearly on his work. And then he moved his hand away and turned the page of his notebook. She waited for him to take her hand again but he never did.

Brian was the most senior medical officer on board the plane. It was his responsibility to screen the patients before each flight and make sure it was medically safe for them to travel. Somewhere out there, under the wings of their plane, were hundreds of people who would rely on him to save their lives. He didn't have time to hold her hand because she was afraid of flying.

The plane shook violently and Andrea gripped her seat tighter, the blood rushing away from her face.

'Deep breaths,' said Nicole. 'Remember, this is normal. They told us this would happen before we boarded, remember?'

Andrea tried to take a deep breath but couldn't. Her heart was beating fast.

Nicole added, 'Close your eyes and imagine we are on a rollercoaster, like that day in Detroit a couple of years ago. Remember us holding on for dear life and screaming with joy?'

'I wasn't screaming with joy. I was screaming with terror.'

'Little Leon loved it so much,' whispered Nicole, her eyes dimming with sadness.

Andrea smiled, momentarily forgetting all about the turbulence at the thought of her nephew. 'He kept asking to go on the rollercoaster one more time. And one more, and one more. I had to buy him the biggest candy floss in the world just to get his mind off it. I remember telling him he would never finish it. But he did. And then he asked me to take him on the rollercoaster again.'

'It was one of the happiest days of my life,' said Nicole. 'Only I didn't know it then.'

Coming to Europe to be a nurse had been an easy decision for Andrea. Thousands of wounded needed her. Her husband needed her. But she knew it was the hardest decision of Nicole's life. There were nights when she heard her sister crying in her bunk before finally falling asleep. She never went anywhere without a photograph of Leon in her pocket. Andrea wondered if Nicole regretted volunteering for the front. Andrea regretted it sometimes and she didn't have a small child waiting for her at home.

When she first arrived at the front, Andrea was stunned by the sheer volume of human suffering, by destruction, fear and death everywhere she turned. It was not what she had expected when she boarded the *Santa Elena*, a former Grace Line cruise ship, while a brass band belted out 'Pistol Packin' Mama' and sailors welcomed the nurses with doughnuts and champagne. They played cards, they danced late into the night, they talked about their past and their hopes for the future. Andrea learnt how to play the guitar and dance a tango. The start of their journey had been one big celebration of life and purpose and doing something worthwhile, until one dark moment ten days into their crossing, when the *Santa Elena* was passing through the Strait of Gibraltar and enemy fighter planes suddenly appeared. Later that day, a torpedo fired by a submarine just missed the bow of the ship as it changed its course, hitting another vessel in their convoy. As sirens wailed and people screamed, Andrea realised she was not prepared for what lay ahead.

But every day she woke up feeling needed. The patients raised their pained eyes to her and asked for help. And when she helped them, they took her hands in theirs and thanked her, tears running down their cheeks. In the first week at the front, she experienced a feeling of satisfaction she had never known before. She also experienced profound helplessness.

She would have preferred to be on firm ground instead of working on evacuation flights but then she wouldn't be with her husband. Her fear of flying was nothing compared to her fear of being apart from him. She closed her eyes and tried to envision herself many years from now, safe in her house in Detroit with Brian by her side, having grown old together. In her mind, she saw a fire blazing in the hearth, a roomful of visitors, smiles and laughter and the sound of champagne flutes touching. When she was old, would she think fondly of her time at the front? Would she long to relive this time, to be young again? Or would she shudder with horror every time she remembered it?

'Thank God the rain has stopped,' Andrea said to her sister. Storms had grounded the 807th Medical Air Evacuation Transport Squadron for the past few days. After the forced rest, the nurses were keen to get back to work. Andrea heard this was the biggest crew ever sent on one plane. Where they were going, she knew they would need all hands on deck. 'It's nice to see the blue skies again.'

But next time she glanced outside, all she saw was steel grey, the colour of wet pavement, miserable and gloomy. Somewhere in the distance, thunder roared. The plane trembled as it made its way through dark cloud that looked angry enough to swallow it whole.

'Not long now,' said Nicole. 'The boys stationed in Bari promised us dinner when we arrive.'

'Do you ever think about anything other than your stomach?'

'I'm not thinking about food at all,' Nicole said. 'I'm thinking about the dancing. Some of the officers are terrific dancers.' Her feet tapped on the spot, like she was practising her steps.

'What would your husband say if he knew his wife was dancing with handsome officers while he is impatiently waiting for her to return?'

Nicole giggled. 'It's Anthony we are talking about. I bet he hasn't even noticed I'm gone.'

Soon they were out of the cloud but the coast of Catania was no longer visible, concealed behind menacing fog. 'This doesn't look so good,' Andrea whispered, wiping the invisible lint off her trousers, her nervous fingers fiddling with her blue uniform, her short Eisenhower jacket.

Tory and Carrie were no longer playing cards. Carrie, a stunning blonde from Wisconsin, was watching the clouds with a worried look on her face. Tory, an older woman from Texas with an inexplicable British accent, turned to the sisters. 'Would you like me to read your fortune?' Like many other flight nurses, Tory had been an airline stewardess before she joined the Nurses Corp. She wasn't worried about a little turbulence. She had seen it all before.

Nicole chuckled and shook her head. 'Not for me, thank you.'

'Yes, please,' said Andrea, fidgeting in her seat. Anything to take her mind off the flight.

'How will you read her fortune? Coffee grinds? The palm of her hand?' Nicole asked sceptically.

'Why, with these cards,' said Tory, the expression on her face seeming to say, *What's not to understand?*

'They're not even Tarot cards. They are gaming cards. What are you going to do with them?'

'The fortune teller never reveals her secrets.'

Nicole, who didn't believe in fortune tellers, grumbled but didn't turn away.

Tory shuffled the cards. 'Ask a question and choose a card,' she said to Andrea.

'What kind of question?'

'Something you want the universe to reveal to you. Something important.'

Carrie said, 'Like will we survive the landing? Will we get to Bari in one piece?' Her hands were trembling as the plane hit more turbulence.

Andrea glanced at her husband, who was still absorbed in his paperwork. She turned back to Tory and was about to speak when the older woman lifted her hand as if to stop her. 'You don't need to tell us your question. Keep it between you and the universe. Take a card.'

With a shaking hand, Andrea reached for a card when a burst of thunder made her jump. The plane jolted this way and that, like a caged bird desperate to escape. The cards went flying out of Tory's hands all over the floor.

'The universe just answered your question, whatever it was,' Nicole said to Andrea, who remained frozen in her seat as if in shock, a queen of spades clutched to her chest.

One of the two pilots, First Lieutenant Charles Thrasher, appeared in the cabin. He was a member of the 61st Troop Carrier Squadron, tall and imposing, with a mop of dark hair that reminded Andrea of a porcupine, prickly and all over the place. He radiated confidence and every time she saw him, she felt reassured. She knew they were in good hands with Thrasher flying them. But this time, the grim expression on his face did nothing to take her fears away, even when he told them there was nothing to worry about. 'Just routine turbulence, folks, nothing out of the ordinary. We have contacted the control tower in Bari to obtain an updated weather report.'

'And what did they say? Is it beach weather down there? Should we bring our swimming trunks?' shouted one of the medics, the ginger-haired lad from New York called Tim Shearman, who could make anybody laugh. His comical disposition was matched by his appearance. His socks were odd, his caps had holes in them and his beard was matted and long.

'We are still waiting for them to clear the landing.'

'And if they don't?'

'If they don't, we will return to Catania. In the meantime, we will change course and try to fly around the weather system.'

Thrasher returned to the cockpit, leaving the nurses and the medics chatting in low, worried voices. Andrea stared at the card in her hand. The queen of spades glared back at her, like a premonition of bad things to come.

'That's what they always say before the crash, you know?' said Carrie, poking the cards with her foot, trying to reach for them without undoing her seatbelt. 'Nothing to worry about, everything is under control. Remember that movie? What was it called? *Lost Horizon*? Have you seen it? It has Ronald Colman in it. I like him because he looks like my husband.'

Andrea shook her head and glanced out of the window. The sky grew darker as they reached the heel of Italy. In an attempt to stay below the cloud ceiling, they were flying low, only four hundred feet above sea level. The murky waters were churning below them, like a witch's cauldron filled with dark magic. Thick fog enveloped the aircraft, making it hard to see. The plane bounced in the wind, while thunder clapped overhead. 'How will we land in such poor visibility?' she whispered to her sister.

Nicole clasped the tennis racket charm she always wore on a chain around her neck. 'The pilots have trained for this. We'll be fine.'

Andrea tried not to listen to the panicked voices around her. Someone said they had lost all radio communication with the ground. Others were convinced their compass was damaged. She did her best to ignore the rumours, focusing instead on the way her sister's fingers felt inside her hand.

Brian lifted his eyes off the documents. He took her other hand. 'Don't worry,' he said. 'The guys inside that cockpit know what they are doing. You heard Thrasher. It's not the time to panic just yet.'

Andrea felt relief wash over her, like a wave. Brian had that effect on her. One word from him and she instantly felt better.

A moment later, he took his hand away. At the same time the plane wobbled and took a nose dive. 'How about now?' Andrea whispered. 'Is it time to panic now?' She didn't think Brian had heard her. Her voice was lost in the multitude of other voices and in the sound of engines, whistling and whining as the plane made its way down.

Andrea squeezed her eyes shut, not to see the ground hurling towards them at a terrifying speed. Suddenly, the plane straightened out with a screech and climbed above the clouds to escape the storm. Andrea could breathe again. 'Why is it so cold?' she whispered, shivering in her jacket.

'The plane is too high. The higher we go, the colder it becomes,' said Brian.

'Better cold than plunging to our deaths,' said Nicole.

Outside was dark like night, almost black. Andrea could no longer see anything.

'Don't look out,' said Nicole. 'Close your eyes. Play me a melody. Something from Tchaikovsky, your favourite. Pretend my arm is a piano.'

Playing her music never failed to calm Andrea's nerves and her sister knew that. She closed her eyes and pretended she was in her study, sitting in front of her grand piano, the present from her beloved grandfather. In her mind she could still see his face when he presented her with the instrument, telling her that music was a superpower, that it could transport her anywhere she wanted, that it could change her life. If there was a time she needed a little bit of magic, it was now. She ran her fingers over her sister's arm, pretending to hit the notes. The sensation was so real, she could almost hear the music. In her mind she could see the Sugar Plum Fairy pirouetting on stage and the little swans holding each other tight as they performed their moves. *Danse des petits cygnes* had always been her favourite. When she was a child, she dreamt of being one of them, of moving gracefully through the air while the crowds applauded. It was not to be but as she thought about her childhood dream, she was no longer on the plane that was flying blindly through the storm. She was far away from the war-torn Italian coast, home with her family where she was safe.

A sudden descent took Andrea by surprise. She gulped for air, the visions of dancing swans vanishing. She could see water just below the wings, roiling like a deathly volcano ready to devour them. In the distance were rugged mountains partially concealed by fog. Brian squeezed her hand again. He was no longer looking at his papers but nor was he looking at her face. She attempted to smile but couldn't. 'It will be all right,' he whispered but she didn't believe him.

She watched the wingtips appear and disappear in the thick cloud. The pilot returned, telling them they were about to attempt a landing. Underneath was a tiny beach, barely a quarter of the length of the runway at their headquarters in Catania. She wondered if a plane this size could safely land on such a small stretch of land and what would happen to them if it couldn't. As if reading her mind, Brian said, 'Land there? It's not enough space. You're going to kill us all.'

Thrasher replied, 'We are short of fuel. And the storm is only getting worse. We lost radio communication and are flying blind. This might be the only chance we have.'

'What about parachuting out?'

'We have thirty people on board and only twenty parachutes.'

'Well, that's just bad planning on your part,' grumbled Brian.

Thrasher said, 'There are twenty-eight Mae Wests. I suggest you put them on, in case we end up in the water.'

'What about you?' asked a nurse Andrea had never met before.

'We had water-survival training back home. We'll be fine.'

Andrea knew no training could prepare one for something like this. She watched the brave pilot, who was ready to risk his life for them, when someone shouted, 'There's an airfield below. Over there, behind that hill.'

The pilot returned to the cockpit. The crew chief moved to a seat by the passenger door to be in position to open it when they landed. The plane changed course. Everyone breathed a little easier. Landing on an airfield would be safer than attempting a water landing. Suddenly, their chances didn't look so bad. Excited voices filled the cabin.

As the aircraft circled the runway, ready to come in for landing, Andrea looked out of the window at small buildings, like doll's houses scattered around the airfield. Between the houses, she saw half a dozen German fighter planes.

'Don't worry. There are abandoned German fighters everywhere we go,' said Brian. 'The most important thing is getting out of the storm. I've never flown in this weather before. I'm sorry your first flight had to be like this.'

Andrea nodded. The German planes were the least of their worries. 'It's almost over. We are nearly there.' She said it to reassure herself, to make herself feel better. It didn't work.

The landing gear lowered and locked into position. They were fifty feet from the ground, ready to touch down. In her head, she counted to ten, once, twice, three times. When she was a child, her mother had taught her to do that whenever she needed to calm down. But this time it did nothing to slow her heartbeat. Her throat was dry. She needed a sip of water but couldn't force herself to let go of her sister's hand and reach for her flask. Any moment now, the wheels were going to hit the ground and they would be safe. And then the terrible nightmare would be over. They would wait out the storm here, wherever it was, and then be on their way. Hopefully she would never have to fly in a storm like this again.

When they neared the end of the runway, something hit the metallic body of the aircraft. At the same time, they heard a deafening roar. At first, Andrea thought it was thunder. But it was something more terrifying than that. With horror she recognised the screeching of anti-aircraft guns.

She heard shouts. 'Someone is shooting at us!'

'The fighters. They're on the move.'

Andrea saw the enemy planes careening down the runway, ready to give chase. The troop carrier began to climb but then the engines coughed and the plane bucked and fell through the air. Andrea panicked. 'What's happening?' she whispered.

'The pilots switched the fuel tanks,' said Brian. His face was impassive and only his fingers gripping her hand were trembling.

For a moment, all was peaceful again. She could no longer hear the enemy planes or the anti-aircraft guns. They had regained altitude and were above cloud cover, flying away from the airfield.

'I was never supposed to be on this flight,' said Tory. 'I switched places with another nurse at the last minute. She was waiting for her fiancé to arrive and begged me to do it. I should have said no.'

'Why didn't you consult your cards first?' asked Carrie.

Tory hid her face in her hands. 'My husband was captured by the Japanese on Wake Island a couple of years ago,' she said. 'He's in a prison camp in Shanghai. Every night I pray to God that he lives long enough to see me again. I never thought I might not live long enough to see him.'

Suddenly, as if out of nowhere, a mountainside appeared and for a moment it looked like they were going to slam into the rocks. Andrea's mouth opened in a silent scream, when the plane turned steeply to the right, nearly scraping the rocks with its wing.

'That was close,' said Nicole.

All Andrea could see now were mountains, and all she could hear was the steady drawl of the twin engines, when suddenly another sound joined in. Another aircraft. A moment later, she spotted a Focke-Wulf Fw 190, the dreaded German Butcher Bird, flying straight at them.

Their trusty plane ducked and dived, desperately trying to outwit the German fighter. But no matter where they went, the Butcher Bird was there, waiting for them. It was faster, more manoeuvrable and better equipped than their C-53D Skytrooper, a variant of the rugged Douglas C-47 Skytrain, designed not to fight but to carry people. Their pilots were experienced but so was the enemy, and there was no escape.

'Is it the same plane? Or is there more than one?' Andrea asked, trembling.

'Does it matter?' asked Brian, looking resigned. 'Either way, our fate is sealed.'

For once, Andrea wished he wasn't so direct. She wanted him to lie to her, to tell her everything was going to be all right. She wondered if these were the last moments of her life. If she were to die right now, she would be surrounded by two people she loved the most, her sister and her husband, and it was a solace to her. It could have been worse, she supposed. She could have been alone. But soon, all thoughts were gone, replaced by blind panic as they weaved through the clouds.

During their six-week training course in air evacuation at Bowman Field Airbase, they learnt how to identify enemy planes and survive in the arctic, the jungle and the desert. They learnt what happened to the body without oxygen at ten thousand feet. They studied aeromedical physiology and chemical warfare. They learnt how to adjust dosages of certain drugs based on the effects of altitude, apply and readjust splints, give sedatives and stimulants, treat shock and administer oxygen. They navigated obstacle courses and crawled under barbed wire with live machine-gun fire in the background. They were pelted with flour bombs to teach them how to take cover. Those six weeks had been the hardest of Andrea's life and yet, none of it had prepared her for this, death coming for them in the form of a German fighter plane.

She could no longer see the mountains. Instead, rolling green fields were all around them, the sight that never failed to take her breath away, only they no longer looked peaceful and calm because she could still hear the enemy plane that seemed to follow their every move. They were running but couldn't get away. Another minute of the mad chase, and another. Breath held, hands in her lap, eyes to the window. Was it her imagination or did the enemy fighter retreat, finally leaving them alone? The buzzing of the engine was not as intense and soon it disappeared altogether. Below was a small lake, with a patch of grey mud between the water and the hills. It was 1.30 p.m. They had been in the air for five hours. Two of those hours they had been fearing for their lives.

Everything in front of her looked fuzzy, blurry around the edges. Wiping her eyes with the back of her hands, she watched the crew chief as he prepared for crash-landing, stashing away the de-icing boots and the ladder used to load passengers onboard. Andrea felt helpless and small, her fate in the hands of the pilots and the enemy aircraft. She moved closer to her sister. 'Where do you think we are?' she asked.

'I don't know. Thrasher and Baggs will know. They're the pilots, they have maps.'

'What's going to happen to us? Once we land, what are we going to do?'

'One step at a time,' Nicole whispered. 'Let's not worry about it just yet.'

Andrea understood. There was no point worrying about what they were going to do next if their plane crashed or the enemy caught up with them. She bit her lips until they bled. Her nails dug into the skin of her hands, drawing blood, though it didn't hurt enough to take her mind off the mad chase. The plane approached the lake, beginning its descent, and Andrea braced herself, holding her knees tight. The land was getting closer, dark slush rushing towards them at blinding speed. Finally, the wheels touched the ground and the aircraft careened to one side. The landing gear sank in the mud and medical bags flew through the cabin. For a few terrifying moments, the plane seemed to hover in the air before falling back to the ground. Shearman was thrown across the fuselage, hitting Carrie in the face mid-flight and finally landing on the floor, a heavy toolbox falling on his head. He lay still, without a sound, without movement, while everyone shouted.

'Are you all right?' Nicole asked Carrie.

'Still in one piece,' she replied, holding her cheek. Blood was trickling from her mouth.

Although the plane continued to slowly move through the

mud, Andrea unclipped her seatbelt and was about to rush to Shearman's side when Brian grabbed her hand so hard, she cried out. 'Sit down right now. Stay in your seat until we know it's safe.'

'He needs our help,' said Andrea, pointing at the medic. Three other nurses were kneeling next to him, checking his pulse.

The plane came to an abrupt stop. 'Now you can go,' Brian said, releasing her.

Shearman was well taken care of by the other nurses. Too stunned to move, Andrea rubbed her hand where Brian's fingers had left angry red marks.

'What a rough landing,' whispered Nicole. 'How are you feeling?'

'I'm fine. Though no one warned us about this at nursing school.' Andrea tried to smile. Her hands were trembling.

The sisters tended to Carrie, who had a cut under her eye and a loose tooth. Shearman groaned and came to. He didn't seem to know where he was. As she bandaged Carrie's eye, Andrea felt disoriented and confused, like it had been her flying through the cabin and hitting her head. Everything swayed in front of her, as if she was still on board the *Santa Elena* sailing towards her unknown future.

She heard the pilot's voice. 'We need to exit the plane as soon as possible. It's not safe to stay here, in case of fire.'

One after another, the nurses and the medics picked up their musettes and medical bags and followed the flight personnel – the two pilots, the crew chief and the radio operator – off the plane. Two men carried Shearman, who was groaning in pain.

'You heard the man,' said Brian, moving towards the exit. He didn't wait for Andrea and didn't help her with her belongings but jumped off the plane into the mud.

Andrea reached for her bags. Nicole did the same. For a moment, the sisters stood close together as if unsure what to do. 'He shouldn't be talking to you with so much anger,' Nicole whispered.

'He's not always like this.' Andrea felt the need to defend her husband in front of her sister, even though she agreed with her.

He shouldn't be talking to her like that. 'He was just trying to make sure I was safe.'

'It upset you. I could tell. And I don't like seeing you upset.'

'He's under a lot of stress. He's been at the front longer than us. The things he's seen.' She shook her head, feeling sad. 'It's not easy for him.'

'It's not easy for any of us. He shouldn't be taking it out on you.' Nicole put the bags down and hugged Andrea. 'I want you to know that you are not alone. I'm here for you. No matter what.'

'I know. It's not like him at all,' she lied. 'He can be caring and loving and kind. When we first met, I thought he was the kindest man I've ever known. I love him.'

'I know that.'

'And he loves me.'

'I know that too. But does he respect you?'

They followed the others, jumping down into the mud, fighting their way to dry land, sinking with each step, while rain was lashing their faces. Behind them was their downed plane, its propellers bent, its sides smashed, its fuselage covered in bullet holes, like a bird with broken wings, defeated and sad. Ahead of them was the unknown land they had found themselves in, forested hills and rugged mountains as far as the eye could see. Andrea was shocked by the damage to the plane. It was a miracle they had survived. Perhaps God was watching over them after all. 'Where are we?' someone shouted, voicing the thought on everybody's mind. All eyes turned to the pilots.

'Deep in enemy territory somewhere,' was the reply.

Eight Years Ago

The grounds of the University of Michigan were magical at all times of year. In winter, the snow sparkled like a bridal gown, fresh and untouched. In summer, the grass was green and cheerful and bathed in sunshine. In spring, the new leaves and flowers screamed of a fresh start. But Andrea's favourite season was autumn, when everywhere she looked she saw all shades of yellow, red and orange, and it made her heart sing. In autumn, she didn't want to study, didn't want to sit in the gloomy theatre listening to lectures, even if it was her beloved professor talking about the latest clinical research. She wanted to feel the golden carpet of leaves under her feet, to breathe the still air, no longer hot but not yet cold either, to amble through the park while humming to herself. She wanted to write poetry under her favourite oak tree, on the bench where a silver inscription read in bold letters, 'To Beryl, from her loving husband of fifty years, until we meet again.' Sometimes, when she sat there, she pretended she could see Beryl and her husband, strolling through these alleyways, holding hands. To be loved like this for fifty years, wasn't it wonderful? But then she imagined the husband walking alone, without his Beryl, his shoulders stooped in grief, and she felt like crying because she realised that even a happy ending meant heartbreak somewhere down the road. Everything was fleeting, nothing lasted forever, not even happily-ever-after.

She knew autumn meant the end of summer, the end of warmth and sunbathing and ice cream in the park. In a few short weeks, winter would be here and white slush would fall from the sky. But to her, it didn't feel like the end. It felt like a glorious, breathtaking beginning.

That morning, she didn't have time for daydreaming, even though the sun was shining and the leaves were calling for her in the breeze. She was late for her midterm. Because she hated chemistry, she had left preparing for the exam until the last moment. Only, the last moment had finally arrived and she had no clue what she was going to do. She would have to find a quiet spot and pray for a miracle, maybe go over her notes one more time. But first, a coffee.

The coffeehouse was bursting with activity, students and staff chirping like overexcited birds. She loved the campus atmosphere, loved the air of expectation and hope. In a few years, they would be doctors, teachers, engineers. They would have the lives they had always dreamt of. Someone once told her that her years at university, with their expectation of great things to come, would be the happiest of her life and she believed it.

She collected her coffee, black, no sugar, and spun around, looking for a place to sit. As she turned, she bumped into a man behind her, spilling dark hot liquid all over him, a brown blotch spreading rapidly across the light-blue fabric of his shirt.

'I'm so sorry,' she exclaimed, her hand flying to her mouth, her eyes travelling from the stain to the stranger's face.

The man saw her dismay and smiled. She thought he had the nicest smile, kind and genuine. It reached his eyes and made her want to smile too. 'Don't be sorry,' he said. 'It was all my fault. I was in your way.'

'Not at all. I should have looked where I was going. Now your shirt is ruined.' She was flustered and nervous, talking fast, tripping over her words.

'Once again, it was all my fault. To make it up to you, please allow me to buy you another coffee. It's the least I can do.'

'I couldn't possibly . . .' she stammered.

But he didn't seem to be listening. With his back to her he ordered two coffees at the counter. He collected the drinks and guided her to an empty table. He was tall, broad-shouldered and wiry, like he played some kind of sport, perhaps squash. His stubble and hair and eyebrows were dark, making him look foreign, exotic. He introduced himself as Brian and offered his hand. She felt a warmth spread through her. 'Andrea,' she said. 'I owe you a new shirt, Brian.'

'This old thing? I was sick of it anyway. I was looking for an excuse to throw it in the trash.'

He asked her what she was studying and what her favourite subject was. She told him she was going to become a nurse. 'I want to help people. My favourite subject? I couldn't pick just one. I enjoy them all. Except for chemistry. I hate chemistry.'

'You do, huh?' He grinned.

'If I never make it as a nurse, it will be because of the dreaded chemistry.'

After their coffees were finished, he suggested they go for a stroll through the grounds. 'It will get cold soon. We must make the most of this weather.'

'I wish I could. But I have an exam this morning. And I'm not ready.'

'Let me guess. Chemistry?'

'How did you know?'

'By the panic on your face and also . . .' He pointed at her bag that had come undone, revealing her chemistry textbook. 'Perhaps I could help?'

'Have you taken this subject before?'

'A long time ago.'

She pulled out her notes, spreading them on the table, and they both leaned over them, their heads nearly touching. One glance at the questions and she felt overwhelmed, like she was on board a tiny ship that was caught in a storm. 'I don't know why I even need it. I'm going to work with people, not molecules.'

'Understanding molecules is important too, especially for a nurse. One day you'll be glad you learnt this.'

'I doubt that very much.'

'Our bodies are made up of molecules after all. So is the medicine you will administer. You can't be a nurse without knowing how it all ties together.'

As he talked about electrons and protons, she watched him. He had the most remarkable face. It seemed to have an expression for everything. Right now it was one of amusement, as if he found her funny and endearing.

'Why does it seem like you are a million miles away?' he asked.

'I'm right here. I'm listening. You were saying something about positive and negative electric charges. And it actually made sense. You should be a teacher. You are good at this.'

'Perhaps I should.' He smiled.

By the time they said goodbye, she was nearly late for her test. She ran through the park, past Beryl's bench, over the fallen leaves, up the stairs and through the front door into the auditorium. Flustered and out of breath, she sank into a seat next to her sister. Nicole looked calm and collected. Nothing fazed her, not even chemistry. She glanced at her watch. 'I thought you weren't coming. The class is about to start.'

'I met someone,' Andrea said happily. 'And I'm seeing him again later today.'

'I thought you were going to the cinema with John tonight? Your first date, remember?'

'John who?' Andrea whispered.

As she watched her sister's teasing face, she heard his voice. 'Good morning, everyone. Professor Wyer is sick today, I'm afraid, and I will be taking the class. My name is Brian Lewis. I apologise for the stain on my shirt, I had a coffee incident this morning. All my fault, of course.'

When she lifted her head, feeling her cheeks burning, he was looking straight at her and his eyes were twinkling.

* * *

Andrea was the last to get off the plane. She hesitated for a moment before jumping into the unknown. Her feet hit the mud and she sank to her ankles, the galoshes she was wearing over her military shoes filling up with water. Her musette and medical bags were pulling her to the ground, making her shoulders sore. 'Let me help you with those,' said Brian, coming closer, reaching for the bags. 'We're safe now. You don't have to worry anymore.' He patted her hand.

Andrea smiled, grateful and relieved. 'I'm not worried.' She glanced at her sister, who was chatting to the other nurses. *See, she wanted to say to her. I told you everything was fine. We are all feeling the strain of the nightmare flight, the chase, the terrifying landing.* She had been so afraid. She was certain Brian was too. But it was all behind them now. She took a deep breath, filling her lungs with air. She could smell salt and distant fires.

For a few moments, the stranded Americans stood still, unsure what to do next, not talking much, not moving, looking at their downed plane, at the lake before them, at the dark forest and grey mountains behind them, their snow-capped hats barely visible in the fog. The mist made the mountains look like bearded ogres, unwelcoming and impregnable, demanding to know who the intruders were, screaming that they weren't welcome in this strange land.

'We might be here for a while,' said the other pilot, Second Lieutenant James Baggs. With his mop of hair the colour of old straw, his solid build, the Thompson submachine gun in his hands, he looked like a fairy-tale giant who belonged in these mountains. Andrea liked Baggs. He had trained as a fighter pilot at Foster Field in Texas before being selected as a troop carrier pilot and had already flown one hundred missions. No matter what the war threw at them, with Baggs on their side they would stand a chance. 'How many rations do we have left?'

'Enough for a couple of days,' said Renee, the head nurse, a tall brunette with the face of an angel and the heart of a Bull Terrier, ferocious and fearless. In the first few days in Catania, Andrea had got in constant trouble with Renee. After that, she tried her best to stay out of the woman's way.

'Better than nothing,' said Baggs.

'And when we run out?' asked one of the medics.

'We'll cross that bridge when we come to it. We need to work out where we are and how we can get back.'

'Why can't we radio for help?'

'We lost all radio communication with the control tower a while ago.'

'Does that mean no one is coming for us?' Renee wanted to know.

Baggs didn't reply. As she looked at the forlorn faces around her, Andrea felt a cold premonition, a fear of things to come. They were trapped in this unknown place, hunted by the Germans, with no means of supporting themselves. What were they going to do?

'Look at the bright side,' whispered Nicole. 'At least we are still alive.'

'Sure, we can be bright and positive for the next two days while we still have food. But then what?' asked Andrea.

'The food is the least of our worries,' said Brian. 'The Germans know about us. They know where we landed. It's only a matter of time before they come looking for us.'

Andrea turned away from her husband. To take her mind off her dark thoughts, she went to check on Shearman. Placing her hand on his forehead, she asked if he could hear her. He didn't reply, resting on a stretcher that the medics had constructed for him out of three airplane seats. His eyes were closed and his skin felt hot to the touch. There were blotches of blood on his dark green field jacket. His peaked hat with maroon piping that indicated he was part of the Medical Department had fallen in the mud. Andrea picked it up and replaced it on his head, covering him with a blanket from the plane's survival kit. The nurses were worried he might have internal injuries but there was nothing they could do for him other than give him some morphine for the pain and hope for the best.

An eerie silence fell over the group. All Andrea could see was water, trees and snow-capped mountains. If it wasn't for their downed plane, like a broken giant laid to rest, it would be peaceful and serene, a perfect scene to put on a postcard. Around her, her comrades were discussing what to do next. Someone suggested burning the aircraft so it didn't fall into German hands. Someone else argued they had no time for that and should hide in the forest. Andrea thought hiding was a good idea. It would give them time to come up with a proper plan. Perhaps there was a village nearby where they could ask for food and shelter and some information as to their whereabouts. She closed her eyes for a moment, listening to their voices, feeling a little dizzy from hunger and lack of sleep.

Suddenly, they fell quiet. One moment, they were talking all at once and everyone had an opinion about the future. The next, as if a button had been hit, the voices faded to nothing. Andrea opened her eyes. Her comrades were staring at the forest. On every face she saw fear. She turned around.

As the wind howled and the rain came down hard, a group of rough-looking men appeared from behind the trees, dressed like peasants in coarse woollen shirts and drawstring pants. Their flat hats were adorned with red stars. Some of them wore jackets, while others had nothing on but threadbare shirts with holes at the elbows. Their thick woolly socks peeked through their sandals. Andrea would have laughed at their comical appearance if every single one of the men wasn't holding a rifle in one hand and a dagger in another.

The Americans moved closer together, their backs to the lake, their faces to the strangers. Baggs stepped in front of them, lifting his machine gun, ready to protect them. A moment later, a dozen rifles were pointing at him. Baggs dropped his weapon and one of the newcomers picked it up. The medical personnel were defenceless in front of the ferocious-looking group, who stared at them with suspicion, not uttering a word. Andrea moved closer to Brian.

The oldest of the group, a man with a matted grey beard and an arrogant expression on his face, said something in a language Andrea didn't understand. 'What is he saying?' she whispered to her husband.

'I don't know. It doesn't sound like German.'

'That's a relief.'

Another man stepped forward. Although his beard covered half his face, Andrea could tell he was younger. For a moment, he observed the Americans, his eyes moving from face to face. Then he said in slow, accented English, 'British?'

'American.'

'Follow us.'

Without further explanation, the man turned on his heels and started walking towards the forest. Faced with a dozen gruff strangers armed to the teeth, the astonished Americans had no choice but to do what the man said. No one dared ask any questions. They were unarmed and exposed, far from home, with no idea where they were or what they were up against and no means to defend themselves.

Under the cover of the trees, the strangers seemed to relax a little. They didn't lower their weapons but exchanged short phrases, occasionally laughing.

Surrounded by the scary men with rifles who were watching her every move, Andrea felt her knees shaking a little as she walked. A few times she stumbled and nearly fell. Nicole didn't seem to have that problem. She was strolling ahead like she was on a promenade in Lafayette Park. Andrea wondered where she got her bravery from. If only she were more like her sister, she could conquer the world.

'If they kill us here in the forest, no one will ever know. Our families will never find out what happened to us,' Andrea whispered to Nicole.

'If they wanted to kill us, they would have done it where they found us,' said Nicole. 'They wouldn't bother to take us away.'

'Where do you think they are taking us?'

'To their lair to eat us, perhaps? They seem the type. Look at their beards and their fierce eyes.'

It was Renee who shouted to the men, 'Where are we going?' Andrea expected the leader to get angry at the head nurse, to hit her with the butt of his rifle perhaps or at the very least to shout at her. To her surprise, he did none of those things. He slowed down, lowered his weapon and smiled. 'Walk now. Questions later. No delays.'

Thrasher, who was walking in front of them, paused and said, 'We have to get back to the plane.'

'No delays,' the stranger repeated. 'Great danger.'

'The IFF. We need to destroy it.'

The leader watched the pilot with incomprehension.

'Equipment that sends the coded signals. We can't leave it behind for the Germans. It's classified. We need to blow up the plane.'

The leader nodded and motioned for Thrasher to follow him back to the lake. 'Bradford needs to come with us,' said the pilot. 'He's our radio operator. I'll need his help.'

Blond and red-faced Bradford joined Thrasher and the stranger. The small group retraced their steps, soon disappearing behind the trees. Everyone waited in tense silence. Ten minutes later, an explosion was heard. Andrea watched the faces around her with a heavy heart. The thought of destroying the only thing that still linked them to the outside world filled her with sadness. Their transport plane was more than just a machine, it represented hope. Now that the plane was gone, it was just them, alone with a group of strangers, lost behind enemy lines, with no means of getting back.

Andrea wanted to move closer to her husband, to ask him how he was holding up, to offer him a bite of her K ration but didn't dare. One of the men was right next to her, his rifle pointing in her direction. She shivered under his gaze.

'I don't like their guns,' she whispered to her sister.

'If the Germans are searching for us, the guns might come in handy.'

'How do you know they are not on the Germans' side?'

'If they were, they wouldn't have let us destroy the equipment.'

It made sense, and for a moment Andrea felt reassured.

When the men returned, they were silent and grim. Andrea could see by their faces they felt just like she did at the loss of their trusty plane. They had brought a box of sugar cubes, some extra blankets, a tarp from the survival kit and more K rations that didn't taste particularly good but were useful in an emergency. They had also taken a parachute off the plane that they cut into pieces to be used as scarves. Andrea accepted her share of the material gratefully, wrapping it around her neck. There was an icy quality to the air and she knew she was going to need it.

Now that everyone was accounted for, they resumed walking through the forest in silence. One after another, trailed by the strangers' weapons, they trudged up a hill, every now and then slipping in the mud. The narrow trail wound its way up the mountain, twisting and turning and disappearing among the pines, like ever-green guards protecting it from trespassers. The track looked unassailable to Andrea, intimidating and impossible to conquer, like Mount Everest on a stormy day. A few nurses wore their raincoats but the sisters had forgotten theirs in their rush to leave the damaged plane. They had jumped out of the troop carrier, afraid it would catch fire, and now they were drenched to the bone. Andrea's hair clung to her face like seaweed. Her boots filled with water and were dragging her down. Her wet uniform felt heavy. Even her underwear was soaked. Her teeth clattered from the cold. She did her best to keep up with the group, even though every step was torture.

A small nurse called Liz had fallen behind. She was crying softly as she walked up the steep path. Andrea watched Renee come up to her. 'Dry your tears. Don't give them the satisfaction,' she said.

Liz sniffled. 'It's too much. First the Germans shooting at us, then the crash. And now this.'

'Remember, you are a member of the Nurses Corps. You represent our Army and our country.'

'I have a small child. And a husband fighting in Italy somewhere. I don't want to die.'

'Many of us have children waiting for us at home. We have to be brave, for them.'

Liz stopped crying and increased her pace. Although the head nurse terrified Andrea, as they trudged through the unknown land surrounded by the group of wild looking strangers, she felt grateful to have Renee on their side.

After an hour of marching through the forest, they came to a small stone hut built into the hillside. A large ox was tethered nearby, munching on grass and occasionally emitting a loud bellow. Andrea supposed he didn't like the storm any more than they did. The Americans watched in surprise as the strangers hitched the ox to a wooden cart and waved at the medics who were carrying the makeshift stretcher. 'To make it easier for you. Hard to carry through the forest,' the leader said. Looking relieved, the men put Shearman on the cart.

Brian pressed Andrea's hand. 'See, nothing to worry about. They are being kind.'

She could think of a hundred things to worry about. 'Perhaps if they pointed their guns away from us, it would be even kinder.'

'Why don't you suggest it to them?'

Before she had a chance to reply, the leader of the rifle-bearing warriors commanded the group to move and the uncomfortable journey continued. After another hour of walking, the rain stopped and the sky cleared. It was no longer black but light grey, with the clouds moving swiftly over their heads, changing shape and shifting as if in a rush to get away from this place, wherever it was. Next thing Andrea knew, the forest was behind them and they were standing in front of a two-storey house with a stone roof. Nearby were a dozen small huts, and people were gathering around, their mouths open in astonishment, their eyes on the Americans. Andrea watched a group of women clad in dark clothes with their hair covered by kerchiefs, carrying sacks on their heads, children running barefoot on wet grass, grim-faced men crouching on the ground and smoking in silence.

'Gjolen,' said the leader. 'We stop here.'

The other men repeated, 'Gjolen, Gjolen.' Andrea realised it was the name of the village. After hours of walking, she felt grateful for a break. She tried to remember when she had last had something to eat. It was hours ago, in the morning, just before they left on their ill-fated journey.

'Women, this way. Men, that way,' said the leader.

'They are separating us?' Andrea felt panic rise inside her. She watched helplessly as her husband and the other men were marched towards one of the huts.

'It's a Muslim village,' said Nicole. 'Look at the way the women are dressed. They probably frown upon socialising between men and women.'

Andrea threw one last regretful glance at her husband. Her eyes filled with tears. Suddenly, she felt lost, as if Brian's presence was the only thing keeping her sane.

'Don't worry. We'll be reunited with them soon enough. Look at the bright side. At least we don't have to walk anymore.'

'Something to eat would be nice. And a warm bed.'

'We'll be lucky if they let us crash on the floor.'

After everything they had just been through, Andrea thought she could sleep anywhere, even standing up if she had to. She wanted to close her eyes and not open them again for a hundred years. And maybe when she woke up, their ordeal would be behind them and by some miracle they would be back home. As she stood in a puddle of water under the ominous skies, waiting for the strangers to decide their fate, she thought of her childhood bedroom, the candles burning by her bed, her soft pillow, her favourite books on the bedside table. An apple pie cooking in the oven downstairs and her mother's voice calling her for dinner.

The leader led the women to one of the houses and told them to leave their bags outside. The women refused. The bags contained their precious supplies. If they lost them, they would have nothing left. But they were quickly silenced by the guns pointing in their direction.

Without their bags, they were taken past a primitive bathroom, nothing but a hole in the wooden floor, and found themselves in an empty room with a fireplace and a dirty rug.

The room was small and filled with smoke, even though there was no fire. Andrea struggled to breathe. There was no furniture in the tiny cabin, apart from a broken chair in the corner. The curtains were tightly drawn and a candle was burning on the mantelpiece. The nurses sat down on the floor, discarding their wet jackets. The leader brought in a flat dish filled with oil and a wick, and placed it on the mantel. 'A lamp for you,' he said. 'Soon, we bring food.'

Outside, the wind howled like a petrified animal. It started raining again. Andrea stretched out her aching feet, wishing the fire was still burning.

The man turned around to leave but paused in the doorway. 'Today is your lucky day. God was looking out for you.'

'The Germans attacked us and we escaped with not a scratch among us. Other than Shearman and Carrie here. I'd say today we won the lottery,' said Renee, smiling.

'Not just the Germans. We were preparing to shoot your plane down, but then we saw a white star on the fuselage. The star saved your lives.'

'Who are you people?' Renee asked.

'My name is Hasan Gina,' the man said proudly. 'I am the leader of the Albanian partisans.'

'We are in Albania?'

'Ay,' said Gina, nodding. A moment later, he was gone.

* * *

Thirteen nurses huddled together on the hard floor. For a few moments, no one spoke. Albania might as well be on a different planet, so lost and out of place they all felt. To take her mind off their uncertain future, Andrea moved to the window, pulled the curtain aside and glanced at the bustling village, trying to spot her husband. One look at his face, even from afar, and she would feel better.

She couldn't see Brian anywhere. A man with a stick was herding sheep, which seemed to be everywhere, dashing this way and that, bellowing and tripping up passers-by, who were shouting at one another in frustration. Women dodged the sheep with heavy baskets balanced on their hips. A dozen barefoot, half-naked children ran happily through the mayhem as if it was summer and not November and nine degrees with wind, pointing sticks at one another like guns. A boy saw Andrea at the window and lifted his stick up, pressing the pretend trigger. 'Pft-pft,' he shouted and she waved at him and smiled.

She sat back down next to her sister, who was busy telling Carrie and Tory all about her son waiting for her at home. Even before she heard the words, Andrea knew Nicole was talking about Leon. Her whole face lit up when she spoke about her boy.

As she listened to her sister, a wave of homesickness washed over her. She closed her eyes and imagined walking hand in hand with her husband on the sand in Waikiki, while the gentle waves whispered under their feet. Their honeymoon in Hawaii was the first time she had been away from home without her parents. That feeling of freedom and love – of their whole lives stretching before them without a care in the world, of being together every moment of every day, of being lost in each other and having nothing to think about and nowhere to be – she had not experienced before and knew she would probably never experience again. It was a new beginning and the time stood still. They made love more times than she could count, their bodies always touching, drawn to one another. She read to him as they held each other in a hammock. He taught her how to snorkel and she looked in awe as a magic world she had never encountered before unfolded in front of her eyes. The tropical waters were warm and inviting, and his smile lit up her heart. It was in Hawaii that she had swum with turtles and touched a dolphin for the first time. There was not a cloud in the sky and there was no war.

It was warm inside the room but Andrea couldn't stop

shivering. If only she had a change of clothes. Her wet uniform clung to her, making her teeth clatter. She wished she'd had the foresight to bring a blanket from the plane's survival gear, like some of the other nurses. Liz, the youngest of the group, was curled up into a little ball in the corner, a warm blanket over her, trembling like a scared kitten and crying softly. Renee sat next to her, stroking her back. Liz looked up at her. 'I'm allowed to cry now. They can't see me here.'

'It's not the time to cry,' said Renee. 'We've been lucky so far. But we need to be strong, for what the next few weeks will bring.'

Liz wiped her face with the back of her hand.

'The warlord with the beard said they are bringing some food. We will all feel better after we've had something to eat and a good night's sleep. We've been through a lot,' said Renee.

'What are we going to do? How will we get back?' Liz cried.

'Let's not think about it today. Let's think about it tomorrow.'

'Like Scarlett O'Hara?' whispered Liz, smiling.

Renee nodded. 'Exactly like Scarlett O'Hara. Everything will look different in the morning.'

'We'll still be here in the morning. We'll still be lost, with nowhere to turn,' muttered Liz, but she was no longer crying.

'I don't think we are that far. Italy is just across the Adriatic Sea.'

'If only we could swim across,' whispered Andrea, moving closer to Nicole. Being next to her sister brought comfort, even here, lost in enemy territory with no hope for the future. 'Does anyone know anything about Albania?'

A large, broad-faced nurse called Frankie, who was sitting across from the sisters removing her wet boots, looked up and said, 'My mother-in-law is Albanian. She hasn't lived here since she was a child but she still talks about this place with love. It's a poor land but the people are proud, with hearts of gold.'

'Perhaps your mother-in-law is right,' said Renee. 'They might look scary but they took us to safety. They promised us food and shelter, even though they themselves seem to have very little.

They are hiding us from the Germans, even though it could get them in trouble.'

Frankie said, 'My mother-in-law calls Albania the land of the eagle. When she tells me about it, it's always with longing in her voice.'

'The land of the eagle,' Andrea repeated. 'Sounds romantic, doesn't it? Hopeful. Like a fairy-tale kingdom.'

'She told me it's been occupied by the Italians since 1939. Two months ago, after Italy surrendered to the Allies, the Germans moved in. The country is predominantly Muslim but there are some Greek Orthodox in the south and Catholics in the north. It's lovely in summer but winters are cold here.'

'As we are going to find out soon,' said Renee.

'Hopefully we'll find a way to get back before then,' said Nicole, ever the optimist. 'As soon as the sun comes up, we need to start walking.'

'Walking where? I'm not going anywhere until I've had something to eat and at least twelve hours of sleep,' said Liz. When she saw the other nurses staring at her, she exclaimed, 'What? I had a long day.'

The girls started laughing, and it was at that moment that Gina walked in, carrying a tray in his hands. 'Good to see you happy,' he said, placing the food on the floor in front of them. 'Happy is good for the soul. Here, cornbread for you and pickled onions.' He pointed at the tray by his feet. 'You eat, you go to sleep.'

Eagerly the women reached for the white flat bread. It looked delicious but when Andrea took a bite, she nearly choked. The bread was heavy and difficult to chew. As they ate, young children appeared in the room and played music for them on their *kavals*, melancholy sounds that filled Andrea with sadness.

A while later, a tray of sour white cheese was brought in, which was as unappetising as the bread. So much so that Andrea didn't take any, even though she was still starving. She felt herself drifting off.

'Please eat a little, you will need your strength,' said Nicole, shaking her awake and putting a chunk of cheese in her hands. 'You can sleep later.'

Gina lit the fire and it crackled and flickered, illuminating their tired faces. Soon there was no bread left on the tray. Even though the women hated it, they had eaten every crumb. The cheese was gone too and so were the onions. One by one the nurses stretched on the floor, covering themselves with their coats. Andrea curled up next to her sister. 'Are you asleep?' she whispered, putting her arm around Nicole, finding comfort in her warmth, like she did when they were children.

'Almost,' Nicole replied.

'Do you remember when we were ten and got lost in the woods?'

Nicole nodded. 'I remember. We walked for hours but couldn't find our way out. We were calling and no one came. It was dark and we were afraid.'

Andrea said, 'We fell asleep under a tree. When we woke up and it was light again, we realised the village was only a hundred metres away. We walked through some trees and there it was. While we slept peacefully in the woods, our parents were up all night, searching for us. I've never seen them so upset.'

'I hope they don't hear about this. I hope they never find out we are missing. I don't want them to worry.'

'We'll be back soon. We'll find a way. Perhaps we'll wake up tomorrow and find that things are not as bad as we thought, just like that time in the woods. Perhaps they will send a search party for us.'

She said it for her sister's sake, to make Nicole feel better, but in her heart she didn't believe it. The coast of Italy, their base, their home seemed forever lost. And no one was coming.

Eight Years Ago

Shivering in her dad's study, Andrea felt small and insignificant. Her strict and successful father had always had that effect on her. He expected too much, from himself and those around him, and as a result, she felt she could never measure up, that she could never be good enough for him. Nicole was good enough. Her marks were better, she was a star tennis player, a champion on the court and off it, the pride of the family. But Andrea wasn't special in any way and her father never failed to remind her of it. She enjoyed a little music and a little art but it wasn't something he could brag to his friends and colleagues about as they sipped their whiskeys and smoked their cigars on Friday nights, regaling each other with stories of their children's achievements. Linda was graduating Harvard and opening a law practice. Darren was taking over the family business. And here was Andrea, training to be a nurse, emptying bedpans and washing floors.

And now she was standing in front of her parents with her head held low and her hands trembling behind her back, disappointing them once again, finally proving that everything her father had ever believed of her was true, that she was good for nothing. He should be pleased. He should be saying to her, I told you so. But he didn't look pleased, only angry and upset, and suddenly she wanted to be anywhere but here, under his dissatisfied glare. She would rather do anything than have this conversation.

Her knees were shaking and her legs felt weak. She looked around for something to lean on but couldn't see anything. She felt like she was suffocating, like the walls were closing in on her. The blinds were down, the curtains shut tight. There was no air and very little light. The furniture was dark, the walls, the bookshelves. From the paintings, her grandparents and great-grandparents looked down on her as if they were deeply disappointed too. Her father was talking, while her mother fidgeted by his side, twisting a handkerchief with her fingers, pacing on the spot and nodding, agreeing with his every word. When the sisters were growing up, their parents had always presented a united front, never disagreed, never argued, not in front of their daughters, anyway. As she watched her father's grim face and her mother's nervous smile, Andrea wished that for once she would stand up for her child.

'You are not marrying this man. Not while you live under our roof,' her father was saying.

Andrea squeezed her fists tight, digging her nails into her flesh to stop her voice from trembling. 'This is where you are wrong, Father. I am *marrying him. He asked me and I said yes.' On the engagement finger of her left hand was a beautiful ring Brian had given her the night before, during the best night of her life, when she had least expected it. Emerald, dark green and stunning, to match the colour of her eyes. Every time she looked at it, she wanted to cry with happiness. She hid her hands behind her back but it was too late, her father had noticed. By the look on his face she knew he deemed the ring unworthy of her, just like he deemed Brian not good enough.*

Her mother shuffled forward. She placed her hand on Andrea's arm. 'There's no rush to marry, honey. You are only nineteen. And this man, how long have you known him? How can you be sure he is the right person for you?'

'Six months,' Andrea replied. She wanted to tell her parents they had been the happiest six months of her life. She wanted to tell them that, when Brian held her in his arms, her heart soared. That when he kissed her, she felt like she was flying. That when she was with him, she felt at home, and when they were apart, she felt like a part of her was missing. That she thought of him every second of every day. And when she thought of him, she felt short of breath, like she was under water. That in the last six months he had become her everything and life without him by her side was not an option. That she was a different person to the one she had been before she met him, that her world had changed beyond

recognition. Wasn't that what true love did? It changed you as a person. She didn't say any of it to her disapproving and judgemental parents. She felt there was little point. They wouldn't understand, their own marriage being one of convenience, more of a business deal than a union of two people who loved each other.

'Of course he is not the right man for her,' her father roared. 'He is ten years older. He's been married before. He has children.'

'None of it matters because I love him. And he loves me.'

'Sometimes love is not enough,' said her mother, shaking her head. 'You'll understand when you are older.'

Andrea watched her mother with incomprehension. Love was all that mattered. What was she talking about?

'Why did he get divorced?' Her mother wanted to know. 'What went wrong?'

'What difference does it make?'

'It makes all the difference in the world,' her father said. 'The way he treated his first wife is going to be the way he treats you.'

Her mother nodded. 'We don't want you to rush into anything, honey. We want what's best for you. We want you to be happy.'

'I am happy. I've never been happier.'

'We don't want your heart to be broken when you are so young.'

'I am a grown-up. I can make my own decisions. I know you think marrying Brian is a mistake but you are wrong. And even if it is, let me make my own mistakes. Let me learn from them. Let me live my life.'

'If you marry him, you will become a stepmother at nineteen. Instead of starting a new life, you will be shackled down with responsibility,' her mother said, rolling her eyes as if marvelling at her daughter's short-sightedness.

Andrea squared her shoulders and looked her parents in the eye. She tried not to flinch when she said, 'I have already said yes to Brian.' It was hard to stand up to her father and mother when her whole life she had let them dictate her every move. But she wasn't a child anymore. And she had never felt more strongly about anything.

For the first time in her life, they were not getting their way.

'You are not to marry this man. I forbid it,' said her father, shaking his fist.

Andrea's eyes filled with tears. She blinked. 'What are you going to do? Marry me off to someone I don't love, like you did to Nicole? Look how happy that made her. Every time I see her, she looks like she's about to cry.'

'Nicole knows her responsibilities. As should you.'

'You don't own us. We are not your toys, to do with as you please. We are human beings, with lives and feelings and dreams. I am marrying Brian and there is nothing you can do to stop me.'

'If you marry that man, you will no longer be our daughter. You won't be welcome in our house.'

She couldn't believe the words she was hearing. It wasn't real. It was a bad dream. She looked at her father, waiting for him to tell her he didn't mean it. She looked at her mother, waiting for her to disagree with him for the first time in her life. But neither of them moved. Slowly, Andrea said, 'Then I will no longer be your daughter.'

She turned her back on her parents and left the room, taking care to close the door as quietly as she could. When she was certain they couldn't hear her, she leaned on the wall and cried.

Chapter 2

Among Strangers

Nicole woke up and found herself on the wooden floor, her body stiff, her arm aching. The room smelt of smoke, even though the fire had long burnt out. The curtains were tightly drawn and only a thin streak of light broke through, playing on the nurses' faces. For a few moments, she didn't know where she was. And then she remembered and her heart fell. She searched for her sister and spotted her nearby, her eyes closed, her head resting on her rolled-up jacket. When she saw her twin, Nicole's heart stopped beating violently. Her breathing slowed down. Everything was all right in the world as long as Andrea was by her side. Her sister was her safe place. She was home.

Leaving for the front had turned out to be the hardest thing Nicole had ever done. Every time she closed her eyes, she saw her child. Her dreams were filled with the images of him, running barefoot through the fields, chasing his dog Clover, learning to ride his bicycle, shouting to her, 'Look at me, Mama. Look what I can do!' She dreamt of him as a three-year-old, chubby and sweet; a five-year-old, discovering the world while holding on to her hand for dear life; an eight-year-old, telling her how proud he was of her. And every morning, when she awoke, she wept.

She volunteered because there was a shortage of nurses, and

thousands of young men across the ocean, in war-torn Europe, were dying without anyone to help. Posters with slogans like 'Become a Nurse: Your Country Needs You' and 'Save his Life and Find Your Own' popped up as if by magic everywhere she turned. Every time she passed one, she felt ashamed. Here she was, safe and content, while on the other side of the world people's lives were being torn apart. Every poster was a reproach and a reminder that it wasn't too late, that she was needed, that this wasn't the time to be selfish. Even the First Lady Eleanor Roosevelt, who had four sons serving in the military, pleaded for her to join. 'I ask for my boys what every mother has the right to ask,' Mrs Roosevelt told her from the pages of the American Journal of Nursing, 'that they be given full and adequate nursing care should the time come when they need it. Only you, nurses who have not yet volunteered, can give it.' That meant her, Nicole. If she went to Europe, she might help bring back someone who otherwise would never return, a young man only a few years older than Leon, someone's son, brother, nephew, grandson. How could she stay home and do nothing? Because she was at the front, a soldier might not perish in a hostile Italy devastated by war. Because she was at the front, a mother might welcome her son back. Because she was at the front, a child might see his father again.

But knowing that didn't make it easier to leave her own child behind.

Of course, there was also her sister. She could never let Andrea go to war on her own. After all, they had never been apart for longer than a few days. Without her sister by her side it would feel like half of her was missing. What if something happened out there and Andrea didn't come home? Nicole would never forgive herself.

She went to the front for all the right reasons. But it didn't mean her heart didn't break with the injustice of it all. To ease her pain a little, to make it possible to breathe freely and not fall into a dark abyss, Nicole wrote to her boy every single day.

Sometimes just a few sentences, to let him know she was thinking of him. Other times, when she had a free moment, pages filled with love and memories of the two of them together. Even though she knew her letters were unlikely to reach him, she continued to write and post them, like diary entries, like confession, every evening without fail.

Nicole stretched and rubbed her eyes. Outside, a rooster crowed. A dog was barking, louder by the second, frantic and excited about something. Somewhere in the distance goats bleated and a cow mooed, the noises peaceful and serene, reminding her of the summers they spent on their grandparents' farm. She smiled at the thought of her grandmother's apple pies in the oven, of the smell of baking waking her in the morning, of fresh milk and daisy chains, and bike rides that lasted for hours, of racing Andrea underwater and sunbathing with a glass of orange juice and a good book.

And then, a loud shriek was heard and the illusion was broken. Nicole jumped to her feet.

'What's happening?' muttered Andrea, opening her eyes. 'Are we under attack? Are the Nazis here?'

The sisters rushed outside, followed by a couple of other nurses.

'Bastards, how dare they?' cried Carrie, shaking her fist. Nicole thought she had never seen the young woman without her makeup before. She was always beautifully put together, even though they were at the front. This morning, however, her hair was a mess and her eyes were red like she had been crying.

'What's wrong?' asked Andrea. 'What happened?'

'I came outside to get a hairbrush from my bag. I found the bag unzipped and everything of value gone. Soap, socks, underwear, toothbrush, lipstick, mascara, some K rations, even the letters Mama wrote me, all vanished. There is nothing left.'

Nicole placed her arm around her weeping colleague's shoulders. 'You can borrow my toothbrush if you like,' she said. 'I always pack a spare one because my sister is absentminded and forgets hers. Here, let me get it for you.'

She went to her bag, only to find it empty too. Dumbfounded, she stared at it for a few moments.

'I knew we couldn't trust these people,' exclaimed Carrie. 'We should have taken our bags to the room with us. Instead, we left everything outside like they told us.'

'What choice did we have? They are the ones with the rifles.'

'And now they are the ones with my toothbrush and spare socks.'

'My bag is fine. I still have all my things,' said Andrea. 'I can share with you girls.'

A terrible thought occurred to Nicole. She unzipped the inside pocket of her bag and put her hand inside. Her fingers found what she was looking for and she exhaled in relief. Pulling out the precious photographs, she pressed them to her heart. She could get new soap and socks. But the pictures were irreplaceable.

'What do you have there?' asked Andrea when they went back inside, leaving Carrie and the other nurses complaining about their stolen belongings.

'Just some photographs. Us as children, Leon, Mother and Father. Sometimes the only thing that gets me through the day is seeing the faces I love.' Nicole pointed at one of the photographs, where a young girl of eight or nine was holding a brown dog no bigger than a rat and just as skinny. 'Look at this one. It was taken the day I turned up with a stray puppy I found in a puddle. Dad was so angry. I can't believe they let us keep him.'

'Pumpkin was our best friend,' Andrea said. 'Mama loved that dog. Dad did too, eventually. Let me see.'

Taking the photographs from Nicole, Andrea spread them on her lap and the sisters looked at the two identical little girls holding tennis rackets and smiling at the camera. And here they were again, throwing a ball to their dog, who loved chasing it but never brought it back. On the next picture their father was teaching them how to ride a bicycle, while their mother was cheering them on. Nicole smiled at the memory of that sunny day when they were six and didn't have a care in the world. It was one of the few occasions they had Dad all to themselves. As an owner of a chain of furniture factories, he never had time for anything that didn't make him money. Even though they rarely saw him, when the sisters were little, they worshipped the ground he walked on. Their mother didn't work but always seemed busy. There was always a charity ball to organise or a fundraiser to attend, and so the girls were brought up by a parade of nannies who never stayed long, scared off by their father's temper. As a result, they had everything money could buy but very little affection. The only thing they could always rely on was each other.

There were a few pictures of Leon, as a newborn, all wrapped up with only his eyes and nose visible, an ecstatic Nicole holding him close to her heart; as a cheeky toddler, pulling a cat's tail; and finally as a serious eight-year-old in his school uniform with his favourite book in his hands.

'What's this one?' Andrea asked, reaching for one of the photographs with a puzzled expression on her face. She looked at the picture, at Nicole, then at the picture again. 'Is this Darren? Does your husband know you carry a picture of your childhood sweetheart in your bag?'

'I don't think Anthony would care.' Nicole peered at the faces in the photograph, her heart beating fast. She saw a handsome young man with the biggest smile on his face. She saw herself, young and wafer-thin, her hair long and blonde, her eyes twinkling with joy. She usually avoided looking at this photograph because, every time she did, she felt like someone had punched her. Everything was in it, joy, heartbreak, longing and regret. 'I found it before we left home. I thought it would bring me luck.'

'You miss him.'

Nicole blushed. 'I still think about him sometimes.'

Ten Years Ago

It was a perfect night, with stars aplenty, moon unusually bright, its silvery light making everything appear magical, the trees, the houses, Darren's smiling face. All was quiet and only the leaves were whispering faintly in the breeze. They were alone together and her heart was singing. When he was by her side, her heart was always singing.

'Do you have the keys?' asked Darren. She showed him the heavy metal key to the tennis courts behind her parents' house. 'The rackets?' She nodded and threw her backpack down. 'Great,' he said. 'Can we turn the lights on?'

'Not if we don't want to get caught.' Nicole giggled, feeling light-headed from the excitement of it. Her father would kill her if he knew she had snuck out of her room after dark to meet a boy. He would be even more upset if he knew the two of them had broken into his precious tennis courts. She would never normally have dared take such a risk but it was Darren's birthday and she was determined to make it special. 'Have you ever played before?'

'Once or twice, never in the dark,' he said.

'Don't worry, there is plenty of light. It's a full moon tonight.'

He pretended to take off his imaginary hat and bowed to her with an exaggerated flourish, his hand reaching all the way to the ground. 'Teach me everything you know, grandmaster Nicole.'

She laughed. 'It's tennis, not chess, silly.'

They picked up their rackets and walked to the opposite sides of the court. Nicole served. She had spent her whole childhood perfecting her serve. There was a wall in her bedroom adorned with medals and trophies, a testament to her father's tyranny. Tennis was like religion in their family. If you didn't play tennis, you didn't belong. And what Nicole wanted more than anything else was to belong. She enjoyed the social aspect of tennis, the camaraderie, the friends she had made over the years. What she didn't enjoy was the gruelling work that left her body sore, or the weight of her father's expectations. Tournaments left her anxious and short of breath, unable to sleep the night before or after. No number of awards could make up for that awful feeling. She wished she was brave like Andrea and could tell her father to his face that she didn't want to play competitively anymore.

No matter how softly she hit the ball, Darren couldn't hit it back. And when he served, the ball got caught in the net. But it didn't matter. As she watched him running across the court, Nicole felt giddy with joy. There was a feeling of anticipation in the air, a sense of a new beginning. Something was happening between them, something different. She couldn't quite put her finger on what it was just yet but it was real and she knew he could feel it too. 'I thought you said you'd played before,' she exclaimed, laughing.

'I said I played. I didn't say I played well. Lucky for me I have the greatest coach in all of Detroit.'

'If you can afford me.'

'I will pay you in books and chocolate. Your two favourite things.'

'Deal,' she said, sending the ball into the far corner, making him run and fall to his knees with a mock expression of horror on his face.

When they were done playing, they sat side by side on the grass. Even though it was the first week of summer, the nights were still chilly. She shivered, wishing she had worn a jumper, but for some reason after ten years of friendship she suddenly started to care what she looked like when he was around, so she had opted for a short skirt and a tight top instead. She opened the picnic basket she had prepared and surprised him with a homemade pie, fruit, cheese and some of her mother's best cold meats.

'You are spoiling me,' he said, grinning and reaching for the pie. If she'd learnt one thing about Darren after all these years, it was that he loved his food.

'Wait till you see the cake. I baked it myself.' He couldn't afford to go out for dinner on his birthday and didn't like the idea of her paying for him, so she had prepared this picnic for him instead.

The hours she had spent baking the cake were worth it, just to see the look on his face.

After she sang 'Happy Birthday' and he blew out the candles, she said, 'As the loser of tonight's tennis challenge, you have to do everything I tell you.' She pinched him.

'You didn't win, you cheated. You're like a cat, able to see in the dark, while I stumble around blindly.'

'How about a rematch tomorrow night?'

'Perhaps a game of chess instead? Or poker? Anything I can beat you at?' He took a bite of his cake and closed his eyes. 'Nicole, this is fantastic. I've never tasted anything like it in my life. You should open a bakery one day.'

'I only ever bake for myself, never for other people. With very few exceptions. Andrea and I are actually thinking of training as nurses.'

'Have you told your parents?'

'Not yet. We know they won't approve. They think nursing is beneath us.'

'You will make a great nurse. You care about people.'

Suddenly, the lights snapped on. They heard someone fumbling with the lock. Exchanging a worried glance, they leapt to their feet. Nicole grabbed the picnic basket, while Darren picked up the backpack, and the two of them dashed towards the fence as fast as they could and climbed over, sprinting down the road and doing their best to ignore the housekeeper's shouts to stop. Out of breath, they collapsed on top of each other in a heap of giggles.

'Do you think she saw us?' she asked.

'Of course she saw us. Why would she be shouting if she didn't?'

'Yes, but do you think she knows who we are?'

'I hope not. Unlike you, she's not a cat and can't see in the dark.'

'Good,' Nicole said. She could feel the heat coming from his body. His face was only inches away. 'Darren?' she whispered.

'Yes?' He turned to her and she moved closer. For a moment it felt like time stood still, as if someone had hit a pause button on a recording. She could see his face clearly in the moonlight. He was

watching her with so much affection, so much kindness, she felt like she was going to cry. Surprising him and herself, she kissed him, lightly at first, barely touching his lips, and then deeper. When she looked up, she saw joy on his face. 'I've wanted to do this for years,' he said.

'How many years?' She wanted to know. Her heart was racing and her hands were shaking, her hair had become loose and fell across her face in a blonde wave, her cheeks were burning. To hide her confusion, she moved away from him slightly and looked at the ground.

'Let's see,' he said, pretending to count on his fingers. 'Ten or eleven.'

She giggled. 'That would make us five years old.'

'I've wanted to kiss you from the moment I saw you.'

'Happy birthday, Darren,' she whispered, touching his cheek with the tips of her fingers, stroking his hair.

They stayed in each other's arms until dawn, talking about nothing and everything, reminiscing about the past and making plans for the future. He was her safe place, Nicole realised. With him she could always be herself. She didn't want the sun to come up, didn't want to see the red sky, the new day being born, because she didn't want the night to end. It had been the happiest night of her life and for as long as she lived, she knew she would never forget it.

* * *

When Gina appeared with another tray of cornbread, the nurses surrounded him, talking all at once, not making much sense. The leader of the partisans, accustomed to facing men who were armed to their teeth, looked ill at ease and unsure of what to do at the sight of so many enraged women. Hands reached for him, fists shook and they hissed like angry cats when they spoke. 'Everything is gone. Only the medical kits remain. We want our things back. All of it. Everything you've taken, we want it all back.'

Gina stood tall and proud in front of them. 'Albanians do not steal,' he said.

'What are we supposed to do without our supplies? We can't continue on our way with nothing.'

'I can't even brush my teeth,' said Carrie. 'And all my makeup is gone. I look a fright.'

Tory said, 'You don't need to brush your teeth. There's barely any food. And what does it matter what you look like? You think the Nazis will care when they shoot you? Me, I lost all the drawings my little girl did for me before I left. I lost all her photographs. It breaks my heart.'

'I can't find my wedding ring,' said Renee. 'I took it off and put it in my bag because it was too loose on my finger in this weather. I was so afraid of losing it. And now it's gone. So is my son's teddy bear. It was my good-luck charm.'

Gina backed away from the nurses, who looked angry enough to strike him. 'Albanians do not steal,' he repeated in a firm voice. 'In our country, penalty is death.'

He raised his hand, like a full stop at the end of a sentence, to show them the discussion was over. Not paying any attention to him, the women continued to shout and even the sight of his rifle was not enough to force them to stop. Finally, he managed to extricate himself from the nurses and slipped out of the room, muttering something about going to check on breakfast. And even after he was gone, they continued to cluck like angry chickens.

Only when local women appeared with trays of cornbread and cheese in their hands did the nurses quieten down and go back inside.

'I've never tasted anything more disgusting in my life,' Nicole said to Andrea as she reached for a slice of cornbread.

'Me neither,' Andrea replied. 'Can I have some more?'

The girls ate in silence. Nicole said, 'You look tired. Didn't sleep last night?'

'Not much. I was so cold, tossing and turning all night, couldn't get comfortable on the floor, couldn't stop worrying.'

'Not me. I slept perfectly well.'

'I wish I was as brave as you. Here we are, half a world away from home, stranded in enemy territory, the Nazis on our heels, and you sleep like a baby.'

'Not brave, just . . . I can't control any of it, so why worry?'

It wasn't strictly true. Nicole could never admit it to Andrea but a mother always worried. What scared Nicole the most wasn't the war or the explosions or the Nazis in pursuit. Her greatest fear was not coming home to her boy. If something happened to her, Leon would grow up without a mother. She wouldn't be there for him when he needed her. She would never hold him in her arms again, feel the warmth of his little body next to hers or hear his voice call for her. What if their goodbye three months ago was the last time they saw each other? Her heart broke at the thought.

Even after all the cornbread was gone, Nicole was still hungry. She wanted to ask Gina if there was more food but he was nowhere to be found. She supposed they had scared him off with their shouting and accusations. Two village women brought a pitcher of water and a basin. When one of the nurses attempted to drink the water, the women laughed and shook their heads, mimicking washing their faces. The nurses took turns to wash. The water was warm and felt nice on Nicole's skin. And when her hands and face were no longer covered in grime, she was ready to face the day. Ready to embark on the journey that would take them back home.

When they left their sleeping quarters and stepped outside, carrying what remained of their belongings, Nicole watched her sister run into her husband's arms and hug him like she hadn't seen him for months. Brian stood still, allowing himself to be hugged. He looked tired, like he hadn't slept either. Andrea bombarded him with questions, wanting to know how his night had been, if he had eaten, if he was well. He responded in short, irritated sentences and didn't ask her anything in return. It didn't seem to faze Andrea, who beamed at the sight of him.

Brian looked in Nicole's direction and nodded. She nodded back. There was an understanding between them. Neither of them liked the other but they put up a polite front for Andrea's sake.

Unlike the nurses, the men had not been robbed. On hearing the women's story, some of them shared their supplies with them. A jolly medic named Greg gave Nicole a piece of soap and his woolly socks. She immediately put the socks on because her feet were freezing.

They were gathered in the village square, surrounded by a group of men wearing dark clothes and holding rifles in their hands. Gina threw worried glances their way like he was afraid they would attack him again. But this time it was the men shouting and talking loudly. Everyone spoke all at once. Everyone had a question for the partisan. 'Are you going to take us to the coast?' 'Can we telegraph our unit?' 'Do you have a boat that can take us back to Italy?' Gina listened quietly for a few moments and then told them he needed to speak to his commandant before he could make any decisions. In order to contact him, he had to send a messenger to a village nearby.

While they waited to hear from the commandant, the villagers brought people with ailments to see the nurses and the medics. A boy had a broken arm. An old man had a bad burn across his face. A heavily pregnant woman had a fever. The Americans did everything they could to help, to repay the villagers' kindness. After lunch of more cornbread and cheese, a group of female partisans came to see them. They carried guns and hand grenades, and entertained them by singing songs and telling stories.

After a short discussion, the group decided to tell Gina they couldn't wait anymore. They had to be on their way. The longer they stayed in one place, the quicker the Nazis would catch up with them. But before they could do so, the commandant arrived on a tall black horse. His name was Kahreman Ylli. He was an imposing man dressed in a black cape and oversized boots, with a long beard and a moustache that reminded Nicole of compass arrows. Half a dozen partisans followed him on foot on either side, bowing deeply at his every word. Gina took his hat off when the man approached. The Americans hesitated for a moment and followed his example.

The commandant spoke no English and relied on Gina to translate. He wanted to know who the Americans were and what they were doing in Albania. Baggs answered all the questions as best he could and asked if the partisans could help them get back to base.

The man nodded and smiled but didn't speak, looking from one face to another, as if trying to read their minds. Then he motioned to Gina to follow him. They spoke privately for a few minutes, while the Americans waited nervously.

'Our destiny is being decided over there,' said Thrasher. All eyes were on the commandant and Gina, whose backs were to the group.

'I don't know why they bothered to walk away. We can't understand a word they are saying anyway,' said Baggs.

'Perhaps they don't trust us. Just like we don't trust them,' said Renee.

When the two Albanians returned, Gina explained the Americans had two options. They could stay in Gjolen and send someone across the country to get in touch with a British pilot who had parachuted out of a plane and was hiding in the hills. 'But village does not have more food for you,' he said. 'And staying in one place is dangerous.' Or they could walk to Berat, a town under partisan control, where they would find additional help. What this help was, Gina wouldn't say. Perhaps it was the language barrier, perhaps the Albanians had no idea what to do about the strangers, but the exchange left the Americans as confused and unsure as before.

'How far is Berat?' asked Nicole, holding her breath. Her feet still ached after yesterday's trek through the woods.

'Two days' walk. But we leave now.'

'Like they are giving us much choice,' muttered Brian as the group gathered their belongings.

Nicole watched her brother-in-law as he walked away, still grumbling, without waiting for Andrea or offering to help with her bags. Sometimes she wondered how her vivacious and cheerful sister – the most easy-going person Nicole knew, who made friends everywhere she went, who couldn't walk past an abandoned puppy without taking it in, who helped the homeless and volunteered to read to local schoolchildren – could have ended up with such a moody, unpredictable husband. It was a case of opposites attract, she supposed, but the marriage never made sense to her. Least of all now, when they were trapped in enemy territory with danger around every bend of the road and Brian was barely paying attention to Andrea.

The whole village turned up to see them off. Women and children waved and smiled, while men watched in silence. The Americans thanked the villagers for their hospitality and followed Gina and his group of partisans towards the forest dressed in autumn colours. Half a world away, across an ocean, it was autumn too. Stepping on yellow and brown leaves under her feet, Nicole could pretend she was back home, ambling through the park with her sister and sharing confidences. She could imagine running down the street towards Darren, his arms around her, his lips on her lips and a giddy sensation of being lifted high in the air and spun round and round, until her sides hurt from laughing and her heart was bursting with joy. But there was little joy on this gloomy morning as they marched in silence, one after another up a mountain trail, mud getting inside their boots.

To everyone's relief, Shearman was feeling better. Although he was still weak, his fever was almost gone. Before they set out, Gina brought a horse the village had provided for the travellers.

Shearman looked like the Emperor Napoleon atop his white stallion, while the rest of them were his foot soldiers trudging dutifully behind him.

'I'd give anything for a shower and a nice pizza,' said Andrea. 'I'm still hungry, even after all that cornbread.'

'I'll be happy if I never see cornbread again in my life,' said Nicole. 'I'd kill for a good coffee, though.'

'I've been telling you for years. All that caffeine is not good for you. Brian says it leads to anxiety and high blood pressure.'

'Well, if Brian says so,' muttered Nicole, making a face behind Andrea's back.

'Perhaps a break will do you good.'

'Are you saying all this is for the best? Never mind that we are lost in Nazi-occupied territory, just as long as Nicole doesn't drink too much coffee.'

'That's exactly what I'm saying.'

Gina walked ahead, followed by the pilots, then the rest of the Americans, while the other partisans surrounded the group, sometimes moving forward, other times falling behind. Nicole was grateful that their rifles were no longer pointed at them. Under the cover of trees, the Albanians seemed to relax and were laughing and talking. Every now and then, Gina would send one of them ahead to scout out the area.

Nicole was worried about Andrea. Her sister didn't seem like herself, barely talking, not smiling, her head held low, her shoulders stooped. Nicole adjusted her bag straps and continued to walk, wishing she was the one riding the white horse. After two hours of making their way through the rocky terrain, walking mostly uphill into the mountains, every step was agony. Nicole had finished all the water in her flask and her lips were burning. She resolved to ration her water in the future and get by on the smallest amount she possibly could. She didn't think she could walk much further, and yet, Gina didn't show any signs of slowing down. She would have asked him if they could stop for a while or whether there was somewhere she could refill her flask, but he was too far ahead and she could never catch up.

She knew she wasn't the only one feeling disheartened and tired. When they first set out, the men and women were chatting happily, reminiscing about home and speculating about what their future held. Now, two hours later, they continued in silence, every now and again slowing down to wait for those who had fallen behind. As the terrain became more difficult, many nurses and medics struggled to keep up. Carrie slipped in the mud. Baggs had to help her up. She continued cautiously, afraid of falling again.

The trees towered above, their dark branches reaching for them, whispering ominously of bad things to come. Nicole tried not to think of what they might hide, of what could be waiting for them behind each bend of the road. She overheard Gina say that the German presence was high in this area. What if they ran into an enemy patrol? Would a handful of partisans be enough to protect them, their rifles notwithstanding? And would they risk their lives for a group of strangers or hand them over happily to save themselves?

All these doubts ran through her mind as she trudged through mud behind Renee, who pushed on like her life depended on it, and her sister, who was watching Brian with a forlorn expression on her face.

Renee turned to the girls. 'I've never met twins before,' she said. 'Do you finish each other's sentences?'

'All the time,' the sisters replied in unison, like a well-rehearsed choir.

'Can you read each other's minds?'

'Most of the time,' said Nicole, laughing.

'Tell me what she's thinking now.' Renee pointed at Andrea, who was puffing as she walked up the hill.

'Let me see.' Nicole appraised her sister. 'She wishes she could sit in the sun by the window in her bedroom with her easel and paints. It's her favourite thing to do. She is hungry and would give anything for a piece of chocolate.'

'Is it true?' Renee asked Andrea.

'A piece of chocolate and a cup of tea,' said Andrea.

'Remarkable. What does it feel like to have a twin? Do you feel like you are looking in the mirror sometimes?'

Nicole thought about their childhood, of growing up side by side with her soulmate who knew her better than she knew herself, of sharing every moment of every day, of always having someone to turn to. 'It feels like you are not alone,' she replied.

After what seemed like many hours of walking, when Nicole was ready to pass out right there on the muddy trail, they heard a swooshing sound. 'River,' said Gina, pointing behind the trees. 'We stop and rest.'

When she heard his words, Nicole placed her bags on the ground with relief, closed her eyes and whispered, 'Thank you, God.' She wasn't religious but speaking to God here, in this majestic forest, felt right. The trees were still and silent and the sun peered through their branches, casting a warm glow around them. If there was one place on earth where God would hear her, it was here.

The Americans cheered up and were chatting happily as they set up a temporary camp by the river. Gina sent two partisans ahead, with orders to prepare their accommodation in the next village. Andrea was resting, her head on Brian's shoulder, her eyes closed. Nicole sat down on the grass next to them, grateful it was no longer raining. She took off her boots and examined the blisters on her feet. Her big toe and little toe were bleeding. She put a plaster over them and replaced her boots, wondering how much longer it would take. How many hours of walking, how many steps, how many days like today. And was she strong enough to make it? Closing her eyes, she listened to the river as it whispered its sad song to her, and wondered where it was flowing. Perhaps, just like them, it was making its way towards the coast in hope of something better.

'Maybe we could spend the night here. It's as good a place as any,' Andrea said, opening her eyes. 'My feet are hurting.'

'It's too early in the day to stop,' said Brian. 'I know it's hard, but we need to keep moving. The sooner we reach Berat, the better.'

Nicole saw the horse drinking eagerly from the stream and remembered how thirsty she was. Grabbing her empty flask, she approached the river. She was about to refill it when she heard Gina's voice. 'Water not for drinking.'

Nicole was about to argue. If she didn't have anything to drink that instant, she might faint. But when she looked at the water, she saw that it was brown with dirt. She knew Gina was right, but she couldn't help feeling disappointed and a little angry at him, as if it was all his fault.

'I have some water left,' said Andrea. 'Have some.' She reached for her flask and held it out for Nicole.

Brian grabbed her hand. 'God knows when we'll be able to refill our supply. Don't give your water away.'

'It's for my sister. She needs it.'

He didn't let go of her hand. 'Your sister should have been more careful with her own water.'

Nicole shook her head. 'I'm fine,' she said. 'Don't worry about me. I can wait.'

Even though Andrea looked upset, she nodded. They sat in silence for a while, resting their aching feet. Brian shared his K ration with Andrea but didn't offer Nicole any. Finally, when he walked away to talk to one of the pilots, Andrea reached for her flask and passed it to Nicole. 'Quick, have a drink before he comes back.'

Gratefully, Nicole took a few sips and then pushed the flask back into Andrea's hands.

'Have some more,' said Andrea. 'I have plenty.'

'Your husband is right. Hold on to your water. You are going to need it.'

Andrea looked like she was about to argue but Brian appeared by her side, and she quickly put the flask away.

The Americans had dispersed, some sitting on tree logs, others on wet grass, munching on cornbread and taking swigs from their flasks, while the partisans watched the trail they had just come along. The men were playing poker, using their K rations as chips. They laughed softly and teased one another. The women chatted in small groups. Renee and Carrie were holding hands, quietly singing lines from Vera Lynn's 'We'll Meet Again'. The popular melody made Nicole feel nostalgic and sad. She closed her eyes, swaying from side to side, wanting to dance on the riverbank, to twirl in a timeless waltz. If only she wasn't so exhausted and her feet weren't aching. The river was whispering by their feet in time to the song, grey like the sky over their heads, framed by tree branches the colour of concrete, like a postcard that had come to life. Somewhere, a coyote was howling, while birds called out greetings to one another. Leon would have liked it here, thought Nicole. He loved nature. Camping had been his favourite pastime since he was three years old. She tried to see it through his eyes, to forget about her fears, to not worry about what lay ahead but enjoy the moment, the serenity, the oppressive skies, the still trees, the rushing water. She was drifting off to sleep when she heard Gina's voice, telling everyone it was time to go.

'Go where?' asked Renee. 'The trail ends here.'

'We don't need trail. We cross river.'

A dozen voices rose in protest, demanding to know how it was possible to cross the river on foot in these conditions.

'It looks deep. Is it deep? Have you seen the current?' exclaimed Liz, tears in her voice. The tiny nurse always sounded like she was about to cry. Nicole didn't blame her. She too felt like crying.

'You want us to swim across? Hardly the weather for swimming.'

That was Baggs, the man who only yesterday had volunteered to go into the sea without a Mae West.

'I can't swim. Never learnt how,' exclaimed Carrie, shaking her head.

Gina raised his hand. Everyone fell silent. He said, 'We don't swim. Mules cross.'

'What mules?' asked Thrasher.

Gina didn't reply, only lifted his hand and pointed. All eyes turned in the direction of the trail. At first, Nicole couldn't see anything. All was quiet but for the breeze whistling in the branches. A moment later, she heard voices. An animal whinnied. Nicole tensed, sensing danger, wondering if it was the Nazis coming after them. But Gina didn't look concerned and she relaxed.

Two partisans she had never seen before appeared from behind a bush, rifles in their hands. Behind the partisans walked half a dozen villagers, each leading a mule on a rope. Gina lifted his hand in greeting.

While the partisans waded across by themselves and didn't seem to mind the cold water, the Americans took turns to ride the mules across the river. Baggs was the first to cross. 'Made it safe and sound,' he called out from the other side. 'Nothing to worry about, folks.'

The other men followed Baggs, while the nurses stood nervously, waiting their turn, throwing worried glances at the river and the animals. In the middle, where the current was the strongest, the water nearly pushed the mules off their feet but they continued to move forward steadily. When it was Andrea's turn, she said, 'See you on the other side,' then smiled and waved to Nicole and the other nurses, climbing her mule and directing it across the river. All was going well until she reached the middle. Nicole watched with horror as her sister's mule lost its footing. Andrea slid off the animal and was thrown into the churning water. As the stream closed over her, she fought for breath, waving her hands in the air. Andrea was crying for help in the river, while Nicole was doing the same on land. Calling her sister's name, her knees shaking, she rushed towards the water, even though she wasn't a strong swimmer. If she entered the river, rather than coming to Andrea's rescue, she would need rescuing herself and she knew it. But her sister was in trouble and she didn't hesitate.

She was knee deep in water when the two pilots jumped in from the other side. With no thought for their own safety, they swam towards Andrea and searched for her underwater, finally locating her and pulling her body to safety, to the opposite bank. The whole operation only took a minute, but it was the longest minute of Nicole's life. She watched with relief as Baggs and Thrasher placed Andrea down carefully, as she coughed and fought for breath. Her eyes searched for her husband and a moment later, Brian appeared, taking her hand.

Nicole took a step towards the river, desperate to see if Andrea was all right. Gina placed his hand on her shoulder and said, 'She is safe. Wait for mule.'

All the mules were busy carrying other nurses across. As if in slow motion, they placed one foot in front of the other carefully. Nicole paced impatiently, while others helped Andrea, who was sitting up and drinking from her flask. Renee placed a blanket over her shoulders. Carrie brought her a bite to eat. Tory kneeled by her side and was saying something to her. And only Nicole remained on the opposite bank, waiting for her turn to cross.

When a mule became available, Nicole sat in the saddle nervously while the stream of water threatened to knock the animal over. Once or twice, the mule stumbled and Nicole grabbed on so hard, her fingers hurt. She crossed without an incident. As soon as her feet touched the ground, she was by her sister's side. 'What a fright you gave me! How are you feeling?'

'Refreshed,' Andrea replied, making an effort to smile. 'What a lovely day for a dip in the river. All that freezing water is good for the immune system.' She was shaking under the blanket and her teeth were chattering.

'Does anyone have any spare clothes?' Nicole cried out. If Andrea travelled in wet clothes in this weather, she was sure to catch a chill.

'I had some socks but they were stolen, remember?' said Carrie. 'And now we are following the thieves blindly into the mountains.'

'I have a spare tunic,' said Renee.

Andrea removed her wet tunic and put the dry one on. Nicole took her jacket off. 'Here, for you. We don't want you getting pneumonia.'

'What about you?'

'I'll be fine for a bit.'

After a short break, they continued on their way. Andrea leaned on Brian's arm, Nicole walked by her side, every few minutes asking if she was all right, if she was hungry or thirsty, if she was warm or needed a rest.

'I'm hungry and thirsty and freezing cold,' said Andrea. 'But I'll live. When we make it back home, we'll laugh about it.'

'*If* we make it back home,' said Liz from behind them. Nicole turned around and glared at the younger girl.

The villagers took pity on the Americans and allowed them to keep the mules for the rest of the day. Andrea and Nicole were among the first to ride the animals down a narrow trail, relieved not to have to walk. Nicole imagined she was on her grandparents' farm, riding one of their horses through the countryside with the wind in her hair. For a moment, there was no war and no fear. Only occasional shouts in Albanian from the partisans broke the illusion.

Higher and higher they climbed into the mountains, Liz complaining every step of the way, Gina looking straight ahead in silence, the pilots humming a war tune and Renee talking about what she would do after the war was over. The trail was mud and slush under their feet. The trees threw shadows on their faces. The sun was high in the sky but provided no warmth. Every time they passed a village of stone houses with red roof tiles, they were welcomed with cornbread and cheese. The male elders who made up the village council stepped out of their huts to greet them, wanting to know everything about them. The Americans were becoming accustomed to curious looks and questions. A couple of times, they were able to refill their water flasks. Nicole made sure she didn't drink her water too quickly, saving it for later.

'They make you feel so welcome, don't they?' Carrie said. 'They greet us like we are their long-lost family.'

'Have you already forgiven them for your stolen socks?'

'I've forgiven but I haven't forgotten. Next time I'm keeping all my socks on.'

When the sun started to go down, they came to a small village called Poshnje and separated into two groups. Gina explained that if they wanted food and shelter, men and women couldn't be seen socialising with one another. Once again, Andrea said a teary farewell to Brian. In a small hut made of stone, a woman dressed in a headscarf, a dark blouse and a long skirt offered them cornbread and raw onions. She wanted to know everything about them, where they served, how the flight evacuation worked, how many patients the planes could carry and if the nurses ever felt afraid.

'I felt so scared when I boarded my first flight, I couldn't hold my flask in my hands,' said Carrie.

'I felt the most scared when our ship was torpedoed in the Atlantic,' said Tory.

'I'm scared now,' said Andrea, resting against the wall with her eyes closed.

When their host heard that Nicole and Andrea were from Detroit, she told them it was where her husband had attended university. 'He's told me so much about it, I feel like I've been there myself,' she said as she poured some soup into a large bowl.

'Maybe you can visit one day, when the war is over,' Nicole suggested.

'The war will never be over,' said the woman. 'The Germans are here to stay. They take our cattle and burn our villages, they kill our men and steal our crops. This is our life now and we might as well get used to it.'

The soup was sweet and a little spicy. The nurses took turns taking a spoonful each from the bowl. They returned again and again and didn't stop until the bowl was empty. It was a nice change to cornbread. Only afterwards they found out the soup was made from sheep intestines. None of them minded. As Nicole lay in the dark on the hard floor next to her sister, she thought it was the most delicious thing she had ever tasted.

This time it was Nicole who couldn't sleep. Her eyes wide open, she listened to her sister's breathing. Her body was aching from walking so much. She was shivering and couldn't get warm, even though the fire was crackling in the fireplace. She knew that in a few hours the sun would come up and they would have to do it all over again, walk until they were ready to drop. And yet, she couldn't get a moment of rest. The day before, they had been pursued by the Nazis and crashed. Today, her sister nearly drowned. What would tomorrow bring?

Chapter 3

Running in Circles

It was still dark outside when Gina woke the nurses up, telling them they had a lot of ground to cover and had to start early if they were to make it to Berat. As they waited for food, Andrea sat on the floor in front of the fireplace with her legs crossed, enjoying the warmth from the fire, while Nicole brushed her hair. A hundred strokes, like their mother had taught them. And then Andrea brushed Nicole's hair. It was a ritual they had shared since they were children. It gave Andrea a sense of belonging, of security and hope.

'I wonder what's for breakfast,' said Nicole. She looked tired this morning, the dark shadows under her eyes making her look older and a little sad, a little uncertain.

'I hope it's some more of that soup. I could eat a whole bowl by myself. Maybe we could ask.'

'Gina said not to beg for food. It's against the Albanian code of conduct or something.'

Their host walked in, wanting to know if they would like some pancakes. The nurses readily agreed. The woman invited them to the kitchen, where she lit the fire on the stone floor, set a ring stand over it and added some fat to a pan. The girls watched as she mixed water and wheat flour into small clumps of batter, ready to drop them into the hot grease.

Andrea was eagerly anticipating the treat when she heard voices outside. Gina appeared in the kitchen, looking like a thing untamed, hair out of place, beard matted. There was no time for breakfast, he said. The Germans had been spotted nearby.

Before they left, the host packed a few pancakes for them to take. As they gathered in the village square, Andrea tried one, finding it delicious. The village had taken their horse and most of their mules back, leaving only two of the smallest animals for the group to use, and once again they were forced to walk. Andrea was glad there were no streams to cross. She felt better on firm ground. The sun was rising when they started on their way, lighting up the horizon, illuminating the mountains, like a magic trick unfolding before her eyes. One minute all was dark, the next the forest was brimming with colour. Andrea walked on bravely, trying to ignore her aching feet. At least they had had a couple of opportunities to refill their flasks, having come across streams of water that appeared safe to drink. Just to be certain, they had added a few drops of iodine from the glass ampoules in their medical kits to sterilise the water.

Andrea noticed that the partisans travelling with them were not the same as the day before. Some were friendly and smiled at her as they walked. Others stared at the group with curiosity but didn't say a word. Then there were those who ignored them and pretended not to see them. They would come and go as Gina sent them to scout the area or relay messages. She felt grateful for everything the partisans were doing for them, guaranteeing food and shelter, protecting them from the Nazis and leading them to safety. She increased her pace and caught up to Gina. 'How much longer to Berat?' she asked.

'A few hours, maybe a day, if there are no Germans.'

She shivered. 'You don't seem too worried about it.'

'Nothing we can do. If we meet them, we hide. If we can't hide, we fight.'

Andrea glanced at the other partisans. There were six of them, holding their weapons, watching the road ahead. The rest of the group was unarmed. She wondered whether six rifles were enough to stand up to a German platoon. To take her mind off it, she changed the subject. 'Where did you learn to speak English so well?'

'When I was small, I went to the Albanian Vocational School. All subjects were in English.'

'What was your favourite subject?'

'I liked sports and algebra but my favourite was history. History teaches many lessons. If only people learnt.'

He looked grim when he said it. Andrea knew he was talking about the war. 'How did you become the leader of the partisans?' she asked.

'By killing the most Germans.'

She watched his impassive face, trying to decipher whether he was joking. She decided that he wasn't. 'And if someone kills more Germans than you?'

'Then they replace me.'

'What has it been like? Since the Germans invaded?'

Gina hesitated before answering. 'Before they came here, our lives were hard but peaceful. Now we are at war. We won't rest until they are out of our country. We work day and night to make it happen.'

'That must be hard.'

'We attacked a German convoy two weeks ago. Next day, the Germans killed a hundred civilians of the town of Borovë and burnt down the villages nearby with flamethrowers. They think it will stop us. But it will only make us fight harder.'

'And your family? Are they partisans like you?'

He shook his head. 'My parents are old. They want a peaceful life. I fight so they won't have to. My pregnant wife is in a different partisan battalion. I haven't seen her since the occupation.'

'You must miss her.'

He nodded. 'When the war is over, we'll be together again. Until then, we have a job to do.'

Andrea tried to match his stride. She found it difficult to keep up with the partisan, who seemed to be made of steel and could walk for hours without breaking into a sweat. 'What is it that you do exactly?'

'Everything to hurt Germans. We destroy infrastructure, disrupt lines of communication.'

'Is that why you are helping us? To spite the Germans?'

'We help you because without us you will die.'

They hadn't been able to stop for food but continued on relentlessly, driven by the fear of a sudden attack. Hour after hour down a muddy path, and Andrea couldn't relax, her eyes on the road, scanning the partisans' faces, trying to discern what was about to happen from their expressions, listening for sudden noises, expecting at any moment to hear the sound of German boots hitting the rocky terrain. After hours of walking on an empty stomach, they paused on top of a hill. The sun had just started to go down and the woods behind them were dim and frightening, as if behind every tree a dark secret was waiting for them. In the valley below, Andrea could see lights that stretched under her like a carpet studded with diamonds. 'Berat,' said Gina, pointing. In silence the group looked at the promised land where they would find help and shelter. It was lit up like a Christmas tree, beckoning the weary travellers. If they hurried, they would make it before nightfall.

It took a further three hours of walking in the dark but they finally made it. As they marched through the outskirts of town, they saw tiny huts, some of them leaning to one side, others in ruins or burnt to the ground. Outside one of the lopsided structures, a miller was grinding cornmeal with a water-powered millstone. A butcher used an axe to chop off pieces of meat from a carcass hanging from a tree branch. He raised his hand in greeting when the group approached. In the hut next door, a blacksmith pounded on a piece of iron, while his apprentice used bellows to pump air into a fire. They didn't look up as the Americans strolled past. Life went on in town, even as the Germans were closing in.

Andrea had fallen behind. Her feet were aching and she couldn't keep up, even though she tried her best, not willing to delay the group. Nicole slowed down and walked next to her. 'It's Mama's birthday today,' she said sadly. 'I wonder what they are doing right now.'

'Having cake and champagne, no doubt. Rosa will cook a lovely meal. They'll have friends over.' At the thought of their housekeeper bringing out delicious meals from the kitchen at one of her mother's famous parties, Andrea felt like she was drowning, like she was still underwater, fighting for her life. When she left for the front, she had been prepared for many things. She had been expecting hardship, hunger, relentless work and sleepless nights. What she hadn't been expecting was the homesickness that hit her the moment she stepped on the ship that would carry her to war, a feeling so powerful, it left her short of breath. 'Dad never even said goodbye to me when we were shipping out,' she said quietly.

'Dad is a stubborn old mule.'

'I remember watching him as he hugged you. I waited for him to turn to me and when he didn't, I called his name. I wanted to tell him there is a war on. What else needs to happen for him to forget the past? But he didn't even glance my way. And now all I can think of is what if it was the last time I saw him? What if we never get a chance to fix things?'

'Of course you will. One day, all this will be behind us. We will come home. And maybe it will teach him a lesson. He'll know we are missing and they are looking for us. And he will finally understand that some things are more important than his pride.'

Was Nicole right? Was there a silver lining in all this? Would their father finally learn to accept her and the choices she had made? She could only hope so.

They caught up to the rest of the group, not because they were walking faster than before but because the others had stopped and seemed to be waiting for something. Everyone was eager to get going, to find a place to sleep, to feel safe. But Gina wasn't moving. He was watching something through his binoculars in the valley below. Andrea turned around and spotted an airfield, a barren strip of land with a runway and half a dozen buildings. In the twilight she saw planes taking off and coming in to land. Trucks darted between them, while people ran around, waving their arms. With horror Andrea recognised Nazi insignia on the planes' fuselages.

'Break is over. Time to go,' said Gina.

No one moved.

'Perhaps you haven't noticed. There is an airfield in the way. A German airfield,' said Thrasher. 'We need to turn back. Find a different route.'

'There is no turning back. No other route.'

Gina began to walk, not waiting to see if the group was following. The other partisans strode after Gina but the Americans remained rooted to the spot, their eyes on the German airplanes.

'He must be kidding. He wants us to cross a German runway, while Germans are all over the place.'

'Does he want us killed or captured?'

'Perhaps he's working for them after all.'

'I'd rather stay here than walk voluntarily into the jaws of a shark.'

The panicked voices reached Andrea, making her shiver, scaring her almost as much as the sight of the enemy planes.

'The man knows what he's doing,' said Baggs, beginning to walk. Slowly, uncertainly, the rest of the group followed.

They crossed a small valley and hid in the bushes while Gina watched the airfield through a pair of binoculars. Perhaps they would get lucky, Andrea thought. Perhaps the Nazi planes would leave and they would be able to cross the airfield safely and enter the centre of Berat. But, instead of leaving, more and more fighter planes seemed to appear as if out of nowhere. Andrea wondered if they would have to sleep here, under the open skies, across the field from the German pilots.

'Are you scared?' Brian whispered, his hand finding hers in the dark.

'Petrified,' she admitted.

'Maybe next time you'll listen to me.'

'What?' She looked up, surprised.

'I told you coming here was a bad idea. I told you to stay home and wait for me. You didn't listen.'

'I came to be with you. And to help people. They need nurses here.'

'And look at you now. Hiding from the Germans under a bush, led across the country by a maniac with a rifle. Don't make me say I told you so.'

How instant it was, the hurt. It scalded her like a sip of coffee that was too hot, making it hard to breathe. Andrea pulled her hand away. It took all she had to stop the tears from coming. She moved away from him and closer to her sister, who put her arms around her and said, 'Don't listen to him. You did the right thing coming here. Everything will work out just fine, you'll see.'

The planes were on the move. One after another, they soared into the air with a great noise and soon disappeared. When the runway appeared empty, the group moved from under the bushes. Andrea felt exposed out in the open, with the German airplanes nearby. She crawled low to the ground behind her husband, not daring to look up or make a noise, afraid the Nazi pilots could hear her heartbeat from the cockpits of their planes. In the distance, she heard bombs exploding. Black smoke and flames rose into the air in an inferno. She increased her speed, even though her legs were trembling.

As they approached the runway, they heard the sound of more planes. Soon they were right above them and Andrea could barely breathe from fear; there was nowhere to hide, not a tree, not a rock between them and the enemy. Any minute now, the Germans would open fire and cut them all down. Suddenly, she heard someone's voice behind her. 'They are our planes! American planes!'

Slowly she looked up, unable to believe her ears. And there, in the sky above her, were a dozen P-38 American fighters. She blinked, wondering if she was dreaming. The planes circled around, so low that, if Andrea waved to the pilots, chances were, the pilots would see her. The Americans shouted with joy and jumped up and down on the spot. Gina raised his hand and ordered them to stop. A moment later, the German Messerschmitts came in to land.

The men and women who were shouting and saluting only a moment ago dispersed, running for cover towards nearby trees. Andrea hid in a ditch. She looked around frantically for her sister and husband but couldn't see them. She felt sick to her stomach and unsteady on her knees as she crouched in the mud. It couldn't get any worse than this, she thought. But a moment later, it did. She heard machine-gun fire. Had they been spotted and were the Germans firing at them?

From her hiding place, Andrea watched the American fighter planes release their bombs. A moment later, she heard a deafening explosion. She cried out, covering her head with her hands. Nearby, the branches were shaking. First, she thought it was from the wind. Then she realised it was bullets. The German planes were strafing them.

She felt someone's arms around her and turned around, expecting to see Brian. But it was her sister, her face muddy, her eyes large like saucers. Andrea cried into her shoulder, wondering what would happen if they never made it to the coast. What if they perished here, near Berat? No one would ever find them. No one would know what happened to them.

The planes vanished just as suddenly as they had appeared. Andrea could no longer hear the sound of war. All was quiet again, as if she had imagined the devastation of a moment ago, if it wasn't for the smoke filling her nostrils, her ears ringing and her hands shaking. Slowly she opened her eyes and looked around. Her sister was saying something to her but she couldn't make out the words. *What?* she mouthed. *What?*

'Are you all right? Can you stand up?'

'I'm fine. I can stand up. Where is Brian?'

Nicole shrugged. 'I lost sight of him when the shooting started.'

All around them, the other members of the group were cautiously emerging from their hiding places. Baggs was helping Carrie to her feet. Shearman was standing up, glancing around like a frightened rabbit, looking shellshocked. Renee was by his side, saying something to him. Gina was talking to the other partisans. Andrea couldn't see her husband anywhere.

Forgetting about the danger, she ran to the spot where she had seen him last, shouting his name. A moment later, she felt a hand on her shoulder. 'What are you doing, screaming the house down? Keep this up and the German pilots will hear you.'

She swung around, her heart bursting with relief, and saw him standing in front of her, unharmed. Her breath caught in her throat. Sobbing, she threw herself into his arms. 'You're alive. I couldn't find you. I thought something happened to you.'

He hugged her. 'Nothing is going to happen to me.'

'I was afraid I lost you.'

'Don't be afraid. I'm fine.' For a long time he held her shaking body, stroking her back. 'Don't cry. I won't let anything happen to you.'

For a moment, in the midst of war and devastation, while others were shouting and airplane engines were buzzing like angry bees, while machine guns fired nearby, she felt safe and warm in his arms. The way she had many years ago, when they first met, when the world was at their feet and he loved her more than anything in his life.

Eight Years Ago

Andrea hesitated at the entrance to the chapel as the piano began to play 'Here Comes the Bride'. It felt wrong to her, to be standing here alone. It wasn't what she had imagined as a little girl, playing make-believe with her twin sister. Her father should be by her side, wearing his best suit, a proud smile on his face, ready to walk her down the aisle. She should be leaning on his arm, anticipating the happiest moment of her life and telling her how much he loved her just as he was about to give her to another man to cherish and take care of for the rest of her life. The chapel should be filled with family and friends. And yet, the pews stood empty. Only her sister Nicole and her husband Anthony were by Brian's side.

She had to take a deep breath before she made the first step towards the rest of her life. At the end of the long, lonely walk, the man she loved with everything she had was waiting for her. He told her she was his life and he would do anything for her, sacrifice everything, face anything. And she would do the same for him. The thought gave her strength.

When she saw his face, her heart skipped a beat and she forgot all about her doubts. He looked besotted, amazed by her. She knew that, after she married him, she would never be alone again. One step after another, she walked to his side, walked to marry the love of her life. It might not be what she had dreamt about as a little girl. But it was all she had ever wanted.

'You look beautiful,' he whispered, not taking his adoring eyes off her. Her mother was wrong. Love was enough. Love was everything.

The celebrant took a few steps forward. He smiled, welcoming them to the most important moments of their life. 'We are gathered here today to unite Brian Lewis and Andrea Connelly in marriage and to bear witness to the celebration of their love.' As he continued talking about trust and commitmeht, for better or worse, in sickness and in health, Andrea wondered about time and how quickly everything could change. Six months ago, she was alone. And now here she was, about to become Brian's wife. The night before, he had told her he never knew what love was until he met her and she believed him. Before she met him, she was a different person. She couldn't even imagine the things she would feel for him. The old her was gone forever and their future started now.

Brian took her hands in his. 'Andrea, when you came into my life, you showed me that miracles were possible. You are my miracle, the best thing that's ever happened to me, and I will treasure every moment with you for the rest of my days. I can't wait to call you my wife.'

When she spoke, her voice was not her own. It sounded unsteady, alien. 'Brian, when we met, it was as if the sun came out and illuminated my life. You fill my heart with joy. I can't imagine myself without you. You are my soulmate, my best friend and I will love you for as long as I live. I will never stop.'

Everything afterwards was a blur. Her sister and brother-in-law congratulating them, driving through night-time Detroit with Brian's arm around her, listening to his whispers of love, dining at their favourite restaurant. She could barely taste the food she put in her mouth. All she could see, all she could think of was him. I have a husband now, *she kept repeating to herself. She felt like a child, dressing up in her mother's gowns and putting on her lipstick. She felt like it was a dream, like she would soon wake up and he would be gone. But it wasn't a dream and she marvelled at the stroke of luck that had brought him into the café that morning when she spilled her coffee and he helped her with her exam.*

At the end of the night, when she could barely keep her eyes open, they danced for the first time as husband and wife and he said, 'I love you, Mrs Lewis.'

'I love you, Mr Lewis,' she replied and started to cry.

He paused on the dance floor and kissed her gently. 'I know you imagined your wedding day differently.'

'It doesn't matter. Everything was perfect. I wouldn't want it any other way,' she said and meant it. There was a simple golden band

on her finger next to her emerald engagement ring. There was a wide white gold band on his. She touched the rings with wonder.

'I know how much you sacrificed to be with me. I will spend the rest of my life making it up to you. I will spend the rest of my life making you happy.'

Outside, she could hear the roar of fireworks, like cannon fire bursting. 'Isn't it lucky?' he said. 'We got married on New Year's Eve. Do you know what that means?'

'It's a new year. A new beginning.'

He held her close, his lips tickling her cheek. 'There will always be fireworks on our anniversary. This way, you will never forget me.'

* * *

Andrea leaned on Brian's arm, her heart racing. It took all she had to keep up with the rest of the group. Only the thought of shelter, of a moment of peace, of leaving this terrifying place behind propelled her forward. They crossed the runway without incident and paused on top of a hill, the centre of Berat stretching below them, its lights calling for them. All was quiet, not a branch rustled, not a voice disturbed the night and only an owl hooted every once in a while from a tree behind them. Andrea couldn't stop her hands from trembling, couldn't stop herself from turning back time and time again, afraid. She knew any moment the mountains could erupt in gunfire. Behind every tree, behind every bend in the road, shadows moved, waiting for them. But she didn't let her doubts slow her down. She knew they had to fight for their survival, and so she placed one foot in front of another, telling herself to stay strong, to keep going, to not let her emotions get the better of her. Later, when they were safe, she would have time to reflect, to feel the fear, to shed those tears. Now was not that time.

From her observation point, she could see the Osum River on one side and a terraced hill of white houses with large windows and red-tiled roofs on the other. In the distance, a castle presided over the large town, like a titan guarding it from evil. Andrea had never seen a castle before and she stood breathless and mesmerised for a few moments, wondering if she had been transported to a magical fairy tale where there was no place for fear or the horrors of war.

Up until now, they had only seen small villages. By comparison, Berat was a metropolis of many thousands of people. 'If we can find help anywhere in Albania, it will be here,' Nicole whispered to her as they entered town. For the first time since they had crash-landed, Andrea felt hopeful. The lights of Berat seemed to be filled with possibilities.

'I'm just glad we made it,' she said. 'I didn't think we would.'

'It truly is a miracle.'

From every direction, malnourished, bare-footed children came running. They followed them like a pack of wolves, gaping with curiosity, chanting something in Albanian, repeating a word over and over again. It sounded to Andrea like they were saying *liberty*. Behind the children came the grown-ups, waving, cheering, shouting out greetings. As they walked through the town, the windows and the doors flew open and the inhabitants spilled out to welcome them. Women threw flowers at the group, while men took photographs with their clunky, old-fashioned cameras.

Stunned by the reception, the Americans slowed down until Gina commanded them to keep moving.

'They sure are friendly,' Andrea said.

'I wish they would be less so,' Brian replied. 'So much attention could be dangerous. Word spreads. Soon the Nazis will know where to look for us.'

'I feel like a celebrity. Why are they so happy to see us?' asked Nicole.

'They know we are American. From what I've heard, they've been waiting for the Allied forces to liberate them from the Germans.'

'And they think we are those forces? Can't they see how few of us there are? And half of us are women?'

'They are used to women fighting alongside men.'

'They think we are here to help them,' Andrea said slowly, 'when it's us who desperately need their help.'

Gina told them to wait in the town square and disappeared somewhere with the rest of the partisans. Andrea suspected he was finalising their sleeping arrangements for the night. The Americans were so exhausted, some slumped on the ground, resting their heads on their bags, while others sat in small circles, chatting and sharing their rations. The locals gathered around, watching them in silence.

Andrea and Brian sat close together away from everybody else, under a giant of an oak tree that looked capable of sheltering an army. The branches reached almost to the ground, and under their cool canopy Andrea felt hidden away from the rest of the world, as if it was just the two of them and not another soul around. A few years ago, before the war and their careers got in the way, they used to enjoy impromptu camping trips and weekends away. They would explore new towns, sip coffee in pretty cafés, browse local markets, sleep in tents, make love all night long and wake up late. Sometimes Brian's sons joined them on their adventures, bringing noise, laughter and light-hearted arguments. Once Brian made her pancakes on a rickety stove at a camp site in the middle of nowhere. She thought they were the best pancakes she had ever tasted. The memory made her feel warm on the inside, even as on the outside she was freezing in her damp uniform.

Even though she was tired and could barely keep her eyes open, she hoped Gina wouldn't be back too soon so she could enjoy this moment with her husband a little longer. Once Gina returned, she knew they would be separated again and she wouldn't see Brian until the next morning. She shuffled closer and placed her head on his shoulder. He moved slightly away. 'We are in a Muslim country, Andie. Show some respect.'

Taken aback, feeling a little deflated, she took his hand. Squeezing his fingers, she touched his wedding ring. 'Remember our honeymoon? Just the two of us in that cabin by the beach, the waves hitting the shore, a black-and-white film on TV, your arms around me.'

'I remember. You got locked in the bathroom. The lock got jammed and I had to use a drill to let you out.'

'I miss those times. We didn't have anywhere to be, didn't have to worry about anything other than the broken lock on the bathroom door and the fact you had never used a drill before in your life.'

He smiled. 'I had used a drill before. And we'll have times like that again. When all this is behind us, we'll go away together, just you and me.'

'What are we going to do when all this is over?'

'What we've always wanted to do. Go back to Detroit. Buy a house. Open our own practice.'

'Maybe take a few months off work first, to recover and spend some time together.'

He nodded. 'It will be fun, just the two of us with not a care in the world.'

She could see it in her mind, a cosy house with a fireplace, long days together doing the things they loved, walking in the park, swimming, playing tennis, reading side by side. No sudden explosions shaking the earth under their feet, no machine guns screaming with anger, nothing but a peaceful sky over their heads. 'It doesn't have to be the two of us forever. Maybe after a little while we could try for a baby. What do you think?' She held her breath, waiting for his response.

'A baby?' he asked, like he didn't know what the word meant.

'Just imagine. A little girl to spoil and love. Or a little boy you could teach how to play soccer. Wouldn't you like that?'

He let go of her hand. 'Andie, we spoke about this. You know I don't want any more children. I already have two wonderful boys. I've done it, I've lived through it. I'm at an age now when I want to live for myself.'

'But I haven't done any of it. And I've always wanted children. Are you saying I will never get to be a mother? I will never hold a baby in my arms?' Something inside her ached at the thought. A fear she couldn't understand or put into words, a longing so strong, it took her breath away.

'You have a nephew and two stepsons who spend every other weekend with us. Perhaps your sister will have another baby.' He spoke coldly, without emotion, as if it had nothing at all to do with him.

'I will never hear a child call me Mama? I will never rock my baby to sleep, sing lullabies, take him or her to school? I don't think I could live with that.'

'What do you want from me? I made it clear from the day we met that I don't want any more children. You knew this about me. Why did you marry me?'

'I married you because I was hoping you would change your mind,' she whispered.

'You made a mistake. I won't change my mind.'

'Not even for me?'

'Don't try to change me, Andie. It's not fair on either of us. If you can't accept me for who I am, then we shouldn't be together. Do you want to be with me? Or do you want children more?'

'Both,' she whispered, heartbroken. 'Both.'

'You can't have both. You knew what you were getting yourself into. It's not like I lied to you.'

She blinked hard, fighting tears. She didn't want him to see her crying. She would cry later, when he wasn't around. She would have all night to cry about this. 'Remember when I wanted to move closer to my sister and you said no? And when I wanted to accept a position at the children's hospital in Boston and you said no?'

'I did what I thought was best. What does it have to do with this conversation?'

She trembled, afraid of his anger but even more afraid of not being heard, of her needs being swept away like they were irrelevant. Like always. 'It feels like there's never any compromise. It's your way or not at all. I was hoping we could compromise on this.'

'Why would you think that? Whether or not we have children is the biggest decision of our lives.'

'Exactly. *Our* lives. It should be our decision, not just yours.'

'I told you I'm done having children. You accepted it. It's not me who is going back on my word, it's you.'

'But . . .'

He turned away from her. 'Let's not talk about it anymore.'

She watched him as he got up to his feet and walked towards the pilots, crouching down next to them, picking up a deck of cards, laughing and chatting, like the discussion that made her heart bleed had never happened. He didn't even glance in her direction, while she never took her eyes off him.

Fifteen minutes later, Gina returned and told the Americans their accommodations were ready for the night. The men were led to someone's house, while the women were taken to Grand Hotel Kolumbo, the best hotel in all of Albania, according to Gina. Andrea waited for Brian to say goodbye to her but he didn't even look up as he followed the rest of the men to their sleeping quarters. *I deserve this*, she thought as she threw one last regretful glance at his back. *Why did I have to bring it up now? This is hardly the time.* But a small part of her thought, *If not now, when?* When could she talk to him about something that meant the world to her and not have her feelings dismissed, and not be ignored and disregarded?

She sighed and walked towards the hotel, her bags dragging her down.

'Are you all right?' asked Nicole as they were about to go up the hotel stairs towards the main entrance. 'You look so sad.'

'Just tired, I think.' She couldn't tell anyone what was in her heart, not even her sister. To say out loud that she might never have children, to hear the devastating words come out of her mouth, to see the look of pity on her sister's face was more than she could bear.

'At least we don't have far to go. I fell asleep right on the road on top of my bag. I would have stayed there all night if the warlord didn't come back for us, that's how exhausted I am.'

The hotel was a tall three-storey building with a red roof and wide windows. Inside, luxury awaited them. Instead of the hard floor, they were given proper beds for the first time in days. 'We'll sleep well tonight,' said Andrea, even though she knew she wouldn't be able to get a moment of rest, not after the conversation she had just had with her husband. She wondered if he was affected by it at all, if he could sense how desperate she was and how afraid, or if he had already forgotten all about it.

Chapter 4

Waiting for a Miracle

When Nicole woke up the next morning, the plate of cornbread from the night before was still next to her. She must have fallen asleep even before she finished her dinner. She could barely remember the previous evening. Everything was an exhausted blur inside her head.

'Breakfast in bed,' said Andrea. She seemed to be in good spirits that morning, and only dark circles under her eyes betrayed a sleepless night.

Nicole poked the bread with her finger. It felt stale but she was hungry, so she took a bite. 'Want some?' She pushed the plate closer to her sister.

'Sure, why not?'

While they were eating the leftovers, their host knocked on the door and invited them for breakfast. The sisters put on their damp uniforms and joined the other nurses in the common area downstairs. The women were gathered at a round table, like King Arthur's faithful knights, staring with suspicion at a stew of unknown origin. When they tried a little bit on the tip of a spoon, they found it so tasty, they filled their bowls up immediately.

The hotel manager, a man in his thirties dressed in black, suggested they pool their money and give it to him. He promised to go to the market and buy some essentials for the group.

'After they stole our supplies, they think we'll trust them with our money,' whispered Renee, who was sitting next to Nicole with her plate of food. Out loud, she said, 'Thank you for your kind offer. We will go to the market ourselves.'

The man shook his head. 'You don't go to the market. They see a foreigner, they will rob you. They see a local, they offer a fair price.'

The girls huddled in the corner, whispering to each other.

'He has a point,' said Andrea. 'They will charge us ten times the price. We don't speak their language. We don't know how much things cost. They will be laughing at us behind our backs.'

'If we give him our money, we might never see it again,' said Carrie.

'We can't eat money. We can't wear money. We can't use money to brush our teeth. This might be the best chance we have to replenish our supplies.'

'I'm with Andrea on this,' said Nicole.

They decided to take the risk and entrusted the manager with their money.

When Gina appeared, they asked him if they should get ready. Gina shook his head. 'We stay here,' he said. 'We wait.'

'For how long? And wait for what?'

He wouldn't tell them. Instead, he taught them the partisan salute, a clenched right fist touching the right side of the forehead, accompanied by the phrase '*Vdekje Fashizmit*,' which meant, 'Death to fascism.' They learnt the proper response, which included the same salute followed by the words '*Liri Popullit*,' or 'Freedom to the people.' He told them a little bit more about life under the German occupation. Many people he knew had been taken away and never seen again. Those left behind went into hiding. Everyone was burying items of value from fear they would fall into German hands. 'The Germans are strong,' he said. 'They think they are in charge. But we fight. We don't give up.'

As they waited, Nicole busied herself with extending the straps on her musette bag using her share of the shroud lines from the parachute. Soon they were long enough to allow her to wear the bag as a backpack. It would make walking so much easier. She showed her invention to Andrea and offered to fix her bag, too. Andrea happily agreed. The sisters worked on the bag together, talking in low voices. Nicole told Andrea about the time a couple of years ago when Leon went ice skating for the first time. He fell within the first few minutes and declared he was never ice skating again. After a few more failed attempts he got the hang of it and soon was spinning on the ice like a professional. For the next five weekends, he didn't want to do anything else. She couldn't get him away from the ice rink.

Talking about her child lit her up inside, filling her with joy and at the same time an indescribable heartbreak. She would do anything to see Leon again. Impatiently, she kept looking at the door, hoping Gina would return and tell them it was time to go. But the door remained shut.

Every now and then, as she worked on the bag, Nicole glanced out the window, where Berat was alive with sound and movement. Cars drove past recklessly and seemingly without following any road rules, young women carried baskets, children and sometimes even livestock on their hips, called out to one another in shrill voices, shepherds rounded up sheep right there, on the city streets among traffic, and dogs wandered aimlessly, looking for scraps. Old women bended under the weight of large bundles of firewood. A group of men sat on the ground talking, while holding prayer beads in their hands. Boys played soccer and raced each other noisily. Despite Italy's surrender to the Allies a few months previously, Italian officers and enlisted men in uniform milled about, looking lost. Occasionally, men arrived on horseback, armed to the teeth, grim-faced, dressed in homespun woollen clothes and parts of German or Italian uniforms they had found or stolen. They exchanged messages, spoke in low voices and passed large wooden crates to one another. Nicole assumed they were the partisans, the selfless men who continued to fight a deathly battle against the Nazis, even though the odds would never be in their favour. The partisans were welcomed by the locals, who greeted them warmly, brought them food and asked for the latest news.

'It feels so far from home, doesn't it? Like a different world,' Nicole said to her sister.

'I feel like it's all a dream and I will soon wake up, safe in my bed in Detroit.'

'Sometimes I feel like we'll never see home again. That we will spend the rest of our lives eating cornbread and walking from place to place. That we'll be trapped here for eternity,' said Nicole, watching the action outside wistfully, while in her mind she was thousands of miles away.

For his fourth birthday, Leon got his first bicycle. He liked the idea of the bike, liked the way it looked, shiny and blue. He insisted on taking it everywhere with him, to the shops, to school, to the playground, but he was too afraid to ride it. The thought of the two of them dragging his little bicycle everywhere they went brought tears to Nicole's eyes. Leon had long outgrown the blue bike but she could never force herself to say goodbye, and so it remained in the garage next to his scooter and his snowboard.

Nicole blinked her tears away and glanced at her sister, noticing her wan appearance and the sadness behind her smile. 'Cheer up,' she said. 'We are still alive. We haven't died in the crash or been captured by the Nazis. God is looking out for us. We'll find our way back one way or another.' Did she really believe it or did she say it to make Andrea, and herself, feel better?

Later that day, the partisans invited them to try raki, a spirit made from distilled fruit. Only Renee agreed, while the other women politely declined. Everyone gathered in a circle to watch the brave nurse sample the drink. When she took the first sip, her eyes bulged and her face twisted. She cried out like she was in pain and spat the raki out. Everyone laughed, the nurses and the partisans alike. When she caught her breath and was able to talk again, Renee exclaimed, 'You are all brave, having a laugh at my expense. Why don't you try for yourselves? It's like drinking fire.'

'I'll give it a go,' said Fiona, a tall woman from Ohio with a round face and the biggest hands Andrea had ever seen. Fiona was a farmer before she decided to join the US Army Corps and become a nurse. She told Nicole she had volunteered because nothing could be as hard as her life back home, back-breaking toil from four every morning until sundown, side by side with her seven brothers. Nicole suspected Fiona was in Europe because she couldn't bear to stay on the farm alone once her brothers had left for the front. 'Back home, no one could outdrink me.'

'We are not in Ohio anymore,' muttered Renee, as Fiona took a quick swig from the glass.

Now it was Renee's turn to laugh, as Fiona spat the drink on the ground and coughed. 'What is in this thing? The devil?' she muttered.

No one else volunteered to try, certainly not Nicole, who didn't enjoy the taste of alcohol.

The hotel manager returned from the market with a sack of goodies for the nurses, like a badly dressed, tobacco-chewing Santa with a rifle. Nicole had never been so happy to see a toothbrush and a bar of soap. They also received woolly socks and warm blankets.

'What about some new shoes? Mine are falling apart,' said Renee.

'Sorry, no shoes,' said the man. 'If you have money, I suggest buying new clothes. What you are wearing now is not suitable for Albanian winter.'

'We don't need winter clothes. We are not staying in Albania for the winter,' said Nicole, trying to sound positive, even though there was a little voice inside her that said, *Winter is only a couple of weeks away. Where do you think you are going?*

'What is your plan?' asked the manager.

'The partisans are leading us to the coast. Once we get there, a boat will take us to Italy.'

'That is impossible. The partisans don't control the coastal areas.'

Nicole felt her hands begin to shake. 'Who controls the coastal areas? The Nazis?'

'Not the Nazis.'

'Who then?'

'The BK.'

'What is the BK?'

The manager didn't reply, looking at them with pity.

* * *

Three days went by thus, with card games and broken sleep, trays of cornbread and cheese, songs and guitar, a little reading, a little daydreaming and occasionally hearing gunshots on the streets of Berat. There was no sign of Gina and no news. What was it they were all waiting for? No one told them anything. They served them food, provided them with beds to sleep in, brought water for them to wash with and drink, but didn't have any answers.

One morning, when one of the partisans, not Gina, came to see them, Nicole asked him whether it was dangerous for them to stay in one place for so long. She led him to the window and pointed at a small crowd of people gathered outside. 'They are always there, waiting to catch a glimpse of us. Everyone seems to know about us. Who we are, what we are doing here. It's only a matter of time before the Nazis hear about us too.' The man glanced out the window, glanced at Nicole's worried face and shrugged. She wasn't sure if he could even understand English.

Every time the hotel manager arrived with a tray of food, they asked to see Gina. Finally, he nodded and said, 'I know exactly what you need.' He returned not with Gina but with a bearded giant carrying a large accordion. As the nurses chewed their cornbread, the large man played cheerful melodies that made them forget all their worries, and for a few fleeting moments took them back in time. They listened to 'Happy Birthday to You', 'God Bless America' and 'Boogie Woogie Bugle Boy'. 'He was a famous trumpet man from out Chicago way,' the man sang in heavily accented English and the girls swung together, holding hands. Nicole danced with her sister, who had barely said a word all day and spent most of her time by the window hoping to see her husband.

The next day, the hotel manager took them to a dark hall with a couch and an old television set that was playing an Italian movie. Even though the nurses couldn't understand a word, by the end of the film there was not a dry eye in the room. Andrea sobbed loudly next to Nicole, while Nicole held her hand and said, 'Sh-sh. It's only a film. We don't even know what it's about.'

Nicole suspected it wasn't the movie that was making her sister upset. She had noticed long ago that Andrea hadn't been her usual self, especially when Brian was around. From a carefree, happy person Nicole had grown up with, she transformed into a subdued, subservient, eager to please individual Nicole didn't recognise. She seemed always on edge, careful with her words, like she was afraid to say the wrong thing. And when she wasn't with her husband, she was silently wilting away like a sad, tearful flower.

When they were not listening to the accordion or watching films, they busied themselves with knitting and playing poker. Nicole won two dollars off Andrea. She suspected she would never get the money but it was worth it just to see her distracted for a while. There was a piano in the dining room and the girls begged Andrea to play. In the evenings they gathered in a circle and listened to Mozart and Tchaikovsky, to Bach and Beethoven. Symphony Number 5 and the *Four Seasons* were everyone's favourites. Just seeing her sister's fingers running over the piano carried Nicole back to the past, to the safety and warmth of their childhood home. When Andrea's hands hit the notes, Nicole was no longer in Berat at war but at her parents' house, nursing a hot cup of tea, while the sound of her sister's music filled the room with joy.

Despite the jolly atmosphere, Nicole couldn't help but feel like they were prisoners here, at the mercy of others, vulnerable and afraid. While outside their window life continued with noise and bustle, inside was nothing but long, fearful faces. And even when they laughed or teased each other or told jokes, they did so in low voices. Often the loudest sound was the clock ticking on the mantelpiece and it seemed to Nicole that time had slowed down, that they were stuck in this day forever, that a thousand years would pass and they would still be here, in Berat, at Grand Hotel Kolumbo, watching the world go by while waiting for Gina to return.

On their fourth morning in Berat, Nicole woke up determined to get some answers. If Gina didn't come to see them, she would go looking for him herself. Every day they stayed here was a day lost. They could have been halfway to the coast by now. Instead, they were sitting on beds, knitting and chatting, and watching the clock on the wall that had seemingly forgotten how to move.

The sun was not up yet and only the fire crackled happily in the hearth, throwing streaks of light across the dark room. Carrie, who shared the room with the sisters, was sound asleep in her bed, arms around her pillow. Nicole was convinced Carrie could sleep through an earthquake or an explosion.

Outside, a rooster crowed happily, welcoming another day, and it surprised Nicole that a busy town like Berat would have roosters and livestock roaming its streets. Once again, she thought of the summers they had spent on their grandparents' farm. One day when the sisters were twelve, they took their grandfather's boat and rowed all the way across the lake. They had a picnic there, picked some blueberries, played some cards, and when they returned it was already dark, and their grandparents were frantic. Despite the punishment from their strict grandfather, that day on the lake with her sister was one of the happiest memories of Nicole's entire childhood.

Wondering what time it was, Nicole got out of bed and made her way to the window. Although it was still dark, Berat was waking up. She could hear voices, men and women calling out to each other, children crying. Somewhere nearby, a door slammed. Nicole closed the blinds and crossed the room, careful not to trip on any of the furniture.

The door opened and she saw her sister's face. 'Hurry up, sleepy head. There's a meeting in the dining hall. I know you need your beauty sleep but you don't want to miss it.'

'What meeting?' Nicole perked up. Perhaps Gina was back and today was the day they would leave Berat and resume their quest for safety. 'What is it about?'

'If you don't hurry up, we will never know.'

Together they woke Carrie, who threw a sock at them and demanded to be left alone, then walked down the long corridor towards the hall where they usually had their meals. Nicole could hear muffled voices and occasional laughter. The girls were talking all at once. As quietly as she could, she opened the door. As soon as she did so, she heard a voice that sounded familiar. It made her stop in her tracks.

'I work for the OSS. And I'm here to help you get back safely,' said a man wearing a US Army uniform with a captain's insignia on his cap and an AAF shoulder patch.

Everyone wanted to know what the OSS was, how long it would take to get to the coast, if it was dangerous, if they would make it.

'The OSS stands for the Office of Strategic Services, America's first national intelligence agency. We work closely with the British Special Operations Executive in occupied territories to undermine and disrupt Nazi activities. You have heard of the SOE, haven't you?'

The girls nodded.

'One of your guides has contacted a senior SOE officer in Albania and told him about your situation. And he got in touch with me. I just arrived from Cairo to take you to the coast where a boat will be waiting for you. Do you have any questions?'

Of course they had questions. And only Nicole stood mutely in the doorway, leaning on the doorframe for support, face pale, hands shaking.

'What's your name again?' Renee called out.

'I am Captain Darren Brown.'

Everything was blurry before her and she realised she was crying. Wiping her tears away with a trembling hand, she glanced at the only man she had ever loved. He looked taller than she remembered, broad-shouldered and strong. Around his waist was a pistol belt with a .45 automatic, his hair was short and his neck was sunburnt. Nicole stared at the face she had seen in her dreams for many years, and wanted to pinch herself, wanted to cross the room and touch him. Instead, she wrapped herself in her scarf and hid behind another nurse.

On her sister's face, she saw the shock reflected back to her. 'Are you all right?' Andrea whispered. Nicole didn't reply. She didn't know if she was all right.

'When do we start?' asked Renee.

'Just before dark,' said Darren. 'It will be safer to leave Berat at night. I suggest you use this time to rest and prepare for the trip. It won't be easy, it will require everything we've got, but we will not stop until you are back on base.'

He turned around and Nicole moved swiftly back into the shadows. When he passed her, she could have stretched her hand out and touched him. She watched him walk across the lobby of the hotel and towards the exit. There he paused and spoke to a group of partisans. When he stepped through the door into the busy street, she approached one of the windows. Her heart in her throat, she stared at him as he crossed the road and entered one of the huts lining the opposite side of the street.

Darren was long gone but she remained at the window, watching the street and thinking of the last nine years without him.

Nine Years Ago

The house was silent and dark. Not a whisper disturbed the perfect night, not a star dared to peek through the clouds. Nicole didn't know whether her parents were in bed or on the terrace enjoying a glass of wine and the balmy weather but she had to take the risk. She couldn't leave Darren waiting on his birthday and the anniversary of their first kiss.

She hid a torch in her pocket and pulled a chair close to the window. She was halfway there, with one leg out and one leg in, when she heard the door open. She froze, petrified. She hoped it was her mother and not her father. Mama listened to reason, while Dad punished first and asked questions later. She tried to think of an excuse but nothing came to mind that could explain why she was about to jump out of her second-storey window in the middle of the night. A second later, the lights snapped on. Nicole blinked, momentarily blinded. When she heard her sister's voice, she almost cried with relief.

'On the run again?' asked Andrea, smiling.

'Please, don't tell.' Nicole knew her parents would never accept Darren, no matter how much she loved him, no matter how much he loved her. In her father's eyes, he was not a suitable match for his daughter, who deserved the best. He wasn't from the right family, didn't have the right education, didn't have the right potential. Marrying his daughters off was a business deal for their father. It had very little to do with matters of the heart.

'I'll never tell, you know that. But I'm not letting you out of here until I know where you're going.'

Nicole grinned. 'It's Darren's birthday today. He's waiting for me.'

'Is he taking you anywhere special?'

'To the tennis courts. He said he'll have a picnic ready. I have a present for him. Would you like to see?' She climbed off the windowsill and showed her sister a silver necklace with a tennis racket charm. 'To remind him of our first kiss,' she said happily.

'It's beautiful,' said Andrea, her feet tap-dancing on the spot with excitement. 'I'm so jealous of you, Nicky. You have your whole life figured out. You know who you want to spend it with.'

'If I had my whole life figured out, I wouldn't be climbing out of my window like an assassin.'

'Maybe you shouldn't be doing that. It's quite high up and . . .'

'I'll be careful. I'd better go. It's so late already.'

But when she arrived and shone her torch around, she found the tennis courts deserted. No one was waiting for her in their special place. She spread the picnic blanket on a pile of leaves and sat down, expecting to hear Darren's footsteps in the dark or his voice calling her name. All was quiet and only the owl hooted in the tree over her head, filling her heart with dread. Darren was never late. It was not like him to keep her waiting.

Ten minutes went by, then half an hour.

'Where are you?' she whispered, hugging her knees close. Even though it was summer, the nights were cold. She remained sitting on the ground, listening to the trees rustling in the breeze, hoping to hear his voice, playing with the tennis racket charm in her hand and trying to convince herself that everything was going to be all right. Any moment now, she would hear his laughter and run to his side. He would put his arms around her and she would no longer feel cold or afraid.

But she didn't hear his steps, nor his voice, and only the wind made the branches of the nearby trees tremble. After another hour of waiting, she got up and walked two miles in the dark to the little house where Darren lived with his family. Occasionally, she saw lights in the distance and a car passed her. Every time she froze in fear, worried it would be someone who knew her and would tell her parents. But no one stopped. No one recognised her.

Darren's family didn't have much money but what they lacked in material possessions, they more than made up with unconditional love. Nicole knew which she would rather have. Every time she had dinner with Darren, his siblings and parents, she was *amazed at their cheerful camaraderie, the laughter they shared, the conversations that flowed so easily between them. No one walked on eggshells, no one had to watch what they said. It was a breath of fresh air compared to her proper, joyless household.*

Her heart beating fast, she made her way down the road towards Darren's little house, ready to knock on the door, prepared to tease him for forgetting about their meeting. He'd been working so hard lately, while looking after his sick mother. Sometimes he didn't have time to eat. There were days when he had to get by on almost no sleep. She'd been worried about him. She decided to talk to her father about it. He didn't need to know they were dating. She would tell him Darren was her friend and he desperately needed a better job.

Even before she knocked, she knew something was not right. What little furniture the Browns possessed was piled up outside. Nicole recognised the chairs and the dining table. The couch where Darren's mother showed Nicole childhood pictures of her son and, to his embarrassment, regaled her with the anecdotes of his early years, was lying upside down in the mud. There was a handwritten sign on top of the furniture. In the light of her torch, she read, 'Free and in good condition, help yourselves.'

She knocked on the door. And knocked and knocked. No one answered. She pushed the door but it was locked. She waited for ten minutes, twenty, half an hour, hoping for a miracle. But all was quiet.

Dejected and confused, she stumbled back home as if in a trance and opened the front door with her key. She didn't care if her parents caught her sneaking in at one in the morning, if her father punished her or her mother told her off. None of it mattered anymore.

No one saw her. Quietly she made her way upstairs and into her bedroom, closing the door behind her.

She was crying softly in her bed when she felt a hand on her shoulder.

'I heard you come in. What's wrong?' asked Andrea, sitting next to her sister. Nicole didn't reply. She was crying harder now,

her shoulders shaking. 'Nicky, what happened? Are you all right?'

It was a few moments before she could whisper, 'He wasn't there.'

'Perhaps he was delayed. Maybe his dad needed him or his mother is feeling worse. You'll see him tomorrow. You two are inseparable. It will do you good to have an evening apart.'

'I went to his house. There was no one there. All the furniture is outside.'

'Perhaps they are redecorating. Or they had to leave suddenly but will be back soon.'

'He didn't say anything. I saw him in the morning. He was happy, looking forward to our evening together. He said he had a surprise for me.' She fiddled with the tennis racket charm in her hand. 'He's been dropping hints about marriage, talking about starting a family. A part of me was hoping he was going to ask me to marry him tonight.' She burst into tears again at the unfairness of it all.

Andrea hugged her and kissed her cheek. 'See, he has plans for the two of you. He wouldn't just leave without talking to you first. It's impossible.'

Nicole nodded, wiping her wet face with the back of her hand. 'I know. It does sound unlikely.'

'Why don't you get some rest? Tomorrow everything will make sense again. He'll get in touch. He'll explain.'

'All right.'

Andrea covered her with a blanket. 'Sleep tight,' she said, getting up.

When Andrea was by the door, Nicole called her. Andrea turned around.

Nicole hesitated, searching for the right words. 'I'm pregnant,' she said finally.

Her sister retraced her steps and perched on the edge of the bed. She took Nicole's hand. 'I know,' she said.

'How do you know?' Nicole blinked rapidly, stunned.

'I'm not blind. You've been pale, off your food, throwing up in the bathroom.'

'You haven't told anyone, have you?'

There was a moment's hesitation and then Andrea shook her head. 'Of course not. Have you told Darren?'

'I was going to, tonight. What if he doesn't come back? Without him, I don't know what I'm going to do.'

'Don't worry about anything now. Wait until tomorrow.' Andrea held her and Nicole lay quietly in her arms, her eyes closed, her face damp with tears. All she could think about was the pitiful-looking furniture on the side of the road. It didn't look like the Browns were coming back any time soon. The little house looked abandoned.

* * *

Chaos reigned in the dining hall. The girls wanted to be ready for anything at a moment's notice, and so they flitted around the room, chirping like overexcited birds, packing and repacking their bags. Everyone was on their feet except Nicole, who sat in silence in the corner with her knees drawn up, staring into space. When Renee told her to get ready or she would slow the group down, Nicole didn't even raise her head. When Carrie sat next to her and asked if she was all right, Nicole nodded but didn't say a word. Carrie soon moved on to finish her packing, while Nicole remained on the floor with her eyes closed.

Andrea sidled up to her and put her arms around her. For a few moments, they sat in silence, while around them items of clothing flew through the air and women shouted. 'It was a shock, wasn't it? Seeing him again?' Andrea whispered.

Nicole nodded. 'I spent years searching for him. Even after I married Anthony, I never stopped. For nine years I dreamt every night about finding him again. I never expected to see him here, in Albania.' She looked up at her sister. There were tears in her eyes.

'Did he see you?'

'I don't think so.' She lowered her gaze, staring at a dark stain on the carpet. 'I hid my face when he walked past me.'

'Why did you hide your face?'

'I panicked. He left all those years ago without a word. I never heard from him again. If he wanted to see me, he would have written.'

'You'll have to talk to him sooner or later. You can't hide forever.'

'I know. But what if he tells me I never meant anything to him? That it was all in my head?'

'At least you'll have all your questions answered. It's better than not knowing.'

'Is it?' whispered Nicole. 'All I have of him is memories. But they are good memories. I don't want anything to ruin them.'

'Nothing ever will.'

'I used to lie awake at night, wondering if he was dead. It was the only possible explanation I could think of. Why else would he never try to contact me, to explain? Every evening, I used to pray. "Please, God, let him not love me anymore but let him live." Isn't it great that God heard my prayers?'

It wasn't Nicole who was crying now, it was Andrea. 'I'm sorry,' she whispered. 'It's been so hard on you. I'm so sorry.'

'What are you sorry for? It wasn't your fault.'

'But it was,' Andrea whispered. Nicole turned to her sister. Andrea's face was red from tears, her eyes staring. She didn't meet Nicole's gaze. 'It was my fault that Darren left all those years ago.'

Nicole shook her head. 'Don't be silly. How is it possible?'

'I've tried to tell you before. This secret was killing me. But every time I stopped myself. I convinced myself I should keep it from you because it would only hurt your feelings. I told myself I did it to protect you. But it was only myself I was trying to protect. I was afraid to tell you because I didn't want you to hate me.'

'Hate you for what?' Nicole whispered. When her sister didn't reply, she added, 'Tell me.'

'Even now I can't find the right words.'

'Nothing you say could make me hate you. You know that. You are my twin sister.'

Andrea took a deep breath, as if searching for courage. 'I told Mama I thought you were pregnant. Two days later, Darren and his family disappeared. For years I tried to convince myself it was a coincidence. I didn't want to be responsible for hurting you so much. But in my heart, I've always known it wasn't a coincidence. Mama must have told Dad. And he must have done something to make them leave.'

Silence fell between the sisters. Andrea was crying, while Nicole watched her, trying to understand. Tory approached them, her musette bag in her hands. 'Are you girls done packing yet?' she asked. Then, after a closer look at their stricken faces, she exclaimed, 'Are you two all right? Why are you crying? We are going home. You should be happy.' The sisters ignored her. They barely heard her.

When Tory walked away, Nicole said, 'Why would you do that, Andie? Why would you tell Mama?'

'We were only seventeen. I was scared. I didn't know how to help you. I thought Mama would know what to do.'

'Oh, Andrea. What were you thinking?'

'I was only thinking of you. I had your best interest at heart. I made a mistake.'

'You should have told me the minute it happened. When I was lying in my bed crying for Darren, you should have told me then.'

'I know I should have. I was selfish. And I'm sorry.'

Nicole moved away from her sister. 'Don't you understand what you've done? Because of you, I lost the love of my life. Because of you, Leon is growing up without his father.'

'He has a father. He has Anthony.' Andrea reached for Nicole's hand. 'He loves him like his own. You are lucky . . .'

Nicole jumped to her feet, pushing her sister's hand away. 'I can't talk to you about it anymore. I can't even look at you.'

'Nicole, wait . . .' Andrea muttered, making a move to get up, to grab her sister, to stop her.

But Nicole didn't wait. 'Don't follow me! You are a terrible sister and I will never forgive you. I never want to talk to you again,' she cried, rushing across the room towards the exit, leaving her bags unpacked on the floor. Andrea remained on the floor in a helpless, tearful mess, while the rest of the girls fell quiet and watched them in shock.

Chapter 5

Under Attack

Growing up, Nicole and Andrea fought about everything. When they were little, fighting was like breathing. But, even as they fought, they knew it was the two of them against the world. They were more than sisters, more than soulmates. Before Andrea could even remember, Nicole had always been there, sharing the same house, the same crib, the same womb. Living the same life. Whenever something happened, it was her sister she ran to. Every dream, every crush, every heartbreak, Nicole had witnessed it all. When Brian asked Andrea to marry him, she called and told Nicole all about it moments after saying yes, even before Brian had a chance to open a bottle of champagne to celebrate.

When Darren left nine years ago, Andrea convinced herself she wasn't responsible. Everything she did was to protect her sister. But, as she lay in her bed at Grand Hotel Kolumbo in Berat, thousands of miles from home, she regretted all of it. Telling their mother in the first place. Not going to Nicole with the truth as soon as she could have. And finally, telling her now, all these years later. She had kept it to herself for so long, why couldn't she stay silent a little longer? Had she not said anything, Nicole wouldn't have rushed outside like wild dogs were at her heels, hating Andrea for what she'd done. And Andrea couldn't stand the thought of her sister hating her.

The packing had been done and the nurses were pacing nervously around the room, obsessively watching the clock on the wall. Only Andrea remained in one spot, hugging her knees, staring into space. Carrie was by the window, observing the action outside. Tory was knitting. She did that when she was stressed or worried or afraid. It calmed her nerves, she said. Frankie was writing a letter. Everyone was in good spirits after the meeting with the OSS officer earlier that morning. Never mind having to cross Albania by foot with the Nazis in pursuit. They all behaved like they had already been rescued.

Renee looked up from her book. 'Where did Nicole go?' she asked. 'You heard the man. We have to be ready at a moment's notice.'

'She'll be right back,' replied Andrea, hiding her shaking hands behind her back. She could barely talk.

'She better be. Did you two argue? I couldn't help but overhear . . .'

Andrea shook her head, not looking at the head nurse.

Leaving her book behind, Renee crossed the space between them and sat down on the floor next to Andrea. 'What happened between the two of you, anyway?'

It took a few moments before Andrea could reply. 'I did something bad. Now she will never talk to me again.'

'Of course she will. You are her sister. She just needs some time.' Andrea didn't say anything. Renee continued, 'It's normal for sisters to fight. It goes with the territory. One day, my sister dug a hole in our garden and covered it with leaves. I fell in and broke my arm.' Renee smiled, gazing into the distance, lost in memories. 'And another time, she locked me in the cellar just so she could eat all my chocolates. And forgot to let me out. I was in that cellar for eight hours, until our parents came home. Oh, and once she put a frog in my tea.'

Andrea stopped crying for a moment. 'She did what?'

'A live frog! I took a sip and there it was.'

'What did you do?'

'I waited till she was asleep and hid a mouse under her pillow. You should have heard her screaming. My parents punished me. They wouldn't listen about the frog. I couldn't leave the house for a week, except to go to school. Growing up together was like a war zone. Still is sometimes. My sister and I are very competitive. But she's also my best friend.'

'Where is your sister now?'

'Back home, teaching at our old primary school. I'd do anything to see her again.' The two women sat in silence for a bit. Finally, Renee patted Andrea's shoulder. 'Don't worry about anything. When Nicole comes back, talk to her. Tell her you love her.'

Andrea hoped with all her heart that Renee was right, that Nicole needed some space and, once she returned, things would go back to the way they had been. She moved to the window next to Carrie and watched the street, hoping to see her sister. Finally, she couldn't wait any longer. She decided to go out there and look for Nicole. She didn't know what she was going to say but when she saw her, she hoped she would find the right words.

She was in the hotel lobby, walking fast towards the exit, when she heard a loud popping noise outside. It came out of nowhere and for a second she stood motionless, wondering what was happening. The noise quietened down, only to come back louder, closer. Gun shots, she realised. A sudden explosion shook the neighbourhood, and machine guns responded, their regular pop-pop-pop sound making Andrea's hand fly to her mouth in shock.

One day, when they were seven, their nanny took the sisters to a funfair. They were eating cotton candy when suddenly the skies exploded. Andrea still remembered the expression on Nicole's face, a mixture of fear and fascination as they watched the fireworks bursting overhead. But this time, Andrea knew it wasn't fireworks. The sound didn't signify joy and excitement. It signified war.

Something was happening on the streets of Berat. Andrea heard shouting and the sound of stomping feet on gravel. Something else exploded, this time much closer than before.

She stood in the doorway for a few moments, watching the mayhem outside. It was as if a tornado had been unleashed in the peaceful town square. Everything was on the move, everyone was searching for cover. The cars couldn't progress down the road but blared their horns insistently, as if performing this simple action could make the traffic disappear, while motorcycles zoomed between them, threatening to knock over the pedestrians, who were running without paying the slightest attention to what was happening around them. The cattle broke loose, frightened cows, horses and sheep dashing in every direction. Somewhere, dogs were howling in tune with the machine-gun fire.

Taking a deep breath, Andrea stepped outside and skipped down the stairs taking two steps at a time, only to bump into Brian on the street. He grabbed her by the hand. 'Where do you think you are going? Can't you hear the gunshots?'

'I'm looking for my sister.'

She pulled away and made a move to get around him. He stepped in front of her. 'Are you out of your mind? Are you trying to get yourself killed?'

'Please, let me go. Nicole could be in trouble.'

But he didn't let her go. Instead, he pulled her hard by the hand and she had no choice but to follow him back to the dining hall of the hotel where eleven women were looking at one another in confused silence. A few minutes later, the other men joined them, closing the door behind them. Andrea heard more gunfire, screams of pain, a sound of another explosion and suddenly it felt like the earth moved beneath her feet, making her stumble. For a moment afterwards, she didn't hear anything at all, as if the world around her had quietened down and everything was peaceful again. She could see Brian talking but couldn't hear a word he was saying. He was like a fish out of water, gasping for air. He looked so peculiar, Andrea stared at his face for a moment, amused, until her hearing returned and she heard him saying, 'It's the Nazis. They are here, in Berat.'

The hotel manager rushed into the room. He looked red in the face, short of breath and panicked. The Americans greeted him with a thousand questions. The man ignored them, peering out of a window and muttering something in Albanian. Finally, he said, 'It is not good. Grab your bags. You need to go.'

The medical team pulled their jackets on and reached for their bags, everyone except Andrea, who stood rooted to the spot, her eyes on the door, praying for her sister to appear. 'I'm not leaving. Not without Nicole,' she said, shaking her head and backing away from Brian.

Swearing under his breath, he picked her up around the middle and carried her through the lobby towards the exit, while she kicked and screamed, trying to break free. Gina was waiting for them outside. Unlike everybody else, the partisan looked calm and relaxed, as if the horror of war hadn't come to the streets of Berat. He wasn't fretting or shouting or waving his hands in panic. When he spoke, his voice didn't tremble. 'We have a truck waiting. We need to leave now, before it's too late.'

A couple of blocks down the road, Andrea saw an orange truck she had noticed the partisans use on a few occasions while they were staying at the hotel. As everyone walked towards it, she pulled on Gina's sleeve. 'My sister is missing. We can't leave without her.' She had to repeat herself three times before he could hear her over the sound of machine-gun fire.

Gina pointed across the road. 'I saw her go inside that hut.'

'What's in that hut?' asked Andrea, looking at a little structure, dilapidated and sad, with a broken fence, overgrown shrubs and shattered windows.

'The OSS officer. We don't have time. The Nazis are here. They will block roads.'

'We can't leave without her. What will the Nazis do to her?' Andrea twisted her hands in despair. 'What if it was your sister?'

Gina nodded, looking at her with pity. 'Don't worry. Get on the truck. I will send someone.' He pointed at the hut.

One after another, the medical personnel climbed inside the truck. Andrea watched from the back of the truck with trepidation as Gina spoke to another partisan, pointed at the place where Darren was staying, then jumped into the driver's seat. While the partisan was approaching Darren's hut, a deafening noise was heard. With horror Andrea saw German tanks crawling down the road. Following the tanks were armoured vehicles. All of a sudden, the streets were teeming with enemy soldiers. Somewhere nearby, machine-gun fire broke out once again. Andrea watched in petrified silence as the partisan who was supposed to bring her sister back fell to the ground, blood turning his white tunic red. She froze, unable to scream or talk or breathe, wondering if what was happening was real or a terrifying nightmare.

But the horror on the streets of Berat was not a dream, and the tanks continued to come, while Nicole remained missing and no one did anything to save her.

With a few sharp words in Albanian, Gina put the truck into gear and it started to move slowly through the crowds.

'Are we going?' exclaimed Andrea. 'What about Nicole? What about my sister?'

'We can't wait. Another minute and we won't be going anywhere.'

She couldn't believe her ears. 'We are leaving them behind? They are going to die.'

'If we don't go now, we will all die.'

As Gina drove through the streets that were churning like a witch's cauldron, Andrea moved to the side of the truck and lifted one leg over, ready to jump, when a strong arm gripped her shoulder.

'What do you think you are doing?' Brian demanded.

'I'm not leaving without my sister.'

Without another word he pulled her inside the truck, throwing her down and nearly dislocating her shoulder. She cried out in pain. 'Don't you hear the shooting?' he shouted. 'Don't you see the tanks? The enemy soldiers? You need to be an idiot to jump off this truck.'

She crawled away from him. 'You want me to leave her behind? She is my sister.' She jumped to her feet and once again swung her leg over the side of the truck. Suddenly, a sharp pain in her jaw made her gasp. She could taste something metallic in her mouth and when she wiped it with her hand, she saw blood. She felt like all the air had left her body and for a moment couldn't breathe. Again, a strong pair of hands grabbed her and threw her carelessly on the floor of the moving truck.

'I can't believe how stupid you are,' screamed Brian, red in the face, his eyes bulging, while the rest of the team watched in horror. 'Reckless and illogical, putting yourself and everyone else in danger.' He bent over her while she curled into a ball, sobbing. 'Don't ever pull a stunt like that again, do you hear me? You are embarrassing me.'

Trembling, she looked up at him. She saw the face of the man she loved, the face she knew by heart. She would be able to pick up a brush and paint it in every exquisite detail, if only she knew how. She saw the man who had once told her he loved her more than anything in the world, who had promised to care for her and make her happy for the rest of her life, the man she trusted with all her heart and would gladly give her life for. And yet, it seemed to her she was looking into the face of a stranger. It was distorted and angry, and she could barely recognise it.

He moved away from her, while she remained on the floor of the moving vehicle, feeling exposed and alone, every bump in the road hurting her shoulder where he had pulled her too hard.

Carrie leaned over her, brushing her hair away from her face, asking if she wanted some water. 'I'm all right, thank you,' Andrea replied, even though she wasn't all right, not at all. She couldn't cry, even though she felt her whole world was cracking apart. The foundations she had built her life on were shifting, and she could sense this shift with every beat of her aching heart.

'Did he hurt you very much?'

'Not really.'

'He'll be over here before you know it, saying sorry, making excuses, telling you it will never happen again. Except it always does. It always happens again.'

Andrea glanced at Carrie, who wasn't looking at her anymore and seemed miles away. 'Sounds like you're talking from experience.'

'My dad used to do it to my mama, my sister and me. That's why I left home when I was sixteen, while Mama is still with him, hoping one day he is going to change.' Carrie sighed and shook her head, like she was staving off a ghost. 'Only they never do. They never ever change. Are you sure you don't want some water? Or something to eat? I have cornbread in my pocket and a slice of cheese tucked away for a rainy day. I think today qualifies.'

Andrea closed her eyes. She wanted to be alone with her thoughts. Seeing the pity on Carrie's face made her want to scream with pain. 'I don't want anything. Thank you.'

'I know you are worried about your sister, honey,' said Carrie. 'We all are. But we couldn't stay there any longer. The Germans were everywhere. As we were driving away, I saw one go into that hut.'

Andrea gasped. 'What hut?' she whispered.

'The OSS officer's hut.'

No, Andrea wanted to scream. *No*.

It's all my fault, she thought, rocking back and forth with her arms around her body, as the truck careened through the outskirts of town, leaving the fighting behind. *It's all my fault*. Perhaps she deserved Brian's harsh words. She had lied to her sister. She had made her run out of the hotel, upset. And now look at them. They were driving away from Berat to safety, while Nicole remained in the occupied city, at the mercy of bloodthirsty German soldiers.

What if she never saw her again? What if God had decided to punish Andrea after all these years for her deception?

When Carrie returned to her book as if the world wasn't exploding around her, Brian sat down next to Andrea and took her hand. 'I'm sorry, darling. I didn't mean to hurt you. I was trying to protect you. You know that, don't you?'

She wanted to reply but couldn't. She had no energy to talk, no desire to hear what he had to say. She remained on the floor, staring straight ahead. Her cheek where he had struck her was throbbing. Her shoulder was in pain. Her heart was breaking.

Eight Years Ago

The patio of Brian's house was lit up like a Christmas tree, filled with champagne flutes, summer dresses and laughter. Andrea felt like she was floating on a cloud, a little hungry, giddy after two glasses of champagne, her heart bursting with joy. Brian had thrown her a surprise party celebrating their marriage. All her friends were here, and so was her sister. Andrea would have been even happier if her parents had come but Nicole told her not to worry about it. 'Once you and Brian have babies, none of this will matter anymore. All will be forgotten.' Andrea hoped she was right. Despite their differences, she couldn't imagine her life without her mother and father by her side.

All around her, people dressed in their best evening attire twirled to a band playing her favourite songs. Every now and then, someone came up to Andrea, touched her hand, congratulated her, made eye contact, as if they wanted her happiness to rub off on them. They wanted to know how the two of them had met, how Brian proposed, what the wedding was like, if they were planning to start a family soon. The later it got, the more the guests had to drink, the more personal the questions.

Andrea spotted Brian across the hall, talking to Nicole and her husband. Suddenly, she wished everything around her would disappear, the lights, the music, the guests, all of it except Brian, so they could be alone together. How handsome he looked in his suit. In a crowd of people, everyone faded away like they were mere shadows, and only he remained vivid and bright. 'We haven't talked about having children yet,' she said to Brian's aunt, who had backed Andrea into a corner and was holding her hostage until she told her everything. 'I want to finish my degree and then we'll see what our plans are.'

It would never be just her plans anymore, she realised. From now on, it would always be their plans. She liked the sound of that.

'Don't leave it too late, dear. Young people these days, putting their careers first, having children late, it's so selfish. Back in my day we knew what was important. When Carl and I were first married . . .'

Andrea pulled away from the woman's grip. 'Please, excuse me. My husband is looking for me.'

She couldn't believe she had a husband. Growing up with her controlling parents, she still felt like a child at nineteen. But she was married now. What was more grown-up than that? She was about to embark on the greatest adventure of them all. In that moment, as people danced to Frank Sinatra and waiters sashayed past with trays of lobster and prawn, she felt like pinching herself but didn't dare to do so, in case she woke up in her bed alone, in case all of it had been a dream.

Adjusting her dress, she crossed the hall, exchanged a few words with a group of friends, waved to Brian's mother, and finally joined her husband by the dance floor. 'There you are,' said Brian, draping his arm around her shoulder. 'You look radiant tonight. Have I told you that?'

'Only a hundred times.'

'Well, you are glowing. I will never tire of repeating that.'

She relaxed into him, no longer overwhelmed by it all. She was finally home, where she belonged. 'I'm happy,' she said.

'Me too. So happy.'

Their eyes met. He pulled her in for a kiss and they remained with their arms locked around each other, forgetting about everybody else, like it was just the two of them, like they didn't have a houseful of guests watching their every move.

'Look at the two of you!' said Nicole, her eyes twinkling. 'Can't keep your hands off each other.'

'Jealous?' Andrea giggled.

'A little,' said Nicole. She glanced at her husband Anthony, who was talking to someone about the audits he had to perform for the end of financial year. 'All I have to look forward to tonight is reading Anna Karenina in bed with a cup of tea and a chocolate biscuit. Thank you for recommending it, by the way. It's a great book.'

'I knew you'd like it.'

'It leaves me speechless. The love, the promises, the betrayal.'

'Even my husband enjoyed it. He was crying by the last chapter.'

Anthony, who had abandoned his conversation and drifted closer, chuckled. 'Crying? Really?'

'You'd be crying too if you read it,' Nicole said coldly. Turning back to Andrea, she added, 'Anthony doesn't read anything other than the financial pages of the newspaper and his accounting books. The man has no soul.'

'I enjoyed Anna Karenina,' said Brian. 'But I didn't cry. My wife has an overactive imagination.'

'Admit it, you had tears in your eyes,' teased Andrea.

They spoke about the food and the music. They gossiped about some of the guests. They tried some spring roll and sipped champagne. To the outside observer, they looked happy and radiant but Andrea knew in her heart that something had changed. The lights continued to shine and the guests continued to dance as the band broke into Ella Fitzgerald's 'Cheek to Cheek'. Andrea would have loved to dance with her lover to her favourite song but he was no longer looking at her and his arm was no longer around her. His eyes were cold and his smile had vanished. Suddenly, she felt a chill run through her veins, even though it was warm in the room.

When all the lights had gone out and the last guest had left after ten minutes of drunken hugs and congratulations, Andrea mustered enough courage to ask Brian if he was all right. 'You haven't said a word to me in the last hour. Did I do something wrong?'

'Of course not. I'm just tired. It's been a long day.'

Without looking at her, he poured himself a brandy. She had never seen him drink anything stronger than a beer or an occasional champagne. Neither of them was a drinker. He kept alcohol in his house for the guests but rarely touched it. She tried to catch his eye. It should have been one of the happiest days of her life but she couldn't shake the feeling that something was terribly wrong. It was as if someone had hit a switch and the Brian she knew and loved was gone. In his place was a cold man who looked at her with disdain.

'Nicole invited us for dinner tomorrow,' she said quietly. 'Just the four of us.'

He took a sip of his drink. 'You go.'

'Without you?'

He was silent for a moment. When he spoke again, she didn't recognise his voice. It sounded snide, angry, unlike him. 'Why do you want me to come? So you can humiliate me again in front of your sister and her husband?' His eyes became slits. The glass trembled in his hand.

Startled, she took a step back. In all their months together, he had never raised his voice. He had never said one angry word to her. And here he was, talking to her like he despised her. She took a deep breath, thinking back on their conversation, wondering if she had said something wrong, something disrespectful, something to offend him. 'Humiliate you? What do you mean?'

'You told them I cried because of some stupid book. They were both laughing at me, like I was some kind of an idiot.'

'No one was laughing at you, darling. I said you had tears in your eyes because the book is so good, so emotional. I didn't mean . . .'

He shouted, 'You embarrassed me! You made me feel like less of a man.'

'It's not embarrassing to cry when something touches you. It's a good thing.' She placed her hand on his arm.

He shoved her away. 'Shut up! You have no idea how your comment made me feel,' he screamed. She was trying to regain her balance when something flew past her face, nearly hitting her. A glass smashed against the wall, spilling brandy all over the white carpet, the stains looking like old blood, the broken shreds glistening like tears. Andrea whimpered in shock, like a wounded kitten. She wasn't hurt, and yet it felt like her whole body was in pain.

Brian pushed past her. 'Don't ever speak about me like that again,' he barked, slamming the front door.

Andrea slid to the floor next to the broken glass and covered her face with her hands. She wanted to cry but couldn't. She wanted to get up but couldn't. In the past few months, whenever she was upset or worried about something, she ran to Brian. He knew exactly what to say to make her feel better. One glimpse of his face and all her troubles melted away. What did she do now, when it was him who had upset her? Who did she turn to?

She must have stayed on the floor for many hours, trembling like a frightened animal, her head on her knees, her eyes dry and staring, because soon it was light outside. When the clock chimed nine, she heard his key in the lock. She didn't look up. His steps resounded in the quiet corridor. His keys jangled as he threw them on the table. There was silence for a moment and then she heard him say her name. In seconds he was by her side.

'What are you doing here, on the floor? How long have you been here?' His arms went around her. She relaxed into them, finding comfort in his warmth, in his kind voice. Had she imagined the shouting, the anger, the broken glass? But no, the pieces were still by her feet like tiny daggers. He kissed her head, kissed the tears off her *face and said, 'Let me take you to bed. You must be so tired. You need rest. Everything will seem better once you've had some sleep.' She broke down in his arms, sobbing into his shoulder. 'Sh-sh-sh,' he whispered like he was comforting a child.*

In their bedroom, he guided her towards the bed. When she was sitting down, he took her hands in hers, looked her in the eye and said, 'I'm so sorry, darling. I'm sorry I got angry and raised my voice.'

Fresh tears sprang to her eyes. She pulled her hands away. 'You scared me. The glass . . . You threw it at me.'

'Not at you. At the wall. I would never hurt you. Do you hear me? I will never do anything to upset you again. You are everything to me. When we met, I was dead inside and you brought me back to life. I'm so happy to be married to you. I can't wait to spend the rest of my life with you.'

'I've never seen you so angry before.'

'And you never will again, I swear. I've been under a lot of stress lately. Work's been a nightmare. I'll make it up to you.'

He made love to her, so gently and lovingly, it made her cry. She trembled in his arms, trying to understand. One moment, he was screaming in anger. The next, he was holding her like she was the most precious thing in his life, as if there were two people inside him, two completely different sides to him. Perhaps it had been her fault after all, she reasoned. Perhaps she shouldn't have said what she said and he had every right to get upset. As he whispered urgently how much he loved her, she promised herself she would be more careful in the future. She would watch her every word, so that he would love her, so that they could be happy. Afterwards, he fell asleep and she lay awake by his side for hours, wondering what their future would bring.

* * *

The truck was driven as fast as the busy roads allowed. Andrea heard artillery shells exploding nearby, and next to her the nurses were whispering to one another, their panicked voices, muffled by the machine-gun fire, reaching her as if through cotton wool.

'Poor people of Berat. What are they going to do? Do they have anywhere to go? What is going to happen to them?' Carrie was saying.

'What will happen to Nicole? I can't believe we left her,' replied Tory.

'We had no choice. Perhaps, when the Germans are gone, we'll come back for her.'

'Does it look like the Germans are going anywhere?'

'What are we going to do? Without Captain Brown, all our chances for a quick rescue are gone.'

'Don't talk like that. We are still alive. We were able to leave Berat. We are safe.'

'For now.'

Andrea wanted to scream, from helplessness, from frustration, from sadness. It made no sense to her that they continued to drive away from Berat instead of rushing back to save Nicole. Soon they left the city. She knew that because she could no longer see the buildings, only trees. Even though she had tried to stay behind and couldn't, even though it wasn't her choice to leave, with every curve of the road, with every structure they were leaving behind, she felt like she was betraying her sister.

As they made their way down the country road, the truck jolting on every bump, Andrea heard the aircraft. Its engines sounded hostile and angry. She looked up and immediately wished she hadn't because right above them was a dreaded German Messerschmitt. A moment later, a torrent of bullets hit the road around them.

'Out, everyone! Take cover,' shouted Gina, jumping from the driver's cabin.

The nurses and medics spilled out of the truck like beans, hiding under the trees and behind the bushes. Brian offered his hand to Andrea but she pushed him away, jumping into the soft mud. As she hit the ground, she felt a sharp blow to her head. She cried out in pain and lifted her eyes. It was one of the partisans, accidentally hitting her with the butt of his rifle. 'Look where you are going,' Brian shouted with anger. The young man turned around and on his face Andrea saw such fear, she felt sorry for him.

Brian guided her under a bush and covered her body with his. She felt like she was going to suffocate. She wanted to crawl away from him but couldn't move.

In the sky above them, there were now half a dozen planes. It seemed to Andrea that they were searching them out and weren't leaving until they were all dead. But ten terrifying minutes later, the machine guns fell quiet. Brian let go of her and she raised her head, looking around. Only one plane remained. It was a Fieseler Fi-156 Storch, a German observation plane. It seemed to hover in the air as if waiting for something.

When the observation plane was gone, they climbed out of their hiding places. Andrea saw that the truck had been hit repeatedly and was completely useless. For a few moments, they stood around it, examining it, hoping for a miracle. Gina tried to start the engine. It coughed once and fell silent. Only when they saw German trucks appear in the distance did they move away from the road and into the little forest nearby.

'We can't stay here. Big danger,' said Gina to the group of dejected and frightened Americans. 'We go to the mountains east from here. We hide there. We look for villages.'

Everyone thought it was a good idea. Everyone except Andrea. 'We need to go back,' she kept repeating. 'We need to go back to Berat.'

But no one paid any attention to her.

'What do we do if the Germans catch up with us?' asked one of the medics.

'Don't tell them anything. Not where we are stationed. Not how many in our squadron. No information that could be useful to them,' said Baggs. 'To all their questions, say you don't know anything.'

'They will see our identity papers,' said Renee.

'Destroy them,' said Baggs.

And they did. At any other time, burning her identification papers would have filled Andrea with sadness. It was like watching her identity turn to ashes in front of her eyes. But on that day, she barely even thought about it. She couldn't get her sister out of her head. Now that the Germans were in Berat, what was going to happen to her?

In a single file, they walked down a narrow trail. Brian was close behind Andrea, breathing down her back, as if afraid she would run the minute he wasn't watching. Every once in a while, he asked her if she was all right but she never replied. Her eyes were on the road in front of her, her hands in tight fists. She concentrated on walking, on putting one foot in front of another. *Step after step, don't slip in the mud, don't slow down, don't think about anything, not your burning cheek where his fist has connected, not the Germans bursting into the house that was sheltering Nicole.* All that mattered was not to fall, to keep moving forward, towards safety. But how could she do that when her sister was still in danger?

As they approached the mountain, it started to rain. It took three hours of walking uphill under the deluge to reach a village. When Andrea saw the buildings, she felt relieved. She was exhausted, not so much from walking but from the thoughts whirring inside her head, driving her crazy. As they were about to approach, they heard gunfire. Bullets flew past like stones, hitting the leaves of the trees where the Americans took cover.

'Are the Nazis here? Have they followed us to the mountains?' cried Renee.

'Not the Nazis,' replied Gina. 'The partisans fighting the BK. We can't go on. We need to turn back.'

'Turn back to Berat and the Germans? And who are the BK?' asked Renee.

Not answering her question, the partisan said, 'We are caught in a crossfire. We need to go.'

As they walked, Andrea could see the valley below, stretching like a postcard before her eyes. In that valley lay Berat, bleeding and besieged. And somewhere in Berat was her sister. It took all her strength not to break down in front of everyone. She couldn't help but feel discouraged. They had walked for miles, only to have to turn back again. They were moving aimlessly, not knowing where to look for shelter from the storm. Ever since they boarded the fateful flight, luck had not been on their side. And now it wasn't just the Nazis they had to worry about. There was a new enemy they hadn't even known existed.

On the bushes around them, small berries glistened in the rain, reminding Andrea of blueberries her grandmother used to grow. She would tell the sisters not to touch them until they were ripe. And when they were ripe, she would give them a bucket and tell them to bring back enough for a pie. The two of them would collect the berries, putting them not in the bucket but straight into their mouths. And when they returned emptyhanded, their grandmother would shake her head and laugh. And the sisters would laugh too. Nicole would point at Andrea and say, 'It's her. She ate all the blueberries.' Even though her own dress would be stained with blueberry juice.

As she looked at the berries in front of her, Andrea thought of the summers long gone, of joy and childhood and her sister. She grabbed a handful of the berries and put them in her mouth. They tasted sour, not at all like her grandmother's blueberries. But she was hungry, so she picked up another handful.

'Don't eat those,' said Gina, coming up to her. Placing his hand on his stomach, he made a grimace, as if he was in pain, then pointed at her. 'You eat too many, bad belly.'

She threw the berries she was holding in her fist to the ground. 'Who are the BK?' She wanted to know.

'Balli Kombëtar,' the man replied, as if it answered all her questions.

She waited for him to say more. He didn't. 'What does that mean?' she prompted.

'The National Front.'

'And they are against you?'

'They are against Albanians, but they don't think so.'

Andrea remembered reading something about the civil war in Albania. 'They are anti-communist?'

Gina nodded. 'They have a slogan. Albania for the Albanians. And yet, they fight alongside the Nazis against the partisans.'

'They don't sound very patriotic.'

'They are ruthless and dangerous. We must avoid them.' He must have seen the expression on her face because he smiled and said gently, 'Don't worry. I will send a partisan to Berat. To look for your sister.'

'Thank you,' she whispered.

When Andrea thought she couldn't walk anymore, they reached a village called Kapinovë and found an empty stone barn. There was no food and, after running for their lives, most of them collapsed on piles of hay, falling asleep instantly. Shaking in her damp clothes, Andrea wrapped herself in her field coat and wondered what her sister was doing, if she was safe, if she was thinking of her. Closing her eyes, she felt for Nicole out there. They were twins. They could do that. They didn't need words to communicate with one another. They didn't even need to be near each other. She tried to imagine Nicole's smiling, happy face, but all she could see was darkness.

She needed to talk to someone about her sister, needed to hear someone tell her everything was going to be all right. In the past, when she needed comfort, she turned to her husband. But she couldn't do it now, not after everything that happened. Brian had spent the day next to her, but he didn't mention anything and didn't apologise. Even though she was hurt by what he had done, she longed for him as she lay alone in the dark. She longed for the other Brian, the Brian she had fallen in love with all those years ago, the man who held her hand, who told her he loved her, who brought her flowers for no reason at all and made her laugh. Not the sullen, cranky man who was always stressed about one thing or another, fighting one battle or another, and barely looking at her most days. Was the man she loved gone forever? Or would he come back one day, when all this was behind them and they were happy? A part of her knew that there would always be a battle to fight. But another, bigger part of her, wanted to believe in him, despite everything.

Her comrades were snoring around her. Baggs was talking in his sleep. Renee was breathing heavily by Andrea's side. On the other side of the barn, one of the medics was whistling a tune Andrea recognised but couldn't quite place. As she was drifting off, she felt someone cover her with a jacket. She heard Brian's voice. 'Are you crying because of your sister? Or because of me?'

She thought of the swarms of German soldiers descending on Berat, overrunning the streets, shooting their guns. She thought of planes with swastikas obscuring the sun, dropping their bombs, and of desperate, panicking people, running away from Nazi tanks. 'What will the Germans do to Nicky?' she whispered. 'What is going to happen to her?'

'She'll be fine. She's a nurse. They have no reason to hurt her.'

'I need to go back and look for her,' she said, even though she knew it was impossible. 'I can't sit here and do nothing.'

'I'm not letting you go anywhere.'

'She's my twin. She's half of me. I can't live without her.'

'I know. We are not giving up. We'll find her again. Somehow, we'll find a way.'

She sat up and looked at him. 'We are walking to the coast so we can get rescued and leave Albania.' She trembled. 'No one is doing anything to find Nicole. What are you even talking about?'

'We can't go back. We need to get to safety and then another rescue party . . .'

'What rescue party? How can I live with myself if I abandon her here?'

'Everything will be all right. It will all work out.'

She wondered if he really believed it or if he was only saying it to stop her from complaining. After a long silence, she said, 'Once, when we were children, Nicole and I had a big argument. I don't remember what it was about but we didn't talk to each other for five days. I hardly saw her, only at mealtimes. I thought she was avoiding me and I was so angry. A few days later, on my birthday, I woke up and found a beautiful dress that my sister made for me. She wanted me to wear it for my party. All those days I thought she was ignoring me, she was locking herself in the shed, working on the dress.' Andrea paused. 'I miss her so much. And all I can think about is, what if I never see her again? How can I continue to live if my twin is gone? How do I get through the day, let alone the rest of my life? How do I face it all without her?'

He placed his arms around her and held her close. She didn't move away. He touched the mark on her face. 'Does it still hurt?' he asked quietly, almost like he was pleading for her to say no, that it didn't bother her at all, that it didn't matter.

But it did matter and she couldn't lie to him about it. 'You've never hit me before,' she whispered. She tried to stop the tears from coming but couldn't. She felt so small, so vulnerable in front of him, so embarrassed, like it had all been her fault. As if it was her who had done something wrong.

'I'm so sorry,' he said. 'I never meant to hurt you. I hope you know that.'

'If you didn't mean to hurt me, why did you?'

'I was afraid you would jump off that truck and I would never see you again. Don't you understand? With everything that was going on, the Germans invading, the explosions, the machine-gun fire, the tanks advancing, I was so afraid of losing you. We only had a small chance of escaping that hellhole. I couldn't let anything happen to you.'

'So you chose to hit me?'

He looked down at his hands, as if he couldn't bear the broken expression on her face. 'I didn't know what to do. I was desperate.

I acted in the heat of the moment.' He turned her to him and scooped her into his arms. She didn't resist, her body going limp in his embrace.

She trembled. 'It's like there are two people inside you. One is loving and kind. I haven't seen him for some time.' *I miss him*, she wanted to add. 'And the other is ...' She hesitated, searching for the right word, finding it, too afraid to say it out loud in case it upset him.

'A monster?' he prompted. When she didn't reply, he said, 'I didn't have a good example of love growing up. I was hurting when you met me. I never thought I could get close to anyone again. You healed me.'

Healed you? she wanted to say. *Look at us.* She was curled up into a ball in his arms, small and afraid. Wishing someone could come and take the pain away. Wishing she could believe him so it wouldn't hurt so much. 'If I healed you, then why are you doing this to me? Why are you so angry all the time?'

'Not all the time. Sometimes ...'

'A lot of the time.'

'I'm so sorry.' Tears were running down his cheeks. She couldn't believe it. She had seen him crying only once before, on the day they were married, when she walked to him in her white dress and promised to love him in sickness and in health, through the good times and the bad, no matter what life threw at them. 'Do you hear me? I'm sorry I hurt you,' he repeated.

'Is that what our life is going to be like from now on? You losing your temper, lashing out at me? Because I don't want that.'

'I don't want that either. I promise you, it will never happen again. I will never hurt you.'

'You've said that before. I don't know if I believe it anymore.'

'Please don't say that.'

'What do you want me to say?' she whispered. His fingertips touched her face, wiping the tears off her cheeks, brushing the hair out of her eyes. His arms moved tighter around her. *That's the way it is*, she thought. *He hurts me, then he makes me feel better. I always turn to him for comfort. Despite everything.*

When he spoke, his voice was quiet. She could barely hear him. He sounded calm and detached, as if he was telling her a story of someone else's life, a story that stirred no emotions or painful recollections. 'Do you want to hear about one of my first childhood memories? One day, my mother was too busy sewing a pair of shorts for me to wear to pre-school and didn't have time to make dinner for my father. He beat her in front of me. Gave her a black eye and a broken arm.'

'Oh, no,' she whispered, horrified. 'You must have been so scared.'

He moved slightly away from her, as if her touch was burning him. 'On my fifth birthday, mother told father to take me to the park. She said it will do us both good to spend some time together, because he rarely did anything with me. He got so angry, he broke her jaw. She had to go to hospital.'

'I'm so sorry,' she said, crying for him and for herself, her finger drawing circles on his hand, big circles and little circles to comfort him, to remind him that he was here with her and not in his past where he was unsafe.

'On my first day of school, mother asked him if he bought flowers for the teacher. He screamed at her to do it herself and threw a glass at her. She needed stitches.' After a few moments of silence, he added, 'I can't remember a single weekend, birthday, Christmas or Easter without my father getting drunk, angry and abusive. Every childhood memory I have is filled with violence and fear. Everything was tarnished, everything was broken.'

She trembled as she thought of the scared little boy cowering in fear in front of his angry father. A little boy who became the man she loved more than anything in the world. She took his hand and kissed the tips of his fingers. 'You never told me any of it.'

'I didn't want to upset you or scare you away.'

'Scare me away? Why? None of it was your fault. You were

just a child. You had no control over what was happening to you.'

And yet, his past had not gone away. It was right there with them, like a spectre threatening their future together. 'Why did your mother stay with him?' And as soon as she said it, she thought, *Why do I stay?* Because leaving was inconceivable. It would feel like leaving her heart and soul behind.

'He was the only provider in our family. She didn't know how she would put food on the table for me and my brother without him. But when he died, she went back to college. She could finally live her life.' He was silent for a while. His shoulders were stooped, his head down, like he still carried his childhood pain with every breath he took. 'My greatest fear is becoming like him one day.'

'You are nothing like him.'

His voice was filled with pain. 'What if I am? Look what I've done.'

'You did it for my own good. We were in danger. I wasn't listening. You did it to protect me.' She couldn't believe she was making excuses for him, defending him when moments earlier she didn't know if she would ever forgive him.

'I carry my childhood trauma with me everywhere I go. But I don't want it to affect our marriage. I love you so much.'

'I know. And it won't.' As she said it, she thought of the glass of brandy shattering above her head and of his hand slapping her hard across her face moments after she had to leave her sister behind in occupied Berat.

'I don't want to lose what we have. To lose you. I will try better. I will try so hard.'

She rubbed the broken skin on her face and placed her hand on her hurting heart. 'You will?'

'Of course. You are the most important thing in my life and I will do anything for you. Do you forgive me?'

On his face she saw pure heartbreak and pain, and his eyes were pleading with her as if his whole life depended on what she was going to say next. 'Of course, I forgive you.'

'Do you still love me?'

'I still love you.'

'And I love you.'

She was no longer crying as she held on to him in the dark. She knew he was telling the truth. He loved her and he would try his best. And she would help him. She would be by his side, supporting him every step of the way. After all, she had made a vow before God to love this man, and love him she would, unconditionally, against all odds, for better or worse.

But she couldn't shake a small doubt, a voice inside her head that whispered, *But what if it happens again?*

Chapter 6

Besieged

Nicole stood at the top of the steps outside Grand Hotel Kolumbo, unsure what to do next. For as long as she remembered, Andrea had been her rock, her constant, the one person she could rely on in any situation. She believed with all her heart that Andrea would never turn her back to her, let her down or tell a falsehood. To have that belief shattered so cruelly, to learn that her sister had been lying to her not for a day or a week or a month but for nine years, left Nicole feeling shaken and empty inside. It seemed to her that the earth itself was shifting under her feet, her ordered universe changing before her eyes. She didn't know how to cope with that and so she chose to do the only thing she could think of – run.

The cold air made her shiver and she realised she had forgotten her jacket. On the streets of Berat, everything was moving in a whirlwind, threatening to swallow her up. A hundred voices, it seemed, collided to form a deafening choir, intent on driving her insane. A hundred cars blared their horns.

When she glanced back at the hotel, Nicole saw a shadow by one of the windows. The curtain trembled and moved aside and for a second she caught a glimpse of her sister's tear-stained face. Perhaps it was the early morning sun, reflecting off the glass and distorting her sister's features. Perhaps it was the tears in Nicole's eyes, blurring her vision. But it seemed to Nicole she was looking at a stranger.

She turned away from the hotel and her gaze fell on the little hut Darren had entered earlier. That instant, she knew exactly what to do. Taking a deep breath, she walked out into the busy road. Cars screeched and drivers shouted at her to get out of the way. She barely noticed. A horse-drawn taxi appeared, the man stopping in front of her and asking if she needed a lift. She shook her head, waved him off with her hand, nearly screamed.

The hut was not unlike Darren's childhood home, small and lopsided, with the paint peeling in places. As she paused outside, she experienced a moment of déjà vu. She had stood like this once before, her knuckles to the door, frantically looking for him. She didn't know it then but she wouldn't see him again for almost a decade. She hesitated, wondering what she was doing here, what she was going to say to him, what questions she was going to ask and if she had any right to, after all these years.

She didn't knock this time but turned the handle and pushed, her heart racing. Pausing to catch her breath, she stepped inside.

She saw him instantly, and for a brief moment remained quiet and trembling. Time itself, it seemed, stood still. She was mesmerised, unable to believe her eyes, unable to move or make a sound. He had his back to her and didn't notice her, nor did he seem to hear the door creak on its hinges. He was sitting at the table, dressed in his uniform, a jar of juice and a book before him. The house was silent and only the fire cracked in the fireplace every now and then. She thought she had carried his image in her heart through all these years, that she remembered every curve of his body perfectly. But she had forgotten how tall he was, how his dark hair curled above his collar, how strong his arms looked. They shared more than a decade of memories together, growing up in Detroit, best friends first, lovers later. They shared an eight-year-old son and he didn't even know it. He still had her heart and didn't even know it. Nine years ago almost to the day, he had left without a word or an explanation. She had spent every night since falling asleep in her bed and dreaming of his face. She had spent nine years praying to see him again. And here he was, in front of her. All she had to do was call out his name. And yet, she was so afraid.

She couldn't remain there much longer, mute and frozen to the spot. Finally, after all these years, she was going to get some answers. He owed her that much. She opened her mouth to say something but no words came out. She cleared her throat. He turned around. Their eyes met. There was recognition on his face, and shock. 'Nicole,' he whispered.

'Hello, Darren.'

He took a step forward, then another. She had to lean on the door because something was happening to her legs. All of a sudden, they were too weak to hold her. He opened his arms and she stepped into them, closing her eyes, feeling the warmth of his body, so close. For a moment, she was no longer in Nazi-occupied Albania but across the ocean where she had once been happy and safe.

'Is it really you? Am I dreaming?' he asked.

'I'm not so sure,' she whispered.

He took a step back to look at her. 'You are one of the American nurses?'

She nodded.

'Why didn't I see you this morning?'

'I hid.' She blushed. He laughed and she laughed, and suddenly her heart felt lighter.

He said, 'You look exactly like I remember you. How is it possible that you haven't changed at all?'

But I have, she wanted to tell him. She was no longer the carefree girl he used to know. She was a wife, a mother. 'You've changed, though. You seem so grown up. Look at you, an officer. What happened to your dream of opening a restaurant?'

'It didn't work out. I'm glad to see you got to follow your

childhood dream. You are a nurse, just like you've always wanted.' They were standing in the middle of the room, unable to take their eyes off each other. A moment later, he shook his head like he was waking up from a dream and said, 'Please, sit down. I saw your face and forgot my manners. Would you like anything to drink? Are you hungry?'

She followed him to a small table and took a seat. 'I'm not hungry. I would love a drink.' Her throat was burning. She could barely breathe.

He gave her a glass of juice and she took a quick sip. The juice was bitter and made her cough. 'What is it?' she asked.

'Grapefruit. Would you like some water instead?'

She shook her head and finished the juice. He offered her some cornbread and cheese. Even though she had eaten nothing at all for breakfast that day, she declined. She couldn't even look at food.

'Eat,' he said. 'You'll need your strength. If we are to reach the coast, we'll need to cover long distances every day.' She took a piece of cornbread. He watched her as she ate. 'You've been through so much. The plane crash. The long hours walking through the mountains. The Germans. You must be so afraid.'

'Not anymore,' she whispered.

'I'll get you back before you know it. It's all arranged. All we need to do is get to the coast.'

For the first time since they crashed, she believed that everything would be all right. Now that Darren was here, it was only a matter of time before they got back to base. Now that he was here, they would see home again. 'What about you? What will you do once we are back in Italy?'

'I'll go where they send me.'

He told her he joined the Army in 1940 and was assigned to the 696th Ordnance Company. 'I was working at a diner, trying to save money to open my own place but hardly making enough for rent and food. It seemed like a dead end. And then the war started. Across the ocean, young men like me were being killed, while here I was, flipping burgers. I knew I had to do something.'

'How did you join the OSS?'

'After a year in Egypt as a commander of a small-arms company of an Ordnance maintenance battalion, the OSS approached me. They told me I could make a real difference working with them.'

'Let me guess. You didn't hesitate.'

'Not for a moment.' He smiled. 'Remember my brother Otis? He's in Europe somewhere, flying a B-26 bomber. I knew if I didn't do something as exciting and heroic, he'd look down on me forever. He'd be really insufferable when he came back home.'

'He must be so proud of you. And you of him. And your parents? How are they?'

'Mama is not working anymore but Dad has a good job. He's an overseer at a winery in Napa.'

'Napa? Is that where you moved when you left Detroit?'

He nodded and didn't say anything else. She waited, hands shaking. The most important question of her life was on the tip of her tongue. *Why did you leave?* she wanted to ask him but couldn't get the words out. 'What's it been like so far? Being here, working with the OSS?' she asked instead.

'I've been in training for the last few months. I just completed a paramilitary course with the British 11th Commando Regiment at Ramat David. Rescuing you and your comrades is my first real mission. I'm so glad I can help *you*.' He touched her hand. 'But enough about me. Tell me about yourself.'

'Not much to tell. Andrea and I have been at the front for a few weeks. This was our first evacuation flight. We were both terrified.'

'With good reason.'

'I can see that now.' Nicole smiled sadly and for a moment they were both silent, studying each other. She couldn't look away from his face, so familiar, and yet, so different. There was something in his eyes that hadn't been there before. A sadness, as if he had seen things he wished he could forget. She wanted to reach out and touch his cheek. She wanted to feel his lips with her fingertips, run her hands through his hair like she used to when they were younger. She remained still, feeling her face burning. She knew her cheeks would be bright red. What if he noticed? What if he knew what she was thinking?

And then she heard the shots outside. They came in short bursts, like angry dogs barking. Someone shouted like they were in pain, like the world was coming to an end. Soon, the screams were drowned by the sound of plane engines. In the distance, something exploded, and suddenly it felt like the floor under her feet was moving.

'What's happening?' whispered Nicole, her voice catching. A rumbling noise was heard outside their windows. She knew it wasn't cars. The sound was deeper, more terrifying. Trucks? When Darren moved the curtain aside, she saw tanks with swastikas painted on them in ominous black. They were slowly moving through the streets of Berat like they owned them. Everywhere she looked, she could see German soldiers, jumping out of military vehicles, walking down the road, knocking on doors. A panic gripped her like strong fingers around her throat, and for a moment she couldn't breathe.

As Darren was stepping away from the window, a bullet hit the glass, shattering it. The window exploded, a million shards falling to the ground and embedding themselves in Darren's face. When he turned around, Nicole saw that he was covered in blood. She shrieked.

'I'm fine. It's just a scratch,' he said.

She rushed to his side. 'You might need stitches.' Her gaze fell on the bullet on the floor. 'You are lucky to be alive.'

'We need to go. Immediately.'

Nicole felt her knees shaking. She knew they shouldn't have stayed in town for four days, waiting for the OSS officer to arrive. They should have hidden in the forest somewhere, in one of the small villages they passed. Instead, they remained in Berat like sitting ducks for the enemy. And now the enemy was here. 'What are we going to do?' she asked.

Darren looked calm, like he was on the tennis court in Detroit and not on the bleeding Albanian streets. Not a muscle moved on his face. His voice didn't tremble when he said, 'We need to find the others and try to get out of Berat before it's too late.' Another explosion shook the ground. Outside, Nicole could hear someone shouting in German. 'If it's not too late already,' he added, taking her hand. 'Don't be scared. I won't let anything happen to you.'

'I know,' she said. And for a moment, when his fingers gripped hers tightly, she was no longer afraid, even though war had come to Berat and bullets flew outside their windows.

They were about to open the door and step into the chaos when it burst open, almost hitting them. A Nazi soldier was on the doorstep, a gun in his hand. He took a step forward and said something in German. Nicole watched him with horror, his crooked mouth, his shaven head, his red face. He seemed to her like a cartoon character that had come to life, the likes of which she and Darren used to watch on her mother's black-and-white television set when they were seven, eight, nine. Except, this was not a cartoon made for children. It was a horror film. Terror filled her heart. The German soldier would see their uniforms and know they were American. He would know they were enemies.

The soldier repeated the same phrase again and again, his eyes jumping from her to Darren. Nicole couldn't understand what he was saying or what he wanted. All those German lessons at school and every word had flown out of her head without so much as a goodbye when she needed them most.

The soldier pointed his rifle at Nicole and cocked it. Like lightning, Darren was in front of her, a gun in his hands, his body covering hers. Two shots sounded. The German fell to the ground and remained there without moving, his eyes staring at the roof, his mouth open like he was screaming for help, only no sound was coming out. But Nicole wasn't looking at him.

Horrified, she watched Darren as he slid down to the ground with a quiet groan. His tunic was covered in blood. His eyes were closed. Screaming as if it was her body torn by a deathly bullet, her heart nearly jumping out of her chest, she stepped over the German officer's body, slipped on the blood and fell, crawling to Darren the rest of the way. With a trembling hand she felt his pulse. He was still breathing. Thank God.

Her hands felt sticky and wet. When she raised them, she saw that they were covered in blood, while the red pool under Darren's body was becoming larger by the second. She couldn't move from the shock, couldn't leave Darren on the floor alone but she knew she needed to do something to stop the bleeding, and fast. With a superhuman effort she got up to her feet, placing Darren's head gently on the floorboards, and rushed to the bedroom, where she looked for a sheet, a clean towel, anything to stem the blood flow. She couldn't find anything, but on the bed she saw a white robe. It would have to do. She rushed back and dressed his shoulder as best as she could, noticing with relief that the wound had an entrance and exit holes, which meant the bullet had left the body.

There was no time to lose. She had to get Darren to the others, so that they could leave Berat. She tried to lift him but it was impossible. He was at least twice her weight. She pushed and pulled and heaved with all her might until they were near the front door. Opening it slightly, she glanced outside. Transfixed, she watched as a cavalcade of German tanks moved through the streets. German soldiers were on every corner, pointing their machine guns at the terrified Albanians. Outside the hotel, people were milling around despondently, as if unsure what to do. The soccer ball the local boys were chasing around only an hour ago lay abandoned in the dust, while the children clung to the grown-ups, their terrified faces peeking out from behind their parents' backs.

She hesitated in the doorway. To get to the hotel, she would have to make her way through a group of Nazi soldiers gathered outside and then cross the road filled with German vehicles and tanks. Leaving the house now would be suicide. A wounded American officer and a nurse in full uniform would not last a minute before they were captured. She could wait until it was dark and the streets were quieter but what if the others had already left by then?

Wiping tears off her face, she stepped back inside, dragging Darren behind her, and closed the door, locking it. She knew the flimsy lock wouldn't prevent the enemy soldiers from entering the little house but it made her feel a little safer. Helpless and lost, she sat on the floor with Darren's head in her lap, whispering his name, asking if he could hear her. He didn't stir, nor did he open his eyes. The bleeding slowed down and he didn't seem hot to the touch. His pulse was strong and she told herself it was a good sign, that everything would be all right, that they were still alive and it was a miracle, but she couldn't stop herself from crying. While the German tanks rolled outside the window, she sobbed, wondering what to do next, what would become of them, what would become of her sister and the others, if she would ever see them again or if the last words Andrea had ever heard from Nicole were that she never wanted to talk to her again.

* * *

The streets rumbled, a terrifying, overwhelming clatter the likes of which Nicole had never heard before. Plane engines, tanks, rifle shots and machine-gun fire collided together to form a deathly symphony. Occasionally it would be interrupted with an explosion and then all would fall silent for a few moments, only to start all over again, louder, more petrifying than before. Nicole wanted to scream from the horror of it all. She wanted to weep and shout and crawl under the nearest rock, where she could be invisible, where she would be safe.

But she couldn't do any of it because Darren needed her. She sat in the middle of the room with his head in her lap, every now and then whispering frantically, 'Darren, can you hear me? Please, wake up.' And when he wouldn't respond, she would wipe the tears off her face and try again. 'Darren, can you hear me? Darren, can you hear me?'

She did her best not to glance at the body of the German soldier on the floor, to forget about his existence, to focus all her energy on the man she was cradling in her arms.

She didn't know how long she sat there like that. It could have been ten minutes or two hours. The sun was high in the sky. The war continued on the streets of Berat but she could barely hear it. All she could see was him. She stroked his face, touched his hair, his closed eyes, his lips, the stubble on his cheeks.

A scar she had never seen before adorned his cheek. *When he wakes up, I will ask him about it*, she decided. She would tell him about her own, invisible, scars. And perhaps she would be brave enough to ask the question that had kept her awake at night for the last nine years.

The first time they made love, the first time she felt his naked body under her fingertips, many years ago when they were teenagers and had their whole lives ahead of them, she was too shy to look at him, at the expression of love on his wonderful face. She had closed her eyes and gave in to his touch, to the torrent of feelings inside her. Afterwards, she wished she had kept her eyes open, so she could see everything he was feeling. They had been each other's firsts in every way that counted. First kiss, first love, first dreams. How she wished she could think back on the memory of his face as he made love to her for the first time. How she wished she could read what was in his heart, while her own heart was bursting with emotion. Afterwards, he had fallen asleep but she couldn't close her eyes even for a moment. She had held his head, much like she was doing now, and stroked his beloved face. She wondered what he was dreaming about. She wanted to know if he was dreaming of her.

And now, in war-torn Berat, while the bullets continued to hit the walls of the little house, she looked into his face and for a breathless moment was transported back to that carefree time when they were together and in love, when they didn't doubt for a moment that they would spend their lives together, when they thought their love would protect them from anything, even heartbreak.

Another explosion sounded, closer, more terrifying than before. It shattered the glass in one of the windows and startled Nicole. She desperately wanted to get to the window to see what was happening outside but didn't want to leave Darren on the cold floor. Where were the others? Was her sister all right? Were they able to escape before the inferno was unleashed on Berat or were they trapped in their temporary accommodation just like she was? And what if they escaped but were stopped on the way? What if they didn't make it?

Suddenly, she felt so small, like a child faced with grown-up choices. She longed for her mother to appear in the little hut in the middle of Berat and make everything all right again. The only blessing in all of this was that her son would not witness this horror, that he was safe at home, waiting for her to return. As she listened to the tempest outside, she wondered if she ever would.

When the gunshots fell quiet for a moment, Nicole heard footsteps, distant at first, then closer and closer, until they stopped outside the door. Her hands tensing around Darren's head, she struggled for breath, her gaze on the dead soldier on the floor. She should have hidden the body when she had a chance but she hadn't thought of it, so focused was she on helping Darren. And now it was too late. If a German patrol burst into the house and saw their dead comrade, they would shoot her and Darren on the spot.

She heard voices and squeezed her eyes shut in fear. The door opened and closed with a loud bang and a floorboard creaked.

Nicole leaned closer to Darren, repeating a prayer to herself. *Please, God, spare us for our son.* She had so much to live for. After all these years, she had finally found Darren. She had her child, who was the love of her life. If she perished in Berat, if she never returned, if she broke his little heart, what would become of him? Who would he grow up to be, without her?

A woman appeared in the doorway, dressed in a long wraparound skirt, a dark blouse and a kerchief. Behind her was a man with an expression of sheer panic on his face. They walked in and quickly shut the door behind them.

Without saying a word, the strangers looked at Nicole and Darren and then at the dead soldier. After a few moments of stunned silence, the woman spoke in Albanian, gesticulating and pointing at the body. Nicole couldn't understand anything, other than that the woman was talking to her and she was angry. 'I'm sorry,' she said softly. 'I didn't mean for any of this to happen.'

'Who are you?' asked the man in surprisingly good English. He barely had an accent.

'My name is Nicole. I'm a nurse.'

'American?'

She nodded. 'And you are?'

The man introduced himself as Nani. His wife's name was Goni. They owned the little house. 'The Germans have won the battle. They have occupied Berat,' he said.

Even though she already knew it, from the sound of war outside, from the sight of the German soldiers on the streets, hearing the horrible truth put into words like this filled Nicole with terror.

Goni spoke again, fast and agitated, her voice shaking and her eyes shooting daggers at Nicole and Darren.

Nani said, 'If anyone sees him . . .' He pointed at the soldier. 'They will kill us all.'

While the machine guns sang on the streets, Nani walked across the living room, moved a dirty brown rug out of the way and pulled a lever. A little trapdoor opened. 'We hide him here,' he said. 'When it is dark, I will get my brother. Together we will get rid of body.'

'Your brother is drunk again,' said Goni. Her English wasn't as good as her husband's but Nicole could understand her. 'I walk to market. I see him in the ditch.'

'Then you will have to help me, woman.'

'I can help too,' said Nicole. 'I'm responsible for this mess. It's the least I can do.'

Nani shook his head. 'It's best if you stay inside. We don't want anyone to see you or, before we know it, the Nazis will be on our doorstep again.'

Nicole had to admit he had a point. She placed her hand on Darren's forehead. He had spiked a fever and felt warm to the touch. 'Do you have any medical supplies? Anything for the fever?'

'We don't. But my brother will,' said Nani.

'If he wakes,' said Goni.

'Do you want to tell us what happened?' asked Nani.

'He just burst in and was going to shoot us, only Captain Brown was faster. He saved my life.' Her trembling fingers touched his burning cheek.

Nani brought some bandages from the bedroom and Nicole applied a dressing to Darren's shoulder, while husband and wife lifted the German soldier and carried him to the opening in the floor, sliding the body inside, closing the trapdoor and replacing the rug. Without the dead Nazi next to her Nicole could breathe easier, as if him not being there meant the horror of the last two hours hadn't happened.

The couple offered Nicole something to eat but she shook her head. She couldn't think of food while Darren lay unconscious by her side and her sister was out there somewhere, on the streets ravaged by the Germans. She stroked Darren's head, whispered to him that everything was going to be all right, even though she didn't believe it, watched Nazi vehicles pass by the window along the main road and listened to husband and wife arguing in Albanian.

Nani said, 'There are hundreds of them outside. A partisan was killed on our doorstep. We will have to move him. It's only a matter of time before the Germans come back here. I will find you something else to wear. You can't stay here wearing this.' He pointed at their uniforms.

He made a move towards the bedroom but Nicole stopped him. 'What will the Germans do to you if they find us here?'

Nani shrugged. Goni remained quiet.

'They will kill you, won't they? They will kill you for hiding an American officer and nurse. They will burn your house and hurt your families.' She shook her head. 'I can't let this happen to you. We will leave. We will find somewhere else to hide. I will not put you at risk.'

The woman spoke fast in Albanian, pointing out the window, then at the two of them, shaking her head. The man nodded and said, 'You are very kind. But you have nowhere to go. The war has come to Berat. And he needs medical attention.'

Nicole's gaze fell on a small wagon outside the window. 'If you help me lift him onto that, we'll be gone in no time. Perhaps to the hotel. They will help us.'

The woman placed her hand on Nicole's shoulder. 'No,' she said.

Nani said, 'When we took him in, we promised him shelter. Albanians never break their word.'

'But if we are discovered here . . .'

'We'll deal with it when it happens.'

Goni went to the bedroom and soon returned with a pile of dark clothes. 'Change,' she said.

Nicole couldn't undress Darren without hurting his shoulder, so she cut his uniform with a knife. It took all her skill to put Nani's old clothes on him, trying hard not to cause him any pain, not to move him too much, not to disturb the torn flesh of his shoulder. Then she went into the bedroom and changed.

Nani took their uniforms and said, 'I will burn these. No one must know who you are.'

Nicole spent the rest of the day helping her hosts clean the blood and the broken glass off the floor, looking after Darren and every once in a while glancing out the window. She saw groups of partisans moving around as if in a daze, men and women shouting to each other before rushing away, German vehicles driving past. She watched the hotel door obsessively, hoping to catch a glimpse of her sister and the others but there was no sign of them.

When it got dark, Nani and Goni carried the German soldier outside. They returned an hour later, telling Nicole that their mission had been a success and with luck no one would ever find him. As she watched the fire burning in the fireplace, she thanked God for the hosts' kindness. She had only met them a few hours previously and yet, they were willing to risk their lives for her and Darren. Even though war raged outside, a little bit of her faith in the world returned as she sat by Darren's side, listened to his heavy breathing and prayed.

* * *

Curled up next to Darren by the fire, his hand in hers, Nicole couldn't get a minute of sleep. She was afraid that the moment she closed her eyes, something would happen to him. She had lost him once. She couldn't lose him again, and so she watched over him in the near darkness, while the moon shone through the open curtains and the machine guns crooned on the outskirts of Berat.

Goni and Nani were fast asleep in the bedroom, their soft snoring reaching her through a thin piece of board that served as a wall. Before they fell asleep, they spent a long time arguing in Albanian. Once or twice, Nicole heard the word American.

She drifted off in the early hours of the morning and was woken a little later when the sun filled the room with light. She opened her eyes and the first thing she saw was Darren's face.

She smiled and touched his forehead. It felt clammy and warm. His pulse was much too fast for her liking.

Suddenly, she heard voices outside. Someone knocked loudly, aggressively. She heard Nani and Goni shuffle in the bedroom but before they emerged the door flew open and an old woman appeared, followed by a man around Nani's age and a young boy of sixteen or seventeen. The woman looked like she was bursting with nervous energy. Dressed from head to toe in black, her hair hidden under a kerchief, she twitched on the spot, her eyes darting this way and that and finally coming to rest on Nicole. She put her hands on her sides and said something fast in Albanian, while the man watched mutely, rubbing his head like he was in pain. The boy didn't even glance at Nicole but walked over to the window and looked outside.

Nani and Goni appeared at the bedroom door, looking exhausted and frightened, and exchanged a few words with the newcomers. Nani pointed at Nicole and then at Darren, speaking fast. Nicole recognised the word *infermiere*, which meant nurse in Albanian.

The old woman sank to her knees by Darren's side. She looked him over and touched his head. 'I will help. I have herbs, I'll make special tea.'

Nani turned to Nicole. 'Meet my family. My mother, brother and nephew. They are loud and scary but they won't bite.'

'We come bearing food,' said the brother, falling heavily into a chair as if his legs could not hold him. 'I'm Agron. If you need anything, anything at all, you come to me.' He shook his head, like he was disappointed with the world. 'I woke up this morning and saw a German tank outside my house. I thought I was hallucinating.'

'I told you the drink will be your ruin,' said the mother, who introduced herself as Agnesa.

'But I wasn't hallucinating, Ma. The tank was really parked outside my house.'

Agnesa crossed herself. 'What is the world coming to? What are we going to do?'

'What we always do,' said Nani. 'We will keep our heads down and wait. In the meantime, we'll have breakfast.'

Agnesa began to cry. 'If only your father lived long enough to see this. It would kill him, absolutely kill him. He always had a weak heart.'

Goni approached her mother-in-law, gently guiding her to a chair. 'It will be all right, Mother. Please, don't cry.'

The young boy, Flamur, said something in Albanian.

'He is always hungry, this one,' said Nani, slapping Flamur on the back. 'Even the enemy on the streets of his hometown can't spoil his appetite.'

Nicole helped Goni set the table, while the family spoke in loud, argumentative voices. Soon they had laid out some boiled eggs on plates, and a chunk of bread. Agnesa opened the sack she had brought with her and pulled out some pickled onions and mutton. Nicole barely touched her food, watching the animated faces around her. The easy camaraderie between them reminded her of dinners she had had with Darren's family when they were young. Everyone was teasing one another, everyone was laughing. It was a world away from her own upbringing with her proper and strict parents, who never teased and rarely laughed.

Agnesa had a thousand questions for Nicole, who answered them as best she could.

'A plane? You don't say,' the old woman exclaimed. 'I don't go on planes. Devil's work, they are.'

'You don't go in cars or trucks. Agron has been trying for years to get you on the back of his motorbike.' Nani turned to Nicole. 'Mama has a fear of things that move faster than her.'

'And that's why I'm still alive. Do you know what happened to my good friend Mateo? A tyre blew on his car and he crashed into a tree. Now he doesn't have a car or a leg.' She turned to Nicole. 'I have the greatest respect for nurses. It takes a special person to become a nurse. Selfless and kind. Someone who cares.' She placed her hand on Nicole's. 'You stay with us for as long as you want. You and your husband are always welcome.'

'He's not my husband.'

'Your sweetheart then.' Nicole was about to protest but the older woman raised her hand. 'I can see the way you look at him. Like you would do anything for him. I've been alive for eighty years and I still remember that feeling.'

Nicole wanted to know where the family had learnt to speak English so well. Nani and Agron had traces of a British accent. Agnesa's English was heavily accented but fluent.

The older woman said, 'My husband was from Liverpool, God rest his soul. When we first met, he didn't speak a word of Albanian. And I didn't speak any English. We taught each other. Despite the language barrier, he understood me better than any man I've ever met. When the boys were little, we spent every summer in England.'

'Did you like it there?'

'I loved it. But there's no place like home. I could never leave Albania. And he stayed here, for me.'

Flamur, who had eaten his breakfast in record time and was watching the road through the window, said something in Albanian. As if by magic, everyone fell quiet. The laughter and camaraderie of a moment ago evaporated. Agnesa was no longer looking at Nicole. Her eyes darted from the window to the door. There was fear on her face. Goni stopped cutting cheese, her knife frozen in front of her face. Nani stopped talking to his brother. A moment later, footsteps resounded outside, followed by a loud knock.

Nani opened the door to two German officers, who marched inside, the sound of their boots deafening in the heavy silence. '*Papieren*,' barked the taller of the two. When no one moved, the shorter said something in Albanian. Her heart in her throat, Nicole glanced at Darren, who was lying on the floor with his eyes closed. She wished she could pick him up and whisk him away, far from the enemy officers.

Nani and Goni disappeared inside their room and soon returned with their identity papers. Agnesa, Flamur and Agron reached inside their pockets and showed their papers to the grim-faced officers. The Germans took their time studying them, looking from the documents to their faces and back again. Finally, they nodded, returned the papers and pointed at Nicole, who was still sitting at the table, mute and afraid.

The fork shook in Nicole's hand, finally falling to the ground, rolling across the room and coming to rest in the exact spot where the secret trapdoor was hidden under a rug. She couldn't talk, couldn't look at the officers, couldn't stand up.

Nani spoke fast in Albanian, pointing at each of them in turn, while Goni placed her finger over her lips when the Nazis weren't looking. Nicole realised she didn't want her to talk, so that the Germans wouldn't know she was American. Nani opened the cupboard and presented the officers with a bottle of wine.

The Germans seemed satisfied. They nodded, took the wine and, after a quick check of the bedroom and the kitchen, were on their way.

Only after the door closed behind them could Nicole breathe again. 'I don't understand. We don't have any papers on us. Why didn't they arrest us or at least question me?'

'I told them you were my cousins from Durrës. That your house burnt down, your papers with it. I said you have a disability and can't talk.'

'And they believed it?'

Nani shrugged. 'My family is in the wine-making business. We supply them with wine. They like it. They leave us alone.'

'But they might not leave us alone forever,' said Agron. 'You will need papers. I can help with that. And we need to think about getting you out of here.'

Nicole hesitated. 'There was a group of us, American nurses

and medics. We were staying at Grand Hotel Kolumbo. I need to know what happened to the others.'

'I'll see what I can find out.'

The little house fell quiet after the family left. Nicole helped Goni tidy up and tended to Darren, cleaning his wound that looked angry and red and reading to him from one of Nani's books she had found on a shelf.

Men marched asleep. Many had lost their boots,
But limped on, blood-shod. All went lame; all blind;
Drunk with fatigue; deaf even to the hoots
Of gas-shells dropping softly behind.

She recited the ominous words by Wilfred Owen almost by heart, written in another time, about another war, another heartbreak. When they were younger, Nicole and Darren devoured books about war. They raced each other to complete *All Quiet on the Western Front* and *War and Peace*, arguing late into the night about whether Napoleon was a positive force in history or the scourge of Europe and what had really triggered the Great War only decades earlier but seemingly a lifetime ago. Who could have thought back then that another war was looming only a few years later, more terrifying, more unfathomable than before?

Nani sat down next to her, a knife and a piece of wood in his hands. As he whittled, his hands moving fast, he seemed to hang on her every word. 'It's my favourite poem. I bought this book in America,' he said.

'You've been to America?'

'I worked in Pennsylvania as a cleaner. I was saving to open my own business. I was very close. I'm careful with my money, you see. Another five years, maybe seven . . .' There was longing in his voice. He spoke about Pennsylvania like it was home.

'What made you come back here?'

'I came back for my wife. We were going to move to America together and start a family. But then the Italians invaded and we were trapped in Albania.'

'You can still move to America one day, when the war is over.'

'I went across the ocean to find a better life for me and Goni. But as long as we have each other, we are happy. It doesn't matter where we are. My wife taught me that. Even though there is a war on, she looks for blessings everywhere she goes.'

'She is a wise woman.'

'She is pregnant, you know? All this time I thought America was my destiny, I thought my life would only start when I got there, but the greatest blessing of my life is happening right here, in Berat. In a few months, I'm going to be a father.'

'I'm happy for you, Nani.'

'She still doesn't believe me when I tell her about America. She doesn't believe I've cleaned hotel rooms with private bathrooms, that there are telephones and televisions, that you can have milk delivered to your doorstep. She thinks I made it all up. Maybe you can tell her it's all true. Maybe she'll believe you.'

'I'll try.' Nicole paused. 'Was your brother telling the truth? Do you think he can get us out of here?'

Nani nodded. 'He is an important person in the BK. If anyone can do it, it's him.'

'The BK? Aren't they the bad guys?'

'Bad guys? Hardly. It's all relative. We all do what we need to survive. We all fight for what we believe in,' said Nani, as he whittled a little cradle out of wood, wishing more than anything for peace for his unborn son or daughter.

143

Chapter 7

The Blessing

Andrea woke up the next morning, her face damp with tears. She called Brian's name but he didn't answer. She was alone on the cold floor of the barn. The others were getting up, exchanging terse sentences in low voices, dreading another day of fighting their way through the rain and mud up into the mountains. Around her were nothing but tense faces and dull eyes. They had only had four hours of sleep, it had been a night and a day since they had had anything to eat, and they knew they had a long journey ahead of them. The glimmer of hope they had felt in Berat was gone, giving way to anxiety and ill humour.

Andrea found Brian by the stream, washing his face in icy water.

'Be careful, you'll get frostbite,' she said. Putting her arms around him, shivering a little, she added, 'I'm not used to this cold.'

'I am. We used to go skiing with the kids in Canada every winter.'

His casual mention of his children and their skiing adventures tugged at her heart. Because of him, she might never have children of her own. She might never teach a child how to ride a bicycle or ice skate or play tennis. She might never hold a little baby in her arms. She turned away from him, so that he wouldn't notice the sadness on her face. But he wasn't looking at her.

'I refilled our flasks,' he said. 'Have you eaten anything? What do they have for us today? More cornbread? I can't bear the sight of it.'

'It's your lucky day. There is no cornbread.'

'If not cornbread, then what?'

'Gina said there is no food. Not till the next village, I suppose.'

'They want us to walk on empty stomachs?'

'They are not obligated to feed us. Or shelter us. Or take us to safety. They are doing it out of the goodness of their hearts. No need to complain and appear ungrateful.'

'Who's complaining?' muttered Brian, turning away from her.

Suddenly wanting to be alone, she started walking back to the barn. Brian followed her, holding both their flasks in his hands. 'I have some K rations left. Not many. Only two, I think. Would you like to share them?'

'All right,' she said, wondering what they were going to do when the emergency rations ran out.

They ate the remaining K rations, sitting side by side on a fallen tree branch, listening to the stream as it rushed happily by. Nothing interrupted the peaceful morning, not the gun shots, nor the machine-gun fire. Only the birds were chirping cheerfully and the branches were whispering in the wind, as if there was no war and all was well in the world.

'I've always wanted to travel,' Brian said thoughtfully, his gaze on the water. 'I've always wanted to see Europe.'

'And now your dream has come true.'

'When Laura and I first married and before the children were born, we spent three months travelling in Italy, Spain and the South of France. It was the best time. We were young, with no obligations, no responsibilities. We could go where we pleased, do what we pleased.'

'The best time, huh?' she said, trying to sound teasing and not show what she was really feeling.

'Except for the time I spent with you, of course.' They were silent for a bit, lost in thought. 'It's beautiful, isn't it? Like a Monet painting that has come to life.' He pointed at the river framed by trees, the cobalt sky and grey mountains, their snow-capped tops glistening like precious gems. 'You can almost forget there's a war on.'

Andrea was grateful for these moments alone with her husband before their gruelling day started. When they rejoined the group, Gina told everyone to start walking. The Nazis were in the area and there was no time to lose. One after another, they began to move, wrapped in their scarves up to their noses, their cheeks flushed from the cold, like mountain climbers ready to conquer Everest. The trail was wet and slippery. For the first part of the trip, Andrea leaned on Brian's hand, and when he left her behind to talk to Gina, she walked next to Renee for a while, listening to stories about her son. Her shoulder was bothering her. Her boots were hurting her feet. Every step was torture but she knew there would be a million more steps before they reached their destination and she had to endure each and every one. She couldn't afford to fall behind, couldn't let the rest of the group down.

It was midday before they could finally eat. They reached a tiny village of a dozen huts that were leaning towards the ground. They were met on the road by a few cows and a goat that looked malnourished and sad. The village elders welcomed them like they were there to liberate them from the Nazis. Everyone came out of their houses to greet them, to offer them presents and food. A woman gave Andrea a bar of soap. It was yellow and smelt terrible but Andrea was touched and thanked the woman from the bottom of her heart. She longed for a bath, wanted to feel water on her body, to feel clean. They were offered mutton with cloves of garlic and after their hungry morning it felt like they were having a feast.

They passed three villages that day and at every one Andrea asked if anyone had any news of an American nurse left behind in Berat. No one had heard anything.

In the third village, an old man approached them and offered them figs for sale. Andrea would have bought some but her money had been stolen from her bag on their first night in Albania. She asked Brian to get her some but he refused. 'He's asking for a lot of money for some wilted figs,' he said. 'I will not be taken advantage of.'

Andrea watched with envy as the others from the group purchased the figs and cut them open with knives. 'It's been months since we last had fruit,' she said sadly.

'I'd rather go without than feel like an idiot,' Brian replied.

* * *

The longer they walked, the steeper and narrower the trail became. Their uniforms were soaked and their boots felt heavy on their feet but on and on they trudged deeper into the mountains. When they conquered a particularly high ridge, Andrea looked behind her and gasped. The view from above was breathtaking. The mountains that looked impregnable on their approach now lay beneath them. The majestic forest they had just crossed was like a green carpet under their feet.

The higher they climbed, the colder it became. It was the third week of November, winter was a few weeks away, and Andrea could feel its icy breath on her cheeks. It had been raining for days but this morning the rain felt especially cold, getting under her clothes, running inside her boots, making her shiver. When they resumed their journey after a meagre lunch at one of the villages, Andrea looked down at the ground and noticed something white on the limp grass. For a moment she thought it looked like washing powder. And only when she touched it did she realise that it was snow.

By late afternoon the snow was falling in a thick veil, making walking even more difficult, freezing them so that their hands shook and their feet felt numb. But how beautiful it made everything look! In a matter of minutes the world had transformed into a white wonderland, untouched and unblemished, filled with hope. When they were children, Nicole and Andrea would often wake up early on Christmas morning and rush to the window, hoping to see Santa's tracks in the snow. As if by magic, waiting for them would be long marks where the sleigh had been and a cluster of little footprints where the reindeer had trampled the ground. There would be imprints of large boots, deep and determined, and an outline of a sack by the front door. Only when they were older did they realise it had been their grandmother all along, making the tracks in the snow to bring the magic of Christmas alive.

They had a family tradition growing up. Every Christmas Eve, they had a snowball fight. In her mind, Andrea could still see herself and Nicole bundled up in scarves, picking up snow, crunching it in their tiny fists and throwing it at each other with glee. And then they threw it at their parents and grandparents, Christmas having brought them all together, like a miracle. They squealed with delight at the annoyed expression on their father's face, at their mother's laughter, and rolled around in the snow, emerging white and freezing, like two miniature overexcited snowmen. What wouldn't she give to travel back in time to those carefree, happy days of her childhood.

If she survived this, if she lived to see home again, she would run to her parents' house and hug them. She would tell them she understood why they acted the way they did before she married Brian. She had thought they tried to control her, to dictate how she lived her life, to ruin her future. Now she could see clearly. They were only trying to protect her because they loved her and worried about her. She was rushing into a marriage, blinded by love, and they wanted her to slow down, to take her time, to think it through. Wouldn't she do the same for her child? The ache of not seeing much of them for the last eight years, of all the precious memories they hadn't built, of happy times they had missed out on broke her heart. Here, at war, she saw firsthand how precious and fragile life was, that a mere moment was enough to extinguish it like a candle in the breeze, that it could all be snatched away when one least expected it. What if she was too late? What if she didn't make it and would never hold her parents in her arms again?

Seeing fresh snow here, in Albania, brought back that childish feeling of a fairy tale coming to life. Except, it was ten times harder to walk through the snow and the trail became more slippery. The visibility became so bad, Andrea could barely see what was in front of her face. Gingerly she put one foot in front of the other, afraid of slipping. At first, she was walking in the middle of the formation, in front of Brian. Then she fell behind. She expected him to slow down but he didn't. Finally, she was the last one of the group, pushing her way through the snow, trying to keep up. It was Renee who dropped back and waited for her. 'How are you holding up?' she asked.

'It's these boots. My feet are killing me.'

'Mine too. Do you want me to walk with you, so you don't feel so alone?'

Andrea nodded. Mile after mile, mountain ridge after mountain ridge, and the snow was so deep in places, they fell through to their knees and had to crawl their way out. The distance they had once covered in an hour now required three or four, while the effort they expanded increased ten-fold. By the end of the day, Andrea could barely move her legs. She could barely step on her right foot. When she took her boot off, she saw angry red blisters on her big toe.

They had been walking for hours, without food, with hardly any water, when they saw the stone structures of a village. Gina motioned for the group to follow him into a large brown building. Everyone did so gladly, hoping for something to eat, but there was no food waiting for them inside the large room. Instead, they saw a tall bearded man wearing a long robe and a black hat. He sat in a wooden chair that looked like a throne and when he saw them come in, he raised his hand.

'Bow,' said Gina, bending down in front of the strange man with a beard.

They followed his example, bowing as low as they could. A few nurses exchanged puzzled looks but no one dared ask any questions. For a few moments, the room was silent. And then the man began to speak. He talked for a long time but no one could understand a word he was saying, and Gina wasn't translating but listening in silence with his head bent.

Finally, the man raised his hand and dismissed them. When they were outside, Renee asked, 'Who was that? And what did he want from us?'

'Imam. Great honour,' said Gina.

'Does he have any food for us at all?'

'No food. Blessing,' replied Gina.

Half an hour after they arrived, they were told to continue walking. Andrea didn't know if she could move another step. Her vision was blurry. Her head was heavy. Her limbs were aching.

'Cheer up,' said Brian, offering her his arm. She took it. 'Perhaps meeting an imam will bring us luck.'

'What is an imam?'

'In Islam, it's someone who's been to the holy city of Mecca.'

'I'd prefer something to eat. And a place to sleep.'

Brian didn't seem concerned. 'Don't worry. We'll rest at the next village.'

But at the next village, they weren't even allowed to enter. There was no welcome committee, no presents, no trays of food. The village elders came out to meet them on the road and shouted something in Albanian, shaking their fists at the Americans. Gina tried to reason with them but they refused to listen.

The group had to continue walking in the dark. A couple of times, Andrea slipped on the ice and would have fallen if Brian hadn't caught her.

'I can't do this anymore. I can't walk any further,' she said. But she didn't stop, trying to keep up as best she could, her fists clasped tight, her feet aching like she was walking on sharp swords. To fall behind, to be left alone in the dark was a prospect too scary to contemplate.

'Remember when we went camping in the woods and lost our way? And we had to walk for hours?' asked Brian.

'I remember. It was one of our first dates.' The memory of that night was like a light warming her from inside out. His hand in her hand. His voice guiding her on. Telling her not to be afraid. The happiness she felt, despite being lost in the woods, because she had finally found him, before the war, before the arguments, before the doubt.

'It was on that trip that I realised you were the one I wanted to marry. You were so strong. You never complained.'

'And if I complained? You wouldn't have married me?' she asked.

'Of course I would.' He took her hand. 'This is a little bit like that trip. We are afraid now. But once it's all behind us, we will think about it and smile.'

Andrea wanted to tell him it was nothing like that trip. Everything felt different. Back then, she had thought they would be happy forever. That nothing could stand between them.

When it got dark, they heard horses' hooves, muffled by thick snow. Someone was chasing after them, shouting in Albanian. Gina ordered everyone to stop. Suddenly scared, Andrea clung to Brian, who moved in front of her, as if to shield her from invisible danger.

'What's happening?' Renee asked.

No one replied. Gina lifted his torch. Andrea saw two men approaching on horseback in a cloud of white dust. When they reached the group, they stopped and jumped off their horses. Andrea thought they looked angry enough to attack them with the butts of their rifles. They gesticulated wildly as they spoke to Gina in Albanian.

Gina listened patiently, bowing his head. Then he addressed the Americans, who were waiting fearfully nearby. 'Did any of you take a holy relic from the imam's house this morning?'

Everyone looked at one another in surprise. 'A holy relic?' asked Baggs.

'A small stone from Mecca. Very precious. If you took it, there will be no more food or shelter. No village will allow us in.'

'You mean this small stone?' exclaimed Shearman, reaching into his pocket. In his palm was a little brown rock.

When the villagers saw it, their faces changed. They stared with horror and reverence at the pebble Shearman was carelessly holding up.

The medic shrugged, looking sheepish. One of the men snatched the relic out of his hand. The two of them turned their horses around, jumped into the saddles and sped off.

'Sorry,' muttered Shearman.

They were refused entry at the next village and had to sleep under the open skies, with snow falling on their faces, getting under their coats, making them shake from the cold. As the temperature plummeted, they hoped they would make it through the night.

'Why did you do such a thing, Shearman? Because of you, we are hungry and cold,' demanded Baggs, sitting in a snowdrift, blowing into his hands to warm up.

'I thought it was just a pebble. My sister and I collected pebbles like that at the beach growing up.'

'Do you always grab every rock you see?'

'I had a cousin like you,' said Renee. 'Couldn't enter a store without putting something in his pocket. He's still in jail, I think.'

Shearman blushed. 'I took it for my sister. She was eight months pregnant when I left. I haven't heard a word from home since. I don't know if she had a boy or a girl. If I have a niece or a nephew. I miss my family so much.'

The jibes ceased and they fell quiet, each lost in their own sadness. They had all left a piece of their heart back home. Every one of them understood. Finally, Baggs said, patting Shearman on the back, 'Don't be sad, Tim. Tomorrow we'll find you a new pebble.'

They huddled close together. Brian put his arm around Andrea and they all sang under the open skies, trying to cheer each other up, even though they felt anything but cheerful. Andrea leaned into Brian, finding solace in his warmth. His lips were in her hair and he spoke about their past, each happy memory warming her like campfire. He spoke about the life they would have after the war, just the two of them.

'The imam blessed us and we stole his precious relic. Does it mean we are doomed?' Andrea asked.

'Not us. Shearman. We didn't do anything wrong.'

'Shearman is not the only one sleeping under the open skies with no food in his belly. What if we never make it back home?'

He kissed the inside of her hand and said, 'Don't be so superstitious.'

What she wanted to say to him was, *What if I never see my sister again*? But for some reason, even though she was desperate to talk to someone about Nicole, even though she could hardly think of anything else, she couldn't mention her sister to her husband. Perhaps it was because he didn't seem at all concerned about Nicole and wouldn't understand how Andrea was feeling. But the real reason, she knew, was because of what had happened between them on the truck. She couldn't bear to utter her sister's name in front of Brian because she knew how Nicole would feel had she known about the way he had treated Andrea. If Nicole knew he had hit her, pushed her and spoken to her with such anger, she would never forgive him. She would feel the heartbreak of what happened deeper than if it happened to her. Andrea knew that for a fact because, if someone had done it to Nicole, she would have been distraught. She would tell her sister to leave immediately. As she lay in Brian's arms, listening to his voice as he talked, she wondered why it was so easy to give advice to others but so hard to follow that same advice.

Chapter 8

The Awakening

Nicole spent most of her time on the floor in front of the fireplace, cradling Darren in her arms. She rocked him like a child, trying to ignore the terrifying symphony outside, of machine-gun fire, rifle shots and explosions singing in unison and filling her heart with dread. His skin felt hot to the touch. The wound on his shoulder was still angry-looking and red around the edges, oozing blood. She read to him and spoke to him, wondering if he could hear her. She shared memories of the two of them together, hoping he would dream of her and feel happy. Every now and then, she touched his forehead, longing for a miracle. But there was no place for miracles in Nazi-occupied Berat. Only fear.

Agnesa arrived on their doorstep every morning, with herbs and parchments for Darren. Nicole was grateful to the old woman, even though it wasn't camomile flower and sage that Darren needed, it was morphine and sulfa. As she applied her remedies to Darren's shoulder, Agnesa regaled Nicole with stories of horror, murder and torture inflicted on the local population by the Nazis. Someone she knew had lost their entire family. Someone else had their house burnt down or had been arrested, never to be seen again. The older woman's tales made Nicole's hands shake with fear. She was afraid to go near a window, afraid of seeing what was happening on the streets of Berat. And yet, they were still alive. They hadn't been killed. She wasn't rotting away in a prison cell somewhere. Darren was still with her. What was it if not a miracle?

In a minute, she would be up and helping Goni fetch water from the well. Then she would wash Darren's face and prepare breakfast. She would mop the floors and wash the linen. It was the least she could do to repay their hosts for their generosity. But for now, she remained on her knees, whispering to Darren, begging him to wake up.

'Soon this will all be behind us. You will get better. We will find the others and return home. We will see our son.' She took his hands in hers. They felt like burning coals. 'Remember when we were teenagers and I climbed a tree, fell and broke my leg? You called Mama and the two of you took me to the hospital. You waited all day by my side, holding my hand, until it got dark and the nurses told you to leave. You did as you were told but ten minutes later climbed through the hospital window and stayed with me all night. I didn't want you to get in trouble but you said you didn't care. You told me I needed you and you were going to be there for me, no matter what. That you were not going anywhere.' Through her tears she smiled. 'You spent hours reading a book to me, even though it was a romance and you hate romances. And when the book was finished, we played cards and talked. I've never talked with anyone like that before or since, except my sister. When the nurse came to check on me, you hid in the closet. You slept in a chair by my bed that night and in the morning I asked you if you had to go to work that day and you told me work wasn't important, I was. That you didn't want me to be alone.' She lifted his limp hand to her lips and kissed his fingers. 'I want you to know that I'm not going anywhere either. You need me and I'm here for you. You are not alone.'

She read to him from some of the books she had found on Nani's shelf. A little bit from *Pride and Prejudice*, which Darren wouldn't care for, and a little bit from *Don Quixote*, which she knew he loved. 'To dream the impossible dream, that is my quest,' she whispered to him, her eyes on the book. He had been her dream for so many years. And she refused to lose him.

The bedroom door opened and Nani came in. Pouring himself a glass of water, he glanced at Darren. 'He doesn't look so good.'

'We need something for the pain. Some morphine perhaps. Something to get the infection under control.'

'My brother went to the hospital yesterday to see if anyone could help us. Our cousin works there. He's a doctor.'

Nicole looked up. 'Nani, that's fantastic.'

Nani shook his head sadly. 'The hospital's been taken over by the Germans. They threw Albanian patients out and are treating their own wounded. We couldn't find our cousin. Not at the hospital, nor at his house.'

'Oh, no,' Nicole whispered. 'I hope your cousin is safe.'

'So do I.'

She returned to the book but couldn't read a word because for some reason the letters in front of her became hazy and illegible. Nani sat next to her. 'You look so sad. I wish I could help.'

She looked into his kind face and smiled. 'You've done so much. We will never forget it.'

'I have good news for you. It will cheer you up. The other Americans, the nurses and the doctors and the medics . . .'

She perked up. 'Yes?'

'They were able to get away in a truck.'

Nicole's breath caught in her throat. 'How do you know?'

'My uncle supplied them with the truck. He saw them driving out of Berat. There was one nurse who refused to go. She was shouting to stop the truck, even tried to jump out. The whole town square heard her. They had to restrain her so they could leave.'

'Andrea,' whispered Nicole, her heart breaking for her sister.

'Sounds like someone is missing you very much. That's why we take good care of you. We Albanians understand the value of family. You have other relatives in America, no?'

Nicole smiled and thanked the host with all her heart, telling him about her loved ones who were waiting for her half a world away. Thanks to Nani and Goni's kindness, perhaps one day she would see them again.

Nani's news had put a spring in Nicole's step as she tended to Darren and helped Goni around the house. But there was a little voice inside her head that was never quiet, that didn't let her rest even for a minute, didn't let her forget about the dangers facing all of them. How far was it from Berat to the coast? How many Nazi patrols were on the way? How many German machine guns stood between the Americans and freedom? Just because her sister was able to get away, didn't mean she was safe.

* * *

Nazi patrols were a daily occurrence in occupied Berat. To keep everybody safe, Nani suggested the Americans should stay in the cellar, away from the enemy who knocked on the door every morning with German punctuality, hoping for more wine. Without identity papers, it was only a matter of time before they were discovered, putting every inhabitant of the little house in danger. Nicole helped Nani lower Darren through the little opening and from that moment on they lived in the dark, with only a small candle to light the wine bottles on the walls around them, the floor of rocks under their feet, the threadbare carpet and Darren's pale face.

During the time she spent upstairs with Nani and Goni, she had stopped looking out the window at the stream of German vehicles and the swarms of Nazi soldiers. There was turmoil inside her and she could not bear the terrifying sight of war in Berat.

One morning, three days after he had been shot, Darren's fever spiked. He was shaking and thrashing around, shouting something unintelligible, making Nicole's job difficult because every time she tried to dress his wound, he pulled the dressing off. The infection was poisoning his blood and there was nothing she could do about it. Even Agnesa didn't bring any ointments that morning, as if she too understood the futility of everything she had been doing.

Nicole wished Brian was there. She never liked her sister's arrogant and unkind husband. It broke her heart when he raised his voice and spoke to Andrea like she wasn't good enough. But she had to admit that he was a surgeon from God. His hands had saved many lives. And had he been there, he would know how to save Darren's.

Nicole spent all her time by Darren's side, forgetting to eat or sleep. She no longer read to him but simply sat next to him, holding his hand and crying. She changed his dressings. She bathed his face in cold water. And she prayed. From the recesses of her mind, she recollected all the prayers her religious grandmother had taught her when she was a child, wishing she had paid more attention, gone to church more often, called on God more often, so that He would hear her voice among all the others when she needed Him the most. She repeated the Lord's Prayer time and time again until her throat was sore, her hand on Darren's hot cheek.

In the afternoon, his breathing became heavy and laboured, as if every breath was a struggle. 'Please, live,' she whispered, her tears falling on his face. 'I searched everywhere for you. I spent nine years dreaming of seeing your face. Don't leave me now.'

Hours passed. She got up once, to have a sip of water. It was cold in the cellar but she felt like her skin was burning. Every now and then Darren groaned and said something but he never opened his eyes. 'Please, don't die. You have someone to live for. You have a son,' she pleaded with him.

Even from the cellar, she could hear someone pounding on the front door. It was just her and Darren in the house. Nani and Goni had gone out, telling her they would be back late. She was grateful for Nani's foresight to place them in the cellar. With luck, the Nazis wouldn't find them down here, hidden underground.

She could hear footsteps above her head. Had the strangers broken down the door and were they now searching the little house? She trembled. A moment later, the trapdoor flew open and a man descended. He was dressed in a military uniform she didn't recognise. In his hands he held a semi-automatic gun and a torch.

She froze, expecting to be interrogated, arrested, taken away. For a few seconds, Nicole and the intruder stared at each other in silence.

The man pointed at Darren and said something in Albanian.

'I'm sorry, I don't understand,' said Nicole, her heart pounding.

'Nani?'

She shook her head. 'Not here.'

The man placed his machine gun on the ground and opened a rucksack. As if by magic, vials of morphine appeared, some syringes and bandages, and, finally, sulfa.

'Tell him his cousin visited,' said the man before turning on his heels and climbing up the ladder. When she could breathe again, Nicole rushed after the mystery man to thank him but he was already gone.

Nicole didn't waste any time. As fast as she could, she administered the morphine and the sulfa, and almost instantly Darren's breathing became calmer. He no longer thrashed on the floor, screaming in pain. She sat by his side, her hand on his heart, her own heart racing.

When Nani returned, she asked, pointing at the medical supplies, 'How did your cousin get all this?'

'He might have borrowed it from the Nazis.'

'And they let him?'

'I don't think he asked their permission.'

She laughed. Seeing some colour return to Darren's face made her feel light-hearted and happy. 'Nani, you and your cousin have to be more careful.' She touched his shoulder. 'How can I ever thank you?'

'No thanks necessary. You stay in my house, you are family. And we Albanians will do anything for family.'

* * *

For the first time since the Nazis arrived in Berat, Nicole slept soundly next to Darren. In the morning, she was overjoyed to find that his fever was almost completely gone. When she touched his forehead, it no longer felt like burning coals. When she changed his dressing, the flesh around his wound didn't look as angry.

In the dark cellar, Nicole thanked God for Nani and his family, who had saved their lives, and counted the days on her fingers. How long had it been since they crash-landed in Albania? How long since they arrived in Berat? How long since the Nazis occupied the city? Where were Andrea and the others? Were they on the way to the coast or hiding somewhere, waiting for an opportunity to get away? She wondered how much longer she and Darren would stay at Nani's house and what the future held for them. With the Germans in Berat, where could they go? How could they escape?

She was wiping Darren's face with a wet cloth when she heard his voice. 'Nicole,' he whispered, so faintly, she thought she had imagined it. When she dropped the cloth and brought the candle closer to look at him, she saw that his eyes were open and he was watching her with surprise, like she was the last person he had expected to see.

She stroked his cheek and touched his forehead, tears running down her cheeks. 'Darren,' she whispered. But he didn't hear her. His eyes were closed again.

She spent the day by his side, listening for the faintest sound from him. In the afternoon, to take her mind off the dark thoughts inside her head, she read out loud from *The Companions of Jehu*, a novel by Alexandre Dumas she had never heard of before. She read on autopilot, every few seconds checking on Darren. While the noble highwaymen robbed government carriages on the pages of the book and the brave Roland was trying to expose them, all she could think about was, *What if*. What if Darren had been killed? What if Nani's cousin hadn't brought the medicine? What if they never made it to safety? What if something had happened to her sister and she didn't even know it? Here she was, reading books, helping Goni with cooking, changing dressings and waiting for Darren to wake up, when she should be grieving. Soon she couldn't read at all but was crying into her kerchief.

Suddenly she heard his voice. 'Why did you stop? I was eager to hear about Roland's mysterious companion. I'm convinced it's Napoleon himself.'

Instantly she sat up. Her tears vanished as if by magic and she twisted the kerchief in her hands. 'How do you know?' she whispered. She was crying again but this time from happiness.

'Why are you bawling your eyes out? I'm not dying, am I?' His voice sounded croaky and strained. But there was the biggest smile on his face.

She took both his hands and squeezed. She wanted to lean closer to him, to kiss his lips, his face, his eyes. 'Of course, you are not dying. You are going to be just fine. All you have is a scratch. Before you know it, we'll be playing tennis again.'

'Yes, because you need all the advantage you can get to beat me at tennis.' He watched her for a few moments. 'What happened to me?'

'You were shot,' she said. Quietly, she added, 'You saved me.' She owed him her life. For some reason the thought warmed her heart, like a thick woolly blanket.

'When I first woke up, I didn't know where I was. I thought we were at my parents' house and I was teaching you how to play chess,' he whispered.

'Unfortunately, we are in Berat and the Germans are here. For the record, you did a great job teaching me chess. I've never lost a game. Granted, I only get to play an eight-year-old boy.' Our boy, she wanted to add.

She fed him some mashed potato on a spoon and made sure he drank plenty of water. He slept, while she sat next to him with the book in her lap but couldn't read a word. All she could do was watch his sleeping face.

Goni came home from the market and Nicole went up the ladder to talk to her as she unloaded her purchases. 'I'm glad he is better. I always knew he will be,' Goni said.

'Did you?'

'I have a good feeling about you. You are good people. Nothing bad will happen to you. Are you hungry?' Goni pointed at the tiny potatoes she was able to buy.

Nicole shook her head. 'I'm not hungry at all.'

'You must eat. I was lucky to get these. Since the Germans came, I can buy nothing. They are taking all food. And it's almost winter. In summer, we have fresh tomatoes and cucumbers from Agnesa's garden. We have blueberries. If you are still here, you help me make blueberry pies and compote. It will be warm and we go swimming in the river. Everything better in summer.'

For the last week or so, Nicole's whole world consisted of the cellar underneath the little house and the corner of the street she could see from the window in the kitchen. Her world was Darren and the quiet moments they shared, while outside chaos reigned. While on the streets children cried and men shouted, sometimes in Albanian and sometimes in German, sometimes in anger and sometimes in fear, Nicole tended to Darren and prayed, listening to his breathing and trying to read his face. They didn't belong here, in this strange country torn by war, with a language they didn't speak and customs they did not understand. Yet, here they were, relying on strangers for all their needs, not knowing what tomorrow would bring. Nicole couldn't imagine another six months in Berat, couldn't fathom another hundred and eighty days of hiding inside the house and fearing for their lives. She couldn't imagine living like this until summer. But all she did was nod politely. She would take it one step at a time. First, she would worry about Darren. When he was better, she would think about leaving Albania.

When she returned to the cellar, Darren was awake. 'Those potatoes look good,' he said, pointing at the plate she had brought.

'They are not cooked yet. I'm just peeling them.'

'I'm so hungry, I'll be happy to eat them raw.'

'Your appetite is back. It's a good sign.'

'How long have you been watching over me?'

'Not long. A few days.'

'Did you tell me about the time when you broke your leg and we took you to hospital? Or was it a dream?'

'It wasn't a dream.'

When he took her hand, Nicole noticed that his fingers were trembling. When he spoke, he didn't sound like himself. 'You told me I had a son. Was that a dream?'

'It wasn't a dream,' she whispered.

'I have a son?' He watched her with awe and disbelief, tears in his eyes.

She couldn't help it, she started to cry too. She had been dreaming of this moment for many years. For a long time, she believed she would never get a chance to tell Darren about their amazing boy. 'We have a son,' she whispered.

He was silent at first, like he couldn't put into words everything he was feeling. 'How old is he? What is his name? Tell me everything.'

They didn't have a wink of sleep that night. And when the morning came and she heard the first explosion, for the first time since she arrived at the front, she didn't feel afraid.

Chapter 9

Chasing Shadows

On the last day of November, as the group of Americans moved one after another down a narrow mountain trail, a blizzard started. As hard as she tried, Andrea couldn't see anything in front of her but a twirling white wall. She couldn't hear anything other than the howling wind. It was like wading through a black box, with no idea where she was or which direction she was headed in. After the night under the open skies and hours of trudging through white slush, the winter wonderland had lost its magic. The fresh snow no longer made Andrea feel like she was caught up in a Christmas fairy tale, with nothing but joy and happiness waiting for her around the corner. Every time she fell through the snow that was knee deep in places and had to pull herself out again, she wanted to cry. As they faced zero visibility and impassable terrain, Andrea wondered if Gina would order everyone to stop. But no, blinded and wearied, they continued on, propelling themselves forward with everything they had. A few of them had caught bad colds, which was not surprising in the weather, and the head nurse was concerned about pneumonia. Two women had twisted their ankles, slipping on the ice, and were limping behind the group, complaining every step of the way. Their progress was slow and painful, but on and on they went, encouraged by Gina's promises of shelter and food.

Finally, when Andrea thought she would fall down in the snow and never get up again, the partisan leading the way sat down and began to sing. Everyone stopped.

'What is happening? Are we under attack? Are we in danger?' they wanted to know.

'Everything is fine. He can no longer see the trail in front of him, so we must wait,' said Gina.

So they waited, while the snow danced around them in a maddening waltz. Andrea remained close to Brian. Even though she had no energy to talk and he didn't seem to be in the mood for conversations, his proximity made her feel less alone. While the Albanian sang his melancholy song, they sat in silence, watching the wall of white in front of them, until, an hour later, the snow cleared a little and the partisan got up, motioning for everyone to follow. One after another they trudged through the blizzard behind two mules they were given by one of the villages a few days ago. The animals pushed through the snow first, making it easier for the people to walk.

It wasn't long before one of the mules fell on the ice. The group stopped. Andrea saw Gina shake his head, like he was disappointed. Because of the weather, they were falling behind the partisan's schedule, leaving themselves vulnerable to an attack. It took half an hour for the mule to finally get up and when it did, they set off again, up the slippery trail, into the mountains, towards the coast.

After three hours of fighting their way through the storm, the snow stopped but it began to rain. *I can't do it*, thought Andrea. *I can't take it anymore.* There was not a bone in her that didn't hurt. She was shaking from the cold in her damp uniform. Her stomach was aching with hunger. She wondered what her sister would do if she was in her position. Nicole would continue walking, she thought, ignoring the pain, to get to their destination, to not let the others down. Instead of focussing on how difficult it was, she would marvel at the glittering snow, at the trees adorned with ice like teardrops. Andrea decided to do the same as she put one foot in front of the other gingerly, trying not to fall.

Finally, after two more hours of torture by snow, rain and wind, Gina had mercy on them and proposed they stop early, at a village called Gerenice. The exhausted Americans waited in the town square, while the partisans spoke to the village elders. Leaning on Brian's shoulder, Andrea thought she would fall asleep, right there in the rain, when Thrasher raised his hand. 'I know you are all tired. But before the partisans return, there is something we need to discuss,' he said. Everyone gathered in a circle around the pilot, who held a compass in one hand and a map in another. 'Since we left Berat, we've been travelling west.'

'West towards Vlorë, right?' asked Carrie. 'Towards the coast. To get rescued.'

'That's the thing.' Thrasher shook raindrops off the map and pointed with his finger. 'Vlorë is east from here. All this time we've been walking away from the coast, deep into the country.'

Since they crashed in Albania, most of their days had been the same, an early start, hours of fighting their way through the mountains, without food, without a break, on a few hours of sleep if they were lucky. Every day was a battle and they felt like warriors for coming this far, for surviving this long, for inching their way towards their goal, little by little, step by step. And here was Thrasher, telling them it had all been in vain. They looked at each other in disbelief, not saying a word. On every face Andrea could read the same question. *What do we do now?*

Liz, the nurse who always seemed to have tears in her eyes, exclaimed, 'I can barely stand on my two feet and we are moving away from the coast?' She started to cry.

Renee patted her on the hand. 'If they are not taking us to the coast, where are they taking us?' she asked.

No one replied. Even Thrasher's map and compass couldn't provide any answers.

'I've always known they are not to be trusted,' said Carrie. 'Ever since they stole our belongings.'

Andrea said, 'Perhaps there's an innocent explanation. Maybe we are moving away from the Nazi-occupied areas and will change course soon.'

'How long have you known about this?' Brian asked Thrasher.

'Two days or so.'

'And you didn't tell us?'

'I wanted to be sure. I didn't want people to panic. Just like Andrea, I thought there must be a simple explanation.'

Andrea said, 'For weeks the partisans have been risking their lives taking us to safety, finding shelter for us, making sure we are all right—'

'Yes, taking us away from where we needed to go,' Baggs interrupted.

'They've been protecting us and feeding us and looking after us. Have you spoken to Gina about this?'

Thrasher shrugged. 'All he told me was that we are exactly where we need to be right now. He had no explanation, no concrete plan, no suggestions. Personally, I don't think they have our best interests at heart. Everything they've done for us has been out of self-interest.'

Andrea thought of how protective Gina had been of the Americans since they crashed, how he had dedicated all his time and effort to getting them home safely. Was there a different reason behind his actions, one they hadn't suspected?

'They've been taking us on a propaganda tour around the country and we've been following along willingly like fools.' Thrasher clasped his fists in anger.

'A propaganda tour?' asked Brian.

'From village to village they lead us, so that the villagers see they have the support of the Americans and join their side.'

Andrea shook her head. She didn't want to believe it. It was demoralising not knowing where their next meal was coming from, depending on strangers for food and shelter, having to beg for a piece of bread. It was demoralising waking up with an emptiness in their stomachs and walking mile after mile after mile, until they could walk no more. But it was nothing compared to this, knowing they had been walking in circles, that all their struggles up until now had been in vain. 'They wouldn't use us like that. Gina has old parents he is trying to protect. His pregnant wife is in another partisan battalion somewhere. He is on our side.' She fell quiet. Didn't Gina tell her he would stop at nothing in his fight against the Germans? Perhaps Thrasher was right and the Americans had been nothing but pawns in the partisans' game.

'I don't know about you but I'm done fighting their war for them,' said Thrasher.

For a moment, all was quiet. Only the branches groaned under snow. 'What do you propose?' asked Renee.

'I propose that we set out on our own. We make our own way to the coast.'

Andrea shivered. The thought of being alone in this strange country terrified her, of wandering from village to village, begging for help. As if reading her mind, Renee said, 'You want us to cross Albania by ourselves, without any support from the locals, not knowing where to go, what their customs are, which places are safe, not knowing how to negotiate for food or shelter. Why, that is suicide, Lieutenant Thrasher.'

'What choice do we have?'

'We stay with the partisans. We are safe with them.'

'Stay with them and then what? Continue this pointless crusade around Albania indefinitely? We need to get back. We are not making any progress with Gina and his men.'

Renee said, 'On our own, we will die. The Nazis, the BK, the weather or the hunger will kill us.'

'The partisans have no interest in helping us get back. At least on our own we stand a chance to get out of here alive.'

Suddenly the town square erupted with voices. Everyone was shouting, everyone had an opinion.

Baggs raised his hand. 'That's enough. We will take a vote. Everyone in favour of setting out on our own, raise your hand.'

All of the men and most women voted to leave the partisans and follow Thrasher to the coast. Only Renee, Andrea and three other nurses opted to stay with Gina. 'It's agreed,' said Thrasher. 'After a few hours of rest, we will leave. Finally, we can be in control. We can make our own decisions.'

'Wait a minute,' said Renee. 'I'm not going anywhere. I didn't agree to anything.'

'Nor me,' said Andrea, shaking her head, doing her best to ignore Brian's angry eyes on her.

Thrasher said, 'The majority has decided.'

'You can go,' said Renee. 'But we are staying. I have a son back home. I want to survive, for him. I'm not doing anything rash.'

'We took a vote. We made a decision. I believe it's best for the group.'

Renee said, 'When you wake up one morning and find that you haven't eaten for five days, when you fall to the Nazis because you don't know which roads are safe, when you are lost in the woods and have no idea which way to turn, you'll wish you had stayed with the partisans.'

Thrasher and Renee squared off against each other, their faces red. Andrea saw that neither of them was ready to back down, neither of them was prepared to give way.

'That's enough,' said Baggs, pointing at the partisans walking their way. 'Let's sleep on it and discuss it in the morning.'

As they watched the partisans approach, the Americans whispered to one another, discussing the impossible situation they found themselves in and the two options available to them – to stay and entrust their destinies to the locals or to leave Gina and his men behind and set out on their own. Each option came with its own set of risks and the longer they speculated about it, the more terrifying their future appeared to Andrea. Brian grabbed her by the hand and pulled her away from the group. *Oh no*, she thought. Her hands started to tremble.

'You are not seriously thinking of staying with the partisans, are you?' he asked quietly.

Andrea knew the calm was just the façade. She could see the upcoming storm in his squinting eyes, the thin mouth, the measured voice, as if he was deliberately stopping himself from shouting. She thought to herself, *I shouldn't provoke him. I should agree with everything he says*. But it wasn't just her safety that was on the line, it was his too. And she didn't want him to make a mistake. 'I am,' she said quietly.

'Why?'

'Because Renee is right. Without the partisans we won't last five minutes in this country.'

'Tomorrow we are leaving. And you are coming with us,' Brian said.

She shook her head. 'I'm not.'

'You would stay with Gina without me?'

'I was hoping I could change your mind.'

'I agree with Thrasher. Remaining with the partisans is pointless.'

'And I agree with Renee. Setting out on our own is suicide.'

He turned her towards him like a doll, so that her face was only inches away from his. 'You will come with me. You will do what I think is right. End of discussion.'

'Please, don't talk to me like that. I'm not a child.'

His fingers gripped her wrist tighter. 'Then stop acting like one. Stop acting like a spoilt, unreasonable, illogical, disagreeable child.'

'Let go of me. You are hurting me.'

He let go of her. 'Why is everything so difficult with you? Why don't you ever agree with anything I say?'

'I'm entitled to my opinion. And I happen to think that staying—'

'I don't care what you think,' he snapped. 'Why are you being so stupid?'

For a moment she couldn't speak and watched him in silence. He screamed, 'For once in your life, can you do what I say?'

'Why?' she whispered. 'Because I'm too stupid to make my own decisions?'

'You want to stay in Albania by yourself? Fine. But tomorrow I'm leaving.' He stormed off without a glance or another word. Andrea stood very still, her hand on her heart, trying hard not to cry.

They were separated into groups of five or six and taken into different houses. Andrea sat next to four other nurses by the fire, rocking back and forth like she was in a trance. While the others never stopped talking, she didn't say a word. She was barely listening as she relived the argument, wondering if there was something she could have said or done differently, if she was responsible for his anger and hurtful words. Their host served them some mutton and the soup they had come to love. The hot liquid warmed Andrea, even as her wet clothes made her shiver. The villager looked at them with pity and said, 'What a day to be out and about. You look like you could do with a warm drink. Wait here and I will make you some tea.'

When the tea was ready, he said, 'I can't believe you took the mountain trail at this time of year. Others have died doing it in summer, and here you are, in winter, in this weather.' He shook his head, like he disapproved of their bravery.

'We are trying to reach the coast,' said Renee. 'From there, a boat will take us back to Italy.'

'The coast? You are walking in the wrong direction.'

When she heard the man's words, Andrea's heart fell. A small part of her was still hoping that Thrasher had made a mistake.

The other nurses settled to sleep, while Andrea sat on the cold floor, her head in her hands.

Renee sidled up next to her. 'I spoke to Carrie, Tory and Liz. We are not leaving the partisans, no matter what.'

'You heard what the host just said. Thrasher is right. They are taking us in the wrong direction. And they are not telling us anything. We are following them blindly, hoping for a miracle.'

'I want to live, for my son. Even if it means staying here longer than we planned. Maybe we could talk to Gina. See what he has to say for himself. He seems like a reasonable man.'

'I agree with you. But I can't stay. Brian's made up his mind. And wherever my husband goes, I go.'

'Even if you'll be going to your death?'

Andrea shrugged, her gaze on the fire in the fireplace, dancing its eternal dance like nothing else mattered. 'If we die, we die together. I lost my sister in Berat. I'm not losing my husband.'

'After the way he spoke to you just now, you still want to go with him?'

'You heard that?'

'He was shouting so loudly. We all heard.'

Andrea's shoulders stooped. 'It's just a little argument. It doesn't mean anything. Everyone argues. People say things they don't mean when they are upset.'

Renee reached for her hand. Andrea felt her warm fingers in hers and for a moment felt comforted. Renee said, 'I don't mean to pry but he hasn't been very nice to you lately.'

Andrea tried very hard not to cry. She held her breath but it wasn't helping. She wiped her tears away, annoyed at herself. 'He's not always like this. He's under a lot of stress . . .' *One of these days I need to stop making excuses for him*, she thought. She realised she no longer believed in any of them.

'Think about it carefully,' said Renee. 'If something happens to your sister, your nephew will need you.'

'I don't have to think about it. I need to stay with my husband.'

'Against your better judgement you will stay with your husband?'

Andrea nodded.

For a few seconds, the older woman watched her with pity. 'You can tell me anything, you know?'

'I know.'

'God will take care of you, whatever happens. He will give you strength.'

'I don't need strength. I'm fine. I'm happy.'

'Are you, really?'

Andrea didn't reply. She didn't want to talk about it anymore. All she wanted was to be alone, to have privacy to cry about her marriage so that no one could witness her tears and feel sorry for her. When Renee moved away from her, she lay down on some straw and tossed and turned, waiting for morning.

Andrea must have drifted off because, next thing she knew, she felt her face being stroked and heard someone calling her name. She opened her eyes and before her in the light of the fireplace she saw her husband. 'Brian,' she whispered. 'What time is it? It feels like the middle of the night.'

'It's five in the morning.'

For a moment, she forgot about their argument. All that mattered was that he was here with her, with his hands on her waist. She smiled. 'What are you doing here?'

'Wake up the girls,' he said. 'Thrasher wants to talk to us.'

Together they woke the sleeping nurses who complained loudly and refused to get up. After walking through the blizzard for eighteen hours straight, Andrea couldn't blame them. She could barely keep her eyes open.

'Where are we going?' grumbled Renee. 'I feel like I slept for ten minutes.'

'I need my beauty sleep,' said Tory. 'I have a feeling tomorrow is not going to be a very relaxing day.'

'You mean today? It's morning. Time to get moving,' said Brian, hurrying them along.

Together they made their way outside, careful not to make a sound, not to disturb their hosts, who slept behind a partition. Before stepping out of the house, Andrea stood for a moment, taking it all in. The sky had cleared. The moon and the stars sparkled over their heads, making the white carpet of snow shimmer in the near-dark. The air was crisp, instantly making her face and the tips of her fingers feel numb.

They walked between the huts towards the little wooded area at the back of the village, the snow making a crunchy noise under their feet. A dog barked, startling Andrea. Brian took her hand, pulling her along. When they turned around the corner, Andrea saw a bright light in the woods. It was to this light that Brian led them. When they arrived, she realised it was a torch in Thrasher's hands, burning brightly, throwing shadows on the trees, the white ground and the men's faces. The rest of the group was already there, the medics and the other nurses pacing nervously, waiting for them to arrive.

When they all gathered, Thrasher spoke. 'If we leave now, we'll have a couple of hours' head start. We will reach the next village by nightfall.'

Renee said, 'Some of us don't agree with this and have decided to stay. We will see you back in Italy.' She crossed her arms against her chest and stared at Thrasher, daring him to argue.

Thrasher said, 'We are not splitting our group up. We were forced to leave a nurse behind in Berat.' He glanced at Andrea. 'We are not doing it again. Either we all go, or we all stay. And I believe leaving is our best option for success.'

'I'm not leaving the partisans and that's that,' said Renee.

'What are you afraid of? We know we can climb mountains on our hands and knees, we've done it. We know we can live on cornbread and sour milk, we've done it. We can march in the rain and sleep on hard floors, we've done it all. There is nothing we couldn't do, as long as there is hope ahead of us, as long as we know we are walking to safety, towards the sea, towards our goal.'

'Me and the girls will be safer here, thank you very much.'

'You are wrong. And we can't waste any more time arguing about it. As the most senior officer of the group, I command you to come with us.'

'I don't take commands from you, not here, not when my life is on the line.'

'May I remind you that you are an officer in the US Army, Nurse. You will obey.'

Colour rose to Renee's face and she opened her mouth to argue but no sound came out.

'It's decided then,' said Thrasher, turning away from Renee towards the rest of the group. 'We will set out on our own and go . . .' He unfolded his map and traced a trail with his finger. 'This way.'

Their future thus decided, the crew, including the disgruntled nurses, went in search of Gina. They knocked on the door of the house where he had been staying, only to be told that he had gone out.

'We can't wait for him to come back. We are leaving now,' said Thrasher.

In silence, they picked up their belongings and started to walk through the quiet village. Everyone else seemed to be asleep, people and animals alike, and only the same dog continued barking, as if sensing something out of the ordinary was happening.

'At least the weather has improved,' said Andrea to Renee, who looked upset enough to cry. 'It will be nice to walk in the sun for a while, to not be drenched to the bone.'

'Walk where? Where are we even going?'

'Thrasher knows what he's doing.'

'If he wasn't the most senior officer of the group . . .' Renee made a perfect imitation of Thrasher, making Andrea laugh. 'I would tell him exactly what I thought of him and his plan. We don't even have any weapons. He wants us to cross the country occupied by Nazis armed with a compass and a rock.'

'Here is where you are wrong,' said Baggs, who was listening in to their conversation. He opened up his bag to show them a pistol hidden under his spare socks.

'Where did you get that?' asked Andrea.

'Took it from the plane before we blew it up.'

'Good thinking.'

'Much good it will do you when you are surrounded by a German squadron,' grumbled Renee.

As they set out down the road in a single file, Andrea couldn't help but feel apprehensive. That morning seemed the same as every other. Just like any other day in Albania, they were making their way down a narrow trail, anticipating many hours of walking in the rain and the snow. And yet, everything was different. They no longer had anyone to rely on but themselves.

Andrea tried to catch Brian's eye, to exchange a reassuring look with her husband, so that her hands wouldn't shake so much in fear, but he wasn't looking at her.

They were on the outskirts of the forest when they heard shouts in Albanian. Next thing they knew, they were surrounded by half a dozen partisans on horseback. When they turned around, they saw Gina at the end of the road, standing next to a man dressed in British uniform.

When they approached, Gina said with a smile, 'I'm glad we caught you. This is Captain Victor Smith, an SOE officer. He agreed to meet us here, in Gerenice. He is going to take you to the coast.'

The officer saluted them. 'Greetings, folks. Starting early this morning? How about some breakfast first?'

Chapter 10

Hiding in Plain Sight

It was never quiet in occupied Berat. Machine guns never slept and every now and then, an explosion would shake the city and it would feel to Nicole that the ground itself shifted under her feet. One morning, Nani's cousin arrived with his camera and took photographs of Darren and Nicole for their identity papers. In the meantime, the best course of action was to hide. Outside was war but inside was peace. She felt at home in this unknown country in the little hut damaged by bullets because she was with him. There might be German soldiers outside, the rumble of Nazi tanks as they made their way through Berat and the threat of enemy patrols but one glance at Darren's face and it all faded away.

It was eerily quiet in the cellar. No voices reached them here, no explosions or machine-gun fire, and Nicole could almost trick herself into believing that the world at war no longer existed, that it was just her and Darren, alone against it all. He was recovering well and was able to sit up unassisted and feed himself. His fever was gone and he was no longer sleeping all day, like a wounded lion. Instead, they talked. They had nine years to catch up on.

For as long as she remembered, Nicole had been afraid of the dark. Once, she had convinced her sister to go hiking in the woods and they had lost their way. They had to spend the night under a tree, clinging to each other as the sun went down and darkness fell, turning the woods into a terrifying place alive with whispers and animal noises. It had been the scariest night of Nicole's life as she shivered next to her sister, counting minutes until sunrise. But, even in the woods, there had been stars over their heads and a bright moon. In the cellar, however, the darkness was unlike anything she had ever experienced before, a black nothingness that admitted no light or hope. And yet, to her surprise, she was not afraid. She could sense Darren's presence, could reach out and touch him, could call out to him and hear his voice. Instead of scaring her, the darkness brought comfort. It hid them away from the world with its conflict and never-ending heartbreak, sheltering them from the horrors of war-torn streets. Even though there were times Nicole wished for a window to look out of, so she could see the movement outside, the people and the traffic, men, women and children in their quest for survival, most of the time she was grateful to be alone with him in the dark.

They had some cushions to rest on and a bundle of books she'd been reading to him in the light of a candle. They had a deck of cards and a chess board. And they had each other. Occasionally, she went upstairs to get some food, bring some water to wash with or help Goni with her chores. Every time she left him, she felt a little lost. And every time she returned to their underground nest, she felt at peace.

She was drifting off, wondering if it was day or night. It was impossible to tell in the cellar. Outside, the sun rose in the morning and went down at night, turning the sky over Berat ominously red. Hidden under a wall of bricks, she couldn't see the sun or the stars over her head or the silver moon. Next time she spoke to Nani, she would ask him if she could borrow a watch. She wondered what date it was. Having existed in a vacuum, she had lost count of the days. Had Christmas come and gone? Had the new year arrived? Was it 1944 and she hadn't even noticed?

She heard Darren's voice. 'Can't sleep?' His hand found her

in the dark. His fingers gripped hers tightly. They felt warm and comforting.

'How did you know?'

'I can hear you tossing and turning.'

'I was thinking about Andrea. Before we got separated, we had an argument. I said such terrible things to her.' Often in the dark, Nicole relived her last conversation with her sister. Sometimes one moment had the power to change everything. One word could destroy a relationship. One sentence could take away the trust that took many years to build. How she wished she could take it all back. If she could live through that moment again, she would do it all differently. She wouldn't blame her sister. She would be understanding, not condemning. 'What if I never get a chance to tell her I didn't mean it?'

'Andrea knows you love her more than anything. She knows you said it in anger.'

'I told her I will never forgive her. I told her she was a terrible sister.'

'We all say things we regret sometimes. One day, when all this is behind us, you will tell her you are sorry and it won't matter anymore.'

'You think so?' She tried to think ahead to their future, tried to imagine seeing her sister's face, hearing her words of forgiveness. The vision was so real, it made her heart ache.

'I know so. What did you fight about, anyway?'

'You,' Nicole whispered. 'She told me it was her fault you went away all those years ago. She was worried about me, so she told my mother I was pregnant. A few days later, you were gone.'

'Don't blame your sister,' he said softly. 'She was only trying to help.'

'The day you disappeared, I waited for two hours at the tennis courts for you. I was going to tell you I was pregnant that day. When you didn't turn up, I went to your house but it was deserted. Back home, I went to bed and didn't get up for two weeks. I just couldn't. My family thought I was terribly sick. They didn't know what to do with me.'

'I'm so sorry. I wish I could turn back time and change everything.'

'Why did you leave, Darren?' Finally, she found the courage to ask the question that had kept her up at night for nine years. She held her breath, waiting for his reply.

'Your father came to our house that day. He told my family he would terminate my dad's employment if we stayed. He was transferring Dad to another factory. We had to leave immediately.'

'Why didn't you tell me?'

'Your father made it clear that the condition of my dad's employment was that I never contact you again.'

'So you just left? Without a word, without a sign?'

'I didn't just leave. I fought with my father. I told him I wasn't going. I refused to get on the train. It was my mother who made me see that we had no other choice. My sister had just had another baby. Mother was sick. We could barely afford food. If my father lost his job, we wouldn't have been able to survive.'

'All these years, you knew where to find me. Why didn't you write to me?'

'I wrote to you almost every day but never posted the letters. A year after we left, I went to see you.'

'You did?' She thought of the hours she had spent nursing Leon in the rocking chair on the porch, her eyes on the road, hoping to see Darren. Up and down she rocked, the baby in her arms, his warmth, his need for her reminding her that she was still alive, that life went on, even if it didn't feel like it. The baby cried and Nicole cried too, and she was afraid to take her eyes off the road in case she missed him but the road remained empty, day after day, night after sleepless night.

He touched her wedding ring lightly with the tip of his finger. After a few moments of silence, he said, 'I drove back to your house and sat in my car, waiting for you to come out, so I could talk to you. Then I saw a limo pull up. A few minutes later, you appeared, leaning on your father's arm. You were wearing a veil and a white dress. There was a bouquet of flowers in your hands.'

Eight Years Ago

The church was filled with flowers, white and beautiful and overwhelmingly festive. Nicole had never seen so many roses, tulips and hydrangea in one place before. She had never seen so many people in one room before, either. Her parents had invited all of Detroit, it seemed. As she stood in the back, clutching her bouquet in panic, she spotted a mayor, a bishop, a famous author and a celebrated composer. Four hundred people waited for the bride to arrive and the ceremony to begin.

Outside, the sun was shining. It was a perfect day for a wedding. After weeks of rain, it was as if nature itself was giving Nicole and her groom its blessing. By the altar, Anthony was pacing nervously, every now and again throwing glances towards the entrance. His thinning hair was gelled and brushed away from his face. His lanky legs and arms moved in a jerky manner, as if he couldn't contain his excitement and force himself to stand still. In front of her, seven bridesmaids in stunning emerald dresses clasped lilies to their chests, eager to walk down the aisle. By her side, her father smiled proudly, anticipating the big moment. He looked dashing in his tuxedo, his grey hair stylishly cut, a white rose in his buttonhole, like it was his wedding day and not hers. And in a way, it was. He had organised everything, from guest list to entertainment. Everything was bought and paid for, even the groom.

They were ten minutes late. But wasn't every bride late for her wedding day?

Her father prodded her gently, offering his arm for her to lean on. 'Shall we? It's time.'

The bridesmaids fell into position. The first chords of 'Here Comes the Bride' were heard.

She felt like the floor had moved under her feet. Everything was spinning before her eyes. 'I can't do this,' she cried, extricating herself from her father. She knew she didn't belong here, in this church, wearing this dress, holding these flowers, about to marry the man she didn't love.

'Is something wrong?' her father asked, his voice rising above the music, irritated and a little angry.

Not pausing to reply, she ran out of the church. Her dress dragging her back, flowers falling to the pavement, the veil covering her eyes, she ran across the road, while horns blared and passers-by stopped in their tracks to watch her. A little girl dashed to her side, shouting, 'Look, Mama, a princess!'

She paused to smile at the child and give her the last rose that still remained in her hands, hoping she wouldn't notice the tears in her eyes. The girl jumped up and down on the spot with joy, while Nicole continued miserably on her way.

It took fifteen minutes to reach the tennis courts. Her breath catching, she walked to the spot where two years ago she had kissed Darren for the first time. It should have been him, she thought, her heart breaking. It should have been Darren waiting for her in the church. In her white dress, she sat down on the grass, put her head in her hands and cried. She wondered about time and its ability to change everything, to snatch things away. Only two years ago, she was a different person. She was happy and carefree and in love. And look at her now.

She remembered waiting here for him every night for years, and the way her heart beat faster every time she saw his face. She thought of the one night when he didn't turn up. Did she realise back then that he would be gone for good, lost to her forever?

She heard a noise and turned around. It was her sister.

'There you are. Everyone is waiting for you. Dad is frantic. So is Anthony.'

The panic on her sister's face was contagious. Even now, as adults, they were deathly afraid of their father's temper. 'I just needed a minute. I needed to come here and think,' Nicole said, feeling anxious and resigned. 'But I'm ready now. Let's do this.'

Andrea took her hand. 'Are you sure? You don't have to go through with it if you don't want to.'

'If I don't, Dad will never forgive me. Anthony's family will break all business ties with us. People will talk.'

'Who cares about any of that? All that matters is your happiness. Don't let Dad force you into anything you are not comfortable with.'

The sisters were quiet for a moment. Finally, Nicole said, 'This is where we kissed for the first time, you know? Right there, outside that fence. Feels like a lifetime ago.'

'You miss him, don't you?'

'Every day.'

'Don't marry Anthony, Nicky. Don't throw your life away.'

Nicole shrugged. 'I don't love Anthony. But it doesn't matter because I know I will never love anyone again. What's the point of waiting? Darren is never coming back. This way Daddy will get his business deal. And Leon will have a father. I can't bring up my little boy by myself, Andie.'

On the way back to church, Nicole kept looking back at the tennis courts. Even though she knew it was impossible, a part of her was expecting to see Darren running down the road to stop her from making the biggest mistake of her life. But he didn't appear and she had no choice but to enter the church and lean on her father's hand for the walk down the aisle that was too short and over far too quickly, long before she was ready. It was a good thing her father was there to support her or she would have fallen in front of all these people, fallen on her knees by the altar, unable to get up.

As the priest spoke of love and commitment, Nicole closed her eyes. It wasn't Anthony she saw as she exchanged vows with a man she could never care for. It was Darren. No one thought twice *about the tears running down her cheeks. After all, all brides cried on their wedding day.*

All around her were happy faces. Everyone was smiling. Everyone except her.

* * *

She watched him in the light of a candle as he slept, a book in her lap, one hand on the tennis racket charm around her neck, the other on the bullet that nearly killed him, twisting and turning it in her fingers to calm her nerves. She found his face remarkable and fascinating. She could see in front of her the boy she used to know and, at the same time, the man he had become. His face had a power to transport her to the past, to every happy memory they had shared as children and young adults, to every morning when she woke up and her heart broke because she knew she had to face another day without him.

He opened his eyes and found her staring at him. He smiled and she smiled back, taking a deep breath, filling her lungs with air, feeling alive and happy and on the verge of something new and wonderful. He pointed at the bullet in her hand. 'What do you have there?' he asked. 'Is that what hit my shoulder?'

She nodded. His fingers closed around the small piece of metal. He looked at it, fascinated. 'Seems so harmless, doesn't it?'

'It could have killed you. You are lucky to be alive.'

'I'm lucky to have you to look after me. You saved my life.'

'And you saved mine.'

'Should I keep it?'

'No, don't.' She shivered.

He placed it in his pocket. 'It will be my good luck charm. A reminder of the day I found you again.'

She wanted to touch him, wanted to move closer and feel his arms around her. As if reading her mind, his fingers found hers. All was quiet inside their hiding place. Was it bursting with sound outside? In that instant, it didn't matter. The world seemed to fade away, disappear like it had never existed. 'Tell me a memory,' she whispered.

'What kind of memory?'

'Something that makes you feel happy.'

'Every memory of you makes me feel happy. Let's see.' He hesitated. 'Remember we went for a hike one day and came across an abandoned shed?'

'I remember. It was cold, much like now. Whose idea was it to go on a hike in winter?'

'Not mine. I don't even like hiking.' He laughed.

'We were so exhausted from all the walking, we fell asleep.' It was back in the days when they couldn't take their hands off each other. Before they fell asleep, they made love for what seemed like hours. As soon as she thought about it, she blushed. 'And when we woke up, we realised the shed wasn't abandoned after all. There was a man in the room, shining his torch at us.'

'I've never jumped to my feet or pulled my clothes on faster. But he was friendly and made us some tea.' He brushed a strand of hair out of her face and smiled. 'Your turn now. Tell me a memory.'

Over the years, there had been thousands of memories of him that lit up her heart. It was difficult to choose just one. 'Remember we were at your parents' house and you were teaching me how to make pizza?'

'I remember. You were not a very good pupil. You told me you preferred eating the pizza to making it.'

'I was kneading the dough and it felt sticky and cold on my hands. You put your hands on mine and when we were kneading the dough together, it didn't feel as cold anymore.' She thought about what happened next, of his lips on her neck, his hands on her waist, moving upwards, leaving traces of pizza dough all over her stomach and breasts. 'It was our first time,' she whispered.

He nodded. 'I remember worrying about my parents coming back at first. And then I forgot about everything.'

She was nestled into his arms, her head resting on his chest. She enjoyed listening to his breathing. It was deep and calm and never failed to reassure her if she was worried or afraid. Late at night she loved falling asleep to the sound of his beating heart. It was cold in the cellar but he radiated warmth. She could spend hours in his arms, thinking about their past, wondering about their future and marvelling at the brilliant stroke of luck that had brought him back into her life.

* * *

Nicole was sound asleep next to Darren when she heard the trapdoor open with a creak. She sat up, confused. It was pitch dark in the cellar but every now and then a streak of light lit up the tiny room, playing on Darren's face. She heard footsteps and loud voices and realised someone was walking around with a torch above them. A man shouted in Albanian. The words sounded harsh and angry in the peace and quiet of the night and she felt her heart race in panic. Had they been caught? Was their hiding place discovered?

She reached for Darren, who was sleeping peacefully, unaware of what was happening. She was about to wake him when she heard someone calling her name. On trembling legs, she approached the opening in the ceiling. Above her, in the light of the torch, she saw Nani's face. 'Sorry to wake you,' he said. 'It's Flamur.'

She climbed up the ladder and Nani helped her into the living room. On the rug by the fireplace, she saw the young boy with his eyes closed and his face and hands covered in burns.

'The Germans burnt his shop. He tried to put the fire out and got hurt,' Nani explained.

She asked the boy if he could hear her, if he knew where he was, if he was in pain. Flamur groaned and muttered something in Albanian.

She treated the burns with gentian violet and applied a dressing. 'I will need more morphine,' she said to Nani. 'We are almost out. He'll need it every three hours or so.'

'I'll see what I can do,' said Nani.

She returned back to the cellar and wrapped her arms around Darren's body but, no matter how hard she tried, she couldn't go back to sleep. The next morning, she was up at five, ascending the ladder, opening the trap door, checking on her new patient, changing dressings, singing to herself to take her mind off her fears. The floor was washed even before Nani and Goni were awake. The laundry was hung up before sunrise. It was a bright day, and she pulled the curtains open, slightly dazzled by the light and the bustle outside. With one eye on the door, prepared at the first sign of trouble to run back into hiding, she made everyone's coffee and prepared some food.

Flamur couldn't hold a spoon in his burnt fingers, so she spoon-fed him. He couldn't hold a cup, so she did it for him. And after he had eaten, she would rush downstairs to spoon-feed Darren and hold his cup for him. 'Give me the plate. I can feed myself,' he demanded.

'You are not well. Let me do it for you.'

'It's too hard for you. You've been doing everything around here. When was the last time you slept or ate?'

'Who has the time? Now, let me feed you. I want to look after you.'

'And who will look after you?' But he let her feed him and read him a few pages of his book.

From then on, her time was spent flying up and down the ladder, taking care of her two patients. Darren would meet her with a smile, teasing her, making her laugh, while Flamur would grunt unhappily and watch her in silence. He remained in one spot, barely eating, not saying a word. When Nicole asked him if he needed anything, he never replied, just looked through her, like she wasn't there. Her heart broke at the expression of sadness on his face. She asked Goni to teach her some simple phrases in Albanian, so she could communicate with Flamur. She learnt how to say, 'Are you hungry? Would you like some water? Are you in pain? Can I get you anything?' But no matter how hard she tried, he continued to stare into space as if she hadn't spoken.

Unlike Flamur, all Darren wanted to do was talk. And the only thing he wanted to talk about was Leon. Every time he brought their son up, she wanted to dance on the spot with joy. Nothing made her happier than talking about her boy to his father. 'Leon is the love of my life. When he was born, I was amazed how much he looked like you. He has your smile, your nose, your eyes. Looking at him is like looking at you. You were gone but you left a part of yourself behind. He became my everything, my whole life. He healed me.'

'I'm sorry you had to go through it all by yourself. I should have been there.'

'When Leon was little, he was my shadow. I couldn't go anywhere without him following. When I was studying, he pulled up a chair and watched me. Never disturbed me, never interrupted, just wanted to be close to me. It's one of my most precious memories of his childhood, him sitting by my side, looking at me. Now that he's older, as soon as he gets home from school, he runs to tell me all about his day. He gives the best cuddles and tells the best stories. He's loyal and kind and brave. And he is smart, just like his daddy. You would be so proud of him.' She put her hand on her chest, trying to steady her heartbeat. Missing her boy was a physical ache that never went away, not for a moment. 'At eight years old, he is a chess prodigy.'

'Did you teach him to play?'

'Anthony did. He's been a good stepfather for Leon.'

'It must have been hard to say goodbye when you left for the front.'

She nodded. 'It was the saddest day of my life. I don't think I've ever cried so much in my life. He told me, "Mama, you make me so proud. I wish I was older so I could go with you and protect you from everything." I've been writing to him every day, telling him about everything.'

'I was wondering what you were writing.'

'I'll have to mail the latest letters as soon as we are rescued. I can imagine his joy when he receives all of them, one for every day since the crash.' She took Darren's hands and studied them. It was hard to imagine that they were the same hands that held her when she was a young girl. They looked strong and hard, like they had known hard work. 'In one of my letters, I told him I found you here.'

Darren sat up, watching her. 'Does he know about me?'

She nodded. 'I told him about you because I thought he deserved to know the truth.' Quieter, she added, 'I told him about you because I was hoping you would come back one day.'

* * *

One morning, after she fed both her patients breakfast and tidied up afterwards, Darren suggested a game of poker. They used pebbles from the garden as chips. In no time at all, Nicole's pebbles were gone, while Darren's pile had doubled in size. She sat in front of him with a stunned expression on her face, while he laughed like it was the funniest thing in the world.

'How did that happen so quickly? You cheated, didn't you?' she demanded.

'I didn't cheat. I won fair and square. It's payback for all those times you beat me at tennis.'

She pinched him. 'Let's play again.'

'You can't play again. You are all out of pebbles.'

'Perhaps I can bet something else.'

'Like what?'

'If I lose, I will read to you for an hour.'

'You read to me anyway.'

'I will tell you something you didn't know about Leon.'

'You'll tell me about him anyway. I have an idea.' He pulled her closer. His arms were around her, his lips were in her hair. He lifted her up, so their faces were almost touching. 'When you lose . . .'

'You mean, if?' She giggled.

'*When* you lose, I get to kiss you.' She felt vulnerable next to him, afraid of what was to come. She remembered the heartbreak of those first months without him like it was yesterday. The pain was still there, hidden deep inside, and she knew she couldn't allow herself to trust someone so completely with her heart, and yet, she suspected she did not have much choice. A moment later, he was kissing her and she forgot about everything. She could barely breathe as his lips touched hers and her heart was beating fast inside her chest but all she wanted was for this moment to go on forever and never end. It was like a fairy tale, and she was part of it, and so was he.

When it was over, she took a deep breath, unable to speak at first. 'I haven't lost yet but you are already kissing me,' she whispered.

'Call it an advance.' He looked at her and winked.

'You must be healing fast, Captain Brown,' she said.

'Faster than you can imagine,' he said with a mischievous grin on his face. He was quiet for a moment as he shuffled the cards. Then he said, 'Tell me about your husband.'

'Anthony is a good man. He is kind and he loves Leon like his own son. We are friends.'

'Like you and I used to be friends?'

'Different. He cares about me, just not in that way. He is in love with the girl he dated at high school. I suspect they are still seeing each other.'

'And you don't mind?'

She shrugged. 'We didn't marry for love. We married because it's what our parents wanted, because our fathers were in business together. I can't give him what he needs. I can't love him like he deserves. I can't make him happy. Maybe someone else can.' She twisted her wedding ring nervously. 'What about you? Is there anyone special in your life?'

He put the cards down and shook his head. 'There's only ever been you. After we left, I threw myself into work. I worked eighteen-hour days just to forget. I would get home and fall into bed exhausted, but at night I'd think of you. Sometimes in Cairo, when things got tough, I imagined that we were still together, that you were waiting for me. All my comrades had a wife or a fiancée back home. I needed someone to fight for too. I felt so lonely at times.'

'I felt lonely too,' she whispered. 'In a house full of people, I was completely alone.'

He stroked her hand. 'I'm so sorry, again. Sometimes it felt like my life was on hold. Like I was waiting for something. Waiting for you.'

* * *

Nicole was worried about Flamur. Injured and without purpose, he seemed to lose all interest in what was happening around him. He spent his time by the window, watching the world go by, not saying a word, refusing to eat. 'Don't be so sad,' Nicole would say to him. 'Your burns will heal. You'll be good as new before you know it.'

She didn't know if he could understand her. He didn't acknowledge her words, didn't even look up from the window. But she could swear his lips moved upwards, as if in a smile.

Goni cooked for him, while Nani spoke to him in Albanian late into the night, even though Flamur never spoke back.

One day, she invited Flamur to play poker. To her surprise, he agreed. In the cellar, in the light of the torch, they divided the pebbles into three piles and began. She was even more surprised to find that Flamur seemed to be an expert at cards. In heavily accented English, he knew how to say *call, all in, fold*.

'Where did you learn how to play?' asked Nicole. He didn't reply, winning hand after hand in silence. Before they knew it, all the pebbles had been moved to his side. He nodded with satisfaction, put his winnings in his pocket and went back upstairs.

Darren and Nicole stared at one another, stunned.

'Beginner's luck, I suppose,' Darren said.

'I don't know. He seemed to know exactly what he was doing.'

'Why did he take our pebbles?'

'He won them, didn't he? Don't worry, I'll get some more from the garden.'

The next time they played, Flamur won again. He had the perfect poker face. Nicole could never tell what he was thinking, no matter how hard she tried to read his expression. 'How do you do this? How do you always have a winning hand?' she wanted to know.

He shrugged but didn't say a word.

'Just don't bet any real money,' Darren said. 'Or you'll never see it again.'

'Don't have any money on me.'

'Probably for the best,' Darren said, throwing a look at Flamur, who was busy arranging his pebbles by pushing them with his foot. He still didn't say a word to either of them but seemed a little more cheerful.

* * *

Every morning and afternoon, a young girl called Elora arrived with a basket of food and sat next to Flamur, trying to convince him to eat. They chatted quietly in Albanian, their heads close together. When Nicole entered the room to change Flamur's dressings or administer morphine, they moved away from each other like they were embarrassed.

Almost every day, German soldiers came to the house. At the first sound of the heavy boots hitting the ground outside, before the dreaded knock on the door, Nicole would dash back to the cellar and sit next to Darren, holding his hand, quiet like a mouse, wishing she was invisible. 'Don't be afraid,' Darren would say to her.

'I'm not afraid,' she would reply.

But it was a lie. All the Nazis needed was a dog and they would find her and Darren in no time. Nicole saw them from the window as she tended to Flamur. German Shepherds the size of small ponies pulled on leashes behind angry-looking German officers. All it took was one inspection, one request for the documents they didn't possess, and they would be arrested and taken away.

After one such visit, Flamur said, 'I hate the Nazis.' At first, Andrea thought she had imagined it, so quietly had he spoken. His face was twisted like he was in pain. 'Hate them with all my heart,' he added.

'I didn't know you could speak English, Flamur. Why haven't you said anything before?'

Flamur shook his head, perhaps indicating he hadn't had anything pressing to express, until now. Gritting his teeth and clenching his fists, he said, 'They burnt my store. They took my best friend away and we haven't seen him since. We don't know what has become of him.' His eyes sparkled like he was about to cry.

Nicole put the tray of cornbread down and sat at the table next to him. 'I'm sorry to hear that.'

'All he did was stand up for his sister. You met Elora. One of the Germans was paying too much attention to her. And now Arben is gone. Elora is inconsolable. It makes me feel so helpless. How can I protect her? How can I take care of her?' He caught a glimpse of himself in the mirror and shuddered. 'Look at the burns on my face. They did this to me. We were supposed to get married in spring. Will she even want me, looking like this?'

Nicole pressed his hand gently. 'Of course, she will want you or she wouldn't be here any chance she gets, bringing you food.' As she was talking to Flamur, Nicole noticed out of the corner of her eye a thick envelope on one of the chairs. It had her name on it, scribbled in large, uneven letters, as if the hand that had written it was trembling. She pointed at the envelope. 'Do you know what that is?'

Flamur shrugged. 'Uncle Nani left it this morning.'

Nicole opened the envelope and, to her surprise, found two sets of documents. One had a picture of herself, and the other of Darren. They had been given Albanian names and addresses. The papers looked authentic to Nicole but would they hold up to a Nazi inspection? She hoped so. After all, Nani's cousin knew what he was doing. She approached the fireplace and examined the documents in great detail.

'It will be easier for you, with the Nazi patrols,' said Flamur.

'The moment we open our mouths, they'll know we are not Albanian. They'll know these are fake.'

'Plans are being made to take the two of you out of Berat. It won't be long now.'

Instead of reassuring her, Flamur's words made her tremble with fear. She had been safe in the little house with Darren, hiding underground like an ostrich burying its head in the sand, lost in her feelings and his warm embrace. Against all odds, she had found a home here. There was joy inside these walls, and hope, while outside unimaginable horrors awaited them, their new Albanian identities notwithstanding.

Chapter 11

A Glimmer of Hope

Now that the British officer was with them, it was as if a veil had been lifted. When she looked at her comrades' faces, Andrea no longer saw tension and uncertainty. Although she felt sad saying goodbye to Gina after everything he had done for them, she was also relieved because she knew they were in good hands. And the rest of the group was ecstatic. Everyone, it seemed, was celebrating, as if they were already on board a ship, being whisked away towards the shores of Italy.

'I told you so,' Renee said to Thrasher with great satisfaction. 'Gina wasn't dragging us around Albania aimlessly. He was taking us to the meeting place with the SOE officer.'

'He should have mentioned it,' Thrasher grumbled.

'Perhaps he didn't want to get our hopes up, in case it didn't work out. Say, "You were right, Renee, and I was wrong". I need to hear you say it.'

'I'm glad you are enjoying this.'

'Just because you are the most senior officer, doesn't mean you never make mistakes. Now say it.'

Thrasher grimaced, then in a comically high-pitched voice, mimicking Renee, said, 'You were right, Renee, and I was wrong.'

'Thank you. I accept your apology. With Smith in charge, I bet you a dollar we'll be back in Italy before Christmas.'

'I'll take that bet. I can't lose, you see. Either we'll be back on base, which is great. Or I'll have myself a dollar.' Grinning, he shook the nurse's hand.

The group wanted to know everything about the man leading them to safety. Everybody took turns to walk next to Smith and ask him the same questions over and over again. Where was he from? What was he doing in Albania? How did he learn about the stranded Americans? He didn't seem annoyed by all the attention or by having to repeat the same information a dozen times. He was easy-going and friendly, and radiated a confidence that seemed at odds with his youth, the kind of confidence that only comes from experience. He told them he was a captain in the Lancashire Fusiliers, a British infantry regiment, and underwent training at a paramilitary school in the Scottish Highlands and at the Royal Air Force station at Ramat David near Nazareth. He had been dropped in Albania a month ago. 'It was the only thing I have enjoyed about Albania so far. The parachute jump.' He smiled, displaying a set of brilliant white teeth.

Baggs wanted to know how they prepared British liaison officers before they sent them to their various assignments. Smith told them he had spent many months studying skiing, climbing, weapons and mule management. 'The most useful course of all,' he said, laughing.

Smith made a list of their names and told them his team would send a message to the US military, letting them know that the group had been located. 'Everyone is looking for you,' he said. 'And I'm the one who found you.'

Andrea gave him her name and her sister's name and explained how they got separated.

'Don't worry. We will find your sister. We won't rest until we do,' he assured her.

For the first time since the fateful day when the Nazis overwhelmed Berat like a swarm of locusts, she felt a glimmer of hope.

Smith moved those in the party who were ill or injured to the front, so they could set the pace. He placed the radio equipment and a sack of provisions, including K rations, dry eggs, biscuits and bread, on one of the mules. The sight of so much food cheered Andrea up. Even if they were turned away from every village, they would not perish.

Thick frost covered the ground and the winter air possessed daggers sharp enough to pierce the exposed skin of their faces until it was red, windswept and sore. Just like the day before and the one before that, they set out in a single file, knowing they would have to continue walking until darkness fell, whether they wanted to or not, whether they were capable of it or not. Even before they started their march, they were exhausted. When they got to their destination for the night, they would be drained of all life and barely able to move. They might not find food or shelter, they might meet with enemies along the way, they might not survive the day. Everything was the same as every other morning in Albania, the cold, the hunger, the fear, the narrow mountain trail that seemed to go on forever, without a beginning or an end. And yet, that day something was different because for the first time since they crash-landed, they had hope.

As she walked behind the others, Andrea looked down, careful not to slip. Although it was no longer snowing, the ground was slush, mud and rocks under her feet. Only occasionally she glanced at the mountains ahead of them, impregnable and frightening. The thought of having to brave these mountains left her breathless and afraid. The trees all blurred together, the timid early-winter sun was blinding her but not doing much to warm her up and the rocks she navigated tried their best to trip her up.

A few times they walked through villages that had been burnt down and abandoned. What was left of the huts looked like ghosts in the morning sun, hollow and frightening. Andrea wondered what had happened here, whether the inhabitants had been able to get away, whether they had survived. She imagined families living in these houses, men tending to the gardens, women cooking in the kitchens, children playing outside, their joyful voices calling out to each other as they kicked their ball around. And now it was all gone, whole lives displaced in mere moments, and only the shell of what had once been remained.

Sometimes they saw Italian soldiers sheltering under what was left of the burnt down buildings. They looked desperate and starved, their gaunt faces, their empty eyes following the Americans' every move. With no food available, Andrea knew they would not survive for long. She felt sorry for them and a little embarrassed because she could do nothing to help, because she herself was only one step away from becoming just like them, destitute and resigned, waiting for the inevitable death. If it wasn't for the British officer and the partisans who had been guiding them along the way, they would be in the same position as the Italians, hiding under rubble, begging for food, not knowing if they would live until the sundown.

Brian caught up to her. 'It's hard to walk in these conditions,' he said. 'You must be exhausted. Look at you.'

'I didn't sleep well.' She wanted to tell him it was because of their argument but didn't. The last thing she needed was another conflict with him in front of everyone. It was best to keep her temper in check, so she wouldn't have to see his.

'Why don't you ride one of the mules for a bit?' he suggested, his voice like honey, like his shouting at her the night before was nothing but a figment of her imagination.

'Because others need it more than I do. Liz twisted her ankle. Renee's arthritis is playing up in the cold. And Shearman is still recovering.'

She waited for him to offer to carry one of her bags, but he didn't. 'Hopefully we'll stop somewhere soon,' he said.

They walked in silence for a bit. She kept throwing surreptitious glances his way. She saw the man she fell in love with, the man who swore he would make her happy for the rest of her life. And yet, he was the one causing her the most pain. What happened to his promises? Had he forgotten about them or was her happiness no longer important to him? Was *she* no longer important to him? Since they got married, there was a voice inside her head that sounded just like his, hissing and angry and terrifying, telling her she wasn't good enough or smart enough, that she would never amount to much, that she was lucky to have him because she wasn't beautiful enough, didn't have model looks or a PhD in science like his ex-wife. What happened to the confident and happy person she had once been? 'Aren't you going to apologise to me?' she asked, her eyes to the ground.

'Apologise for what?' he demanded, his voice slightly louder than it should have been.

'When you say horrible things to me, it hurts my feelings. It's not fair and I don't deserve it.'

'I have no idea what you are talking about,' he muttered.

'You called me stupid. You shouted at me in front of everyone and told me I'm acting like a child.'

'Maybe if you didn't act like a child, I wouldn't have said it.'

Suddenly, her eyes were open and she could see clearly for the first time. 'You don't think you are doing anything wrong, do you?' she whispered. 'And that's why things will never change. You will always be like this. You were different when we first met but it was just an act, to lure me in, to confuse me. Now that you have me, you don't have to hide anymore. You don't have to pretend.'

'Lure you in? You were desperate to be with me.'

'I was in love. It doesn't give you the right to put me down or hurt me. I deserve to be treated with kindness and respect, just like everybody else.'

'Why is everything always a drama with you? You can't go a day without causing an argument.'

'I'm not causing anything. I have the right to tell you how your actions make me feel, in the hope that things might change and our marriage can get back on track. I'm not happy.'

'You are never happy,' he said, turning away from her. 'It's exhausting.'

She wanted to tell him it was exhausting to have to walk on eggshells and watch her every word in case it upset him and made him lose his temper. It was exhausting to worry about his reaction every second of every day and to lie awake in the middle of the night, upset and unable to sleep. She wanted to tell him she couldn't live in a warzone anymore. But there was little point. She knew he wouldn't understand.

Finally, after walking for hours through rain and snow, they came to a village that still looked inhabited, in stark contrast to the empty settlements they had passed earlier that day. Everyone perked up at the sight of it. They walked faster, they spoke louder, so eager were they to reach a place where they could pause for a moment, a place that wasn't dead but filled with living souls who might welcome them and greet them. They were exhausted and soaked to the bone. They were shaking from the cold. And they were hungry. Some of them swore they couldn't walk another step, even though they continued on because they had no choice.

But instead of welcoming them, the village council refused them entry. 'We have nothing left. No food to give,' said the elder in broken English. 'The Nazis took everything. What little we have is not enough for us.'

Andrea could see by the man's face that he was telling the truth. He had a gaunt, haunted look about him that she had witnessed so often since they had arrived at the front. There was fear in his eyes, of things to come that were too terrible to contemplate.

Smith said, 'We don't need food. All we want is shelter for the night.'

Andrea couldn't tell if the elder understood. All he did was cross his arms over his chest and shake his head.

'Please, sir,' Renee pleaded, pointing at the nurses. 'Half of us are women. We are tired and cold. We can't sleep under the open skies.'

But that was exactly what they had to do. They settled among the ruins, much like the Italians they had encountered earlier, the snow falling on their faces and seeping into their clothes, making them shiver.

'It will be one hell of a story to tell the grandchildren,' said Brian.

Surprised, Andrea lifted her eyes to him in the waning light. His face was impassive. He wasn't looking at her and didn't see her pain. More than anything she wanted a child of her own. This need was like a knife inside her heart, causing unbearable pain, not easing for a moment. And here he was, bringing it up so casually. She blinked hard, trying to fight tears. *He didn't mean anything by it*, she told herself. *He wasn't thinking*. But the knife remained inside her heart, making it hard to breathe.

'Are you sure you didn't steal another pebble, Shearman?' Baggs wanted to know, his eyes twinkling.

Shearman blushed and shook his head, while one of the medics said, 'The curse of the pebble will continue to pursue us for the rest of our days in Albania. How much longer do we have to gallop across this wonderful country, chief?' he asked Smith.

Smith told them it would take fourteen days to reach Seaview, the caves above the Adriatic that were used by the SOE as a secret base camp, where some of his colleagues were waiting for them. Once they got there, they would radio for a rescue boat and if all went according to plan, they would be across the water and back in Italy within a day.

'Another two weeks of walking,' said Liz tearfully. 'I don't think we'll make it.'

'You made it for many weeks without me,' said Smith. 'You can do another fourteen days with me.'

Some of the men wanted to know what the SOE did at Seaview.

'We evacuate or bring in personnel, deliver weapons and supplies into the country and maintain communications with the outside world,' Smith explained.

'And the Germans haven't discovered you yet?'

'The mountains between the sea and the main road hide us from view. With luck, they will never find us, no matter how hard they look for us.'

'It must be scary in the caves in the dark, all by yourselves,' said Liz.

'We have torches, so we are never in the dark. The only things we worry about are lice, black scorpions and the BK.'

'The BK?'

'Since they are not fighting the Germans anymore, we don't supply them with weapons. And they go out of their way to stop us delivering weapons to the partisans, who are fighting against them.'

They shared some rations and spoke in low voices. Before they settled for the night, Smith said to them, 'I have something for you. An early Christmas gift.'

He presented them with cans of sardines and two loaves of dark bread. The Americans cheered like they had been given precious jewels.

Andrea had never liked sardines but she was so hungry, she devoured every morsel and asked for more.

She got comfortable next to Renee, who said, 'When all this is over, Trevor and I will buy a cabin by the lake in Michigan, away from civilisation. We will grow our own vegetables. What we can't grow, we will buy. And we'll have more children.'

Andrea gazed at Renee with amazement. Her husband was in a prison camp somewhere, and yet, she never despaired, never seemed to doubt for a second that they would be together again. 'How do you do this? How do you stay positive no matter what?'

'I have to, otherwise I will lose my mind with worry. Every morning I wake up and convince myself everything is going to be all right. That he's still alive. That he will come back to me. I say it to myself a thousand times a day until I believe it. I have this imaginary life that I have constructed inside my head for our little family. To me, that life became real. I know we'll live it one day. I just have to have faith.'

'How did you and Trevor meet?'

'We were childhood sweethearts. Together since we were fourteen. The moment I laid my eyes on him, I knew he was the one for me.'

'How could you tell?'

'It's the way he made me feel. Like I was the most beautiful girl in the world. With Trevor, I don't have to pretend or fake anything. I can just be myself.'

That must be nice, thought Andrea. *To be yourself. To not be afraid. To not have to walk on eggshells around the man you love.* She said to Renee, 'The two of you are lucky to have each other.'

While others slept, Andrea stared at the stars, like a thousand diamonds over her head. She imagined other universes, other lives, heartbreaks and happy endings. And she thought of her own happy ending that had been snatched away from her, bit by bit over time, with every angry word, every disparaging comment, every contemptuous glance.

* * *

The next morning, Brian still wasn't talking to her and she desperately needed someone to talk to. She wished she hadn't said anything to him. She wanted to touch his face, to hear his voice, to feel less alone. 'How did you sleep?' she asked.

'Fine,' he grumbled in response, not looking her way.

'Would you like some of my rations? I'm not really hungry.'

'You better eat,' he said. 'If you don't, you won't have the energy to walk and you will slow everybody down.'

'Can we stop fighting?' she pleaded. 'This is hard enough. Walking for hours, battling through the elements. We need to help each other, not be at each other's throats all the time.'

'I'm not the one fighting.'

Not knowing what else to say, she turned away from him and to the trees that were bending in the wind. There was a wall between them and she didn't know where it had come from or what she could do about it. When they first met, they had agreed on everything. When had they turned into two opponents in the ring wearing heavy gloves, going toe to toe, round after round without a break? She felt like she was trapped in the dark, her hands reaching for him and finding nothing but air. He was slipping away from her and no matter what she did, she couldn't stop it. She wondered when it had started, the distance. There was once a time when they couldn't live without each other, when they ran into each other's arms at the end of the day, eager to tell each other everything. But gradually, her partner had disappeared, only to be replaced by someone who looked like him but was a stranger. Andrea mourned his loss acutely but couldn't talk about it to anyone, not even her sister. She didn't know how to put into words what she was feeling. Her husband hadn't died. He hadn't left her. He was still here, by her side. And yet, he was gone, irrevocably and without a trace.

It was the first week of December and the weather had taken a turn for the worse. The snow was coming down hard, making it difficult to see. The temperature had plummeted. They passed villages with domed churches and vibrant frescoes, many of which had been destroyed by the Germans. Andrea's heart broke at the sight of so much beauty gone for no reason other than one people deciding to invade another. Some villages were still on fire. As she slowly put one foot in front of another, she could barely breathe from the smoke. Women and children gawked at them as they passed. There were no men left, only partisans they occasionally passed on mountain trails. Andrea suspected most of the men were hiding from the Nazis, had been detained or killed. When Andrea touched the rubble in one of the villages, she discovered that it was still warm. How close were the Germans? She wanted to ask Smith about it but was too afraid.

In the early afternoon, they walked past a young woman dressed in a beautiful gown, a fairy-tale princess on top of her mule. Her face was carefully made up and in her hands she held a bouquet of flowers. Behind her walked two dozen people, singing happily. They looked so festive in the midst of war and so out of place, Andrea's heart soared at the sight of them.

'Who is this?' she asked Smith. 'I've never seen a woman in Albania dressed like this before.'

'It's a bride on the way to her wedding,' he explained.

'She's not smiling. Everyone around her looks happy but she seems so sad.' The bride reminded her of her sister on her wedding day, walking down the aisle towards Anthony with tears in her eyes.

'Most marriages in Albania are arranged. No one cares if the bride is happy or sad.'

'Women can't choose who they marry here?'

'Not usually. Those who run away to elope are often caught and punished.'

'What's the punishment?'

'I heard a story of a couple from two families involved in a blood feud. They were killed. Some women decide to become sworn virgins to avoid marriage. They choose to live as men for the rest of their lives.'

Andrea felt sorry for the beautiful bride with sad eyes, forced to marry someone she didn't love. And then she thought, *I married the love of my life. And look at me now.*

* * *

Icy daggers came down from above. Andrea could feel them sting the skin of her face and neck. The path was narrow and slippery, every step fraught with danger. Andrea held her breath as she placed her feet gingerly on the ice rink before her. After a couple of near-falls, she called out to her husband, who slowed down, reluctantly. 'My feet are hurting after walking for so long,' she said. 'Can I lean on your arm for a bit?'

'Come on, Andie,' he replied, looking irritated. 'You can see how much I'm carrying.' He had a backpack on his shoulders and a musette bag in his hands.

'I know. I'm sorry to be such a bother. I keep slipping on the ice, that's all.'

'You want us both to fall? No one else is leaning on anyone. Everyone is acting like a grown-up, except for you. You don't need me to hold your hand all the time.'

They continued on the treacherous trail, which had narrowed down so much that they could only walk in a single file, taking extra care not to slip. Andrea did her best not to look at the giant drop to her left, only two feet away. Every time her gaze fell on it, she felt dizzy and short of breath. One wrong step and it could all be over. She overcompensated, sliding on the balls of her feet like she was ice skating, taking slow, careful strides, her body tense, hands shaking, eyes to the ground. Suddenly, a large stone appeared out of nowhere, catching her foot, and a moment later she was careening down the terrifying slope with her arms outstretched and her mouth open in a mute shout. In the few seconds it took for her to fall, many thoughts ran through her mind. She wondered if these were the last seconds of her life and if Brian would regret the way he had treated her. She wondered if he would cry when she was gone, if he would wish that things had been different. That *he* had been different. She didn't have long to ponder her husband's reaction because all too soon she felt a sharp impact on her head and everything went dark.

When she came to, she was lying on a makeshift stretcher in the woods. Snow was falling on her face, melting and running down her cheeks like tears. 'Water,' she whispered. Her throat was burning. Her voice didn't sound like her own.

Someone brought a flask to her lips. 'Look who's awake,' said Renee. 'You are lucky to be alive.'

'My head. Why does it hurt so much?' She touched her forehead.

'You hit your head on a rock. If it wasn't for that rock, you would have fallen to your death. It saved your life.'

Andrea groaned. 'Where is Brian?' she asked.

'He was here somewhere. I'll find him.'

She watched the movement around her, people coming in and out of her peripheral vision, asking how she was feeling, wondering if she needed anything. She didn't reply, only shook her head, wanting to close her eyes and sleep for a thousand years, to not have to walk down treacherous trails or deal with treacherous men ever again.

'What a scare you gave me,' said Brian, leaning over her with a smile on his face. She wanted to smile back but couldn't.

'Sorry,' she whispered.

He took her hand. 'Don't be. I'm so glad you're safe. I thought I lost you.'

'Did you?' His face looked fuzzy. She couldn't focus on his features, could barely recognise him. She realised she was crying. She blinked fast and for a moment it looked like he had disappeared.

'My heart nearly stopped when I saw you hurtling down that hill. But all is well that ends well.'

She waited for him to say something else, to tell her how much he loved her, how her fall made him reconsider everything because he couldn't imagine his life without her. But he seemed content to sit in silence, holding hands. She pulled away from him and whispered, 'Do you remember when you asked me to move in to your place? We had only been dating for two months but it felt so right. Waking up in the morning and seeing your face. Coming home to you at the end of the day.'

'Of course I remember.'

He looked at her with kind eyes and her heart skipped a beat. There was once a time when his kindness was all she saw. He had been a different man then and she had been a different woman. She missed the old him. She missed the couple they had once been. 'Where did it all go, Brian? Where did you go?'

'I'm still here, sweetheart. I haven't gone anywhere.' He stroked her fingers, brought them to his mouth, kissed them. 'Do you need anything? Some water?'

'I don't think I can walk any more. I feel so broken,' she said.

'Fortunately, we are half an hour away from a village. Fingers crossed we can find shelter there. Are you sure you don't want anything to eat?'

She didn't say anything, just watched him through half-closed eyes.

After a short break, Smith told them it was time to go. They had to start moving if they were to reach the village before nightfall. The men took turns carrying Andrea's stretcher. While she was grateful to be able to rest for a while, she couldn't help but feel like she was slowing everybody down. She told the men she was fine and could walk on her own but the minute she got up, she felt dizzy and nearly fell again. Baggs caught her, guiding her back towards the stretcher. 'It's all right,' he said. 'The trail is dangerous here. We don't mind carrying you if it means you're safe.'

She lay back on the stretcher and watched the clouds above her as they changed shape, pushed by the wind. She felt that her life was just like these clouds, shifting in front of her. Nothing was how she expected it to be. The foundation she had built her future on was not concrete but quicksand.

From her stretcher, Andrea noticed that the sunsets were particularly stunning in this part of Albania. She wondered how she had never realised it before. She had been too exhausted by the end of the day, too busy trying to survive, all her senses and willpower dedicated to propelling her forward. For the first time in many weeks, she had an opportunity to admire the sun as it rolled behind the mountains, spilling magic all over the woods. She wondered if walking in the dark, as scary as it was, was not a fair price to pay to witness such a miracle. The breathtaking sight transported her to the past, to the memory of other sunsets, those she had enjoyed with her sister when they were children and those she had seen with her husband when they were first married. She could close her eyes and see her younger self twirling on the grass, while above her the sky was the most luminous purple, laughing, dizzy, out of breath, while Brian couldn't take his eyes off her, until she couldn't spin anymore and collapsed into his outstretched arms. How happy they had once been, how carefree, and now, all these years and heartaches later, the recollection of the two of them together, precious and unforgettable, became like an old parchment, yellow with age, with cracks running across their smiling faces.

An hour later, to everyone's relief, they reached the village of Gjirokastër. The villagers entertained them with songs and music, with stories and anecdotes but very little food. The Americans were forced to resort to their dry food supplies that were dwindling by the day. Andrea slept fitfully, and in the morning, her head was heavy and her body was aching. Somewhere in the near distance, she could hear gun shots and explosions.

Smith appeared with a sack filled with new boots. Like a flock of seagulls, the group descended on the sack, pushing each other, squawking happily, snatching and bickering. After weeks of walking, their old boots were falling apart and having new ones would make the world of difference.

'Where did you get these?' asked Thrasher. 'Is there a shop in the village? Do they sell tobacco? I am all out and desperate.'

'No shop but I have my connections.'

'Do your connections have any cigarettes? I'm not myself without my smokes.'

'Cigarettes are a filthy habit,' said Renee. 'You are better off without them. They are a danger. I'm telling you this as a medical professional.'

'I am a danger to the world without them,' Thrasher muttered.

Andrea tried her new boots on. They were two sizes too big and the hobnails made them heavy and difficult to walk in. She had to borrow another pair of woollen socks to make sure they didn't fall off. But they were a nice change from her old boots that were torn to shreds and offered no protection against snow and slush.

'Thank you, Captain Smith,' said Renee. 'I look forward to trying them out on the trail. Everybody ready for another twelve hours in the snow?'

They had their coats on and their bags behind their backs. All they were waiting for was a word from Smith. 'Not walking anywhere today, folks,' he said. 'The Germans have occupied the villages ahead of us. The trails are teeming with them. We'll have to camp out here until it's safe.'

'We can't stay here,' exclaimed Renee. 'I have a bet running with Thrasher. If we make it back before Christmas, I win a dollar.'

'A dollar or your life, Nurse?' asked Thrasher.

Renee chose her life and the group remained in the village, while a battle unfolded somewhere nearby. As they talked and played cards and read, they could hear its deafening rumble. Andrea asked Brian if the Germans were coming here. 'How do I know?' he snapped, his attention on his poker game with Thrasher and Baggs. They were playing for their last pack of cigarettes. Thrasher was losing and his frustrated voice was louder than the machine-gun fire.

Everyone was disappointed by the delay, except Andrea. Although she was desperate to get away from danger, to no longer spend every day fearing for her life and trudging through snow up mountain ridges, she couldn't imagine leaving Albania without Nicole. How could she run to safety, abandoning her sister for the second time? And yet, what choice did she have? She couldn't stay behind by herself and wait . . . Wait for what? For the Nazis to leave Berat? For Hitler to surrender? Even if she stayed here, what could she possibly do on her own? She wondered what Nicole would do, had she been in her shoes. She had a feeling that her sister, who had stood bravely in front of school bullies to protect Andrea when they were little, would not abandon her without trying everything in her power to get her back. Andrea spoke to Smith and he assured her that the authorities were aware of the situation and plans were underway to rescue her sister. She didn't know if it was true or if he was like the radio, telling her what she wanted to hear. If it was up to her, she would march singlehandedly back to Berat and lead her sister out of the occupied town.

On the second day in Gjirokastër, a woman walked in, carrying a plate of oranges. Andrea couldn't believe her eyes. She peeled the orange with her fingers, broke it into small parts and took her time to eat it, relishing the taste in her mouth. She was grateful to the stranger for this unexpected moment of joy. When her orange was gone, Brian, who didn't like fruit, offered her his.

On the third day, the host let them take a bath. It was their first bath in seven weeks, an early Christmas present that they all enjoyed. Andrea stayed in the warm water for a long time, grateful not to have to rush. She closed her eyes and imagined she was home with her new husband, years before war and heartbreak, when they were happy and in love. She enjoyed taking baths then, with no one to disturb her and long afternoons of joy stretching before her. She would sit for hours with bubbles so tall, she could barely see anything around her, and daydream about her future. There were no bubbles or soap in Gjirokastër and nothing to daydream about other than finding their way back home but the water felt like heaven to Andrea and it was a miracle to be clean again. If only she didn't have to get into her old, dirty clothes afterwards.

Andrea and the other nurses shared the smallest room in the house. They slept close to each other, their arms touching. When someone rolled over or shuffled in their sleep, Andrea woke up. When Renee inquired if there was another room for them, the host, who had been sleeping in the ante-room on a little sofa, took them to the other bedroom and opened the door. Inside, taking up all the available space and blocking the windows, stacked tightly from floor to ceiling, were cobs of corn.

'That explains why we've been having so much corn for breakfast, lunch and dinner. He could feed a whole army with it,' Andrea whispered to Renee. To the host, she said, 'Why do you have all this?'

He replied that his tenants who farmed the land he owned could only pay him with part of their crop. Not knowing what to do with it, he stored it inside his house. 'But the Nazis will come and take it,' he said sadly. 'They will take all my corn.'

'Why don't you sell it?' Renee wanted to know.

The host shook his head dejectedly. 'No one has money to buy it.'

Christmas came and they were still in Albania. Renee lost her bet and Thrasher got his dollar but he wasn't too happy about it. 'I'd rather be back on base,' he said. He spoke for all of them. None of them were in the mood to celebrate, least of all Andrea, but they awoke early on Christmas Day to attend a church service with their hosts. Andrea was surprised to see a small Greek Orthodox church that looked magical with its golden dome shimmering in the sun. A fresh blanket of snow lay on the ground, making everything look festive and new. It was as if nature itself was rejoicing on this special day.

As the Americans huddled in the back, the priest performed the service, and although she couldn't understand a word, Andrea felt tears running down her cheeks. While the choir sang, making her heart ache, she prayed for her sister, wishing for more time together so she could tell her once again how sorry she was. She prayed for her marriage, wishing for a light, a sign to guide her and help her make the most important decision of her life. And she prayed for all of them to make it back safely, to survive whatever this country threw at them.

Seeing the Greek priest pray for peace gave them hope they all desperately needed. In the evening, they had some chicken for dinner and shared a bottle of wine. They raised their glasses and danced to records on a phonograph belonging to the villagers, hugging one another and wishing each other Merry Christmas. For a brief moment in time, they set their fears aside, as they celebrated Christmas among strangers, lost but not forgotten.

On Boxing Day, they got some unexpectedly good news. Smith told them he had been in contact with SOE Cairo on his radio. The Army Air Forces were keen to attempt an air evacuation. The thought of planes coming to their rescue and whisking them off to safety cheered everyone up. 'It's a Christmas miracle,' said Renee.

'I don't want you to get your hopes up,' said Smith. 'The success of the mission will depend on weather conditions and the German presence in the area.'

Smith's words did nothing to deflate their joy. All they talked about was their life after the war and all the wonderful things they would do when they returned to America. Liz was planning the reunion with her husband, who was waiting for her in Italy. Renee was writing to her son, telling him she was coming home soon. Carrie and Tory were swapping stories about their childhoods and wondering if they would find their elderly parents still alive. Only Andrea didn't join in the conversation, not because she didn't believe rescue was on its way but because she had no idea what she was going to do when she returned home.

Smith explained that they needed to tell SOE Cairo their exact location, the type of terrain and the prevailing winds. Once they received this information, the AAF would know where to look for them and how to land. The pilots went out with Smith to check out an airfield nearby, so they could report back to Cairo.

As if nature itself was opposed to their plans, the sun disappeared behind a dark cloud and it started to snow again. Andrea sat with her nose to the window and watched the white slush falling from the sky, like the wrath of God, obscuring trees and nearby houses. She wondered if it was snowing in Berat and if her sister was watching the snow fall too, dreaming of the winter wonderland of their childhood. The other nurses entertained themselves with cards and songs. Someone at the village had a guitar and in Renee's hands, the instrument came to life with melancholy chords that filled every heart with longing. They sang the songs they loved and dreamt of home, so far away, and yet, for the first time since they landed in Albania, they had no doubt they would see it soon.

When the pilots returned, by the look on their faces Andrea knew that the weather had dashed all their hopes of air rescue in the near future. 'We need to wait for the snow to stop. The valley looks like soup. Ground visibility is zero,' said Baggs.

Everyone was disappointed, while Andrea was secretly relieved. Perhaps if they were delayed here because of the weather for a few more days, she would hear something about Nicole.

Others read books, smoked and sang. Andrea remained by the window and watched the local boys as they joined some of the Americans for a game of soccer. One boy, no more than ten or eleven, was particularly good with the ball. He reminded Andrea of her nephew, Leon, who loved soccer more than anything and spent all his free time outside, practising his skills. She closed her eyes, her hand on her chest, and thought of home. She thought of her mother's last words before she left for Europe. 'Take care of yourself out there. Be safe and write to us as often as you can. I know we haven't seen much of each other lately and we haven't always agreed on things, but we want you to know that we love you and miss you.'

'Even Dad?' Andrea asked, surprised by the tears in her mother's eyes. She had never seen her cry, until now.

'Especially Dad. He is stubborn like a donkey but I'm working on him. Perhaps a grandchild will soften his heart. Any plans to start a family?'

To everyone's surprise, the snow stopped a few hours later and the sun peered cheerfully from behind the cloud. Smith spent all evening and most of the next morning trying to contact Cairo, while the rest of the group gathered around nervously, listening to the static. The line was bad and only occasional words reached them, words that made them tremble with hope. Someone out there was looking for them and working hard to get them out. They had not been forgotten in occupied Albania.

It wasn't until the following afternoon that they were able to receive a message. 'The following arrangements will hold for pickup of Yanks. Pickup between 12:00 GMT and 13:00 GMT, Wed Dec 28. If weather prevents will try again some time next two successive days. Have party completely ready at SE corner of field. Signal if safe to land. Confirm OK.'

The girls hugged each other. The men threw their hats in the air. All they had to do was cross a field and the planes would appear as if by magic to whisk them away. The hardships they had faced in Albania, the gruelling hours of walking up icy mountain trails, the risk of running into Nazi patrols, the hunger and fear looked to be behind them.

Only Smith didn't look happy but stood among the jubilant nurses and medics with a frown on his face.

'What's wrong?' asked Andrea.

'We took too long to decode the message. It's nine o'clock in the morning on December 29. We are a day late.'

Where a moment ago were loud voices congratulating one another, now were tense and disappointed faces.

'I didn't hear any planes. Did you?' asked Andrea.

'They didn't come because we didn't confirm their transmission,' Smith said. 'But don't worry. You heard what they said. They will try again. I will radio them right away.'

They contacted Cairo again and again that afternoon but couldn't get through.

* * *

It took another day but finally the details had been arranged. The planes were coming to rescue them in the morning of December 31. After fifty-three days in Albania, they would be on the way back to base. They would be safe. They would be reunited with their friends and colleagues. They would no longer be in enemy territory, relying on the kindness of strangers.

But even after they were gone, Nicole would still remain. 'How can I get on the plane and leave my sister behind?' Andrea asked Smith on the evening before the rescue.

'You are not leaving her behind. You are leaving her to us. If she's still alive, she's in good hands.'

Smith's words, *If she's still alive*, made Andrea wince like she was in pain. Since the day she had been separated from Nicole, she didn't allow herself to admit a possibility that her sister might die. If Nicole died, where would it leave Andrea, her twin, her other half? Nicole was a part of her, and if she was gone, how could Andrea go on?

While they waited for the appointed hour, they were busy sewing yellow parachute panels together. When the time came, they would position the panels in a cross on the ground, signalling to the planes that it was safe to land.

The needle seemed to have a life of its own in Andrea's hands. It kept falling to the floor, prickling her and drawing blood. Her hands were trembling from hunger and exhaustion. Every time she managed a stitch, it looked awkward and crooked, something a child would make. Other nurses were doing much better. Their sewing was almost finished.

Renee moved closer to Andrea. 'Let me help you with that. It's not hard, once you get the hang of it.'

'Thank you,' whispered Andrea, biting her lip, wondering why she had once been afraid of the head nurse. Now that she got to know her, she realised Renee was one of the kindest people she had ever met. The needle flew in Renee's hand. Five minutes later, the parachute panels were finished. 'Where did you learn how to do this?' asked Andrea.

'My mother was a seamstress. She taught me everything she knew. For as long as I can remember, I've been sewing hems for her. I hated it as a child but it was the only way I could spend time with her. She was always working to put food on the table for me and my three siblings. Dad never helped. Even though he was always around, I feel that Mother raised us all on her own. She loved us so much.'

'Loved?' Andrea's needle paused in the air. She glanced at Renee's tired face. 'Where is your mother now?'

'She died when I was eighteen.'

Andrea placed her hand on Renee's. 'I'm so sorry,' she said.

'That's why I volunteered. Mother was the kindest person I knew. If she lived to see this war, she would want to do something about it, if only in her own little way. To help people, to make a difference. I am here to honour her memory.'

'She would have been so proud of you if she could see you now.'

'She would have been proud of my brothers too. They are out there somewhere, fighting the Nazis and the Japanese. Haven't heard from any of them in over a year.'

'When the war is over, you will.'

'I hope so. But what if I don't? What if the war is over and they never come back?'

'I bet our loved ones back home and our colleagues in Catania think the same thing about us. And yet, here we are, safe and alive and waiting to get back. I bet your brothers are out there, counting days until they can come back home, just like we are.'

The night before the rescue, Andrea barely slept. Her dreams were filled with death spirals and deafening explosions. In the morning, she couldn't eat a bite.

'Are you ready to go home?' asked Brian. Unlike her, he was chipper and excited.

Her ankle was throbbing. Her head was aching. 'I'm dreading the walk to the airfield. Smith said it's four hours away.'

'If all goes according to plan, this will be the last march we will ever have to do.'

On the way to the airfield, everyone was singing and laughing, telling jokes and teasing one another. They were all walking faster than normal, as if the prospect of rescue gave them wings. Andrea's ankle was throbbing when she put her weight on it but she did her best to keep up, limping after the rest of the group as quickly as she could. And all through that final march, she waited for a miracle. She was watching the road behind them and the road ahead of them, hoping to see a messenger approach Smith with news of her sister. But there was no messenger and no news. They continued ahead without interruption.

She wondered if Brian noticed her reluctance as she walked down a mountain trail that morning. While the others were celebrating, she looked down at the snow under her feet and barely said a word. She waited for him to ask if she was all right, if something was bothering her, but he didn't even look at her, too busy chatting with the pilots. It was Renee who said, 'I know it's hard. Getting on the plane when your sister is still in Albania. But you are doing the right thing.'

'I feel like I'm betraying her. Leaving her behind.'

'There is nothing you can do for Nicole while you are stuck here. But once you are back on base, you can go to the general, you can demand that they send a rescue party to Berat. What did Smith say to you?'

'That they are looking for her.'

'Then you have nothing to worry about. They will find her.'

'How do you know?'

'They found us, didn't they?'

They stopped in the woods for a bite to eat. It started snowing again, large fluffy flakes falling on the grey slush under their feet, landing on their shoulders and their smiling, hopeful faces. Smith offered them some cornbread. Andrea thought this might be the last time they would break bread in Albania. If the planes came for them, in a matter of hours they would be back in Italy.

'How many planes are we expecting?' she asked Smith.

'They didn't say but it will be several. You girls will be the first to board, then the men.'

'What about you? Are you coming?'

'I'm staying behind. My job in Albania is not done yet.'

When all the cornbread was gone, they packed up and continued to walk. The ground was grey, the trees silver with frost. After four hours of walking, they didn't talk much, so focussed were they on not slipping on ice. Andrea was at the back of the procession, listening to Carrie talk about her short ballet career. 'I danced on stage in front of thousands. Everyone in my hometown knew my name. They all thought I was meant for stardom.' To prove her point, she performed a pirouette in the snow and nearly fell.

'What happened?'

'I got married. He didn't want me to dance in front of people. It made him jealous. So I stopped and became a nurse. Now I wish I hadn't listened to him. Dancing had always been my dream.'

'Can you go back to it after the war?' Andrea asked.

'My husband won't like it. Sometimes we have to clip our wings to get our happily-ever-after,' said Carrie.

Why can't you have both? Andrea wanted to ask, thinking of all the ways she had had to clip her wings, of the friends she no longer spoke to, the special occasions at her parents' house she had missed, the Christmases, birthdays and Thanksgivings, the children she'd never had.

When Andrea turned around the bend in the road, she found that everybody had stopped.

'We are here,' said Smith.

In the valley below lay the airfield. Andrea saw vehicles zooming around, looking like toy cars from above, with tiny people jumping in and out. Smith surveyed the scene through his binoculars. He looked frustrated and upset.

'What? What can you see?' Everyone wanted to know.

'German tanks, armoured cars, trucks and soldiers all over the place.'

Andrea's heart fell. The rescue had been so close. They had risked their lives to get here and now all that was left was descending into the valley below and waiting for the planes to pick them up. But it was impossible. The Germans stood between them and safety. Everything they had hoped for, everything they had worked for had been dashed by the enemy presence.

Smith looked at his watch. 'It's almost time. The planes will be here any moment.'

'What are we going to do?' Renee whispered.

No one replied and the only sound was the wind rustling the crosses they had made out of parachutes.

Suddenly, they heard the engines. The deafening roar made the Germans stop what they were doing and look up into the sky. Andrea couldn't believe her eyes when she saw two P-38s circling the area. A British Wellington bomber and two C-47 transport aircraft followed. The Lockheed P-38 Lightning fighters kept them company to make sure they were safe.

The planes flew low over the hill and circled the area once, twice, three times, searching in vain for the parachute crosses on the ground. Andrea saw heartbreak on every face as they watched the rescue party, so close and yet, unattainable. If they ran down the hill and waved, the pilots would see them. But so would the Germans with their machine guns. Minutes passed and no one moved. As the planes buzzed overhead, not a word was spoken. Finally, not seeing the agreed signal, the pilots turned back. Soon, the roar of their engines fell quiet but the group of Americans remained as if frozen to the ground, looking at the spot in the sky where the last of the planes had disappeared.

After a long silence, Smith commanded a retreat into the mountains. 'We can't stay here. We have to keep moving or the Germans will catch up with us.'

'What a glorious sight though,' said Thrasher, his face grim.

'If I live for a thousand years, I will never forget it. All these planes, just for us.'

'Don't worry. It was our first attempt. The good news is, a lot of effort is being thrown into your rescue. If they did it for us once, they will do it again. They won't give up and neither will we. We will return to Gjirokastër and once the Germans are gone, we can try again,' said Smith.

But there was no more trying after that. Dark clouds moved into the area, a snowstorm broke out and the wind howled outside their windows. The ground visibility became non-existent, extinguishing any hope of air evacuation.

Chapter 12

Frozen in Time

As suddenly as he had appeared, Flamur was gone one day, without so much as a thank you or a goodbye. Nicole woke up one morning and went up the little ladder to change his dressings but he was no longer there. She was worried at first but Nani assured her his nephew was feeling better and had returned home to try and rebuild his shop. Bizarrely, he took the pebbles he had won during their game of poker and the poems she had read to him. Even though he rarely spoke, the house seemed quieter without him.

Now that Flamur no longer needed her, Nicole barely left the cellar. During those long days and even longer nights, Darren became her world. She fell asleep and woke up in his arms. She lost every card game but took her revenge at chess. They read to each other and talked, grateful the German voices didn't reach them in their quiet haven, or the machine-gun fire, the rifle shots, the screams of terror.

It was nine in the morning and in the living room upstairs, the sun would be peering through the badly drawn curtains, filling the house with light and life. But in the cellar, it might as well have been the middle of the night. It was always dark and damp and cold. In the light of the candle, Nicole was looking at Darren's sleeping face, wondering why she hadn't told him about the documents yet, or the plans to take them out of Berat. What was she so afraid of?

He stirred and opened his eyes. 'Have you been watching me?' he asked.

She nodded. 'I hadn't seen you for nine years. I want to remember what you look like.'

He reached for her. 'I never forgot what you looked like. Not for a moment.'

The candle flickered and died. The cellar plunged into darkness. She felt his arms around her, pulling her close. His lips on her lips, his hands growing more impatient, stroking her hair and face, slowly moving down. To be touched again, to feel the long-forgotten fire stirring inside her, was a miracle and a revelation. She had not felt this way since the day he left her, but here it was again, instant and burning, her desire making her forget the years without him, as if no time had passed at all, as if they had never been apart.

'I don't want you to hurt yourself. You are still recovering,' she whispered, feeling breathless and frightened, like a virgin on her wedding night.

'I'll be fine.'

But she put up her hand, trying to stop him, even though every fibre of her body was screaming for him to continue. It didn't feel right and she needed to tell him that. If only she could find the right words. She couldn't speak because he was kissing her like his life depended on it, and so she kissed him back, passionately, hungrily, like she was starving and he was here to feed her. She had forgotten what it felt like, to be loved and desired, but her body seemed to remember exactly what to do. As he held her in his arms, it remembered every touch and embrace of the past, and the memory of it made her burn. It was impossible to stop, to tear herself away from him, not when she needed him more than anything in the world, and he needed her. But she had to stop. She placed the palm of her hand on his chest and whispered, 'I'm sorry, I can't.'

His hands moved away from her. Instantly she felt cold and sad inside. 'Am I moving too fast?' he asked. 'Is it too soon?'

Not fast enough, she wanted to tell him. *Not soon enough.* 'It's not that. I want to do this right. I want to speak to Anthony first, tell him everything, ask for a divorce. Even though neither of us wanted this marriage, even though we were forced into it, we married in church, before God.'

'Didn't you tell me he hasn't exactly been faithful to you over the years?'

'I'm not doing it for him. I'm doing it for me. For my conscience. What if God sees me break my wedding vows and turns away from us? What if we do this and something bad happens?'

'Nothing bad is going to happen. I promise.'

'I'm sorry.'

'You have nothing to be sorry for. I understand and I'm happy to wait.'

'You are?' She searched for his hand in the dark and brought it to her lips.

'Of course. We have our whole lives to be together. I waited for nine years. I can wait a few more months.'

'Thank you,' she whispered.

It was quiet in their cellar, the air so still, so peaceful. The real world, the terrifying, soul destroying place embroiled in a war that felt like it would never end, the place that was burning, exploding and tearing itself apart, seemed a universe away. It was just the two of them in their special place, safe and content. Love instead of hatred, hope instead of fear. Her hand was on his heart and she could feel how fast it was beating. It hadn't been easy for her, coming here, doing her bit, leaving her son behind. This road had been hard but it had led her to *him*. Somehow, she was exactly where she was supposed to be. After all these years, it felt like a miracle, God's blessing.

'I can't wait to introduce you to our son. You are going to be amazed by him. He's an incredible boy.'

'Takes after his mother,' he whispered. 'I know I missed eight years of his life but I want to be a real father to him. I want us to be a family. I want to marry you.'

'You do?' She let go of his hand and started to cry.

'If I knew my marriage proposal would upset you so much, I would have kept quiet.'

'I'm just so happy,' she whispered, nestling into his body, relishing his warmth and the way his arms felt around her.

'I want to be there for my son. Two weeks ago, I didn't even know he existed. But now he's the most important thing in the world. You and him both.'

'Is that the only reason you would be marrying me? For our son?' She pinched him to show she was only joking.

'Of course not. I would be marrying you because you are the love of my life. What do you say? Will you marry me?'

'Of course I will.' She buried her head in his shoulder and cried harder, whispering to him that these were tears of joy, that it was one of the happiest days of her life, that the thought of Darren, Leon and herself living together like a family was more than she could take, that it was all she had ever wanted.

Darren said, his arm around her, 'We will buy a house by the sea, just like you've always wanted. We can live somewhere warm, just the three of us. But it won't be the three of us forever. We'll have more children. Would Leon like a brother or sister?'

'He's been asking for one for years.'

'We'll give him two or three. Maybe four.'

'Four, really?' She giggled.

'When all this is behind us, we'll do nothing but have babies. What do you think?'

She thought it was the most wonderful thing anyone had ever said to her. For the first time since she had left home and crossed the ocean to war, she had a clear vision of her future. When she imagined her life back home, the life she had been dreaming of in the dark of night, the mundane and the routine, everything she had missed so much, she saw the faces of people she loved. Darren, her son, her sister. And she was comforted and no longer afraid.

* * *

In the morning, Nani came down to the cellar with some goat's cheese on a plate. He watched them eat without a word. When they were finished, he said, 'I have good news for you. We've been in touch with SOE agents at a place called Seaview. They located a group of Americans and are expecting them any day.'

Nicole perked up. 'They are safe?'

'They are safe.'

She jumped to her feet and hugged Nani, who seemed stunned. 'Thank you, Nani. As long as I live, I will not forget your kindness.'

He laughed. 'I haven't done anything. And I haven't told you the best part yet.'

'There is something better than this?'

'Two SOE officers are on their way here. They will take you out of Berat in a truck, drive you to the coast and put you on a boat to Italy.'

'There are patrols on every road. How will we leave?'

'My brother will help. He has connections in this town. Do you still have the papers he gave you?'

She nodded, overjoyed.

'I want you to know that you are always welcome here. When the war is over, we might meet in America,' Nani said.

'We'll be delighted to see you.'

Nani's words gave her wings and she felt like flying, soaring with joy above the fear, above the war. In a few days, they would be on their way to safety. She would find her sister. They would return home, where a new life with the man she loved would begin. Sometimes she had to pinch herself because it seemed like a dream. And other times the worst of her would get the better of her and she would doubt everything. It was war. Every day, people died. All she had to do was climb the little ladder to hear the screams of pain outside their windows that left her scared and ashamed because she could do nothing to help. What if her happily-ever-after was snatched away when she least expected it? During these moments of doubt, she would look at Darren and instantly feel better. One glimpse of his face was enough to make her believe in miracles.

She wondered when they would leave. Every time she pressed for details, Nani told her they had to wait. They had their identity papers. Their bags were packed. They were ready to go at a moment's notice. She didn't have any belongings with her, only the few items of clothing Goni had lent her and a book she received as a gift from Agnesa. Leaving the house that had become like a safe haven for them, even in the midst of the German occupation, the house where she had encountered so much kindness and love, where she had lived some of the happiest days of the last ten years, filled her with blinding, debilitating fear. She didn't think she could find the courage she needed to venture outside where danger lurked behind every corner. She didn't want to shatter the illusion of peace they had created. There were times when she wanted to stay like this forever, hidden away from it all with Darren by her side. But she knew it was impossible. They had to leave so their lives could begin.

To take her mind off her fears, she busied herself with cleaning and cooking, anything to help Goni who in her condition was feeling unwell and exhausted. What free time she had she spent with Darren, who was getting stronger every day.

She must have been especially tired one afternoon because she had fallen asleep at the table with her head on her hands. The sun was just beginning to set, throwing its last rays her way from the open window. Through the drowsy mist inside her head, she heard Nani's voice. For a few confused moments, she didn't know where she was. She had been dreaming of her childhood home, of her dog Grizzly playing with his favourite toy, growling and snarling like he was a ferocious lion instead of a miniature poodle. When she opened her eyes, for a second she expected to find herself in her bedroom, with the blinds down and her fairy princess light on. Suddenly, there was Nani's face leaning over her. She almost cried out.

'Be ready tomorrow morning,' he said. 'My brother received a radio transmission from Seaview. Before the sun comes up, you will leave.'

She sat up, all traces of sleep gone. 'We'll be ready.'

'If they stop you, look down while they examine your documents. You don't want them to see your blue eyes and question your identity. Whatever you do, don't speak. Or they will know right away you are not who you are pretending to be. And be brave.'

'We'll be brave,' said Nicole, hiding her shaking hands behind her back. She took a deep breath, trying to calm herself.

She spent the morning reading to Darren and helping Goni sew the hems of some dresses. She wasn't good at it but it passed the time and took her mind off the next morning when the truck would come and they would be forced to leave the safety of the house that now felt like home. At midday, Agnesa came over, bringing a small gift for Nicole and Darren. Nicole looked in wonder at the kitchen towel with a map of Albania embroidered on it. Agnesa had marked their journey across Albania on the map in red stitches and placed a heart where their house in Berat stood. 'Don't forget, even after you leave, this will always be your home. Our door is always open,' she said.

Nicole thanked her with tears in her eyes, tracing the intricate needlework with her finger. 'I will treasure it forever.' She knew it wasn't just the towel she would treasure but the memories she had made with these people, strangers only a few weeks ago who in a short period of time had become more than friends. They had become family. It occurred to Nicole that she might never see them again. She would never know if they survived the war. The thought broke her heart. 'Take care of yourself,' she said to Agnesa. 'Stay safe. I will leave you my address. Write when it's safe to do so.'

After a tearful farewell, Agnesa left. Goni and Nani went out on their daily quest for food. It was just Darren and Nicole in the house, curled up next to each other on the cold floor of the cellar, counting down minutes until sundown.

'In the truck, stay low in case there is a shooting,' he said. 'And stay close to me. Once we are out of Berat, it will be easier for us.'

'What if something goes wrong? What if we are discovered?'

'Don't be afraid. Think of Leon. We are doing this for him.'

She decided she would do that from now on. Every time she felt afraid, she would imagine her son's face.

She was upstairs, getting some food for Darren and herself when she heard a loud knock. An angry German voice demanded she opened the door or else. Another knock was heard, followed by the sound of stomping boots. Nicole froze with some cornbread in her hands, afraid to make a sound. She was certain the intruders could hear her beating heart. How could they not? It sounded deafening inside the little house. A second later, a sharp blow broke the door down. Nicole opened her mouth to scream, only no sound came out.

Two Nazi officers marched inside, similar like brothers, with their blond hair, blue eyes and matching expressions of resentment on their faces. Nicole felt for the documents in her pocket. She was about to offer them to the officers, only they never asked. They barely looked in her direction. For a moment, she was grateful Darren was in the cellar, hidden away under a layer of rocks. They didn't have dogs with them. They would never find him and soon would be on their way, leaving Darren and Nicole to prepare for their departure. This time tomorrow, the two of them would be in a truck, moving away from Berat, and with luck would never see another German patrol again. All this she was telling herself, trying to convince herself it would all work out, that their lives didn't hang on the thinnest of threads, when, suddenly, something terrible happened. The Germans barged past Nicole, kicked the rug out of the way and pulled the trap door open.

Gasping with horror, she watched as they descended the ladder and said something to Darren, a barrage of angry German words she didn't understand. He said something back and they laughed, a terrifying sound that made her gasp. Next thing she knew, Darren appeared in the living room, pushed up the stairs by the two officers.

Her heart nearly flew out of her chest. She struggled to breathe, like there was no oxygen left in the house. 'Stop,' she cried in Albanian, the unfamiliar word coming out with difficulty. 'He is wounded. He can't walk.'

'Wounded, is he?' said the older and scarier looking of the officers in bad English, staring straight at Darren. 'Looks fine to me.' He yanked Darren by his arm. 'Move, Captain. We don't have all day.'

They shoved him towards the door and a pair of handcuffs closed around his wrists.

Nicole was paralysed with fear. A scream of terror died on her lips. She knew she had to do something. She couldn't remain there while they took Darren away and broke her heart. She opened her mouth to shout at the two officers, to throw herself at them, to singlehandedly fight two heavyweights armed to their teeth. She was prepared to do anything as she watched her future be snatched away from her when Darren whispered in her ear, so that only she could hear, 'Stay quiet, for our son.'

Shaking, petrified, silent, she watched them pushing him out of the house and into the churning cauldron of Berat's main road. When the door closed behind them, she emitted a pain-filled shriek and rushed to the window but before she even got there, she heard the sound of an engine. She pulled the curtain aside and saw a truck drive off. And only when it disappeared around the corner did she drop to her knees and cry.

She remained like this, in a desperate heap on the floor with her head in her hands and her eyes shut, in her mind seeing his face as he was taken away in handcuffs. She heard his voice, telling her to be brave for their son. But she couldn't be brave, not without him by her side. What were the Nazis going to do to him? Why did they take him away but leave her behind? A sudden realisation chilled her to the bone. This had not been a random patrol. They had known exactly who they were looking for.

Chapter 13

Towards the Light

It took another three days of reading and poker and strumming their guitar, of reminiscing and daydreaming and wondering what their future would bring before they got a chance to leave Gjirokastër. Finally, when the Germans moved on from the nearby villages and the roads were safe, Smith gathered them together and told them they would continue their journey towards Seaview. To make up for the lost time, they would have to walk faster and cover more distance each day. Easier said than done when some of them were injured and others sick, and snow continued to fall in white clumps the size of a fist onto the grey, frozen ground. Fortunately, Smith was able to procure more mules from the villagers and those who couldn't walk were able to take turns riding. The group was overjoyed but when they set out, they found that, instead of making things easier and speeding things up, the mules slowed their progress down. The animals were old and kept falling in the snow, dropping the gear they carried, which then had to be retrieved and repacked.

Andrea was grateful for her mule because she didn't think she could take another moment of trudging through heavy snow. But even riding in these conditions was challenging. The wind made it hard for her to breathe. The skin on her face was red and peeling in places. Her clothes were damp. She had forgotten what it felt like to be dry, warm and full.

In the evening, after many hours of battling with the elements, they arrived at a tiny dot on the map by the name of Tërbaç. Just like in many other villages, the men were gone and only women and children remained. The closer the group got to the coast, the sadder the settlements became, most of them burnt to the ground or destroyed by shelling. No one came out to meet them. No one welcomed them or offered them food. The children were no longer playing ball but sitting outside their houses, staring at the newcomers with empty, hungry eyes. Even though it was the middle of the day, the villages seemed dark to Andrea, filled with sadness and suffering.

The little house they had been taken to was almost as cold as the woods had been. There was a hole in the roof and a large part of one of the walls was missing. The wind howled inside the rooms and the snow fell on the floor, the furniture, their tired faces as if they were still out in the open, fighting for every inch, every step along the slippery trail. A woman clad in black came in and offered them some olives from a barrel. It was an unexpected treat, and the nurses refilled their bowls again and again. Only after they had had their fill did they notice that the olives were rotten.

After dinner, Smith gathered them together. 'We are very close to the coast. We could stop here or we could keep going in the dark and get there in a few hours. I suggest we push on.'

'The people are exhausted. So are the mules,' said Baggs.

'The village has no blankets and no food. We won't get a good rest here anyway. The Nazis are not far off. We are not safe here. If we reach the caves tonight, we will be.'

As always in a moment of doubt, they took a vote. On one hand, there was the promise of rest, a cold and uncomfortable floor but somewhere they could stretch out and close their eyes, for a few hours forgetting all about the cold and the Nazi patrols. On the other hand, an opportunity to reach their goal. No matter how tired they were, the choice was clear and the vote was unanimous. They all opted to continue walking. They would march in the dark, they would risk collapsing from exhaustion but they would not stop.

'It's settled,' said Smith. 'We set out in half an hour.'

When it was time to go and they lined up by the side of the road, the moon hid behind the cloud and they could barely see each other's faces, let alone the trail in front of them. No one complained, even though Andrea suspected many of them wanted to. Even Liz, who was usually the first one to cry, seemed determined to make it to the coast, the promised land that was suddenly within their reach. Smith accompanied them for a while and then moved ahead to make sure the path was clear and there were no German patrols on the way. The trail was steep and their progress was slow, while the night air grew colder. It hurt Andrea's throat to take shallow, frequent breaths as she rode her mule.

Brian walked next to her, his shoulders slumped under the weight of his bags. Taking a closer look at him, Andrea wondered when he had become so thin, when his beard had become so grey. He seemed tired, his eyes black with lack of sleep. 'Why don't you put your bags on the mule?' she suggested, feeling sorry for him. 'It will be easier for you.'

'I don't want to overload the poor animal.' But he placed his bags on the mule anyway. 'Freezing, isn't it?' He rubbed his hands together and blew into them. 'When we come back, I will never live anywhere cold again. We can buy a cabin in Hawaii where it never snows. We'll have summer all year round. We'll never wear winter coats. Can you imagine?'

'Never go ice skating or skiing? Never build a snowman? Never have a white Christmas again? No, I can't imagine.'

'We'll go surfing and sailing. We'll swim in the sea and sunbathe on the black sand of Maui, while sipping cocktails. We'll have a swimming pool. We'll buy a boat. What do you say?'

She shook her head, afraid of this new plan, in case he meant it this time. If Brian made up his mind, there was no hope in the world of talking him out of it. 'I want to be close to my parents. I lost so much precious time. I have barely spoken to my dad since you and I got married. I want to fix it. This ordeal showed me what's important.'

'And what is that?'

'Family. The people we love.'

'I thought I was your family,' he barked, before picking up his bags and marching off.

The moon appeared from behind the cloud, shining its cold light on the group, and Andrea watched Brian for a few moments as he trudged through the snow, which grew ankle deep by the time they reached the crest of the mountain trail around eleven o'clock that night. He fell behind and she continued alone for a while, until Renee caught up to her. Andrea enjoyed the older woman's company. Her optimism was contagious. Renee had an ability to reach through the darkness of Andrea's mood and take her mind off her worries.

Despite their best efforts, they didn't reach the coast that night. When they arrived at the village of Dukat at four in the morning, they were forced to stop because they couldn't walk another step, and nor could the animals. They collapsed on the floor of their temporary accommodation and were asleep in seconds, even before their hosts had a chance to offer them some food.

When Andrea woke up a few hours later, she felt like she had spent the night inside a boxing ring. Her whole body ached. Her stomach was hurting. She felt dizzy and unwell. She tried to remember the last time she had eaten a proper meal and couldn't. Luckily, the villagers invited them to breakfast and offered them the stew they had come to love and some cornbread that no longer seemed as terrible as the first time they tried it.

Smith allowed them to stay in the village all day, resting and recovering. Setting out while it was still light was too dangerous. They had to wait for the cover of darkness to avoid being spotted by a German patrol. After a meagre dinner, the group gathered in the town square, eager to get going. Even though their feet were a bloody mess and they were malnourished and weak, the proximity of the coast filled them with the strength they needed to make it to their destination. To their surprise, Smith told them they would not be walking that evening. He pointed to a vehicle parked nearby. 'The village elders are kindly allowing us to borrow their truck. It will save us hours of travelling.'

The vehicle was old, its hood orange with rust, the back covered with mud. But at that moment, it looked to Andrea like the most advanced piece of machinery she had ever seen. She stared at the miracle on wheels in front of her, unable to believe her eyes, while her comrades were cheering and congratulating one another.

Smith raised his hand and the voices fell quiet. 'We will make two trips,' he said. 'The nurses will go first.'

'Not possible,' said the driver, one of the villagers who welcomed them when they had first arrived. 'I only have enough gas for one trip.'

They piled in as best as they could. They would all have to stand shoulder to shoulder the entire trip but no one seemed to mind. The thought of not having to walk through the blizzard, of covering the difficult terrain not on foot or mule but on wheels, cheered them all up.

It was seven in the evening when the truck barrelled down a rough and winding road, leaving the village behind. Andrea only had three hours of sleep but she didn't feel tired. If she stood on tiptoes, over Carrie's shoulder she could see the shadows of the trees zooming past at a great speed.

'Beats walking, doesn't it?' said Renee, grinning.

'Beats riding a mule, for sure,' replied Tory. 'Mine was evil and kept trying to bite me.' She showed the girls a red mark on her hand where the mule had snapped at her.

'I wish they'd given us this truck at the start of our journey,' said Andrea. 'We would have been there by now. Look how fast we are going.'

As soon as she said that, the truck slowed down and then stopped altogether. The engine fell quiet. They asked each other what was happening but no one could tell for sure. Then they heard Smith's voice, ordering them to jump out and hide.

They did as they were told, crawling under bushes and behind trees. Andrea's heart was pounding. She watched through the branches as a German soldier rode past on his motorcycle, not stopping to look at the abandoned truck on the side of the road. They waited a few minutes for the rumble of the motorbike engine to quieten down and climbed back on. A few minutes of driving later, however, they had to do it all over again when a German truck appeared on the road.

'At this rate, we'll never get there,' said Carrie. 'The mules were faster.'

This time, the driver noticed the truck and stopped, using a large spotlight mounted over the cab to pore over the area where they were hiding. Andrea tried to stay as still as she could. What would happen to them if the German spotted them? They were so close, they could smell freedom. The scent was carried on the breeze, the salt of the sea, the seagulls' woeful cries. She held her breath and prayed.

Thankfully, a few moments later the light disappeared and the soldier continued on his way. For the next half an hour, the truck drove like the devil was chasing it, flying over the bumps in the road, shaking and screeching and bouncing, while they huddled in the back, watching dark shapes of pine trees and oaks flying past. Andrea held on for dear life, petrified of the speed and the icy roads, and at the same time, wishing the driver would go faster.

Suddenly, the truck stopped again. Andrea asked, 'What is it this time? Another German vehicle? I didn't hear the sound of an engine.'

But it wasn't a German vehicle. They were almost at the

safe house and the truck couldn't go any further. Smith told them they would have to walk a quarter of a mile though the shrubbery. Andrea leaned on Renee's arm because her ankle was bothering her. Brian came over and offered to take her bags. She agreed.

The sky was the darkest indigo over their heads as they hiked up a steep trail. Andrea was grateful for Renee. If it wasn't for her, she would have fallen. She needed sleep and something to eat but all she could think about was Seaview – and safety – only a quarter of a mile away.

'What is all that?' she asked Smith when they stopped on top of a hill. The valley below was studded with lights, like shimmering diamonds in the dark.

'That is Vlorë.'

Vlorë, the coastal town they had crossed the country to find. Andrea stood still, her hand on her heart, looking at the darkness before her that hid the waters of the Adriatic. They had fought the elements for two months to reach them. For many weeks they had seemed unattainable, ephemeral like a dream. And yet, here they were, right in front of them, and across them was freedom. They almost made it, even if this last stretch felt tougher than anything they had ever done before.

Smith dispatched a messenger to Seaview to tell the men to prepare for the party's arrival. Slowly they made their way down the mountainside. As they descended, Andrea's knees threatened to buckle under her.

'Not long now,' Renee said, patting her hand.

It took an hour of hobbling in the dark, tripping over rocks, sliding on ice. But when Andrea saw the caves, when she heard Smith telling them it was the promised Seaview, she forgot all about how exhausted she was. And so did the others, it seemed. They laughed and joked and teased one another. 'Hey, Baggs,' cried Thrasher. 'You promised you would roll down the hill all the way to the water when we got to the coast. Here is your chance.'

'That was seven weeks ago,' Baggs replied, chuckling. 'I'm too tired now.'

They watched with excitement as three SOE agents rushed to greet them, shaking their hands, giving out chocolate and cigarettes, welcoming them to their headquarters. Although everyone was desperate for some sleep and food, they were eager to know when they would be taken across the sea. No one wanted to stay in Albania for a minute longer than was absolutely necessary.

'The moonlight is too bright,' said Smith. 'The German patrol will spot the boat right away. We need to wait for a darker night. It will take a few days.'

They were so close, they could see the waters that would carry them to freedom. They had waited for two months for this moment. They had walked for hundreds of miles and suffered hunger and cold and the German bullets. And still they had to wait.

They grumbled with disappointment at the injustice of it all as they settled down to rest. Many were too exhausted to wait for food and fell asleep right where they were sitting, on the floor. Unexpectedly, Andrea received the best news of her life. Smith came over and told her someone had been in touch from Berat about her sister. Two SOE officers were on their way to retrieve her. Andrea was so happy to hear it, she forgot all about how tired she was and jumped and danced on the spot to the amusement of the rest of the group. When she was done celebrating, one of the British officers offered her his own bed made of cardboard with a thin mattress and blanket. It felt to her like she was resting on a four-poster bed in a luxury hotel, the likes of which Brian used to take her to when they first met. For the first time since she had been separated from her sister, she was asleep in seconds, without a care in the world.

When she woke up, Andrea couldn't tell what time it was. The caves were illuminated by torches and unless she walked outside, she wouldn't know if it was day or night. When she asked, she was surprised to learn she had slept for eighteen hours. 'You needed it,' Brian said.

'What about you? Did you sleep?'

'A little.'

He looked like he hadn't slept at all. He hadn't shaved in two months, and the beard and the black circles under his eyes gave him a crazed look, like he was a treasure-mad pirate. 'Have a rest. We are almost there. Nothing to worry about now,' she said.

'I can think of plenty to worry about,' he mumbled, getting comfortable on the floor.

Others played cards, smoked, spoke about their lives back home, ate food out of tin cans and drank tea, while Andrea had only one thought on her mind. She found Smith and asked if he had any more news of her sister. He told her no, not since the day before. After a bite to eat, Andrea opened the book she had been carrying in her backpack when they crash-landed. *Anna Karenina* had been her favourite novel since she was a teenager. All that angst and suffering, all that drama and longing for something one couldn't have, she couldn't get enough of it. There was one line she kept coming back to. 'All happy families are alike; each unhappy family is unhappy in its own way.' Based on years of observation, watching her parents grow further and further apart in a marriage of convenience; watching her sister come to terms with her loveless marriage and trying to make the most of it by dedicating herself to her son; watching her friends struggle in their quest for love, she came to understand that happily-ever-after was nothing but a myth, a phantom they were all chasing but would never find.

And yet, everyone who knew them believed Andrea and Brian were the happiest of couples. They were the couple everyone aspired to be. She hid her doubts well, almost like she was ashamed of them. Almost like she blamed herself for what was happening in her marriage. No one knew what was in her heart, not even her sister. When she met Brian, what she felt for him blinded her to everything else. She didn't pause to think if they were compatible, if he would ever compromise with her, if life with him would bring her joy. She donned a set of rose-coloured glasses and overlooked all the obvious warning signs, finding an excuse for all of them. Nothing mattered except him. He was a miracle she had never expected. How could their relationship be wrong when she had finally found true love?

And only recently she began to wonder if perhaps her mother had been right all along, if love wasn't enough after all, if love wasn't everything.

When Brian woke up, hours later, she said, 'Why did you divorce Laura?' She had been wondering about his ex-wife. In all the years they had been together, he had never mentioned anything about their relationship. And she had never asked.

'Why are you bringing it up?' He looked tired, cranky, belligerent. Perhaps it wasn't the right time for this conversation. But she was done walking on eggshells.

'We've never talked about it. It's a big part of your life.'

'I didn't divorce her. She divorced me.'

'What went wrong?'

'When the children came, she changed. She became more demanding. Nothing I ever did was good enough for her. She was never happy. We were always arguing about one thing or other. Who changes the nappies. Who stays up when the baby is crying. Who is clearing the dishes. Our life became one big scorecard.'

'She changed for no reason?'

'Of course she changed for no reason. I hadn't cheated on her. I hadn't lied to her. I hadn't hit her.'

'You haven't cheated on me either,' Andrea whispered, turning away from him.

'I did nothing wrong,' he said.

What about all the things you didn't do? she wanted to ask. But there was little point. It was clear to her that Brian was a man who would never see things from someone else's perspective. He would only ever see himself.

After two months of marching through mud and snow, suddenly they had found themselves with nothing to do but eat and sleep. For the next two days, Andrea didn't move from her bed. She read and wrote in her diary, until Brian came over and tried to read over her shoulder, and she was forced to stop. She thought about her sister. And she wondered about the future.

It was January, a month when everything was in slumber, waiting for a better time, for a new beginning, just like they were waiting for their lives to resume, to pick up where they had left off when they crash-landed in Albania.

Finally, early in the morning of their third day at Seaview, they got the long-awaited news. The wireless operator told them a boat had been sent for them from Italy and the party should be at the water's edge, ready to embark at midnight. The man had barely stopped talking when everyone in the group, even the sullen Brian, jumped up and cheered as loudly as they could. There were fist bumps and hugs and even hats thrown up in the air. Sixteen more hours and they would say goodbye to Albania and all the hardships they had faced.

'Where do you think they will send us next?' Andrea asked Brian as they waited. Andrea could swear the hands of the watch on Brian's wrist had forgotten how to move. 'I don't think I could ever get on another plane. Not after what happened to us.'

'I think this is it for us. We'll be going home.'

Home. Saying the word in her mind filled her with longing, for all the little things she had once taken for granted, for all the things she had missed. In Detroit, much like in Albania, the streets would be hidden under a foot of snow and the trees would be bare, their pitiful, skinny branches reaching for the sky. The snow would no longer be white but muddy slush under her feet. If Andrea were to paint Detroit in winter, she would choose the least attractive of colours, grey, oppressive and dark. And yet, her heart wept for it all as she hid in the cave in Albania and waited for someone else to decide her fate. 'Why do you think we'll be going home?'

'We've spent two months in enemy territory. There are rules in the army about this sort of thing. They won't let us stay in Europe.'

'I'm not leaving Italy until Nicole is back.'

'You might not have much choice,' he said, not looking at her, his voice cold and indifferent, like he was discussing what he wanted for dinner.

At ten-thirty, Smith told them it was time to move. After days cooped up inside the cave, the air outside was brisk and fresh, and made Andrea feel a little dizzy at first. She stood still for a bit, taking big, nervous breaths, wondering if she would always remember this moment. Their time in Albania coming to an end, a new chapter awaiting them.

The party plodded down the steep trail to the small beach. The British SOE officer who carried one of the Handy-Talkies tried to get in touch with the crew on the boat to let them know they were on their way. He pointed the antenna in various directions and even banged the unit on his knee while muttering under his breath that the device was useless and why couldn't he have a walkie-talkie instead. He finally picked up a transmission halfway down the trail. 'I'm getting something. They are out there!' he told them.

It took forty-five minutes to walk from the caves to the beach. It was the easiest walk the group had done since ending up in Albania. After three days of rest, they felt strong and ready for anything. The hope of rescue was like wings behind their backs, propelling them forward, not letting them fall. When they finally reached their destination, some of the nurses ran to the shore and touched the water. 'I can't believe we are here. I can't believe we made it,' they repeated.

'Is the water nice? Warm enough for a swim?' shouted

Shearman, grabbing a nurse closest to him, carrying her to the sea and pretending to throw her in. The nurse shrieked, while Shearman laughed.

'Not so loud, Shearman, or the Nazis will hear you all the way in Berat,' said Thrasher mock-sternly, fighting a smile.

They lit a few signal fires that flickered in the dark, throwing streaks of light across the water.

Brian took Andrea's hand. 'Excited to leave?' he asked. 'I know I am. Finally, we can get on that boat and forget about this place.'

She took her hand away. 'I'm not excited because my sister is staying behind. I can't forget about this place until she's back safely.'

'I know, I didn't mean . . .' He stumbled over his words, was silent for a moment and then added, 'Sorry. I'm just happy we can finally start living the rest of our lives.'

Andrea wanted to tell him she didn't know what the rest of her life was going to look like. Things seemed one way when they came to Albania. They looked completely different two months later, on the night they were leaving. This experience had changed her. It had changed their marriage. It had been a journey not only of survival but of self-discovery. And it was just beginning.

'Look, Shearman, rocks! Why don't you take a couple for your sister?' cried Baggs, throwing a pebble at the red-headed medic.

Shearman bent over and picked up a rock, then another and another.

'I'm just teasing you. You don't have to take any,' said Baggs. 'I don't think your sister will like these. They are grey and dirty, not at all like the holy relic you stole that time.'

'I don't care, I'm taking them. They will always remind me of this moment. What a memory!'

The rest of the group thought it was a great idea. Everyone picked up a pebble. Andrea found one shaped like a heart and placed it inside her pocket.

The men shouted something about a boat, even though Andrea could see nothing but darkness before her, could hear nothing but the waves hitting the shore and their excited voices. She squinted, staring at the black mass of water, until a small rubber boat appeared, manned by a crew of two smiling, waving officers. 'I bet you are happy to see us,' they said, as they helped them into the boat one after another. They made a few trips, taking four or five people at a time to the larger boat that sat idling further out.

Andrea was the last to leave. Until the moment she boarded the small boat, she was waiting for a miracle. Even though she knew it was impossible, until the end she was hoping to see her sister running towards them on the sand.

As they neared the larger vessel, they waited for a wave to lift the small craft higher so they could grab on to the netting and climb aboard. Andrea's hands shook from the tension as she propelled herself up. As she was climbing, she looked back and saw the dark waves churning below her. She nearly cried out in fear.

As soon as the last group was in, the boat began to move towards Italy. While the rest of the group cheered and congratulated one another, Andrea stood in silence, watching the rugged coast of Albania as it disappeared from view. While the others were weeping with joy, Andrea's heart was breaking. She wondered if she would ever see her sister again.

Soon she could no longer make out the land where they had been in mortal danger even before their airplane had touched the ground. They had fought for their survival every single day, overcoming every obstacle, the risk of capture, of falling to their deaths, of freezing or dying of hunger. They had seen German bombs exploding overhead, German aircraft in pursuit, Nazi soldiers overrunning the streets around them. With so much stacked against them, it was a miracle they were still alive. Every step of the way, they were met with kindness. They were welcomed by strangers like they were family. Even though they had only just met them, people were prepared to part with their last piece of bread and risk their lives to help them. As she watched the bleak waters in front of her, trying to catch a glimpse of the Albanian coast before it vanished forever, never to be seen again, Andrea knew that good would always triumph over evil. Despite all the horrors that were happening around them, despite the war and the suffering and the darkness that had descended on earth with Hitler's hordes, the world was still a beautiful place. Albania had taught her that. There was kindness everywhere one looked.

It was two-fifteen in the morning on January 9, sixty-three days after they crashed. Twenty-nine Americans were returning to the Allied territory, while one nurse remained behind.

Chapter 14

Ice and Fire

On shaking knees, like she was learning how to walk, Nicole stepped out of the house and stood on the porch, while around her people moved in slow motion, their eyes to the ground, as if reluctant to witness the horrors that had come to the streets of Berat. After weeks inside the dark cellar and the dimly lit house, she felt overwhelmed for a moment, by the light, the movement, the brisk air that smelt of smoke and burnt flesh. She had forgotten her coat and her boots, leaving the house in what she was wearing when the Nazi officers arrived. The snow landed on her bare skin, her hair, the fabric of her cotton blouse. Her stockinged feet became wet instantly but she didn't even notice.

After a moment's hesitation, she set off down the street teeming with frightened locals and self-assured Germans. When she turned around the corner, she broke into a run. She knew where Agnesa lived. During one of her visits the older woman had pointed out her house from the window. 'You can't miss it,' she had said. 'It's the only building with an orange roof in all of Berat. My husband was fond of the colour orange, God rest his soul. He used to say it's the colour of the sun, the colour of life. Everything in our house looks like a tangerine, the roof, the walls, the rugs on the floor.'

It took ten minutes to fight her way through the crowd and find the orange house. She knocked on the door as hard as she could.

All was quiet at first and she wondered if anyone was at home but continued knocking until her knuckles were sore. Finally, Agnesa opened, her hair a tangled mess, her eyes like saucers. Her face relaxed when she saw Nicole. 'God Almighty,' she exclaimed. 'You made such a racket, I thought it was the Germans. You can't play tricks like this on an old woman.' Agnesa must have seen something in Nicole's face. She stopped talking, watched her closely for a moment and rushed her through the door. 'Is everything all right, dear? You look so pale. And where did you lose your shoes? Did you run all this way barefoot?'

Nicole opened her mouth to tell the older woman everything but suddenly couldn't say a word. Instead, she covered her eyes with her hands and began to cry.

Agnesa put her arms around Nicole and led her into the kitchen. 'Would you like a cup of tea? There is nothing in the world that tea can't make better.'

Nicole shook her head. Even tea couldn't fix the mess she was in. 'Nani. Is he here?' she managed to say.

'He's gone to the market. He'll be back soon. Why don't you tell me what happened?'

It took Nicole a while to find her voice. When she told Agnesa about the knock on the door, the German soldiers and the sudden arrest, the old woman hugged her tight. 'Don't cry,' she said. 'It will be all right.' But Agnesa herself was crying, her tears falling into Nicole's hair. 'Nani will be here soon. He'll know what to do.'

By the expression on the woman's face, Nicole knew she thought there was nothing anyone could do.

'They took him away in front of my eyes,' Nicole whispered. 'And I didn't do anything. I just stood there. I didn't try to stop them, didn't even say a word. I watched Darren leave and did nothing.' She was sobbing now, her shoulders shaking, while the older woman held her and patted her back, like she was settling a toddler.

'What could you possibly have done, child?' Agnesa shook her head with sadness.

'I could have fought back. I had the gun Nani gave me, I should have used it. Then Darren would still be here.' The *what ifs* running through her head nearly made her lose her mind. What if she had listened to Nani and learnt how to shoot? What if she insisted on coming with them and . . . and what? Hijacked the truck? Helped him escape? Nicole knew Agnesa was right. There wasn't much she could have done. But it didn't make her guilt any lighter.

'Don't beat yourself up. You did the right thing. Darren would have wanted you to be safe. He wouldn't want you to do something silly and risk your life,' Agnesa told her.

When Nani returned from the market and Nicole told him everything, he promised to try and find out as much as he could. Nicole begged him to help, to speak to his cousin, to do all in his power to get Darren back. He assured her he would but in his eyes she saw fear. 'Please, Nani,' she cried. 'I spent nine years looking for him. I can't lose him now.'

When Nani left, Nicole sat by the window, wishing she could erase the last few hours of her life, start the day over, do things differently. Outside, the human river was fast-flowing and never-ending, people running, shouting, fighting, panicking. Children were crying, while grown-ups scuttled past with the expression of terror on their faces. In the distance, machine guns sang their eternal song. Nicole looked into every face, hoping to see someone she recognised, waiting for news. Agnesa clucked over her like a mother hen, wanting to know if she needed anything, if she was hungry or thirsty or tired. To every question she would shake her head without turning away from the window. She couldn't rest or eat or drink until she knew he was safe.

After watching the road for what seemed like hours, she would glance at the clock and realise only ten minutes had passed. Suddenly, the time that until now had rushed past seemed to slow down to a crawl. She wished she had more time with him so she could tell him how Leon was scared of the water as a small boy of three and four. He refused to go anywhere near it, even on their family trips to the seaside in summers, when she would spend hours splashing around in the waves, while he built his castles and tunnels in the sand. One day, when he was five, he fell into the river by accident and discovered that not only could he swim perfectly well but that he enjoyed it. There was no getting him out of the water after that. The memory of her son doggy-paddling in the river while calling her name warmed her heart. 'Mama, look, water isn't scary!' he cried, running to her and giving her a wet hug, his hair glistening in the sun, and she picked him up and clasped him close to her chest, whispering, 'Well, aren't you a brave boy!' How much Darren would enjoy this story. She made a mental note to tell it to him as soon as she saw him.

She heard the garden gate open with a creak. Her heart in turmoil, she waited, hoping it was Nani returning with some news. Instead, she saw Flamur walking across the yard. A moment later, the door opened and he disappeared inside the house. She heard his voice and then Agnesa's. They argued about something in Albanian. Nicole lost interest in them, turning back to the road. It was midday, four hours after the arrest. She wondered where Darren was, what he was doing, whether he was all right, whether he was thinking of her. Her mind conjured terrifying images of jail cells and torture chambers, medieval devices designed to crack bones and drive pins under the fingernails, the likes of which they had read about in *Queen Margot* together, when they were younger. She curled into a ball and cried from helplessness and despair, shivering in her still damp clothes.

As she wiped her eyes with a kerchief, telling herself to stop crying, to get herself together because Darren needed her to stay focused, Agnesa appeared in the room, dragging the reluctant Flamur behind her. It looked almost comical, if Nicole was in the mood to laugh – the giant boy being pulled by his tiny grandmother. Agnesa looked furious, while Flamur's eyes darted this way and that, as if looking for an escape.

'This young man has something to tell you,' Agnesa said, giving him one final push. 'I will leave you two alone.'

She disappeared and Flamur was left in front of Nicole, not saying a word. She waited for a bit and then asked, 'Why is your grandmother upset with you?'

He looked so ashamed, standing with his head held low before her. 'I'm sorry,' he muttered.

'Sorry for what?' she asked, smiling at him affectionately to encourage him, to show him there was nothing to be afraid of. He looked so lost and sad all of a sudden, his hands trembling, his eyes damp, the burns on his face angry and red.

'It was me who told the Nazis about Darren,' he said quietly, without looking at her.

'You did what?' She had heard him. She just couldn't understand him. Her brain refused to focus on his words.

'I told the Nazis where to find Darren,' he repeated.

Nicole watched him in silence. She couldn't think of a single thing to say other than 'Why?'

He shrugged.

'I don't understand. For a week you lived with us. You played poker with us. I fed you when you couldn't feed yourself. I held your glass for you. I changed your dressings and looked after you. Why would you do something like that?'

'I didn't tell them about you. You helped me. I will never forget it. I didn't want anything to happen to *you*.'

'What about Darren? What has he done to you?'

Flamur's eyes filled with fresh tears. His gaze remained on the floorboards under his feet. 'I have five younger brothers and sisters. That's a lot of mouths to feed. It breaks my heart to see them cry because they haven't eaten all day. Because of what I did, my family won't starve. We will have food to eat. We won't be threatened or mistreated. Because of what I did, we will live.'

Something was happening to her. The room was spinning before her, the floor was moving under her feet. She had to lean on a chair to steady herself. 'Because of what you did, Darren will die.'

'I'm sorry,' he repeated. 'Afterwards, I felt so bad. I wasn't prepared for that. If I could take it back, I would.'

But Nicole was no longer listening. She turned away from him to the window but couldn't see anything through her tears.

* * *

Since the day she had arrived in Albania, Nicole had known nothing but kindness from the people she met, who welcomed her and fed her, sheltered her and made sure she was safe. They gave her a place to live, a soft mattress to sleep on and food to eat, even as they themselves were starving. They endured German patrols but even at the risk to their lives they wouldn't let her leave. If it wasn't for these people, she might have been arrested, perhaps killed. And yet, she could see how much they were struggling. What Flamur did broke her heart but she couldn't hate him. He wasn't a bad person for choosing to denounce a complete stranger so that his family could live. He was human.

Nicole didn't blame Flamur. She blamed the war.

She remained by the window without food or water until it became dark outside and she could no longer see anything. Nani returned when she had lost all hope of seeing him that evening, when the clock on the wall chimed ten. He sat next to her and watched her face in silence, as if he couldn't bring himself to tell her what he had learnt. Fire was burning bright inside the fireplace, throwing shadows on his face that made him look sad one moment and content the next. 'Nani, what is it? Did you see your brother?'

'I did.'

Once again, silence. She waited. When he didn't say anything, she prodded, 'What did you find out? What did Agron say? Please, tell me. I can't stand the uncertainty.'

All of a sudden, Nani was crying. At first, she thought it was a trick of light. Her own tears made the world around her appear washed out and blurry, like an expressionist painting. She reached her hand out and touched his face. His cheeks were damp. 'What happened, Nani? What's wrong? You can tell me anything.'

But he didn't tell her. He didn't even raise his eyes.

'Nani?' She, too, was terrified. Just like Nani, she wanted to prolong this moment, to cling to hope for as long as she could, before this hope was dashed to pieces. Her voice broke when she asked, 'Where is Darren? What did they do to him?'

He put his hand on hers. She trembled. 'They shot him,' he said. 'The Germans shot him.'

The world seemed to stop for a moment. She could no longer hear the voices outside the window and the traffic moving past. All she heard was the buzzing inside her head. 'No,' she whispered, twisting a handkerchief in her hands until it was torn to pieces. *No, no, no*, she wanted to scream. What Nani told her made no sense. She couldn't believe it without breaking down completely, so she chose not to. 'It's not true. Why would they do such a thing?'

She moved closer to him so she could see his eyes. But he wasn't looking at her. 'I'm so sorry,' he whispered.

'Perhaps Agron was wrong. Perhaps he was talking about someone else. Perhaps he heard rumours that weren't true.'

'He saw it with his own eyes. The truck stopped at an intersection. Darren used it as an opportunity to jump out. He was trying to escape when they shot him in broad daylight.'

Her legs could no longer hold her. She would have fallen to the floor if Nani hadn't caught her. 'Are you all right? Do you want anything? Some water?'

She shook her head.

'Should I get my mother?'

The thought of being alone even for a second filled her with horror. 'No,' she cried. 'Don't go.'

They sat in silence. Only her sobs were heard and the shouts outside. 'Where is he?' she asked. 'Where is Darren?' Saying his name out loud hurt her physically and she groaned in pain. 'Can I see his body?'

'The Germans took it away.'

She rubbed her eyes with her fists and shook her head with such vigour, it hurt her neck. 'I don't believe you. Your brother made a mistake. It's not true.'

'I wish it wasn't.' He took her hands, shaking them, squeezing her fingers. 'I'm so sorry. He was the kindest man. When he first got here, he helped Goni get to the doctor when she thought she was losing the baby. She fainted and he carried her all the way to the hospital. For two hours he carried her and then he stayed with her until it was safe to take her home. Because of him, Goni was fine, and so was the baby. We all loved him.'

'We have a child together,' she whispered, staring into the distance and not seeing a thing. 'His name is Leon. He has never met his father. And now he never will.'

* * *

It was summer and they were on her grandfather's farm, their arms around each other, the sky a bottomless blue above their heads, the sun burning, the river swooshing. Everything was peaceful, the song of the birds, his lips touching the tips of her fingers, the whisper of the leaves, like a poem about first love.

'I've always known you would be my first,' he said, pulling her closer, chest to chest, face to face, his hair mixed with her hair, both dishevelled and out of breath. It was so quiet, she could hear his heartbeat, boom-boom-boom like a runaway train.

'How did you know?'

'Because I couldn't imagine it ever being anybody else.'

'When did you first realise you had feelings for me?'

'I always knew, I think. But the moment I knew for sure was when you broke your arm and I took you to hospital. I couldn't leave you,

not because you needed me but because I needed to know you were all right.' He rubbed the palm of her hand in circles, fast and slow, making her heart race. *'What about you? When did you realise?'*

'The moment I first saw you.'

'We were six. How could you possibly know?'

'Girls just know these things.'

He chuckled, shook his head, smiled. *'You want to hear what else I know?'*

'Yes?'

'I know you are going to be my last.'

She looked into his face, surprised and pleased. *'How?'*

'Because I can't imagine being in love with anybody else,' he whispered to her, when they were young and the summer breeze was warm on their faces.

* * *

The fire went out in the fireplace. Nani had gone out, thinking she was asleep. She remained in the dark, rocking back and forth, wishing she had said yes when Darren wanted to make love to her in the cellar. She longed to touch his face, his arms, his shoulders, to feel the warmth of his body, to run her hands through his hair. She had a chance to do all of that and now she never would again. She covered her mouth with a pillow and screamed, not caring if anyone heard her. On and on she screamed, and punched the wall until her knuckles were red and bruised. She sobbed and screamed some more but when she finished screaming, it still hurt, just like before.

At four in the morning, when the sun was still down and the moon threw its dim light over the street outside, Goni came in with a pile of dark clothes. 'It's time to get dressed,' she said. 'The truck will be here soon.'

Nicole shook her head. 'I can't do it. I can't get dressed.'

'You have to. You need to get up, have something to eat and be ready at a moment's notice.'

'I can't get up.' Her grief was like bricks pushing her down. She felt she couldn't move a finger, let alone her body.

'I brought your things. Your papers.'

'My papers?' asked Nicole, as if she couldn't understand the words. 'I can't go through with it, Goni. Not without him.'

Goni sat next to her. 'What about your son? Darren wanted you to live, for Leon. He told me about him. He said he loved him more than anything, even though he had never met him. Your little boy can't lose his mother too.'

Nicole cried in Goni's arms, shaking her head, repeating, 'No, no, no.'

Goni whispered, 'He wanted you to save yourself.'

As if in a trance, Nicole allowed Goni to change her and tie the headscarf around her head but refused to even touch the food she had brought.

'You have to eat. You need your strength. You have a long journey ahead of you,' Goni said.

'I'm not hungry.'

'I'll pack some food for you to take with you. Promise me you'll eat.'

'I promise.' She repeated the words but had no idea what she was promising, what the woman was talking about, what she wanted from her. On autopilot, she leaned on Goni's hand as she led her out of the house. If it wasn't for Goni, her knees would have given out and she would have fallen to the ground.

Outside, Nani was waiting by the truck. The couple hugged Nicole and said their goodbyes. She thanked them for everything, tears running down her cheeks. Agnesa appeared, carrying a small sack in her hands. 'I packed you something to eat on the road,' she said.

'I gave her food, thank you, Mother,' Goni said to her mother-in-law.

'Now she'll have more. She is going to need it.'

The women watched her, their faces creased with worry. 'Do you think she'll be all right without us?' asked Agnesa.

'I don't know but what can we do? We can't go with her,' said Goni.

Their kindness pulled on Nicole's heart. 'Thank you,' she whispered. 'Take care of yourselves. And stay safe.'

The truck was waiting for her. She stood up straight and took a step and then another and another. Suddenly, she stumbled and fell, and on the ground she started to cry. Goni rushed to her side and helped her up. Together they made it to the passenger door. Goni gave her a push and Nicole climbed up. Her bags of food and belongings were by her feet. In her lap she held Darren's books, his deck of cards and his chess set. She pressed them hard to her chest as if it could bring him back. Goni offered to put Darren's things in the back but Nicole refused. They were all she had left of him. From the driver's seat, Nani's brother asked if she was ready.

She nodded, even though she wasn't ready, not at all. As if in a trance, she watched Goni, Nani and Agnesa wave until they disappeared, giving way to trees, their dark blurry shapes flying past her window as she was whisked away from Berat. There should have been two of them, riding to safety. Instead, she was all alone.

Chapter 15

The Long Way Home

Andrea sat by the table in the mess room with a book in front of her. Other than the round circle of light from her torch, all was dark. It was after midnight and deserted. The other nurses and doctors were asleep in the sleeping quarters. There was little to do for the medical personnel rescued in Albania but rest, sleep, play cards and wait for someone else to decide their fate. Andrea kept to herself, wondering what she would do when she was ordered to leave Europe without her sister.

For a week the group remained at the 26th General Hospital in Bari, their original destination during their ill-fated flight in November. Even though Hitler's troops continued to trample Europe under their boots, their time at the front had come to an end. Policy dictated that any medical personnel who had been in enemy territory for longer than eight days would be sent back to the States. They could not remain in war-ravaged Italy, even if they were needed now more than ever, even though thousands of wounded called for them from their muddy trenches. Even if they were waiting for their lost sister. As Andrea perched on the edge of her chair, staring at her book in the light of the torch but not seeing a word, she wondered what she would tell her mother and father about Nicole. What would she tell Leon?

After a nauseating journey across the sea back to Italy, Andrea thought the worst was over. But then the interrogations began. They questioned them together and one at a time, trying to catch them on a lie or a contradiction, examining them like insects under a magnifying glass, searching for inconsistencies and imperfections, doing their best to prove their story was nothing but a fabrication. There were times in the last week when Andrea almost believed it had all been a terrifying dream. Crossing Albania on foot, surviving on cornbread and not much else, running for their lives with the Nazis on their heels and finding their way back with only one nurse missing was something one would read in a novel. No wonder the high command didn't believe them, calling them into the room with the large desk and an overbearing officer again and again, asking the same questions over and over, trying to trip them up.

During one such interrogation, the lieutenant-colonel pulled out a map and showed them that the distance between the crash site and Seaview was about sixty miles, while their estimated route was three hundred and forty miles. Given the mountainous terrain, the Intelligence officer surmised they had walked two to three times that amount. Andrea remembered every step, every village where they sheltered, every bite of food they had taken, every morning when they woke up with sore bodies and fear in their hearts, every night when they fell to the ground exhausted. 'You are our local celebrities,' the officer said to them. 'Even President Roosevelt insisted on daily briefings on your situation.'

When they couldn't catch them in a lie, they forced them to sign papers stating they could not reveal where they had been or who had helped them, in order to protect their benefactors.

As she sat in the dark mess room, Andrea heard footsteps but didn't turn around. 'Andrea, is that you? Why are you sitting alone in the dark?' The lights snapped on, momentarily blinding her, and she saw Brian staring at her. He looked dishevelled and unkempt, like he had just gotten out of bed. His hair was messy, his eyes bloodshot. 'Are you all right? Have you been crying?' he asked. 'I haven't seen you for days. I've been looking everywhere for you.'

In Bari, they had been staying in opposite wings of the hospital and it suited Andrea. It made avoiding him that much easier. She needed time to think, to understand what she was feeling, so new and unexpected these emotions were. But space didn't bring clarity. 'Hello, Brian,' she said, her voice flat and tired. 'Can't sleep?'

He shook his head and sat opposite her. 'Are you still reading that book? Ever since I met you, it's always with you. You know there are other books in the world, don't you?'

She pushed her copy of *Anna Karenina* away. 'I wasn't reading, just . . .' She hesitated. 'Looking at pages. It's so familiar, it makes me feel a little bit like home.'

'Rumour has it they are sending us back to the US soon. Personally, I'm glad it's over.'

She raised her eyes, watching him with disappointment. 'I can't go. My sister is still missing. I told the lieutenant-colonel as much last time I saw him.'

He didn't try to comfort her, didn't reach his hand out to touch hers. 'And what did he say?'

'He said I don't have a choice in the matter. I would be in breach of policy if I stayed.'

'And what did you say to him?'

'That I don't care about their policy. I only care about my sister. To which he reminded me that I'm an officer in the US Army.' She sighed sadly. To change the subject, she said, 'You know who I ran into in Detroit just before we left for the front?'

'Who?'

'Nancy Brown.'

'Your friend from university?'

Andrea nodded. 'My best friend from primary school. My best friend since we were six. But we went to university together, yes. That day in Detroit, we spent hours talking. We had a lot to catch up on. I asked her where she's been. Why I haven't heard from her in eight years. And do you know what she told me?' Andrea fell quiet, studying him. He didn't say a word but the expression on his face changed. It became wary, defensive. She continued, 'She told me my husband approached her one evening and told her never to speak to me again. My husband threatened her. Is that true?'

'I didn't threaten her,' he said, his eyes flashing with familiar anger. 'I simply told her she hasn't been a good friend to you and that you deserve better.'

'And why would you say that to someone I've known for most of my life? Could it be because she told me I shouldn't let my partner put me down in front of others or throw things at me? That it will never get better and I'm deluded if I think I can change you? That I should leave before you ruin my life? Is it because she said that to me one day and you overheard?'

'What kind of friend says something like that?'

'One who cares about me and doesn't want me to get hurt. What kind of husband threatens his wife's best friend and drives her away?'

'You don't need toxic people like Nancy in your life.'

'It's not up to you to decide who I'm friends with. It's not your place to choose who I talk to. You had no right.'

He sighed, clearly annoyed. 'Why are you doing this? We are going home. Finally, we can start living our life. Why are you always looking for arguments?'

'I'm not looking for arguments. I haven't been happy and I have every right to tell you so.' She hesitated. What she was about to say would change her future forever. Once spoken, she would not be able to take the words back. 'We can start our lives. But not together,' she whispered.

'What do you mean?'

'I want a divorce.' She looked him straight in the eye and made her voice sound firm, even if inside she wanted to curl into a ball and hide under the table.

'You don't mean that.' He took her hand. She wanted to pull away but didn't. He said, 'We've been through a lot. We are both hurting. The war took its toll on us. But we'll fix everything. Once we are back home, we will work it all out, I promise. I'm willing to try. Are you?'

For most of their marriage, she had been longing to hear these words. She had been willing to try a year ago, six months ago, even six weeks ago. All these years, she had been willing to forgive, to look to the future, to hope for the best. To see the best in him, to hope he would change. But not anymore. 'I want children,' she said. 'And I can't have them with you.'

'I'll have a child with you. I don't want another one, but all right, let's do it. I don't want to lose you and if that's what it takes . . .'

'You don't understand. I couldn't have a child with you, even if you wanted one.'

'What are you saying?'

'I can't bring a child into this.' She made a frantic gesture with her hand, pointing at him and at herself, at the two of them together, at the relationship they had built. 'Children need love and kindness and beauty in their world. They need stability. A calm environment where they can feel safe. They can't live in anger or aggression, or they will grow up . . .' Like you, she wanted to say but didn't. 'I don't want my child to see you lose your temper. I don't want them to get hurt.'

'I would never hurt our child,' he whispered.

'Your father never hurt you. He only ever hurt your mother. And look what it's done to you. I don't want it to happen to our children.'

'I only hit you once. It will never happen again. I promised you then and I never broke my promise.'

'You hurt me every time you speak to me in anger. Your neglect, the distance between us, your cold face, your indifference, they all hurt me.'

'We can see a psychologist. We can work it out.'

'It's too late. There's a wall between us and I'm tired of trying to break through it. I finally realised that I can't break through it because I'm the only one trying. I've been so lonely. There is nothing worse than being in a relationship and feeling completely alone.'

'I will try to be better, I promise. Please, Andrea. I don't know who I am without you. I'll be completely lost.'

'I don't know who I am without you either. But I know I'll find my way and so will you.'

'Let's not make rash decisions. Let's get back home first, settle in and then revisit this conversation. One step at a time.'

Rash? It had taken her many years to come to this. She moved away from him, so he couldn't touch her and said, 'For eight years, I was blinded. By my feelings for you, by your promises, by the future I imagined with you. I couldn't take one breath without you in it. I couldn't bear to spend a night away from you. I alienated my friends and family, just so I could be with you. Nothing else mattered. But I can see clearly now. I don't want to be a victim. I don't want to be afraid. I want to live my life, not yours. I want to remember who I am, to be myself again.'

'You can be yourself, with me.'

'I feel like I'm becoming invisible. A little bit longer, and I will disappear altogether. My needs, my dreams, my feelings don't matter to you at all. *I* don't matter to you at all.'

'Of course, you do. You are my life, you know that.'

'Here at the front, I needed you more than ever. There is a battlefield out there. I didn't need a battlefield here with you. What I needed was love, support and kindness. And you gave me anger, contempt and nothing else. I'm scared of you. Scared of your temper, of your reaction, of your judgement. And I shouldn't be.'

'I'm scared of you too. I'm scared of losing you.' He reached for her but she was too far away.

'I'm sorry. There's nothing left.'

Tears were running down his face. 'You are wrong. There is something left. I love you. I've never loved anyone this way.'

'And I love you. I suspect I always will. For a long time, I thought love was all that mattered. The way I feel about you. The way my heart soars when I see you or think of you, the way I am short of breath and light-headed whenever you are around. But it's not enough. It took me eight years to finally understand it.'

'Please forgive me,' he pleaded with her. 'Please stay.'

'I forgive you. But I can't stay.'

She lifted her hand and touched her husband's face, touched the man she had loved for eight years, for most of her adult life. He was crying but her eyes were dry. She felt numb inside. She knew she would never be whole again. What she was doing was going to break her heart forever. But staying with him would break her even more. He was the love of her life. She didn't know how to go on without him, how to breathe, how to get through the day. But she knew she was going to have to learn because, if she stayed with him, she could never be true to herself. She would always have to pretend, to watch her every move, to become somebody else, somebody who would please him. And she could no longer do that.

* * *

The nurses were lined up on the airfield, ready to fly to Casablanca in Morocco, the first leg of their journey to the States. From there, they would join whatever flight was available to take them home. The girls chatted happily, laughing and teasing one another, and only Andrea stood solemnly like a dark cloud, not laughing or teasing but staring into the distance, lost in thought. Her soon-to-be-ex-husband wasn't with her. She had spent so long by his side, thinking about him every step of the way, she felt his absence acutely, like a limb was missing or a part of her heart. 'Look, Brian,' she wanted to tell him. 'We are going home. It's finally over.' But she couldn't tell him that because they were not together and never would be, even though she still felt him close to her, like a ghost that would not let go.

She touched the spot on her finger where her wedding ring had once been. She had been doing it a lot lately, reaching for her non-existent ring, to twist it, to play with it like she used to when she was fretting or afraid. Every time she didn't find it, a sharp pain inside her chest made her gasp. The missing ring was a stark reminder that her life as she knew it was over.

It was sunny in Bari. Not a cloud marred the perfect sky that stretched as far as the eye could see, at odds with the war, with death, with Andrea's heartbreak. She wanted it to rain, wanted the Albanian snow to fall and cover everything in sight, wanted nature itself to mourn her shattered marriage. She yearned for gloomy skies to match her gloomy mood. How could everything sparkle in the sun, as if in celebration of life and hope and love, when inside her everything was dying, when she felt numb and shellshocked, a shadow of her former self?

After their conversation in the mess, Brian had tried to speak to her again, to change her mind, to talk her out of getting a divorce and into working things out. But there was nothing left to work out. The first night after their talk, she cried. And the second night she cried. But since then, she hadn't cried anymore, even though she wanted to, if only to fill the emptiness inside her.

Whenever she thought of her future, a dark panic gripped her. She didn't know what she was going to do. After eight years together, she had no idea how to be alone. Without him, she was lost like a ship in the storm. She didn't know how to behave, where to turn, how to speak. It was like being a child and learning to walk all over again. To walk alone, without leaning on his hand. She knew she would find herself again, even if it took some time. In the meantime, she would go to her parents' house. She would tell them they had been right all along. She would be safe in her childhood home. She would no longer be at war. She would no longer have to walk on eggshells. With her mother and father by her side, she would find peace. One day in the distant future, she would step outside and take a deep breath of fresh air. She would savour a morning coffee, enjoy a book or a movie, go for a stroll by the river and not feel the excruciating pain inside her. Until that day came, she would wait and heal. And she would live her life.

The voices around her grew impatient. The girls couldn't wait to board the plane that would take them home, while Andrea had no intention of going anywhere until her sister was found. She only came to the airfield that morning to tell their commander that.

'Where is this plane?' grumbled Renee. 'How long are we supposed to wait?'

'We've waited for almost three months. You can wait ten minutes, surely?' asked Carrie.

'I can't, not even ten minutes. I want to hug my son.'

Tory said, 'I hope I never see another plane after all this is over. From now on I will only travel on trains.'

Even though she didn't say anything, Andrea agreed wholeheartedly with Tory.

'I won't travel anywhere at all,' said Renee. 'Nothing will take me away from home. I will find a job in a local hospital and spend the rest of my life never leaving the state or my family again.'

'I'm done with hospitals. I couldn't work as a nurse anymore,' said Carrie. 'I want to be a teacher, to work with children, to inspire a new generation. It took a near-death experience to make me realise that nursing is not for me.'

'I couldn't live without it,' said Andrea. 'Sure, it's hard to see people suffer. But when the patients look at you with tears of gratitude in their eyes, when you know you helped someone, made a real difference to someone's life, there's no other feeling like it. When I return, I want to study to become a doctor.' As soon as she said it, she knew that there it was, the thing she had been looking for, the way forward. And no one would tell her that she didn't have what it took, that she wasn't good enough, that she wasn't cut out to be a doctor. Yes, losing Brian hurt more than anything she had ever experienced. But she was finally free.

Renee said, 'Remember that moment on the plane back in November when the Nazi fighter was after us and we thought we were about to die? Remember the moment just after the crash, when we didn't know where we were or how we would survive? Did you think back then that we would make it, that we would be standing here, about to go home?'

The girls shook their heads and then everyone looked at Andrea. They didn't say a word but by the sadness on their faces she knew what they were thinking. Not everyone had made it. Not everyone was flying home today.

A sound of the engine was heard, deafening and shrill, a promise of a new life that was waiting for them. 'There's our plane,' cried Carrie. 'Are you ready, girls?'

'After walking hundreds of miles, all we need to do is cross this airfield and we'll be on our way back,' said Tory, tears in her eyes.

'Let's promise each other something. No matter where life takes us, we will find each other again. We will always stay in touch. After what we've been through, we are family,' said Renee.

They stood in a circle, their heads close together, their hands joined. 'We promise,' they repeated. When she looked at the other nurses, Andrea saw it all in their eyes. The miles they had walked, the explosions they had heard, the shots that had barely missed them. They were about to leave it all behind, and yet, she knew for a fact it would stay with them forever.

'Cornbread, anyone?' asked Renee, reaching inside her pocket.

'That's old, Renee. How long have you been carrying that?' asked Andrea.

'Since our first week in Albania, I think.'

'I'll take some,' said Carrie.

In front of them was the plane that was going to whisk them away from war-torn Italy, to rejoin their families. Behind them were mountains, rugged and grey, not unlike those they had left behind in

Albania. Suddenly, as they were crossing the airfield, a car pulled up and the door opened. Andrea watched as a young woman climbed out, holding a small rucksack. She was petite and unsure in her movements and although she was facing away from Andrea, by the curve of her neck, by her slender figure, by the way her hair curled down her back, she recognised her instantly.

'Nicole!' Andrea shouted. She started to run, nearly knocking Renee off her feet.

Nicole turned around and her hand flew to her mouth. She dropped her bag to the ground and rushed towards her sister. *In a moment I will put my arms around her,* thought Andrea. And in a moment, she did. And she was no longer alone.

Epilogue

Two and a Half Years Later

The officer walked through the streets of one of the most affluent suburbs of Detroit, his pace nothing more than an uncertain shuffle, as if he needed some time to collect his thoughts before he reached his destination. Around him were sprawling houses and manicured lawns, flower beds that seemed to compete with one another for the title of the most ostentatious and flamboyant, and the man seemed fascinated by it all, like he was looking at something exotic and otherworldly, like he hadn't seen anything like it in a very long time. Every now and then, his glance would fall on the piece of paper in his hands, where someone had scribbled an address with an unsteady hand. Then he would pause and pull a map out of his pocket, his finger tracing the winding lines on the page, while his eyes scanned the signs on the street corners. He looked a little flustered and out of breath but that was to be expected on a hot summer day like today, when the sun was blazing and not a leaf rustled in the wind.

Finally, after walking for over an hour, the man stopped outside a two-storey Mediterranean-style home and consulted the piece of paper in his hand, comparing the number on the letterbox to the number on the piece of paper. Half a dozen medium-sized pine trees framed the house like it was a postcard from Lapland, and below them were roses and lilies, white and perfect like fresh snow. On the porch was a swing big enough to accommodate half a soccer team and in the front yard, positioned away from the flowers to prevent little feet from treading on them, was a soccer goal. A boy of ten or eleven was kicking a ball around, occasionally shouting, 'Mama, come and look at this! Look what I can do.' His hair was blond and curly, his legs and arms a little too long, as if they had grown overnight and his body hadn't had a chance to catch up yet. His focus was on the ball and he didn't see the officer, who was watching him from a few paces away.

At the sight of the child, the man froze as if he had forgotten what he was doing. The piece of paper he was holding trembled and flew out of his hands, like a white butterfly released from its cage. The officer didn't even notice, so captivated he seemed by the boy, who was kicking the ball up in the air, his face red with the effort.

'What's your record?' the man asked, coming out of the shadow of the trees with a smile on his face.

'Excuse me?' Startled, the boy stopped in his tracks and dropped the ball to the ground.

'Kick-ups. How many can you do?'

The boy looked the man up and down, sizing him up. 'Ten,' he replied proudly. 'But my buddy Kevin can do twelve. I'm practising so I can beat him.'

'Ten is a serious number. You must be proud of yourself. Try using both your feet. Here, let me show you.'

The child passed the ball to the officer and watched as he skilfully balanced it on his toes and kicked it up. And up and up. It was as if an invisible rope connected the ball to his foot.

'That was amazing!' exclaimed the boy, clapping his hands excitedly. 'Where did you learn how to do that?'

'They teach us all sorts of things in the army.' Grinning, the man returned the ball, his eyes never leaving the boy's face.

'What uniform is that?' the boy wanted to know.

'A captain's in the AAF. But I'm not with the AAF, I'm with the OSS.'

The boy seemed puzzled by that. 'Why are you wearing the wrong uniform?'

'I used to wear it in case the Germans captured me. Being in the AAF is my cover story.'

The boy seemed to forget all about his ball and it rolled away into the bushes. 'Why do you need a cover story?' he wanted to know.

'Because the Nazis treat prisoners of war much better than they treat the spies they catch,' explained the officer. 'Without my cover story, I'd be shot on the spot.'

The boy's eyes became large and round. 'The OSS are spies?'

'They certainly are.'

'Are you a spy?'

'I was until this morning.' The officer extended his hand. 'I'm Darren, by the way. What's your name?'

The child shook the hand as hard as he could. It was clear he wanted to impress this mysterious man, who happened to be a spy and a soccer expert. 'I'm Leon. Darren was my father's name. But he died in Albania. He was in the army too. Mama still cries about it sometimes. She tries to hide it but I always know when she's been crying. Her eyes go red.'

It took a moment for the man to reply. When he spoke, his voice cracked. 'I'm sorry to hear that.'

'I've never met him.' The boy looked at the ground, as if embarrassed to show his emotion. 'I wish I did.'

'It's a nice house,' said the officer, pointing at the porch and the swing and the two columns that framed the front door. 'Do you live here with your family?'

'It's just me and Mama. My stepdad lives across the road with his new wife and baby. They visit all the time. And my aunt lived with us for a while but then she met someone and moved out. They are getting married soon. She is Mama's twin, can you believe it? Very few people can tell them apart. I'm one of them.' Somewhere behind them, a door creaked open. The boy whispered, 'Don't tell Mama I've been talking to you. She doesn't like it when I speak to strangers.'

'Your Mama is right. But I promise I won't tell,' said the officer, turning towards the house, his face pale, his hands clasping the map tight. A moment later, a woman appeared, wearing a short summer dress the colour of ocean waves on a sunny day. The dress clung to her slender figure and her long blonde hair was blowing in the wind. She looked serene and beautiful and when the soldier saw her, his hands began to shake.

'It's time for lunch, Leon,' the woman called, brushing the hair out of her eyes. And then she saw the man standing side by side with her son and the plates she was carrying fell to the ground. The sound was deafening, like a small explosion shaking the house, and the broken crockery was everywhere, even on the woman's bare feet, but she didn't seem to care. Both her hands flew to her mouth and she began to cry. For a few moments, the man and the woman watched each other in silence, as if they were frozen in time and unable to move. Then, as if a spell had been broken, she was running and he was running too, and soon they were in each other's arms. While the boy watched with amazement, the officer stroked the woman's back, saying, 'Sh-sh. Nicky, don't cry!' He repeated it again and again, even though he was crying too.

'How is it possible?' she managed finally. 'You are here. How can it be?'

'I flew in from Europe this morning. I came to find you as soon as I could.'

She couldn't stop touching him, as if she couldn't believe her eyes and needed proof that he was real. 'Nani told me you died. The Nazis shot you. His brother saw it happen.'

'Nani lied.'

'Why would he lie to me?'

'Because I asked him to.'

She took a step back, away from him, so she could see his face. 'You asked him to? When?'

'The cell I was in had a little window. On my first night in prison Nani came to see me. He told me the next day the Nazis were going to transport me to a prison camp and the partisans were planning to attack the vehicle I was in and help me escape.'

'You escaped?' she asked, beaming.

He nodded. 'Thanks to Nani.'

'How can we ever thank that man?' she said. 'But I don't understand. Why would you ask him to lie to me?'

'Because I knew you would never leave Berat if you thought I was still alive. And I needed you to leave Berat. I needed you to be safe.'

Her little hands clasped into fists and she tapped his chest, like she was angry with him. 'It's been two and a half years, Darren. You could have written, no?'

'Do you have any idea how many letters I wrote you?'

She shook her head.

'How many days since you left Berat?'

'Nine hundred and twelve,' she whispered.

'That's how many. You didn't receive them?'

'Not a single one.' She was crying again, her face in his chest. The boy pulled his mother by the hand shyly. Turning to Leon, bringing him into her arms, her voice trembling, she said, 'Leon, meet your father.'

A Letter from Lana Kortchik

Dear Reader,

Thank you for choosing *Sisters of the Storm*. I loved writing and researching this book, and am very excited to share it with you. I hope you enjoyed it.

In November 1943, an American transport plane carrying twenty-six medical personnel and four flight crew from Catania to Bari crash-landed in Nazi-occupied Albania. What followed next was a nine-week-long fight for survival, sixty-three days of battling the hunger, the illness and the elements, while evading German bullets and hiding from German planes. During those sixty-three days, the nurses and medics covered the distance of six hundred and fifty miles. They walked eighteen hours a day, even when they felt they couldn't take another step. They crossed impassable mountains and slept under the open skies during blizzards. Often, their spirits were low and their bodies were weary but they never stopped. Relying solely on the kindness of people they met along the way, they carried on, mile after mile, village after village, mountain ridge after mountain ridge, until they reached the coast and were finally rescued.

This story belongs not only to the stranded Americans but to all those who helped them along the way, risking their lives for strangers and proving that good always triumphs over evil, even in the world turned upside down by war.

Although the events of the rescue are real, most characters in this book are fictional, with a few exceptions. First Lieutenant

Charles Thrasher from Florida was the first pilot and the most senior officer on the flight. Second Lieutenant James Baggs trained as a fighter pilot at Foster Field in Texas and had already flown one hundred missions. When disaster struck, the two pilots took charge of the group, supporting the nurses and medics every step of the way and putting everyone else's safety before their own. Hasan Gina, the leader of a group of partisans, was the first to come across the Americans in Albania. He stayed with them for the first few weeks of their journey, making sure they were safe. Captain Victor Smith, an SOE officer, played an integral part in the rescue efforts of the stranded medical personnel. Thanks to these people and many others like them, the Americans were able to reach their base in Italy without leaving a single person behind, a miracle when you consider everything that was stacked against them on their perilous journey across Albania.

If this story touched your heart like it did mine and you would like to learn more, I highly recommend a wonderful book I came across during my research, *The Secret Rescue: An Untold Story of American Nurses and Medics Behind Nazi Lines* by Cate Lineberry. Drawing on memoirs, diaries, archive materials and interviews with the sole survivor of the group, Lineberry paints a detailed and fascinating picture of the crash-landing and the quest for survival that followed.

I enjoy hearing from my readers and would love to know what you thought about the book. Feel free to reach out by leaving a review or contacting me via my website or social media.

Best wishes,
Lana Kortchik

Twitter: https://twitter.com/lanakortchik
Facebook: https://www.facebook.com/lanakortchik/
Instagram: https://www.instagram.com/lanakortchik/
Website: http://www.lanakortchik.com/

Sisters of War

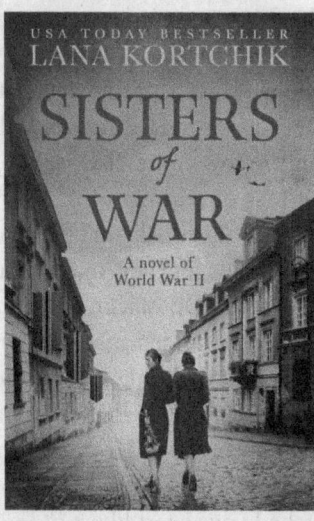

Can their bond survive under the shadow of occupation?

For fans of *The Tattooist of Auschwitz* and *The German Midwife* comes this unforgettable tale of love, loss, family, and the power of hope.

Kiev, 1941: Watching the Red Army withdraw from Ukraine in the face of Hitler's relentless advance, sisters Natasha and Lisa Smirnova realise their lives are about to change forever.

As the German army occupies their beloved city, the sisters are tested in ways they never thought possible. Lisa's fiancé Alexei is taken by the invading army, whilst Natasha falls in love with Mark – a Hungarian soldier, enlisted against all his principles on the side of the Nazis.

But as Natasha and Lisa fight to protect the friends and family they hold dear, they must face up to the dark horrors of war and the pain of betrayal. Will they be strong enough to overcome the forces which threaten to tear their family apart?

Sisters of the Sky

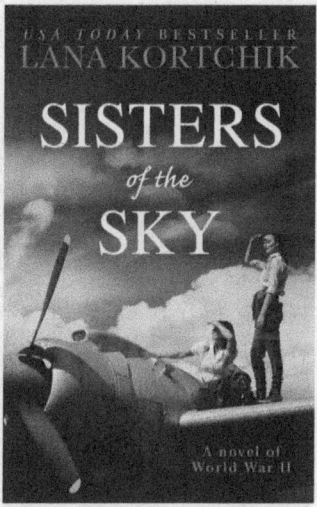

October, 1941

As war rages in the Soviet Union, Nina is devastated as she watches her younger brother being sent off to the front. She has witnessed so many soldiers go to war and never return, and with her father already on the battlefield, her brother is her only family left.

Sick of feeling helpless and determined to fight for her motherland, Nina and her best friend Katya decide to volunteer for the first female-only aviation regiment, led by the legendary pilot Marina Raskova.

But fighting a war is nothing like they expected, and soon the battle lines are no longer restricted to the front – a forbidden love begins to blossom, and Nina is faced with the ultimate betrayal. **Will Nina and her loved ones make it out alive?**

From the bestselling author of *Sisters of War* comes a heart-wrenching novel of love, friendship, betrayal and sacrifice, perfect for fans of Mandy Robotham and Pam Jenoff.

Angels of War

The Philippines, 1941

Rose Williams arrives in Manila on her first assignment as a US Army nurse, enthralled by the new environment and its promise of adventure. Although worlds away from the land she grew up in, Rose feels connected to her father, who worked in the Philippines before he died.

War seems like a distant possibility as Rose takes midnight dips in a warm sea with the other nurses, explores secret corners of the island, and falls in love with a locally stationed US Army officer.

But when Japan bombs Manila, the nurses' lives change. Torn away from the man she loves, Rose faces constant threat, not only to her life, but from those around her she thought she could trust . . .

Will Rose and those close to her survive in the turmoil of war?

Acknowledgements

As I researched the story of the American transport plane crash-landing in Albania, I was blown away by the bravery and resilience of the nurses and the medics, as well as the kindness of those who helped them along the way. This story captured my imagination and it's such a pleasure to share it with readers worldwide. I am grateful to everyone who made it possible.

Thank you to my wonderful editors, Ellie Jardine, Sophia Allistone and Cari Rosen, who with their thoughtful feedback and guidance bring the best out of me as a writer. Thank you to Teresa Palmiero and Michelle Bullock for their feedback, and to Anna Sikorska for creating a cover for this book that brought tears to my eyes. And to the rest of the team at HQ and HarperCollins who worked incredibly hard to make this book a reality.

Thank you to my fantastic agent, Mark Gottlieb, who is only an email away and is always available with words of encouragement and support. I am grateful to have him in my corner.

None of this would have been possible without my family. Thank you to my mum for her kindness and for always being there for me. To my husband Joel for holding my hand every step of the way, and to my children for cuddles and unconditional love. I am a better person and a better writer because of you. Thank you to Sal for being a role model and an inspiration all these years.

Finally, I would like to thank my readers around the world for buying my books, reading, reviewing and reaching out to share their thoughts. Knowing my story touched someone's heart means the world to me.

Dear Reader,

We hope you enjoyed reading this book. If you did, we'd be so appreciative if you left a review. It really helps us and the author to bring more books like this to you.

Here at HQ Digital we are dedicated to publishing fiction that will keep you turning the pages into the early hours. Don't want to miss a thing? To find out more about our books, promotions, discover exclusive content and enter competitions you can keep in touch in the following ways:

JOIN OUR COMMUNITY:

Sign up to our new email newsletter: http://smarturl.it/SignUpHQ

Read our new blog www.hqstories.co.uk

X: https://twitter.com/HQStories

f: www.facebook.com/HQStories

BUDDING WRITER?

We're also looking for authors to join the HQ Digital family! Find out more here:

https://www.hqstories.co.uk/want-to-write-for-us/

Thanks for reading, from the HQ Digital team